英語地雷大冒險

解鎖你不知道的錯誤用法

Preface

　　在我四十多年的英文教育工作經驗裡，常看到許多讀者英文未能學到通透，無論在口語表達、寫作、實務運用等方面，犯錯而不自知；導致在升大學、留學、各類檢定考試與求職，無法達成目標，個人甚感可惜。

　　本書蒐集在英文寫作與運用上常犯的錯誤或易混淆字詞，分別列出正確及錯誤用法並解釋這些字詞巧妙的差異；另輔以適當的例句、插圖，再搭配練習題，希望藉由這樣的方法，幫助讀者理解正確用法關鍵之處，避免再犯同樣錯誤，進而大大提升英文實力。

　　全書共分「生活應用篇」5 大章節，204 個小單元以及「實用文法篇」7 大章節，90 個小單元詮釋。「生活應用篇」包含「常見錯誤用字／用詞／用語」、「字詞辨異」、「常見多種易混淆用字」、「常見卻易用錯的單字／片語／句型」以及「生活用語類」。「實用文法篇」包含「與時態相關的錯誤」、「與否定句相關的錯誤」、「搞懂句子、主要子句、副詞子句、形容詞子句、名詞子句之間的區別及功能」、「名詞子句」、「動狀詞」、「假設語氣」、「其他常見的混淆用法」；每一則都經過我細心考證、再三確認，絕對是能讓讀者收穫滿滿的一本好書！

　　祝大家學習成功！

Instructions for use

使用說明

全書分「生活應用篇」5 大章節共 204 個 Units 及「實用文法篇」7 大章節共 90 個 Units，點出最常用錯的英文單詞 / 片語 / 句型 / 文法！

重點**條列**說明，內容差異一目了然。

Unit 115　awful 及 awesome 怎麼用?

a
- awful *a.* 糟糕的，差勁的 (= very bad)
- awesome *a.* 極好的，很棒的 (= extremely good)

例　Even though the weather is awesome, we still have a lot to do. (✗)
→ Even though the weather is awful, we still have a lot to do. (✓)
雖然天氣很不好，我們仍有許多事情可做。

The concert was so awful that it attracted a capacity audience. (✗)
→ The concert was so awesome that it attracted a capacity audience. (✓)　演唱會太棒了，因此吸引了滿場觀眾。

b　awful 亦可作副詞，與 very (很) 同義，尤用於口語，可修飾正面或負面的形容詞。

例　It's awful / very hot today. (✓)　今天熱斃了。
The little girl there looks awful / very cute. (✓)
那邊那個小女孩看起來很可愛。

c　awfully 是副詞，與 very (很) 同義，多修飾負面的形容詞。

例　It's awfully / awful cold today.　今天冷斃了。
I'm awfully sorry to hear that.　聽到那個消息我很難過。

情境例句、易混淆單詞 / 用法搭配**圖解**，輕鬆學習、一看秒懂！

小試身手

1. Alex's handwriting is so (awesome / awful) that no one can understand it.
2. We went to an amusement park today and had an (awesome / awful) time. I felt really happy!

Ans 1. awful　2. awesome

每個 Unit 後搭配**小試身手**，立收學習成效！

目錄 Contents

>>> 生活應用篇

Chapter 1　常見錯誤用字 / 用詞 / 用語 1

Unit 1	「0 度」是 0 degrees 或 0 degree? 2
Unit 2	「一個半小時」是 one and a half hour 或 one and a half hours? 3
Unit 3	「單詞量大」是 know many vocabularies 或 have a large vocabulary? 4
Unit 4	「我很喜歡」是 I very like it. 或 I like it very much.? 4
Unit 5	「想要」是 feel like to V 或 feel like + N/V-ing? 6
Unit 6	「我認為……不……」是 I don't think he can... 或 I think he cannot...? 7
Unit 7	「忙碌」是 be busy + to V 或 be busy + V-ing? 7
Unit 8	「他和我」是 He as well as I is... 或 He as well as I am...? 8
Unit 9	「我完全同意」是 I can't agree with you more. 或 I couldn't agree with you more.? 10
Unit 10	「一對一」是 one-on-one 或 one-to-one? 11
Unit 11	「正要……」是 be about to V when... 或 be about to V then...? 12
Unit 12	「聯絡」是 contact 人 或 contact with 人? 13
Unit 13	「與……結婚」是 marry 人 或 marry with 人? 14
Unit 14	「與……離婚」是 divorce 人 或 divorce with 人? 15
Unit 15	「與……訂婚」是 engage 人 或 be engaged to 人? 16
Unit 16	「好消息」是 That's good news. 或 That's a good news.? 17
Unit 17	「一個建議」是 an advice 或 a piece of advice? 18
Unit 18	「考試不及格」是 fail the test 或 fail in the test? 19
Unit 19	「考得好」是 do well in the test 或 on the test? 21
Unit 20	「失敗」是 get a fail 或 get a failure? 21
Unit 21	「玩玩具」是 play toys 或 play with toys? 22

Unit 22	「厚衣服」是 thick clothes 或 heavy clothes?	24
Unit 23	「恭喜」是 congratulation 或 congratulations?	24
Unit 24	「遇到麻煩」是 have trouble to V 或 have trouble V-ing?	25
Unit 25	「做……很愉快」是 have fun to V 或 have fun V-ing?	27
Unit 26	「得第一名」是 win first place 或 win the first place?	27
Unit 27	「我喜歡」是 I love it. 或 I am loving it.?	28
Unit 28	「微不足道的人或事物」是 a small potato 或 small potatoes?	30
Unit 29	「照鏡子」是 look into the mirror 或 look at the mirror?	31
Unit 30	「把衣服穿反了」是 wear 物 outside in 或 wear 物 inside out?	31
Unit 31	「住飯店」是 stay at the hotel 或 live at the hotel?	32
Unit 32	「……已無用」是 It is no use to V 或 It is no use V-ing?	33
Unit 33	「不需要」是 need not V 或 need not to V?	34
Unit 34	「很棒的老師」是 so nice a teacher 或 a so nice teacher?	36
Unit 35	「年紀太大」是 too old a man 或 a too old man?	37
Unit 36	「被選為市長」是 be elected mayor 或 be elected the mayor?	38
Unit 37	「總統當選人」是 president-elect 或 president-elected?	39
Unit 38	「估計有兩百人」是 an estimate 200 people 或 an estimated 200 people?	39
Unit 39	「許多的」是 a good many 或 a lot many?	40
Unit 40	「我的一位好友」是 the best friend of mine 或 a good friend of mine?	41
Unit 41	表示「……是必要的」是 It is necessary that he gets… 或 It is necessary that he get…?	42
Unit 42	「英文說得很好」是 speak English very good 或 speak English very well?	43
Unit 43	「減少」是 be reduced to V 或 be reduced to V-ing?	45
Unit 44	「10 層樓的建築」是 a 10-story building 或 a 10-floor building?	46
Unit 45	搭配「市場 market 的介詞」是 on the market 或 in the market?	46
Unit 46	「告訴我這是什麼」是 Tell me what is it 或 Tell me what it is?	47

Unit 47	「較優越的」是 be superior to... 或 be more superior than...?	48
Unit 48	「今天早上」是 today morning、this morning 還是 tomorrow morning?	50
Unit 49	「find 的用法」是 find it to necessary 或 find that it is necessary to V?	51
Unit 50	「別對他期望太高」是 Don't expect him too much. 或 Don't expect too much of him.?	54
Unit 51	「寫日記」是 keep a diary 或 write a diary?	55
Unit 52	「感激」是 I would appreciate you if... 或 I would appreciate it if...?	55
Unit 53	「安排某人從事某事」是 arrange 人 to V 或 arrange for 人 to V?	56
Unit 54	「要用功，那麼……」是 Study hard, you will... 或 Study hard, and you will...?	57
Unit 55	「經過了 3 年」是 Three years have past. 或 Three years have passed.?	58
Unit 56	「回家」是 go home 或 go to home?	60
Unit 57	「依我之見」是 according to me 或 according to my opinion?	62
Unit 58	「照例」是 as usual 或 as usually?	62
Unit 59	「夜幕低垂時」是 when night falls 或 when the night falls?	63
Unit 60	「為何念大學」的簡化句是 why go to college 或 why to go to college?	64
Unit 61	「加入」是 join 人 in V-ing 或 join in 人 to V?	65
Unit 62	「我跟他是朋友」是 I am a friend with him. 或 I am friends with him.?	65
Unit 63	「討論」是 discuss it 或 discuss about it?	66
Unit 64	「在收音機廣播裡」是 on the radio 或 in the radio?	67
Unit 65	事情「發生」要用 happen 或 be happened?	67
Unit 66	「挑剔」是 be particular about... 或 be particular with...?	68
Unit 67	「全新的車」是 a brand new car 或 a new brand car?	69
Unit 68	「有鑑於」是 given that... 或 giving that...?	69

Chapter 2　字詞辨異 ……………………………………………… 71

Unit 69	plenty 及 plentiful 怎麼用?	72

Unit 70	able 及 capable 怎麼用?	73
Unit 71	no such a man 或 no such man 怎麼用?	74
Unit 72	weight 及 weigh 怎麼用?	75
Unit 73	good 及 well 怎麼用?	76
Unit 74	feel good 及 feel well 怎麼用?	77
Unit 75	after 及 afterwards 怎麼用?	78
Unit 76	at the beginning 及 in the beginning 怎麼用?	78
Unit 77	at the end 及 in the end 怎麼用?	79
Unit 78	much money 及 a lot of money 怎麼用?	80
Unit 79	like 及 alike 怎麼用?	81
Unit 80	go on V-ing 及 go on to V 怎麼用?	82
Unit 81	Do you mind if... 及 Would you mind if...?	83
Unit 82	remember 及 memorize 怎麼用?	84
Unit 83	man 及 a man 怎麼用?	86
Unit 84	apart from 及 aside from 怎麼用?	87
Unit 85	to not V 及 not to V 怎麼用?	88
Unit 86	being not 或 not being、having not 或 not having 怎麼用?	88
Unit 87	cannot 及 can not 怎麼用?	89
Unit 88	by far 及 so far 怎麼用?	90
Unit 89	not easy 及 uneasy 怎麼用?	91
Unit 90	a land 及 a piece of land 怎麼用?	92
Unit 91	insist on 及 persist in 怎麼用?	93
Unit 92	on the street 及 in the street 怎麼用?	94
Unit 93	weather 及 climate 怎麼用?	95
Unit 94	failed 及 failing 怎麼用?	96
Unit 95	rob 及 deprive 怎麼用?	97

Unit	內容	頁碼
Unit 96	as day breaks 及 as night falls 怎麼用?	98
Unit 97	lest 及 for fear that 怎麼用?	99
Unit 98	accept 及 receive 怎麼用?	100
Unit 99	compliment 及 complement 怎麼用?	101
Unit 100	principle 及 principal 怎麼用?	103
Unit 101	fun 及 funny 怎麼用?	104
Unit 102	champion 及 championship 怎麼用?	105
Unit 103	「火車離站」是 The train leaves 或 will leave at 2:30 p.m.?	106
Unit 104	「持續地」是 continually 或 continuously?	106
Unit 105	「損害」是 damage 或 damages?	107
Unit 106	be tired of... 或 be tired from... 怎麼用?	108
Unit 107	different 及 indifferent 怎麼用?	109
Unit 108	uninterested 及 disinterested 怎麼用?	110
Unit 109	at all times 及 all the time 怎麼用?	111
Unit 110	none is 及 none are 怎麼用?	111
Unit 111	Neither of us is... 及 Neither of us are... 怎麼用?	112
Unit 112	Either you or he is... 及 Either you or he are... 怎麼用?	113
Unit 113	farther 及 further 怎麼用?	114
Unit 114	then 及 and then 怎麼用?	115
Unit 115	awful 及 awesome 怎麼用?	117
Unit 116	intense 及 intensive 怎麼用?	118
Unit 117	popular 及 prevalent 怎麼用?	118
Unit 118	ashamed 及 shameful 怎麼用?	119
Unit 119	considerable 及 considerate 怎麼用?	120
Unit 120	not to mention... 及 let alone... 怎麼用?	121
Unit 121	prefer to V 及 prefer V-ing 怎麼用?	123

Unit 122	on one's own 及 of one's own 怎麼用?	124
Unit 123	whereas 或 while 怎麼用?	125
Unit 124	「下落」是 whereabouts 或 whereabout?	126
Unit 125	for days 及 hours on end 怎麼用?	127
Unit 126	learn 事物 及 learn about 事物 怎麼用?	128
Unit 127	lovely 及 lovable 怎麼用?	129
Unit 128	far better 及 by far the best 怎麼用?	129
Unit 129	「我突然想起」是 I suddenly thought that… 或 It occurred to me that…?	130
Unit 130	the same… as… 及 the same… that… 怎麼用?	131
Unit 131	give up on 人 及 give 人 up 怎麼用?	132
Unit 132	avenge 及 revenge 怎麼用?	133
Unit 133	cheat 人 及 cheat on 人 怎麼用?	134
Unit 134	interfere with 及 interfere in 怎麼用?	135
Unit 135	deal with 及 deal in 怎麼用?	136
Unit 136	a kind of 及 kind of 怎麼用?	136
Unit 137	drunk 及 drunken 怎麼用?	138
Unit 138	plan to V 及 plan on V-ing 怎麼用?	139
Unit 139	cut down on 及 cut down 怎麼用?	139
Unit 140	「一件行李」是 a luggage 或 a piece of luggage?	140
Unit 141	「鍾愛高雄」是 "We care Kaohsiung." 或 "We care for Kaohsiung."?	141
Unit 142	「想要某人去做某事」是 want 人 + V 或 want 人 + to V?	141

Chapter 3　常見多種易混淆用字 ……………………… 143

Unit 143	a number of、the number of、an amount of、the amount of 怎麼用?	144
Unit 144	due to、because of、as a result of、owing to、on account of 的用法	145

Unit 145	worth、worthy、worthwhile 怎麼用?	147
Unit 146	assure、ensure、insure 怎麼用?	148
Unit 147	live、lively、alive、living 怎麼用?	150
Unit 148	spend、cost、take 怎麼用?	152
Unit 149	not... anymore、not... any longer、no more、no longer 怎麼用?	154
Unit 150	「不再」是 not any more + 名詞 或 not anymore + 名詞?	156
Unit 151	「任何人」是 anyone 或 any one?	157
Unit 152	cannot but、cannot help but、cannot help + V-ing 怎麼用?	158
Unit 153	probable、likely、possible 怎麼用?	159
Unit 154	peek、peep、peak、pique 怎麼用?	161
Unit 155	reply、answer、respond 怎麼用?	162
Unit 156	in a hurry、in a rush、in haste 怎麼用?	164
Unit 157	rubbish、garbage、trash、junk 怎麼用?	164
Unit 158	dislike、unlike、like 怎麼用?	165
Unit 159	lately、recently、in the near future 怎麼用?	167
Unit 160	lightning、lightening、lighting 怎麼用?	168
Unit 161	「修理某物」是 need to be repaired、need being repaired 還是 need repairing?	169
Unit 162	crossroad、crossroads、intersection 怎麼用?	169
Unit 163	even though、although、though 怎麼用?	170
Unit 164	scenery、scene、view、landscape 怎麼用?	172
Unit 165	one... the other...、one... another... the other... 怎麼用?	174
Unit 166	one... another...、some... others...、數字... the others... 怎麼用?	175
Unit 167	last week、this week、next week 怎麼用?	176
Unit 168	on the way、in the way、by the way 怎麼用?	177
Unit 169	pick、pick up、pick out、pick on 怎麼用?	178

Chapter 4　常見卻易用錯的單字 / 片語 / 句型　　181

Unit 170	record 的用法	182
Unit 171	as well 的用法	183
Unit 172	rather than 的用法	184
Unit 173	would rather 的用法	185
Unit 174	other than 的用法	187
Unit 175	none other than 的用法	188
Unit 176	do nothing but 的用法	189
Unit 177	do without 的用法	189
Unit 178	It is time that... 的用法	190
Unit 179	can't... enough 的用法	192
Unit 180	for the past few years 的用法	193
Unit 181	經常與 "on" 搭配的名詞怎麼用？	194
Unit 182	如何連接兩個句子？	195
Unit 183	如何使用現在完成式 the present perfect tense (have / has + 過去分詞)？	196
Unit 184	如何使用過去完成式 the past perfect tense (had + 過去分詞)？	198
Unit 185	如何使用比較級句構 comparative structures？	199
Unit 186	如何使用最高級的句構 superlatives？	201
Unit 187	he who、one who、those who、people who 怎麼用？	202
Unit 188	whoever、whomever 怎麼用？	202

Chapter 5　生活用語類　　205

Unit 189	「幸會」是 Nice to meet you. 或 Nice meeting you.？	206
Unit 190	「當老師不容易」是 As a teacher is not easy. 或 Being a teacher is not easy.？	207
Unit 191	「我的職業是教學」是 My job is a teacher. 或 My job is teaching.？	207

Unit 192	job、work、career 怎麼用?	208
Unit 193	「電話是打來找你的」是 It's your telephone. 或 It's your phone call.?	210
Unit 194	「手機沒電了」是 My cell phone has no electricity. 或 My cell phone ran out of battery.?	210
Unit 195	「你方便……嗎」是 Are you convenient to V? 或 Is it convenient for you to V?	211
Unit 196	「今天星期幾」是 What day is today? 或 What date is today?	212
Unit 197	「你是在跟我開玩笑嗎」是 Are you kidding me? 還是 Are you joking me?	213
Unit 198	「不知道」是 have no idea 或 have no ideas?	214
Unit 199	"do you think" 當插入語要怎麼用?	215
Unit 200	「視若無睹」是 turn a blind eye to 或 turn one's blind eyes to?	216
Unit 201	「充耳不聞」是 turn a deaf ear to 或 turn one's deaf ears to?	217
Unit 202	"how to + V" 要怎麼用?	217
Unit 203	「一小時之後」是 in an hour 或 after an hour?	218
Unit 204	「身上沒帶錢」是 have no money with me 或 have no money on me?	219

>>> 實用文法篇

Chapter 1　與時態相關的錯誤 ……………………………… 221

Unit 1	大眾交通工具(如火車、高鐵、地鐵、公車、飛機等)按時刻表出發或到達時,多使用現在式	222
Unit 2	表示真理或現在仍存在的行動或狀況時,始終使用現在式	223
Unit 3	中文有「(正)在……」時,英文就要使用進行式	223
Unit 4	條件句使用現在式,主要子句使用未來式	225
Unit 5	現在完成式	225
Unit 6	過去完成式	227

Unit 7	未來完成式	229
Unit 8	現在完成進行式	230
Unit 9	過去完成進行式	231
Unit 10	未來完成進行式	232
Unit 11	"be 動詞 + 形容詞" 通常不可能使用進行式，即無 "be + being + 形容詞" 的用法	233

Chapter 2　與否定句相關的錯誤 …… 235

Unit 12	初學者常犯有關否定句的錯誤	236
Unit 13	助動詞後面加 not	237
Unit 14	用 not 還是 no？	238
Unit 15	not any 的用法	239
Unit 16	It is no good 與 It is not good 意思不同	239
Unit 17	避免雙重否定	240
Unit 18	yet 與 already 做副詞的用法比較	241
Unit 19	否定倒裝句	243
Unit 20	用 "否定副詞 / 片語 + 問句" 的倒裝句構表「一……就……」	246
Unit 21	表「如此……以致於……」的句型	248
Unit 22	so... that... 及 such... that... 的倒裝	251
Unit 23	little 做否定副詞時的倒裝	253
Unit 24	"only + 時間副詞" 的倒裝	253
Unit 25	only when、only after 的倒裝	254
Unit 26	only 之後接介詞片語的倒裝	255
Unit 27	比較 only if 與 if only 的不同	256
Unit 28	用 also、too、as well 表「也」	258
Unit 29	用 neither、nor、not either 表「也不」	259
Unit 30	用 Me, too.、Me either.、Me neither. 表「我也是」	260

| Unit 31 | not only... but (also)... 表「不僅……而且……」 | 262 |
| Unit 32 | 感嘆詞 boy 置句首也採問句式倒裝 | 263 |

Chapter 3　搞懂句子、主要子句、副詞子句、形容詞子句、名詞子句之間的區別及功能 ... 265

Unit 33	句子	266
Unit 34	主要子句 + 副詞子句	272
Unit 35	主要子句 + 主要子句	274
Unit 36	命令句 + 主要子句	275
Unit 37	形容詞子句	275
Unit 38	細談關係代名詞、關係代名詞所有格、關係副詞的用法	278
Unit 39	形容詞子句限定修飾與非限定修飾的區別	283
Unit 40	that 取代關係代名詞 who、whom、which	285
Unit 41	who 做形容詞子句受詞時的注意事項	287
Unit 42	關係代名詞 whom、which 做受詞的省略用法	287
Unit 43	關係代名詞 who、whom 接插入語用法	288

Chapter 4　名詞子句 ... 291

Unit 44	何謂名詞子句？如何形成名詞子句？名詞子句有什麼功能？	292
Unit 45	特殊疑問句改成名詞子句	293
Unit 46	一般疑問句改名詞子句	295
Unit 47	「戴慧怡」名詞子句	299
Unit 48	引導 that 子句相關的片語	301
Unit 49	以 it 代替名詞子句	303

Chapter 5　動狀詞 ... 305

| Unit 50 | 動狀詞的種類 | 306 |

Unit 51	原形動詞 / 原形不定詞	307
Unit 52	不定詞片語：to + 原形動詞	308
Unit 53	so as to 與 so that	311
Unit 54	與原形不定詞並用的特殊句構	312
Unit 55	分詞的種類	315
Unit 56	分詞與時態及主被動語態的關係	316
Unit 57	分詞片語的應用與連接詞的使用	320
Unit 58	獨立分詞片語	323
Unit 59	限定修飾的形容詞子句簡化成分詞片語	325
Unit 60	非限定形容詞子句不可簡化成分詞片語	326
Unit 61	簡化副詞子句為分詞構句	327
Unit 62	形容詞＋身體部位名詞變成的過去分詞：描述身體部位	329
Unit 63	分詞作形容詞用	330
Unit 64	主詞補語的誤用：副詞與形容詞的分辨技巧	332
Unit 65	with 引導的情狀片語	333
Unit 66	常用的獨立分詞片語	335
Unit 67	動名詞	335

Chapter 6　假設語氣　341

Unit 68	純條件的假設語氣	342
Unit 69	與現在事實相反的假設語氣	343
Unit 70	與過去事實相反的假設語氣	344
Unit 71	與未來狀況相反的假設語氣	345
Unit 72	使用假設語氣應注意事項	346

Chapter 7　其他常見的混淆用法　349

| Unit 73 | every 連接二個主詞時應用單數還是複數動詞？ | 350 |

Unit 74	everyone 與 every one 的不同	350
Unit 75	「敲門」是 knock the door 或 knock on the door？	351
Unit 76	「在郊區」是 in a suburb 或 in the suburbs？	352
Unit 77	「在城裡」是 in town 或 in the town？	353
Unit 78	「天黑」是 after darkness 或 after dark？	354
Unit 79	「甚至」是 even 或 even though 或 even if？	355
Unit 80	「像家一樣舒適」是 homey 或 homely？	356
Unit 81	provide「提供」與 provided that「如果」的用法	357
Unit 82	「拿給我」是 Give me it. 或 Give it to me.？	358
Unit 83	「比較少」要用 less 還是 fewer？	359
Unit 84	「一分耕耘，一分收穫。」英文怎麼說？	360
Unit 85	「不入虎穴，焉得虎子？」英文怎麼說？	361
Unit 86	「喝湯」是 drink soup 或 eat soup？	361
Unit 87	「如何稱呼……」是 How do you call...? 或 What do you call...?	362
Unit 88	「聖誕節當天」是 on Christmas 或 at Christmas？	363
Unit 89	「回家」是 go to home 或 go home？	364
Unit 90	意志動詞	365

生活應用篇

Chapter 1　Unit 1 >>> Unit 68

常見錯誤用字 / 用詞 / 用語

英文學了好久，總是差那麼一點點就用對了？

本章詳列各種常見錯誤英文用字及文法，幫助你牢記正確的英文用法，不再差之毫釐、失之千里。聽、說、讀、寫皆適用，考試、口說無往不利，英文實力如虎添翼！

Unit 1 「0 度」是 0 <u>degrees</u> 或 0 <u>degree</u>？

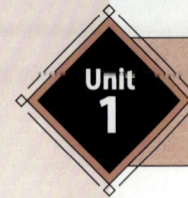

a 注意下列表溫度的英文說法：

例 The current temperature is <u>0 degree</u> Celsius. (✗)
→ The current temperature is <u>0 degrees</u> Celsius. (✓)
目前氣溫是攝氏零度。

理由 0 被視作偶數，故之後接複數名詞，如：
John has zero friends. (✓)
= John has no friend(s). 約翰一個朋友也沒有。

b 0.1 至 0.9 之後亦接複數名詞 degrees。

例 The temperature yesterday was <u>0.3 degrees</u> Fahrenheit. (✓)
昨天氣溫是華氏 0.3 度。

The current temperature on the hilltop is <u>1 degree</u> / <u>2 degrees</u> / <u>25 degrees</u> Celsius. (✓)
目前山頂氣溫是攝氏 1 度 / 2 度 / 25 度。

小試身手

1	Timmy doesn't have any friends. 提示 用數字 0 改寫句子。 Timmy has _____.
2	Q: What was the temperature this morning? 提示 用 0 度回答。 It was _____ this morning.

Ans 1. zero / 0 friends   2. zero / 0 degrees

Unit 2 「一個半小時」是 one and a half hour 或 one and a half hours?

a one and a half 表示「一個半」，既已超過一個，之後應接複數名詞 hours。

例 I'll be back in one and a half hour. (✗)
→ I'll be back in one and a half hours. (✓)
或：I'll be back in an hour and a half. (✓)
我一個半小時就會回來。

注意 但表「兩個半小時 / 三個半小時……」則多採下列說法：
I believe I can finish all the work in two and a half hours / three and a half hours. (✓)

少有人說：
I believe I can finish all the work in two hours and a half / three hours and a half. (罕)

b 半個小時為：half an hour

例 Ken showed up a half hour later. (✗)
→ Ken showed up half an hour later. (✓) 半個小時後肯出現了。

小試身手

選出正確的句子：
Ⓐ I'll be there a half hour later.
Ⓑ Jenny finally arrived at the airport after two and half hours.
Ⓒ In one and a half hours, we will leave town.
Ⓓ Amy will finish her homework in one and a half hour.

Ans Ⓒ

Unit 3 「單詞量大」是 know many vocabularies 或 have a large vocabulary?

vocabulary [vəˈkæbjəˌlɛrɪ] 指「詞彙」或「詞彙量」，也就是你所懂的單詞量 (all the words you know)。

不可說：Tina knows many English vocabularies. (✗)

應　說：Tina has a large English vocabulary. (✓)
= Tina knows many English words.
蒂娜的英文單詞量很大 / 懂許多英文單詞。

例　Reading is a good way to enrich / improve / increase / enlarge your vocabulary. (✓)　閱讀是一個可以增加詞彙量的好途徑。

小試身手

1. The best way to _____ your vocabulary is through reading. (選錯的)
   Ⓐ enlarge　　Ⓑ improve　　Ⓒ add　　Ⓓ enrich

2. My teacher knows a lot of English words.
   提示 用 vocabulary 改寫句子。
   My teacher _____.

Ans　1. Ⓒ　2. has a large English vocabulary

Unit 4 「我很喜歡」是 I very like it. 或 I like it very much.?

very 意思為「很、非常」，用法如下：

a　very 作副詞，可修飾形容詞或副詞：

例　Mary is very beautiful.　瑪麗很美。
　　　　　↱ adj.

Peter works very hard.　彼得工作很努力。
　　　　　　↱ adv.

4

b　very 作副詞時，**不能置動詞前直接修飾該動詞**。若是 very much 則要置句尾方可修飾之前的動詞。

例　I very like music. (✗)
　　　動詞

上句應以副詞 really 取代 very，或在句尾置 very much：
I really like music. (✓)
= I like music very much.　我很喜歡音樂。

注意 一般英美人士會用 a lot 取代 very much，即：
I like music a lot. (更口語)

c　動詞 enjoy (喜歡)、love (愛)、hate (痛恨) 等亦不可用 very 修飾。

例　I very enjoy singing. (✗)
→ I enjoy singing very much. (✓)
= I enjoy singing a lot.　我很喜歡唱歌。

小試身手

選出正確的句子：

1　Ⓐ I like the singer a lot.　　Ⓑ I very like the singer.
　　Ⓒ I very much like the singer.　　Ⓓ I like the singer really a lot.

重組句子：

2　much / very / hates / running
Jennifer _____.

Ans　1. Ⓐ　2. hates running very much

Unit 5 「想要」是 feel like to V 或 feel like + N/V-ing?

feel like 是「想要」的意思，其用法如下：

a feel like + *V*-ing　想要……

上列片語中，feel 是動詞，like 是介詞，故之後應以動名詞 (V-ing) 作受詞，不可接 to 引導的不定詞作受詞。

例 I feel like to swim. (✗)
→ I feel like swimming. (✓)　我想要去游泳。
I don't feel like to eat. (✗)
→ I don't feel like eating.　我不想吃東西。

b feel like + *V*-ing　想要……
= would like to V

例 I feel like to go to the movies this evening. (✗)
→ I feel like going to the movies this evening. (✓)
= I would like to go to the movies this evening.　今晚我想去看電影。

c feel like + *N*　感覺像…… / 想要……

例 I feel like a fool beside you. (✓)　在你身邊我感覺就像個傻瓜似的。
　　　　　　n.
I feel like a drink. (✓)
　　　　　n.
= I feel like drinking.　我想喝點酒。

小試身手

I feel like ＿＿＿ for a walk in the park tonight. Would you like ＿＿＿ me?

Ⓐ going; joining　　　Ⓑ go; join
Ⓒ going; to join　　　Ⓓ to go; joining

Ans Ⓒ

Unit 6 「我認為……不……」是 I don't think he can... 或 I think he cannot...?

表「我認為……不……」在英文中多採下列句構：
I don't think + 肯定的 that 子句 (that 可省略)

例
I think (that) this book is not worth reading. (✗，中式英文)
→ I don't think (that) this book is worth reading. (✓)
我認為這本書不值得一讀。

I think he cannot do it. (✗，中式英文)
→ I don't think he can do it. (✓)　我認為他辦不成這件事。

小試身手

Mr. Wang isn't a liar.
提示 加入 I think / don't think... 改寫句子。
I _____.

Ans don't think Mr. Wang is a liar

Unit 7 「忙碌」是 be busy + to V 或 be busy + V-ing?

busy 意思為「忙碌」，其用法如下：

a　be busy + V-ing　忙著 (從事) ……

例
The kid is busy to do his homework. (✗)
→ The kid is busy doing his homework. (✓)
這個小朋友正忙著做功課。

I'll be busy to write a report this afternoon. (✗)
→ I'll be busy writing a report this afternoon. (✓)
今天下午我會忙著寫報告。

CH 1 常見錯誤用字／用詞／用語

7

補充 英美文法學者對 busy 之後的 V-ing 到底是動名詞還是現在分詞的看法各有堅持，莫衷一是。小弟比較贊成 busy 之後的 V ing 是現在分詞的說法。這一派的人認定："The kid is busy doing his homework." 由下列句子化簡而成：The kid is busy (while he is) doing his homework.。

b be busy with + N　忙碌……

例：Mom is busy with co~~ok~~ing dinner in the kitchen. (✗)
→ Mom is busy with dinner in the kitchen. (✓)
　　　　　　　　　　　　　n.

或：Mom is busy cooking dinner in the kitchen. (✓)
老媽正在廚房煮晚餐。

The kid is busy with his video game. (✓)　這個小朋友正忙著打電動。
　　　　　　　　　　n.

小試身手

1	I was busy ＿＿＿ the dishes when you called last night.
	Ⓐ to do　　Ⓑ to doing　　Ⓒ doing　　Ⓓ with doing
2	Linda will be busy ＿＿＿ her project next month.
	Ⓐ at　　　　Ⓑ with　　　　Ⓒ about　　　Ⓓ of

Ans　1. Ⓒ　2. Ⓑ

Unit 8　「他和我」是 He as well as I is... 或 He as well as I am...?

as well as 表「以及」，其用法如下：

a 可視作連接詞，連接主詞時，動詞按第一個主詞作變化：

例：He as well as I am / are fond of fishing. (✗)
→ He as well as I is fond of fishing. (✓)

He as well as I ~~enjoy~~ fishing (×)
= He as well as I enjoys fishing. (✓)
他和我都喜歡釣魚。

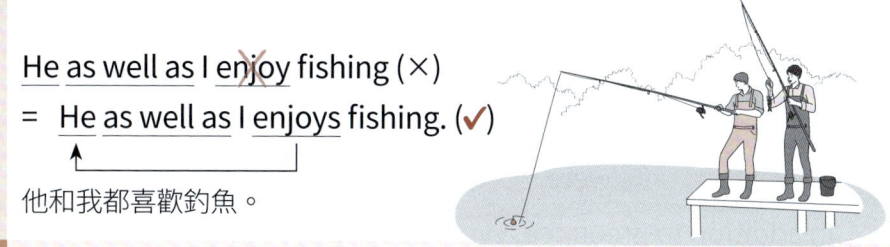

b along with 或 together with 是介詞片語，也表「以及」，之後接受詞。

例 He (主詞) | along with me / together with me | ~~are~~ fond of fishing. (×)
→ He (主詞) | along with me / together with me | is fond of fishing. (✓)
→ He (主詞) | along with me / together with me | ~~enjoy~~ fishing. (×)
= He | along with me / together with me | enjoys fishing. (✓)　他和我都喜歡釣魚。

注意 以上各句最好改用"both A and B + 複數動詞"，即：
(Both) he and I are fond of fishing. (佳)
= (Both) he and I enjoy fishing. (佳)

c as well as 亦可視作介詞，等於 in addition to，表「除……之外尚且……」，通常置句首。

例 As well as ~~sing~~, Jane plays the piano. (×)
→ As well as singing, Jane plays the piano. (✓，少用)
= In addition to singing, Jane plays the piano. (常用)
珍除了會唱歌外，也會彈琴。

小試身手

1. Benjamin as well as the students ＿＿＿ amazed at the view.
   Ⓐ be　　Ⓑ was　　Ⓒ were　　Ⓓ have

2. My friends along with my brother Allen _____ playing baseball in the park yesterday afternoon.
   Ⓐ was　　Ⓑ were　　Ⓒ is　　Ⓓ are

3. In addition to green tea, Lynn also likes root beer.
   提示 用 as well as 改寫句子。
   Lynn likes green tea _____.

Ans　1. Ⓑ　2. Ⓑ　3. as well as root beer

Unit 9　「我完全同意」是 I can't agree with you more. 或 I couldn't agree with you more.?

a 表「我完全同意你的看法／觀點。」，簡單直白的英文說法如下：

例 I <u>fully / totally / completely</u> agree with you. (✓)　我完全同意你的看法。

b 但英文口語中，常用過去式助動詞 "couldn't... more / less" 的結構。

例 A: That girl over there is really pretty.
　B: I <u>can't</u> agree with you <u>more</u>. (較少見)
　→ I <u>couldn't</u> agree with you <u>more</u>. (✓)
　= I fully agree with you.
　A：那邊那個女孩子真美。
　B：我完全同意你的看法。

注意　此處 "I couldn't agree with you more" 按字面的翻譯是「我無法更加同意你的看法了。」，意即「我同意你的看法，同意到了極點，無法復加了。」，是與現在事實相反的假設語氣，故助動詞 can't 應改為過去式較好。

現在事實：I <u>fully agree</u> with you.　我完全同意你的看法。
　　　　　　　現在式動詞

原句實為：I fully agree with you. If you <u>asked</u> me to agree with you
　　　　　　　　　　　　　　　　　　　　　過去式
more, I <u>couldn't</u>.　你若要我再多同意你一點，我做不到。
　　　　過去式

即：我完全／同意你到了極點，無法再更同意了。

A: How's it goin'? (goin' [ˈɡɔɪn] 是 going 的口語說法)
B: (It) Can't be better. (✗)
→ (It) Couldn't be better. (✓)
A：一切都好嗎？
B：好得不得了 / 好極了。（好到無法更好的地步了。）
A: I've heard your ex-girlfriend is getting married next month.
B: I can't care less. (✗)
→ I couldn't care less. (✓)
= I don't care at all.
= I don't give a damn. (俚語)
A：聽說你的前女友下個月就要結婚了。
B：我才不在乎呢。（我不在乎到了極點，無法更加不在乎了。）

小試身手

A: Cats are the most adorable animals in the world.
B: _____ （選錯的）
Ⓐ I couldn't agree with you more.
Ⓑ I completely agree with you.
Ⓒ I could agree with you less.
Ⓓ I totally agree with you.

Ans Ⓒ

Unit 10 「一對一」是 one-on-one 或 one-to-one?

兩者皆為表「一對一」的形容詞，one-on-one 較常被使用，one-to-one 則較少見。

例 I like to play one-on-one half-court basketball.
= I like to play one-to-one half-court basketball.
我喜歡打半場一對一的籃球賽 / 半場鬥牛籃球賽。

It's expensive to find a native speaker to teach you English on a one-on-one basis, but it's worth it.
= It's expensive to find a native speaker to teach you English on a one-to-one basis, but it's worth it.
找母語人士以一對一方式教你英語會很貴，不過很值得。

小試身手

Jenny has a ＿＿＿ meeting with her supervisor to discuss her job performance.

Ⓐ one-on-one　　　　　Ⓑ one on one
Ⓒ one on-one　　　　　Ⓓ one-on one

Ans Ⓐ

Unit 11　「正要……」是 be about to V when... 或 be about to V then...?

a 表「正要……這時……」，不可說：

例　I was about to leave then it started to rain. (✗)
→ I was about to leave when it started to rain. (✓)
我正要離開，這時便開始下雨了。
(此處 when 是連接詞，宜譯成「這時」，不宜譯成「當」。)

理由　then 是副詞，表「當時、然後」，無法連接兩句。
I was busy then.　我當時很忙。
　　　　　adv.

I finished all the work at 5 p.m., then I left. (✗)
　　　　　　　　　　　　　　adv.
→ I finished all the work at 5 p.m., and then I left. (✓)
　　　　　　　　　　　　　　　連接詞
我在下午 5 點把所有工作都做完，然後我就離開了。

b　be about to... when... 亦可被 be on the point of... when... 取代，故：

例　We were about to give up hope when the rescue team showed up.
= We were on the point of giving up hope when the rescue team showed up.
= As we were about to give up, the rescue team showed up.
我們正要放棄希望時，救援小組就出現了。

小試身手

1. Timmy got home at 6:00, ＿＿＿ he made himself some dinner.
　Ⓐ then　　Ⓑ but　　Ⓒ just　　Ⓓ and then

2. 我正要吃晚餐，這時門鈴就響了。
　I was ＿＿＿ ＿＿＿ eat dinner ＿＿＿ the doorbell rang.

3. Judy was on the point of leaving the office when her boss called.
　提示 用 be about to 改寫句子。
　Judy ＿＿＿＿＿＿＿＿＿＿ the office ＿＿＿ her boss called.

Ans　1. Ⓓ　2. about; to; when　3. was about to leave; when

Unit 12　「聯絡」是 contact 人 或 contact with 人？

a　contact 是及物動詞，表「聯絡」或「聯繫」，之後直接接名詞或代名詞作受詞。

例　You can contact with me if you have any questions. (✗)
→ You can contact me if you have any questions. (✓)
你若有什麼問題，可以跟我聯絡。

b　contact 亦可作名詞，表「聯絡」或「聯繫」，有下列用法：
keep in contact / touch with...　與……保持聯絡

13

例　I'll keep contact with you after I go back to my country. (✗)

→ I'll keep in contact / touch with you after I go back to my country. (✓)　我回國後會跟你保持聯絡。

小試身手

Ben tried to ＿＿＿ his classmates after they graduated. (選錯的)
Ⓐ keep in touch with　　Ⓑ keep in contact with
Ⓒ contact　　Ⓓ touch

Ans Ⓓ

Unit 13　「與……結婚」是 marry 人或 marry with 人？

a　marry 是及物動詞 (vt.)，表「與……結婚」，之後直接接受詞。

例　I married with Amy 16 years ago. (✗)

→ I married Amy 16 years ago. (✓)
　　　vt.

= Amy married me 16 years ago.
我與艾咪於 16 年前結為連理。/ 16 年前我娶了艾咪。/ 16 年前艾咪嫁給了我。

b　marry 亦可作不及物動詞 (vi.)，表「結婚」。

例　Miss Roberts | never married. (✓)　勞勃茲小姐終身未嫁。
　　　　　　　　　　vi.
　　　　　　　 | remained single all her life. (✓)

c　過去分詞 married 可作形容詞，表「已婚的」，有下列重要用法：

例　Are you married? (✓)　你 / 妳已婚了嗎？
　　　　　　 adj.

Jane and I got married years ago. (✓)
= Jane was married to me years ago.
= I was married to Jane years ago.
= I married Jane / Jane married me years ago.
= I tied the knot with Jane years ago.　數年前我與阿珍結婚了。

小試身手

1. My mom ＿＿ my dad 30 years ago.
   Ⓐ married to　　　　Ⓑ married
   Ⓒ got married　　　Ⓓ was marrying to

2. Mr. and Mrs. Wang ＿＿ in 1975.
   Ⓐ married to　　　　Ⓑ married
   Ⓒ got married to　　Ⓓ got married with

Ans　1. Ⓑ　2. Ⓑ

Unit 14　「與……離婚」是 divorce 人 或 divorce with 人？

a　divorce 表「與……離婚」，如同 marry「與……結婚」，是及物動詞，之後直接接名詞。

例　Tom divorced with Linda last month. (✗)
Tom divorced from Linda last month. (✗)
→ Tom divorced Linda last month. (✓)
湯姆跟琳達上個月離婚了。

b　過去分詞 divorced 可做形容詞，表「離婚的」。形成 get divorced 的固定片語。

例　Tom and Linda got divorced last month.　湯姆跟琳達上個月離婚了。
Mr. Smith / Ms. Johnson is divorced with a child.
史密斯先生 / 強森女士已離婚，還帶了一個孩子。

小試身手

1. Judy divorced _____ Andy two years ago.
   Ⓐ with　　Ⓑ to　　Ⓒ about　　Ⓓ ×

2. My sister got _____ last week. She's still crying over it.
   Ⓐ divorce　Ⓑ divorcing　Ⓒ divorced　Ⓓ to divorce

Ans　1. Ⓓ　2. Ⓒ

Unit 15　「與……訂婚」是 engage 人 或 be engaged to 人？

a　動詞 engage 無「訂婚」之意，表「訂婚的」只可使用過去分詞 engaged 做形容詞用，不可說：

例　I engaged with Lynn last month. (×)
　　I was engaged with Lynn last month. (×)
　→ Lynn and I got engaged last month. (✓)
　= Lynn was engaged to me last month.
　= I was engaged to Lynn last month.　上個月我和琳訂婚了。

b　engaged 作形容詞時，除了當作「訂婚的」，亦可表示電話「忙線的」或某人「正在忙著從事……」的，有下列用法：

例　The line is engaged now. (✓)
　= The line is busy now.　電話正忙線中。
　Peter is engaged in something important, so let's not bother him now. (✓)
　= Peter is busy with something important, so let's not bother him now.
　彼得正忙著處理一件重要的事情，因此咱們現在就不打擾他吧。

c　engage 也可作不及物動詞，有下列用法：
　　engage with 人　與某人密切互動

例　As a teacher, you should know how to engage your students. (✗)
　→ As a teacher, you should know how to engage with your students. (✓)　身為老師，你應知道如何與學生好好互動。

d　engage 亦可作及物動詞，表「雇用」，等於 hire 或 employ。

例　Andy was once | engaged | by that school as a part-time English teacher.
　　　　　　　　　| hired |
　　　　　　　　　| employed |
　　安迪曾一度受聘在那所學校擔任兼職英文老師。

小試身手

1. Pablo and Amanda ＿＿＿ last month. They'll get married in June.
　Ⓐ got engaged　　　　Ⓑ got engaged to
　Ⓒ engaged　　　　　　Ⓓ got engaged with

2. Since Kelly is ＿＿＿ now, I'll call again later.
　Ⓐ engaging　Ⓑ engaged　Ⓒ engage　Ⓓ been engaged

3. I will be ＿＿＿ by the company as a secretary next month. (選錯的)
　Ⓐ engaged　Ⓑ employed　Ⓒ hired　Ⓓ worked

Ans　1. Ⓐ　2. Ⓑ　3. Ⓓ

Unit 16 「好消息」是 That's good news. 或 That's a good news.?

news 是名詞，表「消息」或「新聞」，是不可數名詞，故不可說 a good news。應說 good news (好消息)、a good piece of news (一則好消息)、some good news (一些好消息) 或 a lot of good news (許多好消息)。

例　I've just received ~~a~~ good news that Peter got promoted to general manager. (✗)

→ I've just received good news / a good piece of news that Peter got promoted to general manager. (✓)
我剛獲悉（一則）好消息，那就是彼得升任總經理了。

No news is good news.　沒消息就是好消息。

小試身手

重組句子：news / Your promotion / is / great / such

_____

Ans Your promotion is such great news.

Unit 17 「一個建議」是 an advice 或 a piece of advice?

advice 是不可數名詞，表「建議」或「忠告」。用法如下：

a　不可說 an advice。應說 a piece of advice（一個建議）、some advice（一些建議）或 a lot of advice（許多建議）。

例　Could you give me some ~~advices~~ on how to improve my spoken English? (✗)

→ Could you give me some advice on how to improve my spoken English? (✓)
有關如何精進我的英文口語，可否請你給我一點建議？

That's really ~~a~~ good advice. Thank you! (✗)

→ That's really a good piece of advice. Thank you! (✓)
那真是個好建議。謝謝你！

b　tip、suggestion 及 recommendation 也可表「建議」，是可數名詞，故可用複數。

例　Could you give me | a few | tips / suggestions / recommendations
　　　　　　　　　　　 | some |
on that issue? (✓)

= Could you give me | some | advice on that issue?
　　　　　　　　　　| a little |

有關那個問題您可否給我一些建議？

注意 a few 之後接複數名詞，a little 之後接不可數名詞，some 之後可接複數名詞或不可數名詞。此外，上列兩句劃底線的 on 均等於 about，表「有關」。

小試身手

1. I really need ＿＿ on how to choose my future career.
   Ⓐ advices
   Ⓑ many advice
   Ⓒ piece of advice
   Ⓓ a lot of advice

2. My parents always offer me many useful ＿＿ when I'm in trouble.（選錯的）
   Ⓐ advice
   Ⓑ recommendations
   Ⓒ tips
   Ⓓ suggestions

Ans　1. Ⓓ　2. Ⓐ

Unit 18　「考試不及格」是 fail the test 或 fail in the test？

fail 可當及物動詞也可當不及物動詞，有「失敗、讓某人失望」等等的意思，其用法如下：

a　fail 作及物動詞時，其中之一的意思為「未通過」，直接以名詞 test（測驗）、quiz（小考）、exam（大考）、final exam（期末考）等作受詞。

例　I felt sad because I failed ✗ in the math test.（✗）
　→ I felt sad because I failed the math test.（✓）
　我數學測驗沒及格，因此心情難過。

b　fail 作及物動詞時還有一個意思為「讓……失望或考試不及格」，用法為：fail 人　使某人失望；使某人（考試）不及格

例　Keep working hard. Don't fail to me. (×)
→ Keep working hard. Don't fail me. (✓)
= Keep working hard. Don't disappoint me.
= Keep working hard. Don't let me down.　繼續努力。別令我失望。
The final exams was so tough that half of the students were failed. (✓)　期末考太難了，因此有半數的同學被當了。

c　fail 作不及物動詞時的其中一個意思為「沒辦法……」，之後接 to 引導的不定詞片語，即：fail to + V　未能……。故 a 的例句亦可改寫如下：

例　I felt sad because I failed in passing the math test. (×)
→ I felt sad because I failed to pass the math test. (✓)
= I felt said because I didn't pass the math test.
You'll be in trouble if you fail to meet my expectations. (✓)
= You'll be in trouble if you don't meet my expectations.
(此處 expectations 恆用複數)　你若未達到我的期望就要倒霉了。

d　fail 作不及物動詞時，亦可指健康方面的「弱化」

例　Dad is aging, and his health is failing.　老爸年事漸高，健康也在弱化了。

小試身手

1　Nick failed _____ the history test today and he has been crying for half an hour.
Ⓐ in　　Ⓑ on　　Ⓒ of　　Ⓓ ×

2　Betty failed to _____ first place in the race.
Ⓐ win　　Ⓑ wins　　Ⓒ won　　Ⓓ winning

3　I'm sorry that I let you down. I'll work harder next time.
提示　將前句用 fail 改寫。
I'm sorry that _____. I'll work harder next time.

Ans　1. Ⓓ　2. Ⓐ　3. I failed you

Unit 19 「考得好」是 do well in the test 或 on the test?

表「考試考得很好」應使用 do well on the test。exam、test、quiz 均指「考試」的試卷，在試卷上作答應使用 on 而非 in。故美語中，下列片語均使用 on：

例 Ted did well on the English test this morning. (✓)
今天早上的英語測驗泰德考得很好。

Hank scored 98 points on the monthly exam in math. (✓)
漢克數學月考考了 98 分。

Anthony was caught cheating on the pop quiz. (✓)
安東尼抽考作弊被逮個正著。

注意 以上各句在英式英語中也有人會使用 in 取代 on。

小試身手

Allen didn't do very well _____ the test this morning.
Ⓐ on　　Ⓑ to　　Ⓒ ✗　　Ⓓ of

Ans Ⓐ

Unit 20 「失敗」是 get a fail 或 get a failure?

failure 是名詞，表「失敗」，fail 是動詞，表「考試不及格」，用法如下：

a 與 pass（及格）對應如下：

例 Regarding the final exams, I got four passes and two failures. (✗)
→ Regarding the final exams, I got four passes and two fails. (✓)
有關期末考，我有四科及格，兩科不及格。

b without fail　務必；總是

例　You must finish the report by 5 p.m. without failure. (✗)
→ You must finish the report by 5 p.m. without fail. (✓)
你務必要在下午 5 點以前完成報告。

Every day, Ed has soy milk and two eggs for breakfast without fail. (✓)　艾德每天早餐都是喝豆漿及吃兩顆蛋。

比較　without failure　若無失敗
There is no success without failure. (✓)　若無失敗就沒有成功。

小試身手

1. Tina got a _____ in the midterm this semester and has to retake the course during the summer vacation.
Ⓐ failure　　Ⓑ fail　　Ⓒ fault　　Ⓓ fall

2. 麥可每天下課總是去打籃球。
Michael plays basketball after class every day _____.

Ans　1. Ⓑ　2. without; fail

Unit 21　「玩玩具」是 play toys 或 play with toys?

「與……玩」動詞為 play，但需要接介詞 with 才接受詞嗎？請見以下說明：

a play 為不及物動詞時，表「把玩、玩弄」(玩具、鑰匙、小器具等等)，之後要接介詞 with，方可接受詞。

例　Little Billy is playing his toys. (✗)
小比利正在演奏他的玩具。
→ Little Billy is playing with his toys. (✓)
小比利正在把玩他的玩具。

Peter tends to play his pen when he feels bored. (✗)
→ Peter tends to play with his pen when he feels bored. (✓)
彼得覺得無聊時，會玩弄他的筆。

b play 作及物動詞時，表「玩」各類球類或比賽性運動如下，之後直接接受詞：

play basketball / volleyball / soccer / badminton / tennis / chess / hide-and-seek...
打籃球 / 打排球 / 踢足球 / 打羽毛球 / 打網球 / 下棋 / 玩捉迷藏……

注意 上列名詞之前不得置 the。

例 I used to play the basketball a lot in my teenage years. (×)
→ I used to play basketball a lot in my teenage years. (✓)
我十幾歲的時候常打籃球。

I'm already sixty, so I guess I'm too old to play hide-and-seek. (✓)
我已六十歲了，所以我想我年紀太大不能玩捉迷藏了。

c 若是表「彈奏」、「吹奏」樂器時，則需要加 the：

play the piano / the flute / the drums / the guitar / the saxophone...
彈鋼琴 / 吹笛子 / 打鼓 / 彈吉他 / 吹薩克斯風……

例 Lily plays guitar very well. (×)
→ Lily plays the guitar very well. (✓) 莉莉吉他彈得很好。

小試身手

Ⓐ × Ⓑ with Ⓒ the

1 Ben likes music, so he wants to learn to play _____ piano.
2 Kelly likes to play _____ chess in her free time.
3 Tommy is playing _____ his favorite toy gun in the living room.

Ans 1. Ⓒ 2. Ⓐ 3. Ⓑ

CH 1 常見錯誤用字／用詞／用語

23

Unit 22 「厚衣服」是 thick clothes 或 heavy clothes?

表「厚衣服」，應說 heavy clothes，而非 thick clothes。heavy clothes 指「厚重的衣服」，有數層保暖衣及外套。thick clothes 則指單層面料厚的衣服。

例 I wear ~~thick~~ clothes when the weather is cold and ~~thin~~ clothes when the weather is hot. (✕，中式英語)

→ I wear heavy / warm clothes in cold weather and light clothes in hot weather. (✓)

天冷時我會穿厚 / 保暖的衣服，天熱時我則穿薄的衣服。

小試身手

那名街友沒有保暖的衣服過冬。
The homeless guy doesn't have any _____ _____ to get through winter.

Ans heavy / warm; clothes

Unit 23 「恭喜」是 congratulation 或 congratulations?

a 表「恭賀」、「恭喜」的名詞一定要使用複數名詞 congratulations。

例 ~~Congratulation~~ on your promotion to general manager! (✕)

→ Congratulations on your promotion to general manager! (✓)

= Congrats on your promotion to general manager! (口語)

恭喜你升任總經理！

Please accept my ~~congratulation~~ on your new job. (✕)

→ Please accept my congratulations on your new job. (✓)

您獲得新工作，請接受我的祝賀。

b congratulate 是及物動詞，採下列結構：
congratulate 人 on + 名詞 / 動名詞

例 I'd like to congratulate to you for passing the test. (✗)
→ I'd like to congratulate you on passing the test. (✓)
= Congratulations to you on passing the test.
(我要) 恭喜你考試及格了。

小試身手

1. ＿＿＿ ＿＿＿ winning first prize!
   Ⓐ Congratulation; in
   Ⓑ Congratulations; in
   Ⓒ Congratulation; on
   Ⓓ Congratulations; on

2. 家裡每個人都恭喜泰迪詩詞競賽獲勝。
   Everyone in the family ＿＿＿＿ Teddy ＿＿ winning the poetry competition.

Ans 1. Ⓓ 2. congratulated; on

Unit 24 「遇到麻煩」是 have trouble to V 或 have trouble V-ing?

名詞 trouble 表「問題、麻煩」等，用法如下：

a have | trouble / difficulty / problems / a hard time | + V-ing （從事）……有困難

例 We have trouble to communicate with that stubborn guy. (✗)
→ We have trouble communicating with that stubborn guy. (✓)
我們跟那個固執的傢伙溝通有困難。

I was surprised when Joe said he had difficulty to work with me. (✗)
→ I was surprised when Joe said he had difficulty working with me. (✓)　當喬說他很難跟我共事時，我很驚訝。

Most Japanese have problems to pronounce English words ending with "l". (✗)

→ Most Japanese have problems pronouncing English words ending with "l". (✓)　許多日本人很難發用 l 結尾的單詞發音。

I've had a hard time to sleep recently. (✗)

→ I've had a hard time sleeping recently. (✓)　最近我一直很難入睡。

b

| have | trouble
difficulty
problems
a hard time | with + 名詞 |

例

I'm having | trouble / difficulty / problems / a hard time | about my term paper. (✗)

→ I'm having | trouble / difficulty / problems / a hard time | with my term paper. (✓)

= I'm having | trouble / difficulty / problems / a hard time | doing / writing my term paper.

我目前寫學期報告有困難。

小試身手

1. I have been having trouble _____ with my boss.
 Ⓐ to communicate　　Ⓑ communicating
 Ⓒ to communicating　Ⓓ into communicating

2. Judy is having a hard time _____ her project. We should help her.
 Ⓐ at　　Ⓑ about　　Ⓒ with　　Ⓓ in

Ans　1. Ⓑ　2. Ⓒ

Unit 25 「做……很愉快」是 have fun to V 或 have fun V-ing？

fun 的意思為「樂趣、開心」等，其用法如下：
have fun + V-ing　（從事）……很愉快
= have a good / great / wonderful / fantastic time + V-ing

例　Mary and I had lots of fun to chat over dinner. (×)
→ Mary and I had lots of fun chatting over dinner. (✓)
我和瑪麗邊用餐邊聊天愉快極了。

I'm having a great time to listen to music now. (×)
→ I'm having a great time listening to music now. (✓)
我正在聽音樂聽得很愉快。

小試身手

Kevin and I had a wonderful time watching movies last night.
提示　用 have fun 改寫句子。
Kevin and I _____ last night.

Ans　had (lots of / a lot of) fun watching movies

Unit 26 「得第一名」是 win first place 或 win the first place？

a　"first place、second place、third place…" 表「第一名、第二名、第三名……」，之前不得加定冠詞 the。

例　Jason won the first place in the speech competition. (×)
傑森在演講比賽贏得第一個頒發的獎。（—— 可能是「舒潔」一包）
→ Jason won first place in the speech competition. (✓)
= Jason came in first（非 came in the first）
in the speech competition.　傑森在演講比賽贏得第一名。

27

b　"first prize、second prize、third place..." 表「首獎、二獎、三獎⋯⋯」，之前也不得加定冠詞。

例　Hank won the first prize in the international chess tournament. (✗)
漢克在國際象棋循環賽贏得第一個頒發的獎。（──可能是巧克力兩片）

→ Hank won first prize in the international chess tournament. (✓)
漢克在國際象棋循環賽贏了首獎。

注意 the first prize 是第一個頒發的獎，未必是首獎 (first prize)。

小試身手

莉莉在 100 公尺賽跑中贏得第一名，而第一名的獎項是現金 20,000 元。
Lily won _____ in the 100-meter race, and _____ was twenty thousand dollars in cash.

Ans　first; place; first; prize

Unit 27　「我喜歡」是 I love it. 或 I am loving it.?

這個問題我們要從動詞種類開始探討，動詞可分靜態動詞 (stative verbs) 及動態動詞 (dynamic verbs)，這兩種差別如下：

a　靜態動詞指一種心理或情感的「認知」，如 know（知道）、want（想要）、admit（承認）、deny（否認）、think（認為）、feel（覺得）、love（愛）、like（喜歡）、dislike（不喜歡）、hate（痛恨）等。感官動詞如 taste（聽起來）、以及表「擁有」的動詞，如 have（有）、own（擁有）等也均包括在內，這些動詞無法用進行式 (be + V-ing)。

不可說：I'm knowing (that) he is trustworthy. (✗)
我正在知道他值得信任。（中文無此說法。）

→ I know he is trustworthy. (✓)
我知道他值得信任。

例　I'm having some money. (✗)　我正在有一些錢。（中文無此說法。）
→ I have some money. (✓)　我有一些錢。

由上得知：I'm loving it. (✘)　我正在愛它。
→ I love it. (✔)　我喜歡 / 愛它。

註　"I'm Loving It." 是麥當勞公司於 2003 年推出的廣告歌曲名，該公司故意以不合語法的曲名成功地引起大眾的注意。英語文法家均認為 "I'm loving it." 是錯誤的句子。但也有人認為 "I'm loving it." 等於 "I'm enjoying it."（我正在享用它。），故大家知道就好，也就不必太介意了。

b 動態動詞指與「動作」有關的動詞，如 eat（吃）、drink（喝）、sleep（睡）、run（跑）、jump（跳）、shout（大叫；咆哮）、cry（哭）等。這類動詞可採用進行式 (be + V-ing)。

例　The baby sleeps now. (✘)　小寶寶目前睡。（中文不通）
→ The baby is sleeping now. (✔)　小寶寶現在正在睡覺。
The baby cries now. (✘)　小寶寶現在哭。（中文不通）
→ The baby is crying now. (✔)　小寶寶現在正在哭。

總而言之，只要中文有「正在」時就可使用進行式（使用 be + 現在分詞），否則就用簡單式（使用動詞即可）。

I'm having money. (✘)　我正在有錢。（中文不通）
→ I have money. (✔)　我有錢。
I'm seldom eating hamburgers. (✘)　我很少正在吃漢堡。（中文不通）
→ I seldom eat hamburgers. (✔)　我很少吃漢堡。
Tom is looking like a monkey. (✘)　湯姆正看起來像隻猴子。（中文不通）
→ Tom looks like a monkey. (✔)　湯姆看起來像隻猴子。
We look for a big house. (✘)　我們尋找一間大房子。（中文不通）
→ We're looking for a big house. (✔)　我們正在尋找一間大房子。
We're considering him a hero. (✘)
我們正在認為他是個英雄。（中文不通）
→ We all consider him a hero. (✔)　我們大家都認為他是個英雄。
I'm thinking (that) he is cut out for the job. (✘)
我正在認為他很適合這份工作。（中文不通）
→ I think he is cut out for the job. (✔)
我覺得 / 認為他很適合這份工作。

小試身手

1. I ＿＿＿ to know if you'd like to go out with me today.
   Ⓐ want　　Ⓑ am wanting　　Ⓒ am wanted　　Ⓓ have wanted

2. The kids ＿＿＿ up and down on the bed now.
   Ⓐ jump　　Ⓑ are jumping　　Ⓒ have jumping　　Ⓓ jumped

Ans　1. Ⓐ　2. Ⓑ

Unit 28　「微不足道的人或事物」是 a small potato 或 small potatoes？

small potatoes 表「微不足道的事物或人」時恆為複數。

例　I'm a small potato compared with that great hero. (✗)
→ I'm small potatoes compared with that great hero. (✓)
= I'm nothing compared with that great hero.
跟那位偉大的英雄相比，我不算什麼。

Your workload is a small potato in comparison with mine. (✗)
→ Your workload is small potatoes in comparison with mine. (✓)
= Your workload is nothing in comparison with mine.
你的工作量跟我的相比算是小巫見大巫。

小試身手

Andy is nothing in this field compared with the award winner.
提示　用 small potatoes 改寫句子。
Andy ＿＿＿＿＿＿＿＿＿＿ in this field compared with the award winner.

Ans　is small potatoes

Unit 29 「照鏡子」是 look into the mirror 或 look at the mirror?

表「照鏡子」應使用 look "into" the mirror，乃因往鏡內透視可看到自己的影像。look at the mirror 則把鏡子當作一個不能透視的物體，兩眼盯著這個物體看，而非照鏡子。

例 Ted looked at the mirror and saw his father standing behind him. (✗)

→ Ted looked into the mirror and saw his dad standing behind him. (✓)　泰德照鏡子看到他老爸就站在他身後。

Nick looked at / looked over the mirror carefully to make sure it was not broken. (✓)
尼克仔細看著 / 檢查鏡子以確定它沒破裂。

小試身手

Linda looked ＿＿＿ the mirror and combed her hair.
(A) at　　(B) over　　(C) into　　(D) to

Ans (C)

Unit 30 「把衣服穿反了」是 wear 物 outside in 或 wear 物 inside out?

a. inside out 表「裡面朝外」，outside in 表「外面朝裡」，但表「把衣服穿反了」，只能說 "wear 物 inside out"，無 "wear 物 outside in" 的用法。

例 Look! Aaron is wearing his T-shirt outside in. (✗)

→ Look! Aaron is wearing his T-shirt inside out. (✓)
瞧！艾倫把 T-shirt 穿反了。

b. know 人 / 物 inside out　對某人 / 某物瞭若指掌
= know 人 / 物 like the back of one's hand

31

例 Don't attempt to fool me. I know you inside out. (✓)
= Don't attempt to fool me. I know you like the back of my hand.
別想唬我。我太了解你了。

I've been living here over the past 30 years, so I know this area inside out.
= I've been living here over the past 30 years, so I know this area like the back of my hand.
我過去 30 年來我都住在這裡，因此我對這個地方瞭若指掌。

小試身手

1	I wore my dress ＿＿＿ today and made a fool of myself. Ⓐ outside　Ⓑ inside　Ⓒ outside in　Ⓓ inside out
2	Amy and I are very close friends, so I know her like the back of my hand. 提示 用 inside out 改寫句子。 Amy and I are very close friends, so I know her ＿＿＿＿＿＿＿＿.

Ans 1. Ⓓ　2. inside out

Unit 31 「住飯店」是 stay at the hotel 或 live at the hotel?

stay 指短暫「居留」，live 指長期「居住」，尤指戶籍所在地。故住在旅館裡動詞應用 stay。

例 I went on vacation in Paris last May and lived in a luxurious hotel. (✗)
→ I went on vacation in Paris last May and stayed at a luxurious hotel. (✓)
我五月份到巴黎渡假，住在一間豪華的飯店。

Starting next week, I'll be on business in New York, and I'm going to live there for half a year. (✗)

→ Starting next week, I'll be on business in New York, and I'm going to stay there for half a year. (✓)
下星期開始，我就會到紐約出差，在那邊我會待上半年。

I've been staying in Kaohsiung ever since I was born. (✗)

→ I've been living in Kaohsiung ever since I was born. (✓)
我從出生起就一直住在高雄。

I used to live in Taoyuan, but now I live in Taipei. (✓)
我以前住在桃園，不過現在則住在台北。

小試身手

我們在泰國旅遊期間住在旅館裡。
We _____ _____ a hotel during our trip in Thailand.

Ans stayed; at

Unit 32 「……已無用」是 It is no use to V 或 It is no use V-ing?

"it is no use + V-ing" 是固定結構，表「……已無用」。

例 It is no use to cry over spilt milk. (✗)

→ It is no use crying over spilt milk. (✓)

= There is no use (in) crying over spilt milk.
（實際用法始終省略 in）

= It is useless to cry over spilt milk.

= It is no use for you to cry over spilt milk.

牛奶灑出來，哭也無用了。——生米已成熟飯，後悔無濟於事。（諺語）

A: I failed the test, and I regret at not having studied hard.
B: It's no use crying over spilt milk. Work harder from now on.
A：我考試沒及格，很後悔沒好好唸書。
B：生米已成熟飯。從現在起要更加努力才是。

小試身手

What is done is done. It is useless to explain it anymore.
提示 用 it is no use 改寫句子。
What is done is done. _____ it anymore.

Ans It is no use explaining

Unit 33 「不需要」是 need not V 或 need not to V？

need 意為「需要」，可當一般動詞也可當助動詞，用法如下：

a need 與 not 並用時，need 視作助動詞，主詞不論是第幾人稱，均使用 need not，形成下列固定用法：
need not + 原形動詞　不必……

例　Tom is at fault, so you need not to apologize to him. (✗)
→ Tom is at fault, so you need not apologize to him. (✓)
湯姆有錯，因此你不必向他道歉。

I'm on leave today, so my wife needs not to mop the floor. I will do it for her. (✗)
→ I'm on leave today, so my wife need not / needn't mop the floor. I will do it for her. (✓)
我今天休假，因此我老婆不必拖地板。我幫她做就行了。

b need 亦可作動詞，之後亦可接 to 引導的不定詞語作受詞，即：
need to + 原形動詞　有必要……

例　Jay need to finish the work now. (✗)
→ Jay needs to finish the work now. (✓)　阿傑現在需要完成工作。

c 由上得知：

例　Tom is at fault, so you need not apologize to him. (✓)
　　　　　　　　　　　　　助動詞
= Tom is at fault, so you don't need to apologize to him.
　　　　　　　　　　　　　　　　　動詞

34

I'm on leave today, so my wife <u>need not mop</u> the floor. I'll do it for her. (✔)
　　　　　　　　　　　　　　　　助動詞

= I'm on leave today, so my wife <u>doesn't need to mop</u> the floor. I'll do it for her.
　　　　　　　　　　　　　　　　　　　　　　　動詞

注意 "didn't need to + 原形動詞" 與 "needn't have + 過去分詞" 的不同。

{
  didn't need to + 原形動詞　　當時沒必要做某事，也就未做此事
  needn't have + 過去分詞　　　當時沒必要做某事，卻做了此事 (與過去事實相反的假設語氣)
}

It was Sunday yesterday, so John <u>didn't need to go</u> to school. He stayed home listening to music.
昨天是星期天，因此約翰沒必要到學校去上學。他待在家聽音樂。

I've already cleaned the dishes, so you <u>needn't have washed</u> them again. (But you washed them again.)
我已經清洗過這些碗筷了，因此你就不必再清洗了。(不過你卻又清洗了一遍。)

小試身手

1. Danny _____ not clean his room because Mom already did it for him.
　Ⓐ need　Ⓑ needs　Ⓒ needed　Ⓓ didn't need

2. You _____ shout; I can hear you perfectly.
　Ⓐ need not to　　　　Ⓑ don't need to
　Ⓒ need to not　　　　Ⓓ don't need

3. My friends didn't stay for dinner, so my mom _____ dinner last night.
　Ⓐ needn't prepare　　Ⓑ don't need to prepare
　Ⓒ needed not　　　　Ⓓ needn't have prepared

Ans　1. Ⓐ　2. Ⓑ　3. Ⓓ

CH 1　常見錯誤用字／用詞／用語

35

Unit 34 「很棒的老師」是 so nice a teacher 或 a so nice teacher?

在 "so... that..."（如此……以致於……）的句型中，so 是副詞，表「如此地、那麼地」，之後須接形容詞，再接 a / an + 單數可數名詞。故形成：so + 形容詞 + a / an + 單數可數名詞

例 Mr. Li is a so nice teacher that we all like him. (✗)

→ Mr. Li is so nice a teacher that we all like him. (✓)

= Mr. Li is such a nice teacher that we all like him.

李先生是那麼好的老師，因此我們都很喜歡他。

a 上列句型不可接不可數名詞或複數名詞。

例 It is so good music that I never feel tired of listening to it. (✗)
　　　　　不可數名詞

They are so good teachers that I respect them all. (✗)
　　　　　　　　複數名詞

此時只能使用 "such + 形容詞 + 不可數名詞 / 複數名詞"。故上列兩句應改寫如下：

It is such good music that I never feel tired of listening to it. (✓)
這音樂真好聽，我百聽不厭。

They are such good teachers that I respect them all. (✓)
他們是很棒的老師，因此我很尊敬他們。

b 但 "so much + 不可數名詞" 或 "so many + 複數名詞" 則合語法。

例 I have so much work to do that I can't go out with you today. (✓)
　　　　　不可數名詞

= I have so many things to do that I can't go out with you today.
我今天有太多的工作 / 事情要做，因此無法跟你外出了。

小試身手

1. 選出語法錯誤的句子。
   - Ⓐ Judy had so much work today that she couldn't get off work on time.
   - Ⓑ Spot was such a great dog that I'll remember him for the rest of my life.
   - Ⓒ Rick and Dave are my so good friends that we hang out almost every day.
   - Ⓓ Debra is so kind a lady that everyone respects her.

2. Joe is a very handsome guy. Many girls want to be with him.
   提示 用「so＋形容詞＋a / an＋單數可數名詞」合併句子。
   Joe is ＿＿＿＿＿＿＿＿＿＿＿＿＿ many girls want to be with him.

   Ans 1. Ⓒ 2. so handsome a guy that

Unit 35 「年紀太大」是 too old a man 或 a too old man？

"too... to..." 表「太……而不能……」。此處 too 是副詞，表「太過於」，之後須接形容詞方可接不定冠詞的 a / an，再接單數名詞。

故不可說：My neighbor is a too old man to walk. (✗)
應　　說：My neighbor is too old a man to walk. (✓)
我的鄰居年紀太大，走不動了。

注意 1 在 "too... to..." 的句構中，"too + adj." 不可接不可數名詞或複數名詞。

例 They are too old people to walk. (✗)
　　　　　　　　複數名詞

→ They are too old to walk. (✓)
他們年紀太大，走不動了。

It is too difficult work to handle. (✗)
　　　　　　　不可數名詞

→ The work is too difficult to handle. (✓)
這工作太難，無法處理了。

注意 2 "too much + 不可數名詞" 或 "too many + 複數名詞" 則合語法：

I have too much work to deal with today to go out with you. (✓)
　　　　　不可數名詞

= I have too many things to deal with today to go out with you.
我今天有太多的工作 / 事情要處理，無法跟你出去玩了。

小試身手

選出語法正確的句子。
Ⓐ These are too easy jobs to finish.
Ⓑ The swimming pool is too cold to swim in.
Ⓒ It is too hot water to drink.
Ⓓ There were so many people at the party to move around.

Ans Ⓑ

Unit 36 「被選為市長」是 be elected mayor 或 be elected the mayor?

想表達「被選為……」或「競選……」時，表「職位」的名詞之前不得置冠詞 the 或 a / an。

例 Mr. Smith was elected the mayor of the city. (✗)
→ Mr. Smith was elected mayor of the city. (✓)

It is said that the businessman will run for the president again. (✗)
據說這位商人會再次為該總統跑步。（不合邏輯）
→ It is said that the businessman will run for president again. (✓)
據說這位商人會再次競選總統。

小試身手

丹尼今天被選為班長。
Danny _____ _____ class leader today.

Ans was; elected

Unit 37 「總統當選人」是 president-elect 或 president-elected？

表「總統當選人」應為 president-elect，非 president-elected。

例 The president-elected is scheduled to give a victory speech this evening. (✗)

→ The president-elect is scheduled to give a victory speech this evening. (✓)

= The newly-elected president is scheduled to a victory speech this evening.
總統當選人預定今晚發表勝選演講。

小試身手

總統當選人將於下週拜訪立法院。

The _____ is going to visit the Legislative Yuan next week.

Ans president-elect

Unit 38 「估計有兩百人」是 an estimate 200 people 或 an estimated 200 people？

an estimated + 數字　估計有……

例 An estimate 200 people were killed in the air crash. (✗)

→ An estimated 200 people were killed in the air crash. (✓)

= It is estimated that 200 people were killed in the air crash.
這次空難估計有兩百人死亡。

The building is worth an estimate $10 million. (✗)

→ The building is worth an estimated $10 million. (✓)

= It is estimated that the building is worth $10 million.
這棟大樓估計值一千萬美元。

39

小試身手

It is estimated that the company is worth $5 million.
提示 用 The company 開頭改寫句子。
The company _____ $5 million.

Ans is worth an estimated

Unit 39 「許多的」是 a good many 或 a lot many?

a good many 表「許多的……」，後接可數複數名詞。
a good many + 複數名詞　許多的……
= a great many + 複數名詞
= a large number of + 複數名詞
= | a lot of | + 複數名詞
　| lots of |

例　I saw a lot many people at the concert. (✗)
→ I saw a good many people at the concert. (✓)
= I saw a large audience (非 many audiences) at the concert.
我在演唱會上看到好多人 / 一大群觀眾。

小試身手

Although Patty is very sad about the breakup, luckily she has _____ friends to keep her company.（選錯的）
Ⓐ lots of　　　　　　　Ⓑ a good many
Ⓒ a lot many　　　　　Ⓓ a large number of

Ans Ⓒ

Unit 40 「我的一位好友」是 the best friend of mine 或 a good friend of mine?

在英文中要如何表達「我的一位好友」？請見以下說明：

a 英文中並無 "the best + 名詞 + of + 所有格代名詞 (mine、yours、hers、his、theirs、ours 等)" 的用法，故不可說：
Jack is the best friend of mine. (✗)

應說：Jack is one of my best friends. (✓)
傑克是我最要好的朋友之一。

或：Jack is my best friend. (✓)
傑克是我最要好的朋友。

b 除 the 以外，其他如冠詞 (a / an)，數詞 (two、three...)，數量形容詞 (no、a few、some、any、several、many、most)，指示形容詞 (this、that、these、those) 及疑問詞 (which) 均可與所有格代名詞並用，稱作「雙重所有格」，結構如下：
不定冠詞 / 數詞 / 數量形容詞 / 指示形容詞 / which (哪一個) + 名詞 + of + 所有格代名詞

例 A friend of my is coming to visit me this afternoon. (✗)
→ A friend of mine is coming to visit me this afternoon. (✓)
我的一位朋友今天下午會來看我。

注意 在本句型中，不要使用數詞 one 取代 a / an，即：
I ran into one old friend of mine this morning. (✗)
→ I ran into an old friend of mine this morning. (✓)
= I ran into one of my old friends this morning.
今天早上我碰到我的一位老友。

Two friends of mine are very good at singing. (✓)
= Two of my friends are very good at singing.
我的兩位朋友歌唱得很好。

Which car of your can I use? (✗)
→ Which car of yours can I use? (✓) 你的哪一輛車可讓我使用？

You can use these pens of mine. (✓)　你可以使用我的這些筆。
Are you a friend of Tom? (✗)　你是湯姆的朋友嗎？
→ Are you a friend of Tom's? (✓)
I've read some books of yours. (✓)　我曾看過你的一些書。
No friends of mine will ever do things like this! (✓)
我的朋友沒一個會做這樣的事！

小試身手

1. _____ friends of Jay's will come visit him in the hospital this afternoon. (選錯的)
Ⓐ Some　Ⓑ These　Ⓒ Any　Ⓓ Two

2. Are any friends of _____ artists?
Ⓐ you　Ⓑ your　Ⓒ yours　Ⓓ to your

3. Three of my friends are also Linda's friends.
提示 用 Three friends 開頭改寫上列句子。
_____ are also Linda's friends.

Ans　1. Ⓒ　2. Ⓒ　3. Three friends of mine

Unit 41　表示「……是必要的」是 It is necessary that he gets... 或 It is necessary that he get...?

表「需要的、必要的、重要的」形容詞在下列句構出現時，that + 子句中的動詞之前應置助動詞 should（應該），should 可予省略，保留之後的原形動詞。表「必要的」這類形容詞常用的如下：necessary（必要的）、imperative（極有必要的）、important（重要的）、crucial（至關重要的）、essential（必不可少的）、vital（極其重要的）、urgent（緊迫的）、advisable（明智的）、desirable（值得做的）等等。

例　It is necessary that Andy must get to work on time. (✗)
→ It is necessary that Andy (should) get to work on time. (✓)

→ It is necessary that Andy get to work on time. (✔)
安迪有必要準時上班。

It is imperative that Ed must tell the truth. (✘)

→ It is imperative that Ed (should) tell the truth. (✔)

→ It is imperative that Ed tell the truth. (✔)　艾迪非說實話不可。

It is desirable that we must team up if we want to win the game. (✘)

→ It is desirable that we (should) team up if we want to win the game. (✔)
我們若想贏得比賽就須團結合作，此舉是明智的。

小試身手

Ben has to brush his teeth at least twice a day. It is important for him to do it.

提示　用 It is important... 開頭合併上列句子。

It is important that _____
at least twice a day.

　　　　　　　　　　　　　　Ans　Ben (should) brush his teeth

Unit 42　「英文說得很好」是 speak English very good 或 speak English very well?

a good 是形容詞，表「優秀的、很好的」，可置**名詞前**修飾該名詞。well 是副詞，表「很棒地、很好地」置**動詞後**，修飾該動詞。

例　Ann speaks English very good. (✘)
　　　　　　　　　　　　adj.

→ Ann speaks very good English. (✔)
　　　　　　　adj.　　n.

43

= Ann speaks English very well. (✔)
　　　　vt.　　　　　　　adv.

= Ann has a good command of spoken English. (✔)
　　　　　　adj.　　n.

安英語說得很好。

註 此處 command 是名詞，表語言方面的「造詣、知識」。

b good 作形容詞，表「身體安好的、健康的」，與 well 同義。

例 A: How're you feeling?
　 B: I'm not feeling good / well. I'm afraid I have to ask for sick leave.
　 A：你感覺怎麼樣？
　 B：我感覺不舒服，恐怕要請病假了。

c 注意下列打招呼的用法：

例 A: How're you doing today?
　 B: I'm doing g~~oo~~d / gr~~ea~~t. (✗，good 及 great 是形容詞，無法修飾 doing。但口語可以接受 doing good 的說法。)

→ A: How're you doing today?
　 B: I'm doing well. (✔)
　　　　　　　adv.

A：你今天還好嗎？
B：我還好。

小試身手

珍妮說得一口好日文。

Jenny ＿＿＿＿＿＿＿＿＿＿ (d) Japanese.
= Jenny ＿＿＿＿＿ Japanese very (w)＿＿＿＿.

Ans speaks / spoke; good; speaks / spoke; well

44

Unit 43 「減少」是 be reduced to V 或 be reduced to V-ing?

a reduce 為及物動詞，表「減少」。其用法如下：

reduce + 物　減少……

例　You should reduce your spending and save up for a rainy day. (✔)

→ You should cut down on your spending and save up for a rainy day. (✔)

你應減少花費並存錢以備不時之需。

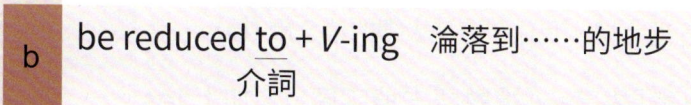

b be reduced to + V-ing　淪落到……的地步
　　　　　　　介詞

例　Twenty years ago, Mr. Johnson was a billionaire, but much to my surprise, he is reduced to beg now. (✘)

→ Twenty years ago, Mr. Johnson was a billionaire, but much to my surprise, he is reduced to begging now. (✔)

二十年前，強森先生是個億萬富翁，可是令我大吃一驚的是，他現在已淪落到乞食維生的地步了。

小試身手

1. After he was fired, Ted was reduced to _____ on the streets just to make ends meet.
   Ⓐ beg　　Ⓑ begged　　Ⓒ begs　　Ⓓ begging

2. To save money for the trip, I decided to cut down on my food expenses.
   提示 用 reduce 改寫句子。
   To save money for the trip, I decided to _____ my food expenses.

Ans　1. Ⓓ　2. reduce

Unit 44 「10 層樓的建築」是 a 10-story building 或 a 10-floor building?

a story（英式英語採用 storey）及 floor 均表樓層，story 指大廈的總樓層，floor 指某人所居住或辦公的某一層樓。

例 This is a 6-floor building in front of us. I live on the 5th story of that building. (✗)

→ This is a 6-story building in front of us. I live on the 5th floor of that building. (✓)

我們前面有一棟 6 層大樓。我住在這棟大樓的第 5 層（樓）。

b story 在英語中表「故事」，複數要去掉字尾 y，加上 ies。

例 Peter is good at telling stories. (✓) 彼得很會講故事。

小試身手

這棟 15 層樓的辦公大樓的電梯壞掉了，所以這些員工只好爬樓梯。

The elevator in the _____ office building was broken, so the employees had to use the stairs.

Ans 15-story

Unit 45 搭配「市場 market 的介詞」是 on the market 或 in the market?

market 意思為「市場」，與其搭配的介詞 in 或 on 都有，用法如下：

{ 人 + be in the market for sth　　某人有意購買某物
  人 + put sth on the market　　　某人要出售某物

例 I'm on the market for a used car. (✗)

→ I'm in the market for a used car. (✓)

→ I'm interested in buying a used car. (✓)

我想買一輛中古車。

I put my house ~~in~~ the market in May last year, and it hasn't been sold yet. (✗)

→ I put my house on the market in May last year, and it hasn't been sold yet. (✓)　去年五月我就拋售我的房子，迄今尚未賣掉。

小試身手

1	I put my car ＿＿＿ the market last week, but I haven't gotten any inquiries yet.	
	Ⓐ on　　Ⓑ in　　Ⓒ at　　Ⓓ above	
2	Dan is ＿＿＿ the market for a new scooter because his old one has broken down.	
	Ⓐ at　　Ⓑ on　　Ⓒ in　　Ⓓ for	

Ans　1. Ⓐ　2. Ⓒ

Unit 46　「告訴我這是什麼」是 Tell me what is it 或 Tell me what it is?

Tell me what it is.（告訴我這是什麼。）才是正確的。

理由　"What is it?" 自成一個問句，表「這是什麼？」。

本問句中 it（這）是主詞，is（是）是動詞，疑問詞 what（什麼）作主詞補語。形成問句時，疑問詞 what 置句首，並改成大寫 What，it is 改成倒裝 is it，再加問號（?）。

任何由疑問詞（如 who、when、where、why、how、which）形成的問句稱作特殊疑問句，這些疑問句自成獨立的問句，不可直接作句中動詞的受詞。必須先變成名詞子句，方可作動詞的受詞。

特殊疑問句：When did Ed call you?　艾德何時打電話給你？

名詞子句：when Ed called you　艾德何時打電話給你

例　Tell me when did Ed call you? (✗)

→ Tell me when Ed called you. (✓)　告訴我艾德何時打了電話給你。
　　名詞子句（作 Tell 的直接受詞）

特殊疑問句：Why is Hank crying?　漢克為何在哭？

名詞子句：why Hank is crying　漢克為何在哭

Do you know why is Hank crying? (✗)

→ Do you know why Hank is crying. (✓)　你知道漢克為何在哭嗎？
　　　　　　名詞子句 (作 know 的受詞)

小試身手

1	Can you tell me _____? Ⓐ what is it time　　Ⓑ what time is it Ⓒ what time it is　　Ⓓ what it is time
2	How are you doing? Please tell me. 提示 用 Please tell me 開頭合併上列句子。 Please tell me _____.

Ans　1. Ⓒ　2. how you are doing

Unit 47　「較優越的」是 be superior to... 或 be more superior than...?

a
superior 表「較優越的」，為 -ior 結尾的形容詞，其用法如下：
-ior 結尾的形容詞一定與介詞 to 並用，不可套用在 "more...than..." 的比較級結構中。常用的這些形容詞如下：
superior (較優越的)、inferior (較差的)、senior (級別較高的)、junior (級別較低的)、prior (先前的)

例　This product is far more superior than that one in quality. (✗)

→ This product is far superior to that one in quality. (✓)

= This product is far better than that one in quality.
這項產品的品質要比那項產品優越多了。

As far as quality goes, this pen is more inferior than yours. (✗)

→ As far as quality goes, this pen is inferior to yours. (✓)
就品質而言，這支筆比你的筆差一些。

A captain is ~~more~~ junior ~~than~~ a major. (✗)
→ A captain is junior to a major. (✓)　上尉官階要比少校低。
The general manager is ~~more~~ senior ~~than~~ the assistant manager. (✗)
→ The general manager is (far) senior to the assistant manager. (✓)
總經理的地位要比協理高很多。

Prior to / Before the war, Mr. Li taught English in a small rural junior high school.　戰爭前，李先生在鄉下一所國中教英文。

b senior 及 junior 可作名詞，分別表「年長者」及「年輕者」。

例 Patty is senior to me by two years. (✗)
　　　　　adj.
→ Patty is two years senior to me. (✓)
　　　　　adv.　　adj.
= Patty is two years my senior.
　　　　　　　　　　n.
= Patty is older than I by two years.
= Patty is two years older than I.
派蒂比我大兩歲。

Carl is junior to me by two years. (✗)
　　　　adj.
= Carl is two years my junior.
　　　　　　　　　　n.
= Carl is younger than I by two years.　卡爾比我小兩歲。
但 Carl is two years junior to me. (罕)　卡爾比我小兩歲。
　　　　　　　　　adj.

Carl　Patty
22 years old　24 years old

小試身手

1　That company lost some customers because their products are _____ my company's.
　Ⓐ inferior than　　　　Ⓑ more inferior than
　Ⓒ more inferior to　　　Ⓓ inferior to

49

2　Mr. Wang is five years older than I.
提示 用 ... my senior 改寫句子。
Mr. Wang _____ my senior.

> Ans　1. Ⓓ　2. is five years

Unit 48 「今天早上」是 today morning、this morning 還是 tomorrow morning?

a 表「今天早上」一定要使用 this morning，無 today morning 的說法。同理，表「今天下午」要說 this afternoon，表「今天傍晚 / 晚上」要說 this evening / tonight。

例　I met Peter on my way to work today morning. (✗)
→ I met Peter on my way to work this morning. (✓)
今天早上我在上班途中遇見彼得。

What are you planning to do today afternoon? (✗)
→ What are you planning to do this afternoon? (✓)
今天下午你打算做什麼？

I'm going out with Mary today evening. (✗)
→ I'm going out with Mary this evening. (✓)
今晚我將與瑪麗外出約會。

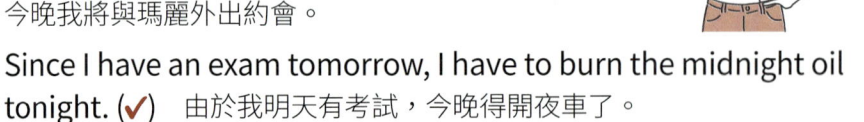

Since I have an exam tomorrow, I have to burn the midnight oil tonight. (✓)　由於我明天有考試，今晚得開夜車了。

b 表「明天早上 / 明天下午 / 明天傍晚 / 明天晚上」要說 tomorrow morning / tomorrow afternoon / tomorrow evening / tomorrow night。

例　I'll discuss the issue with you tomorrow morning / tomorrow afternoon / tomorrow evening / tomorrow night. (✓)
我明天早上 / 明天下午 / 明天傍晚 / 明天晚上再跟你討論這個問題。

c 表「昨天早上 / 昨天下午 / 昨天傍晚」要說 yesterday morning / yesterday afternoon / yesterday evening。表「昨天晚上」不可說 yesterday night 應說 last night。

例 What did you do last morning? (✗)
→ What did you do yesterday morning? (✓) 你昨天早上做了什麼？
I went fishing with David last afternoon. (✗)
→ I went fishing with David yesterday afternoon. (✓)
昨天下午我和大衛釣魚去了。
I heard the couple next door quarreling late last night. (✓)
我昨天深夜聽到隔壁的夫婦吵架。

小試身手

Ⓐ tomorrow morning　Ⓑ last night　Ⓒ this morning

1. David and I went out for dinner ＿＿＿, and we had a wonderful date.
2. Ken's alarm clock didn't go off ＿＿＿, so he didn't get up on time to catch his school bus.
3. I'll be on the train to Hualien ＿＿＿, heading for my dream vacation.

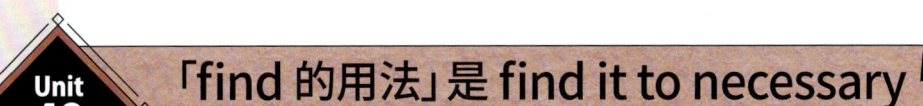

Ans　1. Ⓑ　2. Ⓒ　3. Ⓐ

Unit 49　「find 的用法」是 find it to necessary 或 find that it is necessary to V?

find 表「發現、認為」，其用法如下：

a find 可作完全及物動詞，表「發現」，之後接名詞或 that 引導的名詞子句作受詞。

例 I found the key under the table. (✓)
　　完全 vt.　　n.
我在桌底下發現了這支鑰匙。

I <u>find</u>　(that) French is fun to learn. (✓)　我發現學法語很有趣。
完全 vt.　　　名詞子句

b find 亦可作不完全及物動詞，表「覺得；認為」，使用時結構如下：find + 受詞 + 形容詞或名詞 (作受詞補語)

例　I <u>find</u>　　the little girl　　very cute. (✓)　我覺得這小女孩很可愛。
　　不完全 vt.　　受詞　　　形容詞 (作受詞補語)

We all <u>find</u> Ted　　a genius when it comes to drawing. (✓)
　　　不完全 vt.　名詞 (作受詞補語)
說到畫畫，我們全都認為泰德是個天才。

c find 作不完全及物動詞時，不得直接用 to 引導的不定詞片語作受詞，即不可說：

例　I <u>find</u>　　to cooperate with him necessary. (✗)
　　不完全 vt.　　不定詞片語

此時，find 之後應置虛受詞 it，代替實受詞（即 to 引導的不定詞片語），再將該不定詞片語放在句尾，即：

I <u>find</u>　　it　necessary <u>to cooperate with him</u>. (✓)
不完全 vt.　虛受詞　　　　　實受詞

= I <u>find</u> (that) it　is necessary <u>to cooperate with him</u>.
　 完全 vt.　　虛主詞　　　　　　　實主詞

= I <u>find</u> (that) <u>cooperating with him</u> is necessary.
　 完全 vt.　　　　實主詞

我發現跟他合作有必要。(to cooperate with him 移至 that 子句句首時，宜變成動名詞片語 cooperating with him)
由上得知：

I <u>find</u>　　to learn French　fun. (✗)
不完全 vt.　　不定詞片語

→ I <u>find</u>　　it fun <u>to learn French</u>. (✓)
　 不完全 vt.　虛受詞　　實受詞

= I <u>find</u> (that)　it is fun <u>to learn French</u>.
　 完全 vt.　　虛主詞　　　實主詞

= I <u>find</u> (that) <u>learning French</u> is fun.
　 完全 vt.　　　　實主詞

我發現學法語很有趣。（to learn French 移至 that 子句句首時，宜變成動名詞片語 learning French）

d 表「認為」的動詞（如 consider、deem 及 think）用法如 find，可作完全及物動詞，亦可作不完全及物動詞。

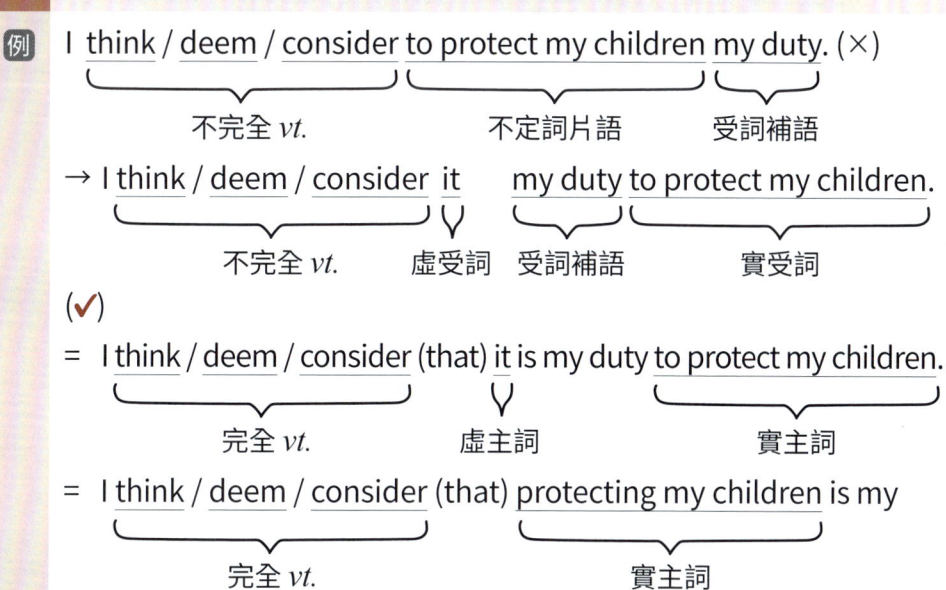

例 I think / deem / consider to protect my children my duty. (✗)
         不完全 vt.   不定詞片語   受詞補語

→ I think / deem / consider it my duty to protect my children.
     不完全 vt.   虛受詞 受詞補語   實受詞 (✓)

= I think / deem / consider (that) it is my duty to protect my children.
     完全 vt.   虛主詞   實主詞

= I think / deem / consider (that) protecting my children is my duty.
     完全 vt.   實主詞

我認為保護我的孩子是我的責任。

小試身手

選出錯誤的句子。

Ⓐ I found my keys in your bag.
Ⓑ I consider my job to do the dishes.
Ⓒ I deem that feeding my cats is my responsibility.
Ⓓ I think it my duty to teach my students well.

Ans Ⓑ

Unit 50 「別對他期望太高」是 Don't expect him too much. 或 Don't expect too much of him.?

expect 為「期望」之意，表「對某人有所指望」或「對某人沒有指望」應採下列結構：

a　expect 物 of 人　對某人有所期望。

例　All parents expect their children something. (✗)
→ All parents expect something of their children. (✓)
所有父母都對子女有所期望。

b　expect nothing of 人　對某人沒有期望

例　I expect nothing of Peter because he goofs around all day. (✓)
彼得整天打混，因此我對他沒有期望。

c　expect too much of 人　對某人期望太高

例　Don't expect Andy too much. After all, he is just a ten-year-old boy. (✗)
→ Don't expect too much of Andy. After all, he is just a ten-year-old boy. (✓)　別對安迪期望太大。畢竟，他是個 10 歲小男孩。

小試身手

1. I expect a lot _____ my students because I am sure they have the potential to succeed.
   Ⓐ in　Ⓑ on　Ⓒ at　Ⓓ of

2. I've learned it the hard way that I should expect _____ of others and count only on myself.
   Ⓐ too much　Ⓑ a lot　Ⓒ nothing　Ⓓ anything

Ans 1. Ⓓ　2. Ⓒ

54

Unit 51 「寫日記」是 keep a diary 或 write a diary?

表「寫日記」，應說 keep a diary，而非 write a diary。

例 I have the habit of writing a diary every day. (×)
→ I have the habit of keeping a diary every day. (✓)
我每天都有寫日記的習慣。

注意 但若提到在日記裡「寫」了什麼，則動詞要用 "write"。
What did you write in your diary yesterday? (✓)
你在昨天的日記中寫了些什麼？
I wrote about my father in my diary yesterday. (✓)
我在昨天的日記中寫到有關我老爸的事。

小試身手

小提米每天都寫日記；他寫關於學校生活的一切。
Little Timmy _____ a diary every day; he _____ about everything he does at school.

Ans keeps; writes

Unit 52 「感激」是 I would appreciate you if... 或 I would appreciate it if...?

appreciate [əˋprɪʃɪ˙et] 為「感激、欣賞」之意，用法如下：

a appreciate 可作及物動詞，表「感激」，不可用「人」作受詞。

例 I really appreciate you for helping me so much. (×) —— 受詞為人
→ I really appreciate your help. (✓) —— 受詞為物
= I am really thankful / grateful for your help.
= Thank you very much for your help.
非常感謝你的幫助。

I would appreciate you if you could help me write the paper. (✗)
── 受詞為人

→ I would appreciate it if you could help me write the paper. (✓ ── 受詞為物，此處 it 是代名詞代替之後的整個 if 子句)
你若能幫我寫這份報告我會很感激。

b　appreciate 另一意表「欣賞、賞識」，可用「人」或「事物」作受詞。

例　John left the company when he found his boss didn't appreciate him / his contribution. (✓)
約翰發現老闆並不賞識他 / 他的貢獻時，便離開公司了。

小試身手

選出錯誤的句子。

Ⓐ I appreciated Tom for helping me move last weekend.
Ⓑ The boss appreciated Linda's hard work and gave her a raise.
Ⓒ I would really appreciate it if you could come and give me a hand with the project.
Ⓓ Children should learn to appreciate everything in life and be grateful.

Ans　Ⓐ

Unit 53　「安排某人從事某事」是 arrange 人 to V 或 arrange for 人 to V?

arrange 為「安排」之意，用法如下：

a　表「安排某人從事某事」，須採下列結構：
arrange for 人 to V　安排某人（從事）……

例　I'll arrange somebody to pick you up at the airport. (✗)
→ I'll arrange for somebody to pick you up at the airport. (✓)
我會安排某人到機場接你。

The boss was sick, so he arranged his secretary to preside over the meeting. (✗)

→ The boss was sick, so he arranged for his secretary to preside over the meeting. (✓)
老闆生病了，因此他安排他的祕書主持會議。

b 表「安排某活動」，arrange 之後直接接受詞。

例 I've arranged a meeting with Mr. Smith for eight tomorrow morning. (✓)　我已與史密斯先生安排在明天早上 8 點碰面。
　　　　 vt.

c arrange 之後亦可接 to 引導的不定詞片語或 that 子句作受詞。

例 I've arranged to meet Mr. Smith at eight tomorrow morning. (✓)
= I've arranged that I will meet Mr. Smith at eight tomorrow morning. (✓)　我已安排好明天早上 8 點要與史密斯先生見面。

小試身手

1. Dana asked her assistant to arrange ＿＿＿ somebody to take care of her dog while she was on the business trip.
   Ⓐ about　　Ⓑ ×　　Ⓒ for　　Ⓓ at

2. Jane has arranged ＿＿＿ a magic show for her son's birthday party.
   Ⓐ ×　　Ⓑ for　　Ⓒ on　　Ⓓ to

Ans　1. Ⓒ　2. Ⓐ

Unit 54　「要用功，那麼……」是 Study hard, you will... 或 Study hard, and you will...?

命令句 (以原形動詞起首的句子) 之後不能直接接主要子句。

不可說：Study hard, you will pass the test. (×，兩句無連接詞連接)
　　　　　命令句　　　　主要子句

應　說：Study hard, and you will pass the test. (✓)
　　　　　── and 為連接詞
要用功，那麼你考試就會及格。

= If you study hard, you will pass the test. (✓)── if 為連接詞
你若用功，考試就會及格。

例　Study hard, or you will fail the test. (✓) —— or 為連接詞
要用功,否則你考試就會不及格。

= If you don't study hard, you won't pass the test. —— if 為連接詞
你若不用功,考試就會不及格。

Be nice to me, and I'll marry you. (✓) —— and 為連接詞
要善待我,那麼我就會嫁給你。

Be nice to me, or I'll ditch you. (✓) —— or 為連接詞
要善待我,否則我會把你甩掉。

小試身手

Ⓐ If　Ⓑ and　Ⓒ or

1	Treat your pet well, _____ it will love you back more.
2	Put your toys away, _____ I'll throw them away.
3	_____ you're always under great pressure, you'll get sick.

Ans　1. Ⓑ　2. Ⓒ　3. Ⓐ

Unit 55 「經過了 3 年」是 Three years have past. 或 Three years have passed.?

past 與 passed 發音相同,也都有「經過」的意思,但是詞性與用法大不相同,請見以下說明:

a past 是介詞,必須置動詞之後,方可置受詞:

例　Don past me without saying hello to me. (✗)
　　　　介詞

→ Don walked past me without saying hello to me. (✓)
　　　動詞　介詞

阿丹走過我身旁,並沒跟我打招呼。

I drove ~~passed~~ the bank on my way to work. (✗)
　　動詞　　動詞

→ I drove past the bank on my way to work. (✓)
　　　動詞　介詞

我上班途中開車經過銀行。

b　pass 則為動詞：

例　Three years have ~~past~~, and I haven't heard anything from Tom yet. (✗)
　　　　　完成式助動詞　介詞

→ Three years have passed, and I haven't heard anything from Tom yet. (✓)　三年都過去了，我一直都沒接到湯姆的任何音訊。
　　　　完成式助動詞　動詞

A: What time is it now?　現在幾點了？
B: It's half ~~passed~~ two. (✗)　兩點半。
　　　　　動詞

→ It's half past two. (✓)
　　　　介詞

The old movie star is ~~passed~~ his prime.
　　　　　　　　　　動詞　過去分詞
(✗，is passed 表「被經過」，無意義)

→ The old movie star is past his prime. (✓)
　　　　　　　　　　　動詞　分詞

這位老影星已過氣了。

小試身手

1　I walk (past / pass) a park on my way home every day.

2　So many years have (past / passed), but the old lady is still looking for her missing daughter.

Ans　1. past　2. passed

Unit 56 「回家」是 go home 或 go to home?

a home（家）可作副詞，如同副詞 here（這裡）、there（那裡）一樣，直接置動詞之後，且 home 之前不置任何介詞。

例 When did you get ~~to~~ home last night? (✗)
→ When did you get home last night? (✓)
　　　　　　　　　vi.　adv.
你昨晚幾點到家？

I arrived home at 6 p.m. (✓)
　vi.　　adv.
= I got home at 6 p.m.
　vi.　adv.
我晚上 6 點到家。

b home 亦可作名詞，直接作及物動詞 reach（抵達）或 leave（離開）的受詞。

例 By the time I reached ~~to~~ home, it was already 1 a.m. (✗)
→ By the time I reached home, it was already 1 a.m. (✓)
　　　　　　　　vt.　　n.
= By the time I got home, it was already 1 a.m.
　　　　　　vi.　adv.
= By the time I arrived home, it was already 1 a.m.
　　　　　　　vi.　　adv.
= By the time I | reached my home, | it was already 1 a.m.
　　　　　　　　　vt.　　　n.
　　　　　　　　got to my home,
　　　　　　　　介詞　　n.
　　　　　　　　arrived at my home,
　　　　　　　　　介詞　　n.
等到我到家時，已經是凌晨 1 點了。

I left home at 8 this morning.　我於今天早上 8 點離開家門。
　vt.　n.

John left home at the age of 16.　約翰於 16 歲便離家在外了。
　　　vt.　n.

C home 作名詞時可作介詞 at 或 from 的受詞，但不可作介詞 in 或 to 的受詞。

例　I'll go to̶ home early tonight. (✗)
　　　　　介詞　n.

→ I'll go home early tonight. (✓)
　　　　　adv.

我今晚會早點回家。

但 I'll go to his home tonight. (✓)
　　　　　　　　n.

我今晚會去他家。

I'll stay at　home listening to music over the weekend. (✓)
　　　　介詞　n.

→ I'll stay home listening to music over the weekend. (✓)
　　　　vi.　adv.

整個週末我都會待在家裡聽音樂。

Once you contract COVID-19, it's best to work from home. (✓)
　　　　　　　　　　　　　　　　　　　　　　介詞　n.

一旦你感染 COVID-19，最好居家上班。

小試身手

選出錯誤的句子。

Ⓐ If you arrive home by 7, you will be able to have dinner with us.
Ⓑ I plan to stay at home tomorrow, playing online games all day.
Ⓒ Jane got home very late last night. I'd really like to ask her why.
Ⓓ I used to go my friend's home to chat with him when I was little.

Ans　Ⓓ

61

Unit 57 「依我之見」是 according to me 或 according to my opinion?

according to 表「根據」，之後應接第二人稱或第三人稱作受詞，故表示「依我之見」，不可說：According to ~~me~~ / According to ~~my opinion~~, Peter is not cut out for the job. (✗)

→ According to him / John / them, Peter is not cut out for the job. (✓)

= In his / John's / their opinion / view, Peter is not cut out for the job. (✓)

根據他／約翰／他們的看法，彼得不適任這工作。

例 In my opinion / view, Peter is not cut out for the job. (✓)

= I am of the opinion / view that Peter is not cut out for the job. (✓)

依我之見，彼得不適任這工作。

According to you, we must cancel the meeting. Is that right? (✓)
根據你的說法，我們必須取消會議。對嗎？

小試身手

Judy is of the opinion that we should give customers more discounts.

提示 用 According to 開頭改寫句子。

_____, we should give customers more discounts.

Ans According to Judy

Unit 58 「照例」是 as usual 或 as usually?

as usual 表「照例」、「像往常一樣」。無 as usually 的用法。

a as usual 可擺放句首、句中或句尾。

例 David came to work late this morning, as ~~usually~~. (✗)

→ David came to work late this morning, as usual. (✓)

= David, as usual, came to work late this morning.
= As usual, David came to work late this morning.
大衛跟往常一樣，今天早上上班又遲到了。

b as always 亦表「一如往昔」，比 as usual 語氣強，as usual 偶有例外，as always 完全沒有例外。

例 As always, Peter got full marks on the English test.
一如往昔，彼得這次的英文考試又得了滿分。（一成不變）

As usual, Peter got full marks on the English test.
跟往常一樣，彼得這次的英文考試又得了滿分。（有時未必得滿分）

小試身手

選出錯誤的句子。

Ⓐ As usual, Tony rode a bike to school.
Ⓑ Tony usually rode a bike to school.
Ⓒ Tony rode a bike to school, as usually.
Ⓓ Usually, Tony rode a bike to school.

Ans Ⓒ

Unit 59 「夜幕低垂時」是 when night falls 或 when the night falls?

表「夜幕低垂時」，應說 "when night falls" 不可說 "when the night falls"。

例 In this area, it's dangerous to go out when the night falls. (✗)
→ In this area, it's dangerous to go out when night falls. (✓)　在這個地方，天黑外出很危險。

The night was falling when I got home. (✗)
→ Night was falling when I got home. (✓)
我回到家時天快黑了。

注意 表「破曉時」，應說 "when day breaks 或 when morning breaks"，不可說 "when the day breaks 或 when the morning breaks"。

They set out for Kaohsiung when the day broke. (✗)
→ They set out for Kaohsiung when day broke. (✓)
= They set out for Kaohsiung at daybreak / sunrise / dawn.
他們在破曉時就出發往高雄去了。

小試身手

選出錯誤的句子。
Ⓐ My friends and I hit the road when night falls.
Ⓑ The police broke into the criminal's house at the daybreak.
Ⓒ We started the hiking trip at dawn.
Ⓓ Night was falling when the party began.

Ans Ⓑ

Unit 60 「為何念大學」的簡化句是 why go to college 或 why to go to college?

副詞 why (為什麼) 之後可接原形動詞，由下列問句化簡：

例 Why should I / you go to college? (✓)
= Why go to college?
不可說：Why to go to college? (✗) （我 / 你）為何要念大學？

Why don't you join us? (✓) （你）為何不加入我們的行列？
= Why not join us?
不可說：Why not to join us? (✗)

小試身手

你何不養隻寵物？
_____ keep a pet?

Ans Why don't you / Why not

Unit 61 「加入」是 join 人 in V-ing 或 join in 人 to V?

join 表「加入」，可作及物動詞，之後接人或某組織（如俱樂部等）作受詞，常用 "join + 人 + in + V-ing (動名詞)" 的結構。

例 Would you like to join ~~in~~ us ~~to~~ watch the baseball game this afternoon? (×)

→ Would you like to join us in watching the baseball game this afternoon? (✓)　你要不要跟我們去觀賞今天下午的棒球賽？

We are going to watch the baseball game this afternoon. Would you like to join us? (✓)

我們今天下午會去看棒球賽，你要不要跟我們去？

小試身手

你週末想不想跟他們去打籃球？

Would you like to join _____ basketball on the weekend?

Ans　them in playing

Unit 62 「我跟他是朋友」是 I am a friend with him. 或 I am friends with him.?

"be friends with 人" 表「與某人是朋友」，此處 friends 恆為複數。

例 Jane is ~~a friend~~ with Peter. (×)
→ Jane is friends with Peter. (✓)
= Jane and Peter are friends.
阿珍與彼得是朋友。

65

小試身手

Roland and I are friends.
提示 用 be friends with 改寫句子。
I _____ Roland.

Ans am friends with

Unit 63 「討論」是 discuss it 或 discuss about it?

discuss 表「討論」是及物動詞，之後直接接受詞。

例 This issue is too complicated. We'll discuss about it later. (✗)
→ This issue is too complicated. We'll discuss it later. (✓)
= This issue is too complicated. We'll talk about it later.
這個問題太過複雜。我們稍後再討論。

注意 talk 也有「討論」之意，用法為：
talk it over with 人　與某人詳細討論某事

This issue is too complicated. I have to talk over it with my advisor first. (✗)
→ This issue is too complicated. I have to talk it over with my advisor first. (✓) 這個問題太過複雜。我必須先和我的顧問商討一下。

小試身手

選出錯誤的句子。

Ⓐ Choosing a college major is very important. I need to discuss it with my parents.
Ⓑ Buying a car is a huge matter. You need to talk over it with your wife.
Ⓒ Let's talk about your trip and make sure you have everything you need before you go.
Ⓓ I'm going to have a meeting with my group members and discuss the theme of our project.

Ans Ⓑ

Unit 64 「在收音機廣播裡」是 on the radio 或 in the radio?

{ on the radio　　在收音機廣播時
{ in the radio　　在收音機機體裡面

例　I heard in the radio that a typhoon is approaching. (✗，不合邏輯)
我人在收音機裡面聽說有颱風要來了。（人進入收音機裡面是不可能的事）

→ I heard on the radio that a typhoon is approaching. (✓)
我在收音機上聽說有颱風要來了。

小試身手

我今早上學途中在廣播裡聽到這首歌。

I heard this song _____ _____ _____ on my way to school this morning.

Ans　on; the; radio

Unit 65 事情「發生」要用 happen 或 be happened?

表「發生」的動詞如 happen、occur 或 take place 均為不及物動詞，無被動語態。

例　What was happened? (✗)　被發生了什麼事？

→ What happened? (✓)　（剛才）發生了什麼事？

= What's (= What is) happening?　正在發生什麼事？

A car accident was happened / was occurred / was taken place early this morning. (✗)　今天清晨一起車禍被發生了。（語意不通）

→ A car accident happened / occurred / took place early this morning. (✓)　今天清晨發生了一起車禍了。

67

小試身手

今天早上我家隔壁發生意外，幸好沒有造成傷亡。

An accident _____ next door this morning; luckily, no one was injured.

Ans happened / occurred

Unit 66 「挑剔」是 be particular about... 或 be particular with...?

a particular 是形容詞，表「特別的」。

例 You should pay particular attention to John's behavior. He is a bit odd today. (✓)
你要特別注意約翰的行為。他今天有點怪怪的。

b particular 亦可表「挑剔的」，與介詞 about 並用。

例 Mary is particular with her clothes. (✗)
→ Mary is | particular | about her clothes. (✓)
　　　　　 choosy
　　　　　 fussy
　　　　　 picky

瑪麗對穿衣服很講究 / 挑剔。

小試身手

1. I don't like John because he is choosy about what he eats. (選同義詞)
   (A) exciting (B) weird (C) particular (D) special

2. Jane is very particular _____ the tea she drinks.
   (A) with (B) in (C) for (D) about

Ans 1. Ⓒ 2. Ⓓ

Unit 67 「全新的車」是 a brand new car 或 a new brand car?

要表示「全新的……」可用 a brand new + 名詞：

例
John bought a ~~new brand~~ car last week. (✗)
→ John bought a brand new (= completely new) car last week. (✓)
約翰上星期買了一輛全新的車。

I won't let anyone touch my ~~new brand~~ computer. (✗)
→ I won't let anyone touch my brand new (= completely new) computer. 我不會讓任何人碰我的全新電腦。

小試身手

我哥哥上週剛搬進郊區的全新房屋。
My brother just moved into a ＿＿＿ ＿＿＿ house in the suburbs last week.

Ans brand; new

Unit 68 「有鑑於」是 given that... 或 giving that...?

given 可作介詞，表「有鑑於 / 考慮到……」，可接名詞或名詞片語作受詞。

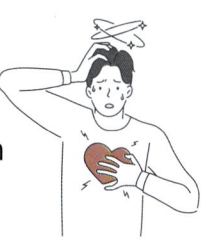

例
~~Giving~~ his poor health, Tom can't handle such a heavy workload. (✗)
→ Given his poor health, Tom can't handle such a
　　介詞
heavy workload. (✓)
= Considering his poor health, Tom can't handle such
　　　介詞
a heavy workload.

常見錯誤用字／用詞／用語

CH 1

69

= In view of his poor health, Tom can't handle such a heavy workload.

考慮到 / 有鑒於湯姆健康欠佳，他無法承擔這麼重的工作量。

注意 given 亦可與 that 連用，視作副詞連接詞，之後接主詞 + 動詞。

G~~i~~ving that he is in poor health, Tom can't handle such a heavy workload. (✗)

→ Given that he is in poor health, Tom can't handle such a heavy workload. (✓)

= Considering that (非 Considering from the fact) he is in poor health, Tom can't handle such a heavy workload.

= Judging from the fact that (非 Judging from that) he is in poor health, Tom can't handle such a heavy workload.

= In view of the fact that (非 In view of that) he is in poor health, Tom can't handle such a heavy workload.

有鑒於湯姆健康欠佳，他無法承擔這麼重的工作量。

小試身手

1. Because Lena was a vegan, we didn't order any meat.
   提示 用 Given... 開頭改寫句子。
   _____, we didn't order any meat.

2. 提示 用 Judging... 開頭改寫句子。
   _____, we didn't order any meat.

Ans 1. Given that Lena was a vegan
2. Judging from the fact that Lena was a vegan

Chapter 2

Unit 69 ▶▶▶ Unit 142

▶ 字詞辨異

沒錯！英文的陷阱就在於微小的差異所帶來的誤解。不論是用錯詞性、介詞或搭配詞等等，都會造成天差地遠的意思。

本章節整理了看似相同或易混淆的單詞和片語。透過這些寶貴資訊，你將學習如何辨別這些相似詞彙的微妙差別，並掌握正確的用法，避免落入近似字詞的囹圄，打造無可撼動的英文地基！

Unit 69 plenty 及 plentiful 怎麼用?

a plenty 是代名詞，表「充分」、「許多」，不可作形容詞用。其用法如下：
plenty of + 複數名詞 / 不可數名詞　充分的 / 許多的……

例　We have plenty work to do this afternoon. (✗)
→ We have plenty of work to do this afternoon. (✓)
今天下午我們有許多工作要做。

Don't worry. We still have plenty eggs in the fridge. (✗)
→ Don't worry. We still have plenty of eggs in the fridge. (✓)
別擔心。冰箱裡我們還有很多雞蛋。

b plentiful [ˈplentɪfəl] 是形容詞，表「充分的」、「豐富的」，之後可接名詞，亦可置 be 動詞之後作主詞補語。

例　There is a plentiful supply of food for those refugees.
　　　　　　　　　　　　　n.
有充分的食物可供應給那些難民。

Bananas are cheap now because they are plentiful.
　　　　　　　　　　　　　　　　　　　主詞補語
香蕉產量很多，因此很便宜。

小試身手

1. I have (plenty / plentiful) of time to finish my work, so I'm not too worried about the deadline.

2. The farmer's market had a (plenty / plentiful) selection of fresh fruits and vegetables for sale.

Ans 1. plenty　2. plentiful

Unit 70　able 及 capable 怎麼用?

a　able 是形容詞，表「有能力的」，用於下列結構：
be able to V　能……，可以……
= can V

例　After months of treatment, the patient is able to walk around now. (✔)
= After months of treatment, the patient can walk around now.
經過幾個月的治療後，病人現在可以到處走動了。

I believe Ted is able to handle the problem himself. (✔)
= I believe Ted can handle the problem himself.
我相信泰德一個人就可處理這個問題。

補充　be unable to V　無法……，不能……
= cannot V

Jim has had a severe sore throat and is still unable to talk now. (✔)
= Jim has had a severe sore throat and still can't talk now.
吉姆喉嚨痛，現在仍無法說出話來。

I was unable to fall asleep all night long. (✔)
= I couldn't fall asleep all night long.　我一整晚都不能入睡。

b　capable [ˈkepəbəl] 亦是形容詞，亦表「有能力的」，多指有潛力勝任未來的工作。
be capable of + N/V-ing　有能力從事……

例　I believe the talented young man is capable to fulfill that huge mission someday. (✗)
→ I believe the talented young man is capable of fulfilling that huge mission someday.

= I believe the talented young man is capable of that huge mission someday.
我相信那位有才氣的年輕人有朝一日一定能完成那艱鉅的任務。

補充 be incapable of *N/V-ing* 沒有能力從事……
Though 9 years old, the kid is still incapable of speech.
= Though 9 years old, the kid is still incapable of speaking.
這孩子雖然 9 歲了，卻仍無法說話。

小試身手

選出錯誤的句子。

Ⓐ With enough resources and time, the team is capable of completing the project.
Ⓑ After months of practice, Helen was finally able to play her favorite song on the piano without making any mistakes.
Ⓒ Due to a lack of money, the company is unable to pay its employees their salaries.
Ⓓ The software is so outdated that it is now incapable to run on the latest operating system.

Ans Ⓓ

Unit 71　no such a man 或 no such man 怎麼用？

no 是形容詞，之後直接接「單數可數名詞」，如 no book、no man、no student。not 是副詞，之後須接冠詞 a，方可置單數可數名詞，如 not a book、not a man、not a student。

例　A: This is Peter Lai. Is Mr. Johnson there, please?
　　B: I'm sorry, but there's no such a man here. (✗)
→ I'm sorry, but there's no such man here. (✓)
= I'm sorry, but there's not such a man here. 
A：我是賴彼得。強森先生在嗎？
B：抱歉，我們這裡沒這個人。

小試身手

There is no such man as the perfect partner—everyone has their flaws.

提示 用 such a man 改寫。

There is _____ as the perfect partner — everyone has their flaws.

Ans　not such a man

Unit 72　weight 及 weigh 怎麼用?

a　weight 是名詞,表「重量」。weigh 則作不及物動詞,表「重達……」。要問某人體重不可說:

例　How much are you weighted? (✗)

應說: How much do you weigh? (✓)

= What's your weight? (✓)
　　　　　　　　n.

= How heavy are you?　你體重是多少?

I weigh at 70 kilograms. (✗, at 是贅字)

→ I weigh 70 kilograms. (✓)　我體重是 70 公斤。

b　weigh 亦可作及物動詞,表「量……的重量」。

例　The nurse weighed me and took my temperature.
護士稱我的體重並量我的體溫。

c　若要說某人變胖或要減肥,則應說:

例　You seem to have added weight. (✗,中式英文)

→ You seem to have gained / put on weight. (✓)
你似乎變胖 / 發福了。

To lose / reduce weight, you have to eat less and exercise more. (✓)
想要瘦下來,你就得少吃多運動。

小試身手

選出錯誤的句子。
Ⓐ How much is your dog weighed?
Ⓑ My son weighed 40 kg when he was 8 years old.
Ⓒ I have put on 5 kg since I moved back home.
Ⓓ Jenny weighs herself every day to make sure she stays slim.

Ans Ⓐ

Unit 73 good 及 well 怎麼用?

good 為形容詞，表「好的」，修飾名詞或置 be 動詞之後作主詞補語，不可修飾動詞。well 是副詞，表「很好地、極佳地」，可修飾動詞。

不可說：Peter speaks English very go~~o~~d. (✗)
　　　　　　　　　　　　　　　　adj.

應　說：Peter speaks (very) good English. (✓)
　　　　　　　　　　　　adj.　　*n.*

= Peter speaks English well. (✓)　彼得英語說得很好。
　　　　v.　　　　*adv.*

同　理：Peter speaks English flu~~e~~nt. (✗)
　　　　　　　　　　　　　　　adj.

→ Peter speaks fluent English. (✓)
　　　　　　　　adj.　　*n.*

= Peter speaks English fluently. (✓)
　　　　　　　　　　　　adv.

小試身手

Dom speaks good French.
提示 用 well 改寫句子。

Dom speaks _____.

Ans French well

Unit 74　feel good 及 feel well 怎麼用?

a well 可作形容詞，表「健康的」、「沒生病的」。通常出現在 be 動詞或 feel 之後，作主詞補語。

例　I'm worried that my dad has not been feeling well lately. (✔)
老爸最近身體一直欠安，令我擔心。

My dad had surgery recently and is well again now. (✔)
= My dad had surgery recently and is up and about again now.
我老爸最近動了手術，現在恢復健康 / 可下床走動了。

b feel well 及 feel good 均可表示「身體好」、「身體無恙」，尤用於下列打招呼用語：

例　A: How're you doing?
B: I feel good (更常用) / great / well. How about you?
A：你好嗎？
B：很好。你呢？

c feel good / great 亦可表示「心情好」。

例　I feel good / great whenever I'm with you. (✔)
每一次跟妳在一起，我就感到很愉快。

小試身手

你應該休息到你覺得恢復健康為止。

You should rest until you ＿＿＿ ＿＿＿ again.

Ans　feel; well / good / great

Unit 75　after 及 afterwards 怎麼用?

after 與 afterwards 均可作副詞，表「之後」，但 after 不能單獨使用，需與 shortly、soon、ever 等等搭配。而 afterwards 可與 shortly、soon、ever 等等搭配，亦可單獨使用。

例　The bank robbery took place early this morning, and the bandits were caught soon after / soon afterwards. (✓)
= The bank robbery took place early this morning, and the bandits were caught shortly after / soon afterwards.
銀行搶案是今天凌晨發生的，沒多久這些匪徒就被逮捕了。

下列是童話故事常出現的結尾語：
And they lived happily ever after. (✓)
= And they lived happily ever afterwards.
從此他們就過著幸福的日子。

We visited some friends and went home after. (✗)
→ We visited some friends and went home afterwards. (✓)
我們拜訪了一些朋友之後便回家了。

小試身手

德瑞克負債，從此他花錢便更加小心。
Derek got into debt, and he was more careful with his spending (e)_____ (a)_____.

Ans　ever; after / afterwards

Unit 76　at the beginning 及 in the beginning 怎麼用?

beginning 是「開端」之意，其用法如下：

a　at the beginning 須與 of 並用。
at the beginning of...　在……開始時

例　Our teacher told us a joke ~~in~~ the beginning of her lecture. (×)

→ Our teacher told us a joke at the beginning of her lecture. (✓)

我們老師在開始授課時先給我們講了一個笑話。

I'm planning to travel (around) the world ~~in~~ beginning of May. (×)

→ I'm planning to travel (around) the world at the beginning of May. (✓)　我計劃在五月初就要環遊世界。

b　in the beginning　起先，當初 (= at first = originally)

例　~~At~~ the beginning, I thought Tom was honest, but it turned out that he was a liar. (×)

→ In the beginning, I thought Tom was honest, but it turned out that he was a liar. (✓)　我原先還以為湯姆很老實，可是他竟然是個騙子。

小試身手

1　演講一開始時，琳達談到她的童年。
　　_____ the speech, Linda talked about her childhood.

2　我原先沒有任何銷售服飾的經驗，所以沒有很多客人。
　　_____, I didn't have any experience of selling clothes, so I didn't have many customers.

Ans　1. At the beginning of　2. In the beginning

Unit 77　at the end 及 in the end 怎麼用？

end 為「結束、結尾」之意，其用法如下：

a　at the end 須與 of 並用。
　　at the end of...　在……結束時

例　We'll take a trip to Tokyo ~~in~~ the end of this month. (×)

→ We'll take a trip to Tokyo at the end of this month. (✓)

這個月底我們會到東京走一趟。

79

Having a good wife like you, I believe I'll have no regrets ~~in~~ the end of my life. (✗)

→ Having a good wife like you, I believe I'll have no regrets <u>at the end</u> of my life. (✓)　有妳這樣的好老婆，我相信我死而無憾。

b　in the end　最後，到頭來 (= eventually)

例　Originally, I thought about taking in a movie this afternoon, but I went fishing ~~at~~ the end. (✗)

→ Originally, I thought about taking in a movie this afternoon, but I went fishing <u>in the end</u>. (✓)
原先我想在今天下午看場電影，最後我卻釣魚去了。

小試身手

1　學期結束時，學生們會將教室徹底清掃。
_____ the semester, the students will clean their classrooms thoroughly.

2　最後，正是他的決心讓 Ray 獲得了勝利。
_____, it was his determination that led Ray to victory.

Ans　1. At the end of　2. In the end

Unit 78　much money 及 a lot of money 怎麼用？

a　much 是形容詞，表示「許多的」、「大量的」，之後接不可數名詞（如 water、money、air、information 等），且多用在否定句中。

例　John has much money. (✗)

→ John <u>doesn't have much money</u>. In fact, he is as poor as a church mouse. (✓)
約翰錢並不多。事實上，他是個窮光蛋。

b 在肯定句多以 a lot of 或 lots of 取代 much。

例　I have much work to do today. (罕)
→ I have lots of work to do today. (✓)　我今天有許多工作要做。
但：I have so much work to do today that I can't go out with you. (✓)
= I have too much work to do today to go out with you.
我今天有好多工作要做，因此不能跟你約會了。

小試身手

選出錯誤 / 較不常見的句子。
Ⓐ It is dangerous to let strangers know you have a lot of money.
Ⓑ Judy has so much work that she needs to work overtime.
Ⓒ If I had much money, I would buy a house for my family.
Ⓓ John had lots of work, so I helped him.

Ans Ⓒ

Unit 79　like 及 alike 怎麼用？

a like 表「像」時是介詞，使用時之前應有 be 動詞或感官動詞 (如 sound, look, feel, taste, smell)，且 like 之後一定要有受詞。

例　The twin brothers are very like. (✗)
　　　　　　　　　　　　　介詞
→ The twin brothers are very much like each other. (✓)
　　　　　　　　　　　　　　　　　　　　　受詞

注意 ❶ very 是副詞，之後須接另一副詞 much 方可修飾介詞 like。
上句 = The twin brothers look very much like each other. (✓)
這兩個雙胞胎兄弟長得很像。

This fabric feels like silk. (✓)　這個布料摸起來像絲一樣。

❷ like 引導的介詞片語亦可置句首，修飾之後的主詞。
Like me, my sister sings well. (✓)　我妹妹跟我一樣很會唱歌。

b　alike 是形容詞，表「相像的」，在句中置 be 動詞或感官動詞之後，作主詞補語，之後不得接名詞或代名詞。

例　The twin brothers are very alike each other. (✗)
→ The twin brothers are (very) much alike. (非 very alike)
= The twin brothers look (very) much alike.
這兩個雙胞胎兄弟長得很像。

小試身手

選出錯誤的句子。
Ⓐ It looks like it's going to rain soon.
Ⓑ Although Jenny and Linda are not real sisters, they are very much alike.
Ⓒ Like my father, I also love to eat dumplings.
Ⓓ Because the two girls are twins, they are very like.

Ans Ⓓ

Unit 80　go on V-ing 及 go on to V 怎麼用？

go on 是「繼續」的意思，其用法如下：

a　go on + V-ing　持續不停地從事……

例　Tina went on to talk on the phone as I entered the room. (✗)
→ Tina went on talking on the phone as I entered the room. (✓)
我進入房間時，蒂娜繼續在講電話。

b　go on + to V　（做完某事件後）接著（從事）……

例　After doing the dishes, Mom went on mopping the floor. (✗)
→ After doing the dishes, Mom went on to mop the floor. (✓)
老媽洗碗後，接著便拖地板了。

小試身手

1. After Joan graduated at the top of her class, she went on (going / to go) after her dream job.
2. When I entered Mr. Johnson's office, he went on (talking / to talk) without noticing me.

Ans　1. to go　2. talking

Unit 81　Do you mind if... 及 Would you mind if...?

mind 為「介意」的意思，其用法如下：

a Do you mind if + 主詞 + 現在式動詞？　……你介意嗎？（較不客氣）

理由　句首的助動詞 Do 為現在式，故 if 子句中的動詞亦應使用現在式。

例　Do you mind if I op~~e~~ned the window? (✗)
→ Do you mind if I open the window? (✓)
= Do you mind me opening the window?
我把窗戶打開你會介意嗎？

b Would you mind if + 主詞 + 過去式動詞？　……您介意嗎？（較客氣）

例　Would you mind if I op~~e~~n the window? (✗)
→ Would you mind if I opened the window? (✓)
= Would you mind me opening the window?
我把窗戶打開您會介意嗎？

c 上列問句中主詞是同一人時，可採下列問句結構：

例　Do you mind if you turn on the light? (✓)
　　　↑　　　　↑
　　　主詞相同

→ Do you mind turning on the light, please?（更常用）
勞煩你開燈，可以嗎？

Would you mind if you open the window? (✓)

　　　　　主詞相同

→ Would you mind opening the window, please?（更常用）
勞煩您開窗戶，可以嗎？

小試身手

1. 您介意把門關上嗎？
   _____ You _____ _____ the door?

2. 你介意我晚點打電話給你嗎？
   _____ You _____ _____ I call you later?

Ans 1. Would; mind; closing　2. Do; mind; if

Unit 82　remember 及 memorize 怎麼用？

remember、memorize 都有「記得」的意思，其用法及差異如下：

a remember 是及物動詞，表「記得」，可接名詞、名詞子句或名詞片語作受詞。

例　Do you remember my name?　你記得我的名字嗎？
　　　　　　　　　　n.

I remember that we met before / where you live / how pretty you were when young.
我記得我們曾見過面／你住在哪裡／妳年輕時有多美。（皆為名詞子句）

Do you remember how to spell that word / what to do this afternoon?
你記得那個字是怎麼拚的嗎／今天下午要做什麼嗎？（皆為名詞片語）

b { remember to V　　　記得要……
　　 remember V-ing　　記得曾經……

例　Remember ca~~ll~~ing me when you arrive. (×)
→ Remember to call me when you arrive. (✓)
你到的時候記得要打電話給我。

I don't remember t~~o~~ have seen him somewhere. (×)
→ I don't remember having seen him somewhere. (✓)
= I don't remember seeing him somewhere.
我記不得曾經在某處見過他。

I remember working with you 20 years ago. (✓)
我記得 20 年前曾經與你共事過。

c　memorize [ˈmɛməˌraɪz] 亦為及物動詞，表「將……熟記 / 背起來」。

例　When in elementary school, I used to re~~m~~ember a poem a week. (×)
→ When in elementary school, I used to memorize a poem a week.
我念小學時曾經每一週背一首詩。

If you remember 20 words a day, you'll have a large vocabulary in three years. (×)
→ If you memorize 20 words a day, you'll know many words three years from now. (✓)　你若每天記 20 個單詞，三年後你會認識許多字。

Mem~~o~~rize me forever. (×)　永遠要把我背起來。
→ Remember me forever. (✓)　永遠要記得我。

CH 2　字詞辨異

小試身手

1	In order to pass the exam, Judy has to (remember / memorize) all the vocabulary in the book.
2	The great man will be (remembered / memorized) forever.
3	Hey! Please remember (to buy / buying) some milk on your way home. We need it for breakfast tomorrow.

Ans　1. memorize　2. remembered　3. to buy

Unit 83　man 及 a man 怎麼用?

a　man 之前無冠詞時，表「人類」，尤用於與其他動物比較時；a man 指「某個男子」。

例　Dogs are a man's best friend. (✗)
　　→ Dogs are man's best friends. (✓)
　　狗是人類最好的朋友。

　　Men (世上所有男人) are the only animals that can talk. (✗)
　　→ Man is the only animal than can talk. (✓)
　　人類是唯一會講話的動物。

　　Science has proven that the chimpanzee is man's closest relative. (✓)
　　科學已證實黑猩猩是與人類血緣最近的親戚。

b　不與動物作比較時，多用 human beings (humans)、mankind (humankind) 或 humanity，均表「人類」，之前均不置冠詞 the。

例　John has decided to devote all his life to the service of human beings / humanity / mankind.
　　約翰決定要把畢生奉獻於對人類的服務。

小試身手

1. Compared to (man / a man / men), elephants are much heavier.
2. (Man's / A man's / Men's) character is partially determined by the way he dresses.

Ans　1. man　2. A man's

Unit 84 apart from 及 aside from 怎麼用?

apart from 與 aside from 同義，皆可用於肯定句或否定句中，意義稍有不同。

a 肯定句：此時，apart from / aside from 等於介詞 besides 或 in addition to，表「除了……之外尚有……」。

例 Tony has a car <u>apart from</u> a house. (✓)
= Tony has a car <u>aside from</u> a house.
= Tony has a car <u>besides</u> a house.
= Tony has a car <u>in addition to</u> a house.
東尼除了一棟房子外還有一輛車子。

b 否定句：此時，apart from / aside from 等於 except 或 except for，表「除了……之外均無……」。

例 <u>Apart from</u> a book, there is nothing on the desk. (✓)
= <u>Except for</u> a book, there is nothing on the desk.
桌上除了一本書外，其他什麼東西也沒有。

小試身手

_____ the *Harry Potter* series, I also read every other book in the mini library, so I can answer any question you want to ask. (選錯的)

Ⓐ Except for Ⓑ Apart from
Ⓒ Aside from Ⓓ Besides

Ans Ⓐ

Unit 85　to not V 及 not to V 怎麼用?

to 引導的否定詞片語與 not 並用時，not 應置 to 之前，即：not to V。但當今也有不少英語母語人士使用 to not V。

例　I cautiously tiptoed into the living room in order to not wake Dad up. (口語)

→ I cautiously tiptoed into the living room in order not to wake Dad up. (✓)
我踮著腳小心翼翼地走進客廳以免吵醒老爸。

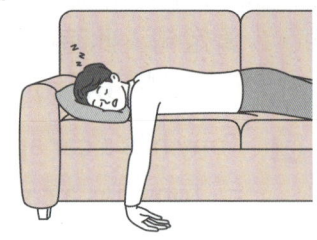

It's raining now, so I've decided to not go out. (口語)

→ It's raining now, so I've decided not to go out. (✓)
現在正在下雨，因此我決定不外出了。

小試身手

重組：to / eat / spicy food / not / the

I told Ted ＿＿＿＿＿＿＿＿＿ if he didn't want to have stomach problems later.

Ans　not to / to not eat the spicy food

Unit 86　being not 或 not being、having not 或 not having 怎麼用?

a　動名詞 being 或 having 與 not 並用時，not 應置 being 或 having 之前。

例　I regret being not able to help her then. (罕)

→ I regret not being able to help her then. (常用)
我後悔當時沒能力幫助她。

I regret having not told you the truth. (罕)

→ I regret not having told you the truth. (常用)
我後悔沒把真相告訴你。

以上 not being 及 not having 均視作動名詞，引導的片語均作及物動詞 regret 的受詞。

b being 或 having 亦可視作現在分詞，與 not 並用時，not 亦應置 being 或 having 之前。

例 Being not satisfied with his report, I asked John to rewrite. (罕)
→ Not being satisfied with his report, I asked John to rewrite it. (✓)
我對約翰的報告並不滿意，便要他重寫。

Having not heard anything from Ann for a couple of days, I started to worry about her. (罕)
→ Not having heard anything from Ann for a couple of days, I started to worry about her. (✓) 我有幾天沒接到安的信息，開始為她擔心。

小試身手

重組：having / sleep / can cause / enough / Not

_____ serious health conditions.

Ans Not having enough sleep can cause

Unit 87 cannot 及 can not 怎麼用？

a 助動詞 cannot 與 can not 同義，均表「不能」，但實際使用時，英美人士多用 cannot，且為較正式用法；少有人使用 can not。

例 You can not go out until you finish your homework. (罕)
→ You cannot go out until you finish your homework. (✓) 你直到做完功課後才可外出。

b can't 是 cannot 的縮寫，多用在口語中，屬非正式用法。故上句亦可改寫如下：

例 You can't go out until you finish your homework. (✓)

You can't use my bike without my permission. (✓，口語，非正式)
= You cannot use my bike without my permission.
未經我許可，你不可使用我的自行車。

For the good of our offspring, we cannot ignore the problem of global warming anymore. (✓，正式)
為了我們後代子孫的福祉著想，我們不能再忽視全球升溫的問題了。

c 過去式 could 與 not 並用時，一定要分開而非連成一個字。

例 I couldnot understand what Ben was talking about. (✗)
→ I could not understand what Ben was talking about. (✓)
= I couldn't understand what Ben was talking about.
班說的話我聽不懂。

小試身手

茱蒂在整理完房間前不能離開。
Judy _____ leave until her bedroom is tidied.

Ans can't / cannot

Unit 88　by far 及 so far 怎麼用？

a by far 視作副詞，表「最、以極大程度地」，置最高級的形容詞之前，修飾該形容詞。so far 亦視作副詞，表「到目前為止」，通常置句首，之後置逗點，修飾之後的整個主要子句。so far 亦可置 be 動詞之後或句尾。

例 Tom is far the best student I've ever taught. (✗)
→ Tom is by far the best student I've ever taught. (✓)
　　　　　最高級　adj.
湯姆是目前我所教過最最優秀的學生。

比較 So far, Tom is the best student I've ever taught. (✓)
= Tom is so far the best student I've ever taught.

90

= Tom is the best student I've ever taught so far.
到目前為止，湯姆是我教過最優秀的學生。

So far, we've only finished one-fifth of the project.
= Up the present, we've only finished one-fifth of the project.
截至目前為止，我們僅完成五分之一的計畫。

b
by far the + 最高級形容詞　最最……的
= far and away the + 最高級形容詞
= very much the + 最高級形容詞

例 Don't you think my girlfriend is by far / far and away / very much the most beautiful girl in the world? (✓)
你不覺得我女友是世上最最美麗的女孩子嗎？

小試身手

1　約翰是我所看過最最高的男生。
John is _____ _____ _____ _____ boy I've ever seen.

2　截至目前為止，我還沒有收到珍妮的回覆。
_____ _____, I haven't received Jenny's reply.

Ans　1. by; far; the; tallest　2. So; far

Unit 89　not easy 及 uneasy 怎麼用？

{ not easy　不容易的 (修飾事物)
{ uneasy　不安的、不自在的 (修飾人)

例 Frankly, it is uneasy to learn French. (✗)
Frankly, French is uneasy to learn. (✗)
→ Frankly, it is not easy to learn French. (✓)
= Frankly, French is not easy to learn.
坦白說，學法語不是件容易的事。

I don't feel easy whenever you sit by my side. (✗)
→ I feel uneasy whenever you sit by my side. (✓)
= I feel ill at ease whenever you sit by my side. (✓)
每次你坐在我旁邊我就感到不自在。

小試身手

1. Math is (uneasy / not easy) for me. I'm just bad at numbers.
2. Judy always feels (uneasy / not easy) when taking pictures.

Ans 1. not easy   2. uneasy

Unit 90 a land 及 a piece of land 怎麼用?

land 作不可數名詞時，表「土地」或「陸地」；land 亦可當可數名詞，表「國家」，常用單數。

- a piece of land　一塊地
- a land　一個國家

例 I bought a land in the countryside. (✗)
→ I bought a piece of land / a plot of land in the countryside. (✓)　我在鄉下買了一塊地。

Mr. Li owns several plots of land in downtown Taipei. (✓)
李先生在臺北市中心擁有好幾塊地皮。

The sailors reached land at midnight. (✓)　這些水手於午夜登上陸地。

I prefer to travel by land rather than by air or by ship. (✓)
我比較喜歡乘車旅遊而不太喜歡乘飛機或坐船旅遊。

It is not too much to say that France is a beautiful piece of land. (✗)
→ It is not too much to say that France is a beautiful land.
法國是個美麗的國家，這樣的說法並不過分。

小試身手

1	Australia is (land / a land) of great natural beauty and diverse wildlife.
2	The rich businessman bought some (loaves / plots) of land to build a new housing development.

Ans　1. a land　2. plots

Unit 91　insist on 及 persist in 怎麼用?

{ insist on + V-ing　堅持要做……
{ persist in + V-ing　持續 (從事) ……

例　I asked John to stay, but he persisted in leaving. (✗)
我要約翰留下來，他卻堅持不懈地離開。
(語意不通)

→ I asked John to stay, but he insisted on leaving. (✓)
我要約翰留下來，他卻堅持要離開。

Whatever Tom decides to do, he insists on doing it. (✗)
不管湯姆決定要做什麼事，他都堅持要做它。(語意不通)

→ Whatever Tom decides to do, he persists in doing it. (✓)
不管湯姆決定要做什麼事，他都會堅持不懈地做下去。

補充　persist 亦可表某症狀「持續存在」。

If the symptoms insist, contact your doctor immediately. (✗)
如果這些症狀堅持下去的話，趕緊連絡你的醫生。

→ If the symptoms persist, contact your doctor immediately.
(✓，此處 persist 等於 continue to exist)
如果這些症狀持續下去的話，趕緊連絡你的醫生。

小試身手

1. Despite facing difficulties, Joan chose to (persist in / insist on) her efforts to learn a new language.
2. My doctor (insists on / persists in) regular exercise and a healthy diet as the keys to maintaining good health.

Ans 1. persist in   2. insists on

Unit 92　on the street 及 in the street 怎麼用?

{ on the street　在街道旁邊
  in the street　在街道中間

例　I live ~~in~~ that street / ~~in~~ Maple Street. (✗)
我住在那條街道中間 / 我住在楓樹街的中間。(三天後會被來往的車輛壓成人乾。)

→ I live on that street / on Maple Street. (✓)
我住那條街上 (街邊) / 楓樹街 (街邊)。

On weekends, there is always a policeman directing traffic ~~on~~ the street. (✗，在街邊)

→ On weekends, there is always a policeman directing traffic in the street. (✓，在街道中間)
週末的時候總會有警察在街道中指揮交通。

During the rush hour, vehicles are moving bumper to bumper ~~on~~ the street. (✗，在街邊)

→ During the rush hour, vehicles are moving bumper to bumper in the street. (✓，在街道中間)
在上下班交通擁擠時間，街道上車輛堵得一輛接一輛寸步難行。

小試身手

1. My mom's clothes store is located (on / in) this street. If you go straight, you'll see it on your right.
2. The children were playing (on / in) the street and had to move when a car approached.

Ans　1. on　2. in

Unit 93　weather 及 climate 怎麼用?

weather 表「天氣」，為不可數名詞，指短期或日常的大氣狀況；climate 則指某區域的長期天氣平均狀況，為可數名詞。

例　What's the climate like today? (✗)
→ What's the weather like today? (✓)　今天天氣怎麼樣？

It's such a good weather that I feel like going swimming this afternoon. (✗)
→ It's such good weather that I feel like going swimming this afternoon. (✓)　天氣這麼好，因此今天下午我想去游泳。

Generally, we have a pleasant weather in Taiwan. (✗)
→ Generally, we have a pleasant climate in Taiwan. (✓)
一般而言，臺灣的氣候宜人。

What was the climate like in San Francisco yesterday? (✗)
→ What was the weather like in San Francisco yesterday? (✓)
昨天舊金山的天氣怎麼樣？

→ What's the climate in San Francisco all year round? (✓)
舊金山全年的氣候怎麼樣？

CH 2　字詞辨異

小試身手

1. How is the (weather / climate) in your city at the moment?
2. Most people believe that humans are to blame for (weather / climate) change.

Ans 1. weather   2. climate

Unit 94　failed 及 failing 怎麼用?

failed 與 failing 均可作形容詞。failed (= unsuccessful) 表「失敗的」；failing (= no longer strong or healthy) 表「逐漸衰弱的」。

例　The ~~failing~~ coup landed the general in prison. (✗)
→ The failed coup landed the general in prison. (✓)　這場失敗的政變讓這位將領鋃鐺入獄。
＊ coup [ku] n. 政變 (字尾 p 不發音)

The world-famous actress had three ~~failing~~ marriages. (✗)
→ The world-famous actress had three failed marriages. (✓)
這位世界知名的女演員有三次失敗的婚姻。

My mom's ~~failed~~ health worries me sick. (✗)
→ My mom's failing health worries me sick. (✓)
我老媽日漸衰敗的健康令我擔心極了。

小試身手

1. In order to save his (failing / failed) business from closing, Jason is trying every possible way to increase sales.
2. The actor has had three (failing / failed) marriages, and he is now going to get married again!

Ans 1. failing   2. failed

Unit 95 rob 及 deprive 怎麼用？

a rob 是及物動詞，表「搶奪」，用法如下：
rob + 人 / 銀行 + of + 金錢

例 The bandit robbed all the woman's money. (✗)
→ The bandit robbed the woman of all her money. (✓)　匪徒搶走了婦人所有的錢。

理由 第一句例句 robbed 的受詞是婦人的錢 (the woman's money)，不是被搶奪的對象，故不合邏輯。第二句中，robbed 的受詞是婦人 (the woman)，是被搶奪的對象，合乎邏輯。之後的介詞 of 有 from (從) 的意味，即匪徒把婦人從她所有的錢推離開，以搶走她的錢。

b 由此得知，有 rob 出現的被動語態中，主詞也應為被搶奪的對象 (人)，而非被搶奪的物 (金錢)。

例 All the woman's money was robbed. (✗)
→ The woman was robbed of all her money. (✓)
婦人所有的錢都被搶走了。

According to the police, three armed men robbed the bank at noon out of the blue. (✓)
根據警方報導，中午突然有三名武裝男子搶劫該銀行。

The police released that 3 million dollars were robbed of the bank. (✗)
→ The police released that the bank was robbed of 3 million dollars. (✓)　警方透露稱該銀行被搶走了 3 百萬美元。

c deprive [dɪˋpraɪv] 表「剝奪」，用法與 rob 完全相同。

例 The court sentenced the criminal to life imprisonment and deprived all his civic rights. (✗)
→ The court sentenced the criminal to life imprisonment and deprived him of all his civic rights. (✓)
　　　　　　人
法庭將該罪犯判處無期徒刑並褫奪所有公權。

The criminal was deprived of all his civic rights. (✓)
人
該罪犯被褫奪所有公權。

小試身手

選出錯誤的選項。
Ⓐ Some bad guy robbed the lady's money on the street.
Ⓑ The First Bank was robbed of one million dollars this morning.
Ⓒ The government deprived the poor people of their rights.
Ⓓ The children were deprived of their basic needs, such as food and water, due to the war.

Ans Ⓐ

Unit 96　as day breaks 及 as night falls 怎麼用?

a　as day breaks 是固定片語，是固定片語，表「破曉時」，此處 day 表「白晝」，之前不得置 the。

例　We set out as the day broke. (✗)
→ We set out as day broke. (✓)
= We set out as soon as day broke.
天一亮我們就動身出發了。

b　as night falls 亦是固定片語，表「天黑時」，night 之前不得置 the。

例　We got to the destination as the night fell. (✗)
→ We got to the destination as night fell. (✓)
我們於天黑時抵達了目的地。

小試身手

天亮時我們就上路了，天黑時我們才到旅程的中途而已。
We hit the road _____ _____ _____, but we were only halfway there _____ _____ _____.

Ans as; day; broke; as; night; fell

Unit 97　lest 及 for fear that 怎麼用？

a lest 為副詞連接詞，表「以免」，用於下列句構：
主要子句 + lest + 主詞 + (should) + 原形動詞

例 I got up early this morning lest I would miss the first high-speed train to Kaohsiung. (✗)

→ I got up early this morning lest I should miss the first high-speed train to Kaohsiung. (✓)

= I got up early this morning lest I miss the first high-speed train to Kaohsiung.
(原形動詞 miss 之前省略了 should)
我今天一大早就起床以免我趕不上開往高雄的第一班高鐵。

Ted should quit smoking immediately lest he will get lung cancer. (✗)

→ Ted should quit smoking immediately lest he should get lung cancer. (✓)

= Ted should quit smoking right away lest he get lung cancer.
泰德應立刻戒菸以免染上肺癌。

b for fear that 亦視作副詞連接詞，與 lest 同義，表「唯恐」或「以免」，用於下列句構：
主要子句 + for fear that + 主詞 + will / may + 原形動詞

例 I burned the midnight oil last night reviewing my lessons for fear that I should fail the math test today. (✗)

→ I burned the midnight oil reviewing my lessons last night for fear that I would / might fail the math test today. (✔)

= I burned the midnight oil reviewing my lessons last night for fear of failing the math test today.

= I burned the midnight oil reviewing my lessons last night lest I (should) fail the math test today.

我昨晚開夜車複習課業以免今天的數學考試不及格。

小試身手

選出錯誤的選項。

Ⓐ Annie studied diligently every night lest she fail the upcoming exam.
Ⓑ Don always locked the doors before going to bed lest any thief break in during the night.
Ⓒ Dina packed an extra sweater for the trip, for fear that the weather would turn cold.
Ⓓ Alex double-checked the directions for fear that he get lost on his way to the interview.

Ans Ⓓ

Unit 98　accept 及 receive 怎麼用？

a　accept 是及物動詞，表同意「接受」；receive 亦是及物動詞，表「收到」。

例　Did you accept the birthday gift I sent you the other day? (✘)
→ Did you receive the birthday gift I sent you the other day? (✔)
我前幾天寄給你的生日禮物你收到了嗎？

I'm sorry to tell you that she refused to receive the birthday gift you sent her. (✗)

→ I'm sorry to tell you that she refused to accept the birthday gift you sent her. (✓)　很遺憾要告訴你，她拒絕接受你寄給她的生日禮物。

Since you've promised not to do that again, I'll receive your apologies. (✗)

→ Since you've promised not to do that again, I'll accept your apologies. (✓)　既然你已承諾不會再做那樣的事，我就接受你的道歉吧。

小試身手

1. I will (accept / receive) the job offer if the salary is reasonable.
2. Anya (received / accepted) a phone call from a stranger, saying that he had kidnapped (綁架) her daughter.

Ans　1. accept　2. received

Unit 99　compliment 及 complement 怎麼用？

a compliment [ˈkɑmpləˌmɛnt] 是及物動詞，表「讚美」，用於下列結構：

compliment 人 on 事物　因某事物讚美某人

例　My teacher complimented my outstanding performance in the speech contest. (✗)

→ My teacher complimented me on my outstanding performance in the speech contest. (✓)　老師讚美我在演講比賽中的卓越表現。

Mr. Wang complimented his daughter for her musical talent. (✗)

→ Mr. Wang complimented his daughter on her musical talent. (✓)　王先生讚美他女兒的音樂天賦。

b 另一表「讚美」的及物動詞為 praise，用於下列結構：
praise 事物　讚美某事物
praise 人 for 事物　因某事物讚美某人

例 My teacher praised my outstanding performance in the speech
　　　　　　　vt.
contest. (✓)

= My teacher praised me for my outstanding performance in the
　　　　　　　　　　　人　　　　　　　　　　事物
speech contest.　老師稱讚我在演講比賽中卓越的表現。

Mr. Wang praised his daughter for her musical talent. (✓)

= Mr. Wang praised his daughter's musical talent.
王先生讚美他女兒的音樂天賦。

c compliment [ˈkɑmpləmənt] 亦為可數名詞，一樣為「讚美」之意，常用單數；亦可表「祝賀、致意」，恆用複數。

例 I take it as a compliment when people say my son looks exactly like me. (✓)　大家說我兒子長得跟我一模一樣時，我認為這是讚美。

Please give my compliments (非compliment) to Mr. Li. (✓)
請代我向李先生致意 / 祝賀。

比較 Please give my greetings (非 greeting) to Mr. Li. (✓)

= Please say hi to Mr. Li.　請代我向李先生問候 / 打聲招呼。

d complement [ˈkɑmpləˌmɛnt] 可作及物動詞，表「配襯、補足」、「使……完美」。

例 The red tie compliments your black suit jacket perfectly. (✗)

→ The red tie complements your black suit jacket perfectly. (✓)

= The red tie goes well with your black suit jacket.
這條紅色領帶跟你的黑色西裝上衣很搭堪稱絕配。

小試身手

選出錯誤的句子。

Ⓐ Jay complemented my quick reaction during the game.
Ⓑ Lanny praised her son for helping the old lady cross the road.
Ⓒ When you get to the party, please give my compliments to Jake.
Ⓓ Your new hair color complements your brown eyes.

Ans Ⓐ

Unit 100　principle 及 principal 怎麼用？

a principle 與 principal 發音相同，均為 [ˈprɪnsəpl̩]，均作名詞；但 principle 指「原則」，principal 則指 (中小學) 校長，使用時不可混淆。

例　John is a man of principal, which is why I trust him. (✗)
→ John is a man of principle, which is why I trust him. (✓)　約翰是個有原則的人，這也是我信任他的理由。
The new school principle is friendly to us students. (✗)
→ The new school principal is friendly to us students. (✓)
新任校長對我們這些學生很和善。

b principal 亦可作形容詞，與 major 或 important 同義，表「主要的、重要的」。

例　Teaching is a principle source of my income. (✗)
→ Teaching is a principal source of my income. (✓)
教書是我收入的主要來源。

小試身手

1　The school's (principle / principal) goal is to provide students with a great education.

2　The school (principle / principal) told us that the annual sports day event will take place next week.

> Ans　1. principle　2. principal

Unit 101　fun 及 funny 怎麼用?

a fun 可作不可數名詞,表「樂趣」。

例　It's <u>fun</u> learning math with Mr. Smith.
　　　　n.

= It's <u>fun</u> to learn math with Mr. Smith.
　　　n.

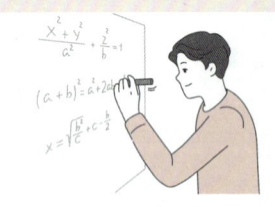

= Learning math with Mr. Smith is <u>fun</u>.　跟史密斯老師學數學很有趣。
　　　　　　　　　　　　　　　　n.

b fun 亦可作形容詞,表「有趣的、好玩的」。funny 亦為形容詞,表「滑稽的」。

例　In my view, hiking in the mountains is <u>a fun thing</u> to do. (✓)
我認為在山中健行是件趣事。

Jay is <u>fun</u> to be with. (✓)　跟阿傑在一起很有趣。
　　　adj.

We had a fun~~n~~y day at the park. (✗)　我們在公園渡過了滑稽的一天。

→ We had <u>a fun day</u> at the park. (✓)　我們在公園渡過了有趣的一天。

Peter looks serious, but he can be very <u>funny</u> when he wants to. (✓)
彼得看起來很嚴肅,但只要他願意,他會非常滑稽。

小試身手

1　滑稽的小丑逗得每個人笑哈哈。
The ＿＿＿＿ clown made everyone laugh.

2. 跟約翰聊天很有趣。
Chatting with John is a lot of _____.

Ans 1. fun / funny 2. fun

Unit 102　champion 及 championship 怎麼用?

champion [ˈtʃæmpɪən] 指「冠軍得主」，championship [ˈtʃæmpɪənˌʃɪp] 則指「冠軍頭銜」。

例　Jane was the championship in the speech competition. (✗)
→ Jane was the champion in the speech competition. (✓)
= Jane won first place in the speech competition.
珍是演講比賽的冠軍。

Mary was the champion in the singing contest. (✓)
瑪麗是歌唱比賽的冠軍 (得主)。

Tammy was the first runner-up in the singing contest. (✓)
潭美是歌唱比賽的亞軍 (得主)。

Susan was the second runner-up in the singing contest. (✓)
蘇珊是歌唱比賽的季軍 (得主)。

小試身手

愛麗絲獲勝並被加冕為冠軍。
Alice won the _____ and was crowned the school tennis _____.

Ans championship; champion

105

Unit 103 「火車離站」是 The train leaves 或 will leave at 2:30 p.m.?

a 大眾運輸工具 (如高鐵、火車、飛機、郵輪等) 每天均按時刻表到站或離站，故均應使用「現在式」表示常態。

例 The train ~~will leave~~ at 2:30 p.m., so let's hurry up now. (✗)
→ The train leaves at 2:30 p.m., so let's hurry up now. (✓)
火車下午兩點半離站，因此咱們動作要快了。

The plane ~~will arrive~~ at 10 a.m. I'll meet you at the terminal. (✗)
→ The plane arrives at 10 a.m. I'll meet you at the terminal. (✓)
飛機上午 10 點到達。我會在航站跟你碰頭。

b 若無到站或離站的時間修飾時，則可使用未來式 (will + 原形動詞)、未來進行式 (will be + V-ing) 或現在進行式 (is + V-ing)。

例 This train | will leave | soon. Let's take the next one instead. (✓)
| will be leaving |
| is leaving |

這班火車很快就要開了。咱們改搭下一班吧。

小試身手

請選出較適合的答案。

1 Our train (leaves / is leaving) in five minutes. We need to hurry!
2 The plane (leaves / is leaving) for New York every Thursday.

Ans 1. is leaving　2. leaves

Unit 104 「持續地」是 continually 或 continuously?

continuously [kənˈtɪnjʊəslɪ] 表無間斷的「持續地」；continually [kənˈtɪnjʊəlɪ] 表動作有間斷的「持續地」。

例 It has been pouring continually for almost three hours, and the river is overflowing its banks now. (✕)

→ It has been pouring continuously for almost three hours, and the river is overflowing its banks now. (✓)

滂沱大雨不停地下了將近 3 個小時，河水現在都漲出堤岸了。

I've been driving continually on the freeway for two hours. I hope you can take over at the next rest area. (✕)

→ I've been driving continuously on the freeway for two hours. I hope you can take over at the next rest area. (✓)

我在高速公路上連續不停地開了兩個小時的車，希望你在下個休息區換手。

How can I keep on talking if you continuously cut in like this? (✕，不停地打岔，一秒都未停過)

→ How can I keep on talking if you continually cut in like this? (✓，隔一陣子就打岔)

你若像這樣持續隔一陣子就打岔，叫我怎麼能繼續講下去？

小試身手

1. The rain fell (continuously / continually) for hours, flooding the streets and causing traffic jams.

2. Tina (continuously / continually) checked her phone for messages, because she didn't want to miss anything important.

Ans 1. continuously 2. continually

Unit 105 「損害」是 damage 或 damages?

damage 及 damages 均為「損害」之意，皆為名詞，可作不可數與可數名詞，差異如下：

{ damage [ˈdæmɪdʒ] n. 損害 (不可數)
{ damages [ˈdæmɪdʒɪz] n. 損害賠償金 (恆用複數)

107

例 The typhoon has done a lot of damages to that area. (✗)

→ The typhoon has done a lot of damage to that area. (✓) 颱風對那個地方造成許多損害。

My car crashed into a tree. Luckily, I was all right, and the insurance company promised to cover my damages. (✓)
我的車子撞上一顆樹。所幸的是我人無事，保險公司也承諾賠償我的損失。

小試身手

The drunk driver crashed into my car and did a lot of (damage / damages) to it. Therefore, he had to pay me (damage / damages).

Ans damage; damages

Unit 106　be tired of... 及 be tired from... 怎麼用？

```
be tired of...    對……感到厭倦 / 厭煩 (指心煩)
= be bored with...
= be fed up with...
be tired from...  由於……感到累了 (指體力累)
```

例 I'm tired of doing the same job day after day. (✓)
= I'm bored with / I'm fed up with doing the same job day after day.
每天都做同樣的工作讓我很厭煩。

I'm tired of Mom / Mom's nagging at me all the time. (✓)
= I'm bored with Mom / Mom's nagging at me all the time.
= I'm fed up with Mom / Mom's nagging at me all the time.
老媽一直對我嘮叨，讓我煩死了。

I'm tired from the intensive physical training, so I need a good rest. (✓)　密集訓練讓我累壞了，因此我需要好好休息一下。

小試身手

1. The children were tired (of / from) playing all day in the park, and they fell asleep as soon as they got home.

2. Judy is fed up with studying for exams and wants to relax for a while.　提示 用 tired 改寫句子。
   Judy is ＿＿＿＿ ＿＿＿＿ studying for exams and wants to relax for a while.

　　　　　　　　　　　　　　　　Ans　1. from　2. tired; of

Unit 107　different 及 indifferent 怎麼用?

a be different from...　與……不同
英美人士認為，be different "from" 是最標準的用法。

例　This car is different from the one I saw yesterday. (✔)
= This car differs from the one I saw yesterday.
這輛車與我昨天看的那一輛不相同。

但在口語中，美國人常使用 be different than，英國人則使用 be different to。

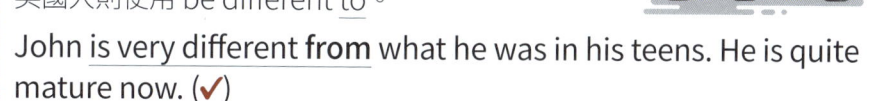

John is very different from what he was in his teens. He is quite mature now. (✔)

= John is very different than what he was in his teens. He is quite mature now.

= John is very different to what he was in his teens. He is quite mature now.　約翰與十幾歲時候的他有很大的差異。他現在成熟多了。

b be indifferent to 人 / 事物　對某人 / 某事物漠不關心 / 不感興趣
indifferent [ɪnˋdɪf(ə)rənt] *a.* 冷漠的

例　To be frank, I'm indifferent from politics. (✗)
→ To be frank, I'm indifferent to politics. (✔)
= Frankly (speaking), I'm not interested in politics.
坦白說，我對政治不感興趣。

CH 2　字詞辨異

109

小試身手

1. 湯尼的繪畫與其他人的不同，他只用少數幾種顏色畫畫。
   Tony's paintings are _____ _____ the others'. He uses only a few colors to paint.

2. 羅伊對去看演唱會的主意不感興趣，他比較想要看電影。
   Roy is _____ _____ the idea of going to a concert. He prefers to watch movies.

Ans 1. different; from / to / than   2. indifferent; to

Unit 108　uninterested 及 disinterested 怎麼用？

{ uninterested [ʌnˈɪntrɪstɪd] *adj.* 不感興趣的
  disinterested [dɪsˈɪntrɪstɪd] *adj.* 公正的 (= fair)；不偏心的 (= unbiased) }

例 Ted is disinterested in watching TV. (✗)
→ Ted is uninterested in watching TV. (✓)
= Ted is not interested in watching TV.
泰迪對看電視不感興趣。

A good judge should be uninterested when handling law cases. (✗)
→ A good judge should be disinterested when handling law cases. (✓)　優秀的法官在處理訴訟案件時應保持公正的立場。

小試身手

1. Ray seemed (uninterested / disinterested) in the speech and kept looking at his phone.

2. As a judge, Ross remained (uninterested / disinterested) in the case and focused on the evidence presented.

Ans 1. uninterested　2. disinterested

Unit 109　at all times 及 all the time 怎麼用?

{ at all times　隨時，任何時候 (有 at any moment 的意味)
  all the time　一直，重複不斷地 (有 repeatedly 的意味)

例　When you are traveling, keep all your belongings with you at all times. (✓)
你旅行時，隨時要看好隨身物品不離身。

Parents have to remind their children to do their homework all the time. (✓)
父母得不斷提醒孩子要做功課。

Ben is busy all the time. (✓)　阿班一直忙個不停。

小試身手

1. You need to remain seated (at all times / all the time) during the speech.

2. Little Hank talks (at all times / all the time). Does he ever get tired of it?

Ans　1. at all times　2. all the time

Unit 110　none is 及 none are 怎麼用?

none 是代名詞，表「沒有一個」，之後接 of，再接複數名詞，動詞可用單數或複數形。

例　None of these pens works. (✓)
　　　　　單數動詞
= Not one of these pens works. (✓)
= None of these pens work.
　　　　　複數動詞
= Not any of these pens work.　這些筆沒有一支能用。

(上列例子源自《牛津英漢辭典》。)

111

不過，也有英美人士認為，"none of" 之後接複數名詞時就使用複數名詞，"none of" 之後接不可數名詞時就使用單數動詞。

None of the water is polluted. (✔)　這些水全都沒受到汙染。

（上列例子源自網站 "Quick and Dirty Tips Grammar Girl"。）

小試身手

我的朋友們沒有人明天要去游泳。

_____ going swimming tomorrow.

Ans　None of my friends is / are

Unit 111　Neither of us is... 及 Neither of us are... 怎麼用？

a　neither 可作代名詞，指「兩者沒有一個」，等於 not either，視作單數，故作主詞時，按正式的文法之後應接「第三人稱單數動詞」。

例　Neither of my parents enjoys singing. (✔)
我爸媽沒有一個喜歡唱歌。

Neither of us likes / is fond of going fishing. (✔)
我們兩個沒有一個喜歡釣魚。

I don't like neither of these two books. (✗，don't 與 neither 形成錯誤的雙重否定)

→ I don't like either of these two books. (✔)

= I like neither of these two books.　這兩本書我都不喜歡。

b　不過在口語中，neither 作主詞時，之後可接第三人稱單數動詞或複數動詞。

正式　Neither of my parents enjoys singing. (✔)　我爸媽都不喜歡唱歌。

口語　Neither of my parents enjoy / enjoys singing. (✔)

正式　Neither of us is fond of going fishing. (✔)　我們都不愛釣魚。

口語　Neither of us are / is fond of going fishing. (✔)

112

小試身手

我的兩個姊姊都不喜歡運動。

_____ of my sisters (l) _____ sports.

Ans Neither; like / likes

Unit 112　Either you or he is... 及 Either you or he are... 怎麼用?

a 下列連接詞連接兩個主詞時，動詞按較近的主詞作變化：

- not... but...　　　　　不是……而是……
- not only... but (also)...　不僅……而且……
- either... or...　　　　　不是……就是……
- neither... nor...　　　　……及……皆不……

例　Not you but Tom are to blame. (✗)

→ Not you but Tom is to blame. (✓)
該怪罪的不是你而是湯姆。

Not only Ed but also I is responsible for the mistake. (✗)

→ Not only Ed but (also) I am responsible for the mistake. (✓)
不僅是艾德還有我對這項錯誤要負起責任。

Either you or Jess are wrong. (✗)

→ Either you or Jess is wrong. (✓)　不是你錯就是潔斯錯。

Neither Danny nor I is supposed to do it. (✗)

→ Neither Danny nor I am supposed to do it. (✓)
該做這事的既不是丹尼也不是我。

b as well as（以及）連接兩個主詞時，動詞始終按第一個主詞作變化。

例　I, as well as my friends, were late for work today. (✗)

→ I, as well as my friends, was late for work today. (✓)

= I, no less than my friends, was late for work today.

= My friends, as well as I, were late for work today.

= My friends, together with me, were late for work today.
　　　　　　　　　　　　介詞 受詞

= My friends, along with me, were late for work today.
　　　　　　　　　　　介詞 受詞

我和我幾個朋友今天上班都遲到了。

小試身手

1 Either my students or I _____ going hiking tomorrow.
Ⓐ is　　Ⓑ am　　Ⓒ are　　Ⓓ be

2 The twins as well as their mother _____ interested in cooking.
Ⓐ is　　Ⓑ are　　Ⓒ be　　Ⓓ am

3 Both Alice and Jake keep pets.
提示 用 Not only... but also... 開頭改寫句子。
_____ pets.

Ans　1. Ⓑ　2. Ⓑ　3. Not only Alice but also Jake keeps

Unit 113　farther 及 further 怎麼用？

farther 是副詞，表「更遠地」，是 far（很遠地）的比較級，指實際可測量的距離。further 指程度「更進一步地」亦是 far 的比較級。

例　Jim lives far away from our school, but I live farther away. (✓)
吉姆住地方離我們學校很遠，但我住得更遠。

114

The farther we traveled north, the colder the weather became. (✓)
我們越往北行（距離可測得出來），天氣就變得越冷。

How much further is it to our destination? (✗)

→ How much farther is it to our destination? (✓)
我們還要走多遠才會到達目的地？

Because of poor management, our company plunged farther into debt. (✗，陷入債務與實際的空間距離無關而是與程度有關)

→ Because of poor management, our company plunged further into debt. (✓)　由於經營不善，本公司陷入債務的程度就更深。

The farther we talked, the more problems we found. (✗)

→ The further we talked, the more problems we found. (✓)
我們談得越深，發現問題也越多。

We'll go a little farther into the details this afternoon. (✗)

→ We'll go a little further into the details this afternoon. (✓)
今天下午我們進一步討論細節。

小試身手

1 I need to drive (further / farther) than this to get to the nearest gas station.

2 Doris will need to do (further / farther) research on the topic before she can come to a conclusion.

Ans　1. farther　2. further

Unit 114　then 及 and then 怎麼用？

a then 作副詞，表「然後」，不可當對等連接詞連接兩個主要子句。

例　I finished all the paperwork by 6 p.m., then I walked all the way back home. (✗，兩主要子句無連接詞連接)
我在下午 6 點前把文案全部處理完畢，然後就一路步行回家。

補救之道

1 在 then 之前置對等連接詞 and，且 and 之前置逗點。

I finished all the paperwork by 6 p.m., and then I walked all the way back home. (✔)

2 用分號 (；) 連接兩句，此時 then 之前不置 and。

I finished all the paperwork by 6 p.m.; then I walked all the way back home. (✔)

3 兩個主要子句各自獨立，形成兩個句子，then 改成大寫 Then，即：

I finished all the paperwork by 6 p.m. Then I walked all the way back home. (非 6 p.m.. Then)

Go straight ahead, then turn left at the first crossroads. (✗)

→ Go straight ahead, and then turn left at the first crossroads. (✔)

= Go straight ahead; then turn left at the first crossroads.

= Go straight ahead. Then turn left at the first crossroads.

往前直走，然後在第一個路口左轉。

*請上網參考網站 English Language & Usage 有關 then 及 and then 的用法。

b 現在許多英美人士在口語甚至在寫作中均將 then 視作對等連接詞，即：

例 I'll take care of this matter first, then I'll call you back. (口語)

我先處理這件事，然後再給你回電。

Go straight ahead, then turn left at the first crossroads. (口語)

往前直走，然後在第一個路口左轉。

小試身手

我吃了晚餐，然後去公園散步。

I ate my dinner, _____ _____ I took a walk in the park.

Ans and; then

Unit 115　awful 及 awesome 怎麼用?

a　{ awful *a.* 糟糕的，差勁的 (= very bad)
　　awesome *a.* 極好的，很棒的 (= extremely good)

例　Even though the weather is awesome, we still have a lot to do. (✗)

→ Even though the weather is awful, we still have a lot to do. (✓)
雖然天氣很不好，我們仍有許多事情可做。

The concert was so awful that it attracted a capacity audience. (✗)

→ The concert was so awesome that it attracted a capacity audience. (✓)　演唱會太棒了，因此吸引了滿場觀眾。

b　awful 亦可作副詞，與 very (很) 同義，尤用於口語，可修飾正面或負面的形容詞。

例　It's awful / very hot today. (✓)　今天熱斃了。

The little girl there looks awful / very cute. (✓)
那邊那個小女孩看起來很可愛。

c　awfully 是副詞，與 very (很) 同義，多修飾負面的形容詞。

例　It's awfully / awful cold today.　今天冷斃了。

I'm awfully sorry to hear that.　聽到那個消息我很難過。

小試身手

1. Alex's handwriting is so (awesome / awful) that no one can understand it.

2. We went to an amusement park today and had an (awesome / awful) time. I felt really happy!

Ans　1. awful　2. awesome

117

Unit 116　intense 及 intensive 怎麼用？

{ intense [ɪnˋtɛns] a. 強烈的
{ intensive [ɪnˋtɛnsɪv] a. 密集的

例　I can't stand the intensive heat in summer. (✗)

→ I can't stand the intense heat in summer. (✓)
我受不了夏天的酷熱。

We guarantee that our six-week intense pronunciation course will enable you to speak perfect American English. (✗)

→ We guarantee that our six-week intensive pronunciation course will enable you to speak perfect American English. (✓)
我們保證我們的 6 週密集發音課程會讓你講得一口完美的美語。

小試身手

1. The language course included an (intense / intensive) study program, with daily classes and a lot of practice.
2. The athlete felt (intense / intensive) pressure to perform well in the competition.

Ans　1. intensive　2. intense

Unit 117　popular 及 prevalent 怎麼用？

{ popular [ˋpɑpjələ] a. (潮流方面的) 流行
{ prevalent [ˋprɛvələnt] a. (到處都存在的，尤指疾病) 流行

例　K-pop is getting increasingly prevalent in Taiwan. (✗)

→ K-pop is getting increasingly popular in Taiwan. (✓)
韓國流行樂在臺灣日趨流行。

At that time, COVID-19 was getting increasingly pop~~u~~lar across the world. (×)

→ At that time, COVID-19 was getting increasingly prevalent / rampant across the world. (✓)

當時 COVID-19（2019 年冠狀病毒）在全球各地日趨盛行 / 猖獗。

小試身手

1. The flu is (popular / prevalent) during the winter months, and many people take extra precautions to avoid getting sick.
2. The restaurant is (popular / prevalent) among locals and tourists.

Ans 1. prevalent   2. popular

Unit 118 ashamed 及 shameful 怎麼用？

a ashamed [əˋʃemd] *a.* 感到羞愧的。使用本字時，主詞一定是人，用於下列結構中：

- 人 + be ashamed of...
- 人 + be ashamed to V
- 人 + be ashamed + that 引導的名詞子句

例 I was ashamed ~~for~~ his behavior. (×)

→ I was ashamed of his behavior. (✓)　他的行為令我感到羞愧。

I am ashamed to tell you that I lied to you this morning. (✓)
我很羞愧地要告訴你，今天早上我對你撒了個謊。

I am ashamed that I didn't tell you the truth this morning. (✓)
我今天早上沒對你說實話，感到很羞愧。

b shameful [ˋʃemfəl] *a.* 令人羞愧 / 可恥的（修飾行為或事情）

例 I'm sha~~m~~eful that you did such an ash~~a~~med thing. (×)

→ I'm ashamed that you did such a shameful thing. (✓)
你做了這樣令人可恥的事使我感到可恥。

Andy's behavior towards the elderly woman was shameful. (✓)
安迪對那位老太太的行為是可恥的。

小試身手

1. It is (ashamed / shameful) that you lied again and again to get what you wanted.
2. I'm (ashamed / shameful) that my son committed such a crime.

Ans 1. shameful   2. ashamed

Unit 119　considerable 及 considerate 怎麼用?

{ considerable [kənˈsɪdərəbl̩] *a.* 大量的
{ considerate [kənˈsɪdərət] *a.* 體貼的，貼心的

例　The company has lost a considerate amount of money because of poor management. (✗)

→ The company has lost a considerable amount of money because of poor management. (✓)
公司因管理不善損失了很多錢。

The flood caused considerate damage to the village. (✗)

→ The flood caused considerable damage to the village. (✓)
洪水對這個村落造成很大的損害。

It was considerable of you to remember my birthday. (✗)

→ It was considerate / thoughtful of you to remember my birthday. (✓)　你還記得我的生日，真貼心。

You should be considerate / thoughtful of other people's feelings. (✓)　你應體諒其他人的感受。

小試身手

1. My (considerable / **considerate**) son gave me a card on my birthday.
2. The construction of the new building required a (**considerable** / considerate) amount of time, effort, and resources.

Ans 1. considerate 2. considerable

Unit 120　not to mention... 及 let alone... 怎麼用?

not to mention... 及 let alone... 均表「更不用說……」，前者可用於肯定句或否定句，後者只用於否定句。

a

not to mention...　更不用說……

肯定句 / 否定句 + | not to mention / to say nothing of / not to speak of | + 名詞 / 動名詞

例　The billionaire can afford that huge mansion, not to mention a Ferrari. (✓)
這位億萬富翁可以買得起那座巨大的別莊，更別說一輛法拉利超跑了。

Mary can't sing, not to mention dance. (✗)
→ Mary can't sing, not to mention dancing. (✓)
瑪麗不會唱歌，更別說跳舞了。

b

let alone... + 原形動詞 / 名詞　更不用說……
= much less...

例　The poor man can't afford a bicycle, let alone / much less a car. (✓)
　　　　　　　　　　　　　　　　　　n.　　　　　　　　　　n.
這個窮人連自行車都買不起，更別說車子了。

Dan can't ride a bike, let alone / much less driving a car. (✗)
　　　　　　　　　　　　　　　　　　　　動名詞
→ Dan can't ride a bike, let alone / much less drive a car. (✓)
　　　　　　　　　　　　　　　　　　　　原形動詞

= Dan can't ride a bike, <u>not to mention</u> driving a car.
阿丹連自行車都不會騎。更別說開車了。

David can't boil eggs, <u>let alone</u> / <u>much less</u> cooking dinner. (✗)
　　　　　　　原形動詞　　　　　　　　　動名詞

→ David can't boil eggs, <u>let alone</u> / <u>much less</u> cook dinner. (✓)
　　　　　　　原形動詞　　　　　　　　　原形動詞

= David can't boil eggs, <u>not to mention</u> / <u>to say nothing of</u> / <u>not to speak of</u> cooking dinner. (✓)　大衛連蛋都不會煮。更別說煮晚飯了。
　　　　　　　　　　　　動名詞

C

「更不用說……」		
主要子句	使用片語	後接
肯定句	not to mention to say nothing of not to speak of	名詞 / 動名詞
否定句	not to mention to say nothing of not to speak of	名詞 / 動名詞
	let alone much less	名詞 / 原形動詞

小試身手

1. I can't walk well after the accident, _____ running. (選錯的)
   Ⓐ to say nothing of　　Ⓑ not to speak of
   Ⓒ much less　　　　　Ⓓ not to mention

2. Jason wouldn't drink any water, let alone eat anything.
   提示 用 not to mention 改寫句子。
   Jason wouldn't drink any water, _____.

Ans　1. Ⓒ　2. not to mention eating anything

Unit 121　prefer to V 及 prefer V-ing 怎麼用？

prefer [prɪˋfɝ] 是及物動詞，表「比較喜歡」，有下列用法：

a　prefer A to B　喜歡 A 勝於喜歡 B
　　　　　　　介詞

例　I prefer coffee than tea. (✗)
　→ I prefer coffee to tea. (✓)　我喜歡咖啡勝過喜歡茶。
　　I prefer hiking than jogging. (✗)
　→ I prefer hiking to jogging. (✓)　我喜歡健行勝過慢跑。

b　prefer to + 原形動詞 + rather than + 原形動詞　寧願……也不願……
　　= would rather + 原形動詞 + than + 原形動詞

例　I prefer to hike rather than jogging. (✗)
　→ I prefer to hike rather than jog. (✓)
　= I would rather hike than jog.　我寧願健行也不願慢跑。

小試身手

1. Jane likes fish better than meat.
   提示　用 prefer... to... 改寫句子。
   Jane ＿＿＿＿＿＿＿＿＿＿＿＿＿＿＿＿＿＿＿＿ meat.

2. I would rather ride a scooter than drive to work.
   提示　用 prefer to... 改寫句子。
   I ＿＿＿＿＿＿＿＿＿＿＿＿＿＿＿＿＿＿＿＿ to work.

Ans　1. prefers fish to
　　　2. prefer to ride a scooter rather than drive

Unit 122　on one's own 及 of one's own 怎麼用?

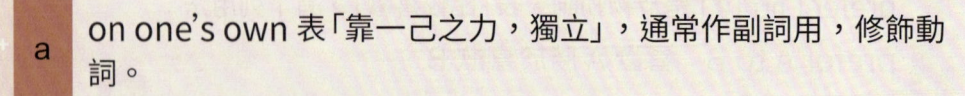

a　on one's own 表「靠一己之力，獨立」，通常作副詞用，修飾動詞。

例　From now on, you'll have to do everything by your own. (✗)
→ From now on, you'll have to do everything on you own. (✓)
　　　　　　　　　　　　　　　　　　　v.
= From now on, you'll have to do everything by yourself.

從現在起，你做什麼事都得靠自己了。

b　on one's own 亦可視作形容詞，表「獨立的，不依賴家人幫助的」，置 be 動詞之後，作主詞補語。

例　John has been of his own ever since he graduated from college. (✗)
→ John has been on his own ever since he graduated from college. (✓)
= John has been independent of his family ever since he graduated from college.　自從大學畢業後，約翰就獨立生活了。

c　of one's own 是形容詞片語，表「屬於自己的」，一定要置名詞之後，修飾該名詞。

例　Though young, Peter has a house on his own. (✗)
→ Though young, Peter has a house of his own. (✓)
　　　　　　　　　　　　　　　　　n.

彼得雖然年輕，卻有一棟屬於自己的房子。

小試身手

1　在湯姆的父母去世後，他必須學會照顧自己並獨自管理家務。
After his parents passed away, Tom had to learn how to take care of himself and manage the household ___ ___ ___ .

2. 我的目標是大賺一筆並且買棟自己的房子。
My goal is to make a fortune and buy a house ___ ___ ___.

> Ans　1. on; his; own　2. of; my; own

Unit 123　whereas 或 while 怎麼用？

a whereas [(h)wɛrˋæz] 是連接詞，表「然而，但是」，與 while 同義，用以對比兩個「相反的事實」。此時，whereas 或 while 可置句中或句首。

例　John and Mark are twin brothers. The former is introverted, whereas / while the latter is extroverted. (✓)
= John and Mark are twin brothers. Whereas / While the former is introverted, the latter is extroverted.
約翰及馬克是孿生兄弟。前者個性內向，後者則外向。

It's January now. It's cold in Taipei, whereas / while it's hot in Sidney. (✓)
= It's January now. Whereas / While it's cold in Taipei, it's hot in Sidney.　現在是一月。臺北很冷，而雪梨卻很熱。

b while 亦可表「當……，與……同時」，此時「不可」用 whereas 取代。

例　You can help me do the laundry ~~whereas~~ I'm doing the cooking. (✗)
→ You can help me do the laundry while I'm doing the cooking. (✓，while 之前不置逗點)
= While I'm doing the cooking, you can help me do the laundry.
我在弄飯的時候，你可以幫我洗衣服。

c while 亦可做動詞，與 away 並用，有下列重要片語：
while away + 時間名詞 + V-ing (如 the time, the hours)
（藉從事……）愉快地打發時間

例　I whiled away the afternoon (by) listening to music. (by 通常省略)
我藉著聽音樂消磨了整個下午。

> 小試身手

1　你在忙著做功課時，我正在聽音樂。
　　_____ you were busy doing your homework, I was listening to music.

2　瑪莉迪絲熱愛閱讀，而她弟弟則較喜歡看電影。
　　Meredith loves to read books, _____ her brother prefers watching movies.

Ans　1. While　2. while / whereas

Unit 124　「下落」是 whereabouts 或 whereabout?

a　whereabouts [ˈ(h)wɛrəˌbaʊts] 是名詞，表「下落」或「行蹤」。無 whereabout 一詞。

例　We don't know his whereabout. (✗)
→ We don't know his whereabouts. (✓)　我們不知道他的下落。
The man refuses to reveal his whereabouts. (✓)
這個男人拒絕透露他的行蹤。

b　whereabouts 作主詞時，動詞可用單數或複數。

例　The celebrity's whereabouts is / are still unknown.
這位名人的行蹤仍然不為人知。

> 小試身手

因為泰迪消失得無影無蹤，他的下落不明。
Teddy's _____ _____ unknown since he disappeared without leaving any clues.

Ans　whereabouts; is / are

126

Unit 125　for days 及 hours on end 怎麼用？

a 本片語 on end 是副詞片語，表「持續地」。for years / mouth / days / hours on end 表「持續好幾年 / 好幾個月 / 好幾天 / 好幾個小時」。這些表時間複數名詞之前「不得置明確數字」。

例　It has been raining here for two days on end. (×)
→ It has been raining here for days on end. (✓)　這裡一連下了好幾天雨。

We chatted over dinner for three hours on end. (×)
→ We chatted over dinner for hours on end. (✓)
我們邊進餐邊聊天，一連聊了好幾小時。

b in a row 亦表「連續地」，可與有「明確數字」修飾的時間名詞並用。

例　It has been raining here for two days in a row. (✓)
這裡一連下了二天雨。

I'll go crazy if I'm locked in the room for 24 hours in a row. (✓)
若被關在房間一連 24 小時，會發瘋的。

小試身手

Ⓐ in a row　Ⓑ on end

1. George worked on the project for days ＿＿ without taking a break, which left him exhausted.
2. Gary has won the championship three years ＿＿.

Ans　1. Ⓑ　2. Ⓐ

Unit 126　learn 事物 及 learn about 事物 怎麼用?

a learn 表「學習」，之後接名詞作受詞。learn 亦可表「聽說」、「獲悉」，之後須接介詞 of / about，方可接受詞。

例　I've decided to learn Spanish next semester. (✓)
　　　　　　　　　　vt.　　　n.
我已決定下學期要學西班牙文。

I was shocked when I learned John's death. (✗)
　　　　　　　　　　　　　　　n.
我學習約翰的死訊時很震驚。(不合邏輯)
→ I was shocked when I learned about John's death. (✓)
= I was shocked when I learned of John's death.
我獲知約翰的死訊時很震驚。

b learn 表「聽說」、「獲悉」時，亦可作及物動詞，之後接 that 引導的名詞子句作受詞。故上句亦可改寫如下：

例　I was shocked when I learned that John passed away. (✓)
　　　　　　　　　　　　　　vt.
= I was shocked when I learned (the news) │ about │ John's death.
　　　　　　　　　　　　　　　　vt.　　　　　　　　　of

小試身手

Ⓐ learn　Ⓑ learn about

1. You have no idea how happy I am to ＿＿ your good news.
2. Peter wants to ＿＿ how to play the guitar so he can join a band.

Ans　1. Ⓑ　2. Ⓐ

Unit 127　lovely 及 lovable 怎麼用?

{ lovely [ˈlʌvlɪ] a. 美麗的 (= beautiful)；令人愉快的 (= pleasant)
{ lovable [ˈlʌvəbl̩] a. 可愛的 (= cute, adorable)

例　What a lovable day! (✗)
　　好可愛的一天！（不知所云）
　→ What a lovely day! (✓)　好舒服 / 棒的一天！
　　What a lovable / cute / adorable baby! (✓)　好可愛的小寶寶！
　　What a lovely baby! (✓)　好漂亮的小寶寶！

小試身手

1. Tonia wore a (lovely / lovable) dress to the party and caught everyone's attention.
2. The rescue dog had a (lovely / lovable) personality and quickly became a beloved member of the family.

Ans 1. lovely　2. lovable

Unit 128　far better 及 by far the best 怎麼用?

a　far 與 by far 均可視作副詞。far 之後接「比較級」的副詞或形容詞，by far 之後接「最高級」的副詞或形容詞。

例　John's English is more better than Peter's. (✗)
　　理由　形容詞 better (更好的) 已經是 good (好的) 的比較級，故之前不可再置副詞 more (更加地)，以避免錯誤的雙重比較。
　→ John's English is far better than Peter's. (✓)
　= John's English is much better than Peter's.
　= John's English is way better than Peter's. (口語)

129

= John's English is a lot better than Peter's. (口語)
約翰的英文要比彼得好多了。

John drives far more carefully than Peter. (✓)

= John drives much more carefully than Peter.

= John drives way more carefully than Peter.

= John drives a lot more carefully than Peter.
約翰開車要比彼得小心多了。

| b | by far 專用以修飾最高級的形容詞。 |

例 Tom is far the best student I've ever taught. (✗)

→ Tom is by far the best student I've ever taught. (✓)

= Tom is by far and away the best student I've ever taught.
湯姆是我所教過最最棒的學生。

In my eyes, Mary is the by far the most beautiful girl in the world. (✓)

= In my eyes, Mary is the by far and away the most beautiful girl in the world.　在我眼中，瑪麗是全世界最最美的女孩。

小試身手

1　Iris is (far / by far) the smartest person I've ever known.

2　Tony is (far / by far) more attractive than Ben.

Ans　1. by far　2. far

Unit 129　「我突然想起」是 I suddenly thought that... 或 It occurred to me that...?

表「某人突然想起……」，應採下列句型：
It occurred to 人 that...

例 I suddenly thought that it is John's birthday today. (可)

→ It suddenly occurred to me that it is John's birthday today. (佳)
我突然想起今天是約翰的生日。

小試身手

Ed suddenly thought that the final exam is next week.

提示 用 It occurred... 改寫句子。

It _____ the final exam is next week.

Ans occurred to Ed that

Unit 130　the same... as... 及 the same... that... 怎麼用?

{ the same... as...　和……相同的……（一共有兩個）
　the same... that...　同一個……（只有一個）

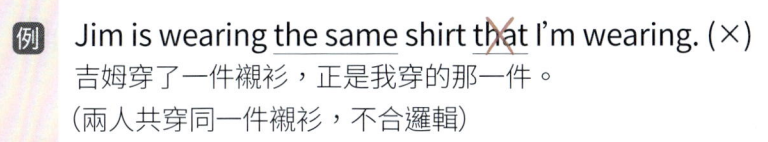

例 Jim is wearing the same shirt that I'm wearing. (✗)
吉姆穿了一件襯衫，正是我穿的那一件。
（兩人共穿同一件襯衫，不合邏輯）

→ Jim is wearing the same shirt as I'm wearing. (✓)
吉姆穿了一件襯衫，與我穿的相同。（兩件襯衫）

Ken will be on the same train that I took yesterday. (✓)
肯將會搭乘我昨天搭乘過的同一班火車。（同一輛火車）

Andy is the same man that I saw this morning. (✓)
安迪就是我今天早上見到的同一個人。

小試身手

1　Sarah is wearing the same dress (as / that) Lucy's wearing!
2　It is the same car (as / that) hit my mailbox last week.

Ans 1. as　2. that

Unit 131　give up on 人 及 give 人 up 怎麼用？

a　give up on 人　放棄某人，對某人不抱希望
　　　 give 人 up　　與某人絕交 / 不再來往

例　John goofs around all day. No wonder his parents have given him up. (✗)

→ John goofs around all day. No wonder his parents have given up on him. (✓)　約翰整天都在鬼混。難怪他爸媽已對他不再抱希望了。

b　give up 亦可視作不及物動詞，表「放棄希望」，等於 give up hope。

例　Ever since she moved to the countryside, Mary has given up all her old friends. (✓)　瑪麗自從搬到鄉下後就放棄與老朋友連絡了。

Hang in there! Don't give up (hope)! (✓)
撐下去 / 堅持下去！別放棄希望！

c　give up / quit smoking　戒菸

例　It's been ten years since Peter gave up smoking. (✓)
彼得戒菸十年了。

d　give oneself up to + 名詞 / 動詞　投身於 / 致力於……

例　Mother Teresa gave herself up to taking care of the sick and poor all her life. (✓)

= Mother Teresa devoted / dedicated herself to taking care of the sick and poor all her life.
德蕾莎修女終其一生都致力於照顧貧病的人。

小試身手

1　即使我犯了錯，我的爸媽也從不放棄我。
Even when I make mistakes, my parents never ＿＿＿＿ ＿＿＿＿ me.

2. 你再不戒菸很有可能會得肺癌。
If you don't ___ ___ ___, it's very likely that you'll get lung cancer.

3. 我的老師致力於教導學生。
My teacher ___ himself up ___ ___ students.

Ans 1. give; up; on 2. give; up; smoking
3. gave / gives; to; teaching

Unit 132　avenge 及 revenge 怎麼用？

avenge [əˋvɛndʒ] 及 revenge [rɪˋvɛndʒ] 兩個動詞均表「報仇」。avenge 尤指為某人因受不公正的迫害而採取的正義報復行動。revenge 則指因仇恨變惡且不太顧正義所採取的報復行動。avenge 不可作名詞，但 revenge 可作名詞。用法如下：

{ avenge 某事　為某事報仇
　avenge / revenge oneself on 人　為某人報仇
　= take revenge on 人

例　Alice vowed to reve~~n~~ge her father's death. (✗)
→ Alice vowed to avenge her father's death. (✓)
愛莉絲誓言要為父親的受害報仇。

John vowed to avenge himself on those bandits who had killed his father. (✓)　　　　　　　　　　　人

= John vowed to revenge himself on those bandits who had killed his father.　　　　　　　　　　　人

= John vowed to take revenge on those bandits who had killed his father.　約翰誓言要向那些殺害他父親的匪徒報仇。

小試身手

選出錯誤的選項。

Ⓐ Instead of taking revenge on those who bullied him, Ned chose to forgive them and move on.

Ⓑ Instead of taking avenge on those who bullied him, Ned chose to forgive them and move on.

Ⓒ Instead of revenging himself on those who bullied him, Ned chose to forgive them and move on.

Ⓓ Instead of avenging himself on those who bullied him, Ned chose to forgive them and move on.

Ans Ⓑ

Unit 133 cheat 人 及 cheat on 人 怎麼用？

a cheat [tʃit] 作及物動詞，表「欺騙」，之後直接接人作受詞。

例 The conman cheated all the old woman's money. (✗)
→ The conman cheated the old woman out of all her money. (✓)
　　　　　　　　　　　　人
這個金光黨徒騙走老婦人所有的錢。

Don't cheat me. I was not born yesterday. (✓)
　　　　　　人
別騙我。我又不是三歲小孩。

b cheat 亦可作不及物動詞，有下列重要用法：
cheat on 人　對某人感情不忠

例 John is a two-timer. He has been cheating his wife for years. (✗)
→ John is a two-timer. He has been cheating on his wife for years. (✓)
約翰腳踏兩條船。多年來他對他的妻子一直感情不忠。

小試身手

1. The company (**cheated** / cheated on) its customers by selling faulty products.

2. Don was sad when he found out that his girlfriend had (cheated / **cheated on**) him for years.

Ans 1. cheated　2. cheated on

Unit 134　interfere with 及 interfere in 怎麼用?

- interfere [ˌɪntəˈfɪr] with...　干擾／阻礙……
- interfere in...　涉入／干預……

例　The rain didn't interfere in the soccer game. (✗)
→ The rain didn't interfere with the soccer game. (✓)
這場雨並未阻礙足球賽的進行。

It's unwise to interfere in other people's business. (✓)
→ It's unwise to get involved in other people's business. (✓)
干預別人的事是不智之舉。

小試身手

1. The loud noise from the construction site interfered (**with** / in) my ability to concentrate on my work.

2. My parents always warned me not to interfere (with / **in**) other people's relationships unless they asked for my advice.

Ans 1. with　2. in

Unit 135　deal with 及 deal in 怎麼用?

a　{ deal with 人　　與某人打交道
　　　 deal with 事物　處理 / 解決事情 }

例　I never deal with people who are calculating. (✓)
　　= I never associate with people who are calculating.　我絕不與很會算計的人來往。
　　This problem is hard to deal with. (✓)
　　= This problem is hard to cope with.　這個問題很難處理。

b　deal in 事物　從事……的買賣

例　John's father is a businessman who deals with used cars. (✗)
　　→ John's father is a businessman who deals in used cars. (✓)
　　約翰的父親是個從事中古車買賣的商人。

小試身手

1　As a customer service representative (客服人員), I often have to deal (with / in) angry customers.
2　Anya is a successful businesswoman who deals (with / in) art.

Ans　1. with　2. in

Unit 136　a kind of 及 kind of 怎麼用?

a　a kind of + 名詞　某種……
　　= a sort of + 名詞
　　= a type of + 名詞

例　Kelly is a kind of ~~a~~ person who never lies. (✗)

理由　a kind of / a sort of / a type of 之後不得加不定冠詞 a / an。

→ Kelly is a kind of person who never lies. (✓)
凱莉是那種從不會說謊的人。

b　what kind of + 名詞　什麼類的……
　= what sort of + 名詞
　= what type of + 名詞

例　What ~~a~~ kind of music do you like? (✗)
→ What kind of music do you like? (✓)　你喜歡哪一類的音樂？

c　kind of 及 sort of 則視作副詞，表「有點、或多或少」，之後置動詞、副詞或形容詞，以修飾這些詞類。

例　It's ~~a~~ kind of hot today. (✗)
　　　　　　adj.
→ It's kind of hot today. (✓)
= It's sort of hot today.
= It's kinda hot today. (口語)
= It's sorta hot today. (口語)
= It's a bit / a little / a little bit / somewhat hot today.　今天有點熱。

I kind of feel like going swimming. (✓)
　　　　　v.
= I sort of feel like going swimming.　我有點想去游泳。
　　　　　v.

David dealt with the problem kind of carelessly.
　　　　　　　　　　　　　　　　　　adv.
大衛處理這個問題有點粗心。

小試身手

1　今天想吃哪一種晚餐？
　_____ _____ _____ meal would you like to eat tonight?

CH 2
字詞辨異

137

2	莉莉是那種不聽搖滾樂的人。 Lily is ___ ___ ___ person who doesn't listen to rock and roll.
3	我現在有點餓了。 I'm ___ ___ hungry now.

> **Ans** 1. What; kind / type / sort; of　2. a; kind; of
> 　　　 3. kind / sort; of

Unit 137　drunk 及 drunken 怎麼用?

drunk（drink 的過去分詞）與 drunken 均為形容詞，也均表「喝醉的」。drunken 通常要置名詞前，修飾該名詞；drunk 則置 be 動詞或 get 之後，作主詞補語。

例　Tom was too drun~~ken~~ to drive. (✗)
→ Tom was too drunk to drive. (✓)
湯姆醉得無法開車。

I don't drink because I get drun~~ken~~ easily. (✗)
→ I don't drink because I get drunk easily. (✓)
我不喝酒因為我很容易喝醉。

My car was hit head-on by a drunken driver. (✓)
　　　　　　　　　　　　　　　　 n.
我的車子被一位酒醉駕駛人迎面撞上。

Drunken driving is strictly prohibited in that country. (✓)
= Drunk driving is strictly prohibited in that country.
那個國家嚴格禁止酒駕。

小試身手

It's very dangerous to drive when you're (drunk / drunken).

> **Ans** drunk

Unit 138 plan to V 及 plan on V-ing 怎麼用?

plan to V 與 plan on V-ing 同義，均表「計劃要……」。無 plan for V-ing 的用法。

例 Jane and John are planning for getting married in May next year. (✗)

→ Jane and John are planning to get married in May next year. (✓)

= Jane and John are planning on getting married in May next year.　阿珍與阿強打算在明年五月結婚。

小試身手

我們計劃下個月去日本旅遊。
We _____ _____ taking a trip to Japan next month.

Ans　plan; on

Unit 139 cut down on 及 cut down 怎麼用?

{ cut down on...　減少……的量 (= reduce the amount of...)
  cut down...　砍倒…… (= cut... down) }

例 You should cut down the amount of sugar you eat. (✗)

→ You should cut down on the amount of sugar you eat. (✓)

= You should reduce the amount of sugar you eat.
你應減少糖的攝取量。

You should cut down on spending and learn to save money for a rainy day. (✓)

= You should cut expenses / cut spending and learn to save money for a rainy day.　你應減少花費學習存錢以備不時之需。

More and more trees are being cut down throughout the world, which can harm ecosystems. (✔)
全球各地遭砍伐的樹木越來越多，這會殃及生態系統。

小試身手

1. We should all try to (cut down / cut down on) the use of plastic bags for the sake of our environment.
2. The people in the neighborhood decided to (cut down / cut down on) a few trees in the park for safety reasons.

Ans　1. cut down on　2. cut down

Unit 140　「一件行李」是 a luggage 或 a piece of luggage?

a　luggage（英式用法）及 baggage 均指「行李」，是集合名詞，包含 suitcase（裝衣物的箱子）、backpack（背包）或其他包包、袋子（bag）。由於是集合名詞（即統稱名詞），baggage 與 luggage 均不可數。不可說 a luggage / baggage、two luggages / baggages、many luggages / baggages…。應說 a piece of luggage / baggage、two pieces of luggage / baggage。

例　A: How many luggages / baggages do you have with you? (✗)
　　B: I have only one luggage / baggage. (✗)
　→ A: How many pieces of luggage / baggage do you have with you? (✔)
　　B: I have only one piece (of luggage / baggage). (✔)
A：你有幾件行李？
B：只有一件。

b　suitcase、backpack、bag 則是行李的分類，是可數名詞。

例　I have two suitcases with me. (✔)
我有兩只行李箱。

I have three backpacks and a large bag. (✔)
我有三個背包及一只大袋子。

小試身手

I took two (baggages / pieces of baggage) with me when I went to Thailand.

Ans pieces of baggage

Unit 141 「鍾愛高雄」是 "We care Kaohsiung." 或 "We care for Kaohsiung."?

care 是不及物動詞，故無法直接接受詞，其後應先接介詞。

例 We care Kaohsiung. (✘)
→ We care for Kaohsiung. (✔) 我們鍾愛高雄。
或:We care about Kaohsiung. (✔) 我們很關切 / 關心高雄。

小試身手

亞曼達很關心這場選舉。

Amanda _____ _____ this election.

Ans cares / cared; about

Unit 142 「想要某人去做某事」是 want 人 + V 或 want 人 + to V?

上個世紀末，由歌星歐陽菲菲唱紅的一首國語歌曲"愛我在今宵"，有一句英文歌詞如下：

I want you love me tonight. (✘)
→ I want you to love me tonight. (✔)

理由 表示「期望、要求」等動詞如 want、need、expect 等之後接人作受詞時，需再接 to 引導的不定詞片語作受詞補語。

例　I want you to finish the report no later than 5 p.m. (✓)
我要你在下午 5 點前完成報告。

Ted asked me to go out with him last night, but I turned him down. (✓)　昨晚泰德邀我約會，但我拒絕了。

I wish you to get well soon. (✓)　我期望你身體很快好起來。

但：I hope you to get well soon. (✗)

→ I hope (that) you'll get well soon. (✓)

小試身手

我需要你幫我個忙。
I need you ＿＿＿＿ ＿＿＿＿ me a hand.

Ans to; give

Chapter 3

Unit 143 >>> Unit 169

常見多種易混淆用字

英文單詞或片語常有非常相近的用法,一點點細微的差異就會造成語意的誤差,進而發生被扣分或是說話被誤解的狀況,防不勝防。

本章節收集了 3 種以上長得很像或用法容易混淆的字詞、片語,幫助讀者把英文讀到通透,不再受近似字詞的魔咒束縛,建構最強的實力!

Unit 143　a number of、the number of、an amount of、the amount of 怎麼用?

a　a large number of (許多的) + 複數名詞 + 複數動詞　許多的……
　　　　　　　　　　　　　　　　　主詞　　　　動詞

例　A large number of students is absent today. (✗)
→ A large number of students are absent today. (✓)
今天有許多學生缺課。

Only a small number of people in that area has contracted COVID-19. (✗)
→ Only a small number of people in that area have contracted COVID-19. (✓)　那個區域只有少數人感染了 COVID-19。

b　the number (數量) + of 複數名詞 + 單數動詞　……的數量
　　　主詞　　　　　　　　　　　　　　動詞

例　The number of stray dogs in my neighborhood are increasing. (✗)
→ The number of stray dogs in my neighborhood is increasing. (✓)
我家附近的流浪狗數量不斷在增加。

c　a large amount of (大量的) + 不可數名詞 + 單數動詞　大量的……
　　　　　　　　　　　　　　　　主詞　　　　動詞

例　A large number of evidence have been collected against Tom. (✗)
　　　　　　　　　　　不可數名詞
→ A large amount of evidence has been collected against Tom. (✓)
已蒐集了大量對湯姆不利的證據。

We need only a small amount of money for the project. (✓)
　　　　　　　　　　　　　　　不可數名詞
我們只需要少許錢就可執行該企畫。

d　the amount (量,數量) + of 不可數名詞 + 單數動詞　……的數量
　　　主詞　　　　　　　　　　　　　　　動詞

144

例　The amount of money aren't enough for my tuition. (✗)
→ The amount of money isn't enough for my tuition. (✓)
　　　主詞　　　　　　動詞

這筆錢不夠付我的學費。

結論　上列句型中，number 要與複數名詞（如 books、trees、cars、people、dogs、schools...）並用；amount 則須與不可數名詞（如 water、evidence、information、money、rice、air、soil...）並用。

小試身手

1. 我的學校的學生數量正在增加中。
   _____ of students in my school _____ increasing.

2. 有許多人看過《鐵達尼號》。
   A large _____ of people _____ seen *Titanic*.

3. 水的數量不夠所有人喝。
   _____ of water _____ not enough for everyone to drink.

4. 已投資了一大筆錢開發新的 APP。
   A large _____ of money _____ been invested to develop a new app.

Ans　1. The; number; is　2. number; have
　　　3. The; amount; is　4. amount; has

Unit 144　due to、because of、as a result of、owing to、on account of 的用法

a　due to 的 due 是形容詞，正確的用法要將 due 置 be 動詞之後，形成下列結構：
be due to + 名詞　……由於……（所引起）
= be caused by + 名詞

例　Ted's failure was due to his laziness.
　　泰德的失敗乃因他的懶惰之故。

b　**because of, as a result of, owing to** 及 **on account of** 亦均表「由於」，但所引導的片語視作副詞片語，修飾句中的動詞或整個主要子句。

例　Ted failed because of his laziness. (✓)　由於懶惰，泰德失敗了。
　　　　　v.

　　John was late for work owing to a traffic jam. (✓)
　　　　主要子句

　　由於交通堵塞，約翰上班遲到。

c　由上得知，because of, as a result of, owing to 及 on account of 不得置 be 動詞之後。不可說：

例　Ted's failure was ~~because of~~ / ~~owing to~~ / ~~on account of~~ / ~~as a result~~ of his laziness. (✗)

d　不過有越來越多的英美人士已將 due to 視同 because of, owing to, as a result of 及 on account of 等副詞片語。他們認為 due to 亦可當作副詞片語，即：

例　Ted failed due to his laziness. (可)
　　　　　v.

　　= Ted failed because of / owing to / on account of / as a result of his laziness.　講求文法的英美人士仍認為上句是錯的。

小試身手

意外因為人為疏失而發生。
The accident happened ＿＿＿＿＿ ＿＿＿＿＿ the man's carelessness.

　　　　　　　　　Ans　due; to 或 owing; to 或 because; of

146

Unit 145 worth、worthy、worthwhile 怎麼用?

a worth [wɝθ] 是介詞,表「值得」,置 be 動詞之後,其後再置名詞或動名詞作其受詞。其用法為:be worth + 名詞 / 動名詞

例 My bike woxths $1,500. (×,worth 不能作動詞)
→ My bike is worth $1,500. (✓)
          prep.
我的腳踏車價值 1,500 美元。

This famous painting is worth a fortune. (✓)
這幅名畫值很多錢。

注意 worth 之後若接動名詞作受詞時,句中的主詞必須當該動名詞的受詞,否則該動名詞之後須另接介詞,使該主詞作其受詞。

This book is worth reading it. (×)
理由 This book 應作 reading 的受詞,故應刪除 it。
→ This book is worth reading. (✓)　這本書值得一讀。
Mr. Johnson is worth working. (×)
理由 working 是不及物動詞 work(工作)變成的動名詞,Mr. Johnson 無法做 working 的受詞,故之後應接介詞 for 或 with,使 Mr. Johnson 作 for 或 with 的受詞。
→ Mr. Johnson is worth working for. (✓)　為強森先生效力很值得。
或:Mr. Johnson is worth working with. (✓)　與強森先生共事很值得。

b worthy [ˋwɝðɪ] 是形容詞,與介詞 of 並用,之後接名詞,用於下列結構:
be worthy of 事物 / 人　值得……的

例 This is a question which is worthy attention. (×)
→ This is a question which is worthy of attention / note. (✓)
這是個值得注意的問題。

Tom doesn't think he is worthy of her. (✓)　湯姆認為他配不上她。

注意 worthy 亦可表示「有價值的」、「值得尊敬的」,之後可接名詞。

147

I really think John is a worthy colleague in our company. (✓)
我真的認為約翰是我們公司值得尊敬的一位同事。

c　worthwhile [ˌwɝθˋ(h)waɪl] 亦是形容詞，表「值得的」。

例　The book is worthwhile to read. (✓)

= It is worthwhile to read the book.

= It is worth it to read the book. (本句中的 worth it 視同 worthwhile，均表「值得的」) 這本書值得看。

小試身手

1	Exercising regularly is (worth / worthy / worthwhile) as it can improve your overall fitness and well-being.
2	The act of helping others in need is truly (worth / worthy / worthwhile) of admiration and respect.
3	The rare painting turned out to be (worth / worthy / worthwhile) millions of dollars.

Ans　1. worthwhile　2. worthy　3. worth

Unit 146　assure、ensure、insure 怎麼用？

a　assure [əˋʃʊr] 是及物動詞，表「向……保證」。使用時，主詞必須是人，受詞也必須是人。

例　I can assure that he is honest. (✗)
　　　人

→ I can assure you that he is honest. (✓)
　　　人　　　人

= I can assure you of his honesty.　我可向你保證他很誠實。
　　　人　　　人

補充 be assured that... 獲得保證……

We are assured (by the boss) that we will get a pay raise starting next month. (✓)　我們獲得 (老闆的) 保證，下個月起我們會加薪。

b　ensure [ɪnˋʃʊr] 亦是及物動詞，表「確保」，通常以 that 子句作受詞，亦可用名詞作受詞。

例　Please ensure that the door is locked before you leave. (✓)
= Please make sure that the door is locked before you leave.
你離開前，請確保要把門鎖好。

We need to buy more facilities to assure the safety of our students. (✗，assure 之後應接人為受詞)
→ We need to buy more facilities to ensure the safety of our students. (✓)　我們必須買更多的設備以確保我們學生的安全。

c　insure [ɪnˋʃʊr] 是及物動詞，表「為……投保 / 保險」

例　Have you insured your car against accidental damage? (✓)
你的車子保了意外險了嗎？

The house is assured for 3 million dollars. (✗)
→ The house is insured for 3 million dollars. (✓)
這棟房子已投了 300 萬美金的保險。

動詞	中文	常見用法
assure	向……保證	❶ 人 assure 人 of 事物 ❷ 人 be assured that...
ensure	確保	❶ 人 ensure that... ❷ 人 ensure + 事物
insure	為……投保 / 保險	❶ 人 insure 物 against... ❷ 物 be insured...

小試身手

1　約翰要瑪麗確保出門前所有的窗子都關好了。
John asked Mary to ＿＿＿＿ ＿＿＿＿ all the windows were closed before leaving the house.

CH 3 常見多種易混淆用字

149

2	我決定要幫我的新車投保失竊與意外險。 I decided to _____ my new car _____ theft and accidents.
3	醫生向病患保證手術成功後會完全恢復。 The doctor _____ the patient _____ a full recovery after the successful surgery.

Ans 1. ensure; that   2. insure; against   3. assured; of

Unit 147 live、lively、alive、living 怎麼用?

a **live** [laɪv] *adj.* 現場演出 / 播出的 & *adv.* 以現場演出的方式

例 I was quite impressed with the living concert last night. (✗)
→ I was quite impressed with the live concert last night. (✓)
　　　　　　　　　　　　　　　　　　　　　　　adj.
昨晚的現場演唱會令我印象深刻。

The show will be broadcast lively. (✗)
→ The show will be broadcast live. (✓)
　　　　　　　　　　　　　　　adv.
這個節目將會現場直播。

b **lively** [ˋlaɪvlɪ] *a.* 活潑的，有生氣的

例 Though close to ninety, my grandpa is healthy and live. (✗)
→ Though close to ninety, my grandpa is healthy and lively. (✓)
我爺爺年近 90，身體卻很健康又有朝氣。

c **alive** [əˋlaɪv] *adj.* 活的，健在的

例 My grandparents are still living and well. (✗)
→ My grandparents are still alive and well.　我爺爺奶奶仍然健在。
注意 alive 不可置名詞前，只能置名詞後。

150

Sadly, the rescuers found no al~~ive~~ miners in the cave-in. (✗)
　　　　　　　　　　　　　　　　　　　n.

→ Sadly, the rescuers found no <u>miners</u> <u>alive</u> in the cave-in. (✓)
　　　　　　　　　　　　　　　　　n.

遺憾的是，救援小組在這次礦坑塌陷事故中未找到任何生還的礦工。

d **living** [ˈlɪvɪŋ] *adj.* 活著的（置名詞前）

例 No al~~ive~~ <u>things</u> can survive without air. (✗)
　　　　　　　n.

→ No <u>living</u> <u>things</u> can survive without air. (✓)
　　　　　　　　　　n.

若無空氣，任何生物都不能存活。

注意 living 可作名詞，表「生計」，與冠詞 a 並用。

Peter teaches for l~~i~~ving. (✗)

→ Peter teaches <u>for a living</u>. (✓)

= Peter <u>makes</u> / <u>earns</u> a living (by) teaching. 彼得靠教書為生。

小試身手

1	The (lively / alive / living) music at the party got everyone up on their feet and dancing.
2	Jamie makes a(n) (live / lively / alive / living) by working as a freelance writer.
3	The TV station will broadcast the badminton match (live / lively / alive / living) for all the fans to watch.
4	The children's laughter filled the playground, making it feel (live / lively / alive / living) with joy.

Ans　1. lively　2. living　3. live　4. alive

Unit 148　spend、cost、take 怎麼用？

a　spend 表「花費」，主詞一定是人，用於下列結構：
- 人 + spend + 時間／金錢 + *V*-ing　　某人花若干時間／金錢從事……
- 人 + spend + 時間／金錢 + on + 名詞　某人把若干時間／金錢花在……之上

例　Many schoolchildren in Taiwan spend at least 2 hours to ~~do~~ homework every day. (✗)
→ Many schoolchildren in Taiwan spend at least 2 hours **doing** homework every day. (✓)
臺灣許多學童每天至少花兩個小時做功課。

I have to spend the whole weekend to ~~prepare~~ for the finals next week. (✗)
→ I have to spend the whole weekend **preparing** for the finals next week. (✓)　我必須花整個週末的時間準備下週的期末考。

John spends most of his salary to ~~buy~~ books. (✗)
→ John spends most of his salary **buying** books. (✓)
= John spends most of his salary **on** books.
約翰把大部分的薪水花在買書上。

Peter used to spend too much time to ~~play~~ video games. (✗)
→ Peter used to spend too much time **playing** video games. (✓)
= Peter used to spend too much time **on** video games.
彼得過去曾花太多的時間打電玩。

b　cost 表「花費」，主詞必須是物，受詞必須是金錢，用於下列結構：
事物 + cost +（人）+ 金錢　某物花費（某人）若干錢

例　~~I~~ cost a lot of money to buy that car. (✗)
人

理由　"I cost a lot of money." 表示「我這個人花很多錢就可以買得到。」不合邏輯。

152

→ That car cost me a lot of money. (✓)
  物   人

= It cost me a lot of money to buy that car.

我花了很多錢買了那輛車。

I cost NT$50,000 to have that car repaired. (✗)

→ It cost me NT$50,000 to repair that car. (✓)

= Repairing the car cost me NT$50,000.

= That car cost me NT$50,000 to repair.

我花了 5 萬塊修理那輛車。

c   take 亦表「花費」，主詞必須是事物，受詞必須是時間，用於下列結構：
事物 + take + (人) + 時間 某事物花費 (某人) 若干時間

例   That math problem took me half an hour to solve. (✓)
   事物

= It took me half an hour to solve that math problem.

我花了半個小時解開那道數學題。

I estimate that it will take at least three days to finish the project. (✓)

= I estimate that the project will take at least three days to finish.

我估計這個企畫案至少要花三天才能完成。

「花費」的用法			
英文	主詞	受詞	用法
spend	人	時間 / 金錢	人 + spend + 時間 / 金錢 { V-ing / on 物
cost	物	(人) + 金錢	事物 + cost + (人) + 金錢
take	物	(人) + 時間	事物 + take + (人) + 時間

153

小試身手

1. It (costs / takes / spends) me forty minutes to walk from home to school.
2. My sister (cost / took / spent) 100 dollars on her lunch today.
3. Fixing my old car (cost / took / spent) me a lot of money.

Ans　1. takes　2. spent　3. cost

Unit 149　not... anymore、not... any longer、no more、no longer 怎麼用?

a　not... anymore　不再……
　　 = not... any longer

例　John doesn't live here no more. (✗，雙重否定)
→ John doesn't live here any more. (✓，少用)
= John doesn't live here any longer. (常用)
= John doesn't live here anymore. (更常用)
約翰不再住這裡了。

The cost of electricity in Taiwan is not cheap no more. (✗，雙重否定)
→ The cost of electricity in Taiwan is not cheap anymore. (✓，少用)
= The cost of electricity in Taiwan is not cheap any longer. (常用)
= The cost of electricity in Taiwan is not cheap anymore. (更常用)
臺灣的電費不再便宜了。

b　not... any more、not... any longer 亦可被 no longer 取代。no longer 置一般動詞之前或 be 動詞之後。

例　John no longer lives here. (✓)　約翰不再住在這裡了。
The cost of electricity in Taiwan is no longer cheap.
臺灣的電費不再便宜了。

| c | 在美式英語常把 any more 寫成一個字，即 anymore 是副詞，與 not 並用，修飾句中動詞，故上列句子亦可改寫成： |

例 John doesn't live here anymore. (✓)
          v.

The cost of electricity is not cheap anymore. (✓)
                        v.

| d | no more 亦表「不再」，英美人士很少人會使用，一般置句尾。 |

例 I'll no more see you. (✗)
→ I'll see you no more. (✓，罕)
= I'll no longer see you.
= I won't see you any longer.
= I won't see you any more.
= I won't see you anymore.　　我不會再見到你。

小試身手

| 1 | Ken will eat chicken no more.
提示 用 not... anymore 改寫句子。
Ken will _____. |
| 2 | Alice no longer works here.
提示 用 not... any longer 改寫句子。
Alice _____. |

Ans　1. not eat chicken anymore
　　　2. doesn't work here any longer

CH 3

常見多種易混淆用字

155

Unit 150 「不再」是 not any more + 名詞 或 not anymore + 名詞?

a   not... anymore = not... any more　不再……
以上結構的 anymore 或 any more 視作副詞，修飾句中動詞，恆置句尾。

例　I enjoyed singing when young, but I don't sing anymore / any more / any longer.　　　　　　　　　　v.
我年輕時喜歡唱歌，不過我現在不再唱歌了。

b   any more 亦可視作形容詞，之後接名詞，即：
not any more + 名詞　不再有……（非 not anymore + 名詞）

例　I'm so full that I can't eat anymore (food) now. (✗)

→ I'm so full that I can't eat any more food now. (✓)

= I'm so full that I can eat no more food now.
我太飽了，現在再也吃不下任何食物了。

Thank you for your clear explanation. I don't have anymore questions to ask now. (✗)

→ Thank you for your clear explanation. I don't have any more questions to ask now. (✓)

= Thank you for your clear explanation. I have no more questions to ask now.　謝謝你清楚的解釋。我現在沒有任何問題要問了。

c   「any more + 名詞」亦可用於一般問句中。

例　Are there anymore questions? (✗)

→ Are there any more questions? (✓)
還有什麼問題嗎？

Is there anymore work you want me to do? (✗)

→ Is there any more work you want me to do? (✓)
還有什麼你要我做的工作嗎？

小試身手

選出錯誤的句子。
Ⓐ I'm so busy that I can't do any more freelance work.
Ⓑ I'm so busy that I can't do freelance work anymore.
Ⓒ I'm so busy that I can't do anymore freelance work.
Ⓓ I'm so busy that I can do freelance work no more.

Ans Ⓒ

Unit 151 「任何人」是 anyone 或 any one?

a anyone 是代名詞，指「任何人」，而非指某個群體的任何一個人。

例 The question is so easy that any~~o~~ne can answer it. (×)
→ The question is so easy that anyone can answer it. (✓)
= The question is so easy that anybody can answer it. (✓)
這個問題太容易，因此任何人／誰都可以答得出來。

b any one 亦為代名詞，指某個群體內的「任何一個人」或同類東西的「任何一個東西」。

例 The question is so easy that any~~o~~ne of the students in my class can answer it. (×)
→ The question is so easy that any one of the students in my class can answer it. (✓)
這個問題太容易，因此我班上的任何一個學生都可以答得出來。

I'll feel worried if any~~o~~ne of you gets hurt. (×)
→ I'll feel worried if any one of you gets hurt. (✓)
你們之中有任何人受傷，我都會感到憂心。

You may choose any~~o~~ne of the (three, four, five...) apples. (×)
→ You may choose any one of the (three, four, five...) apples. (✓)
這些（這三顆、四顆、五顆……）蘋果中，你可以選擇任何一顆。

小試身手

1. You can choose (anyone / any one) of the books from the library to read.

2 You can ask (anyone / any one) for directions; he or she will be happy to help.

> Ans 1. any one   2. anyone

Unit 152 cannot but、cannot help but、cannot help + V-ing 怎麼用？

a 表「忍不住」或「無法克制」，有下列用法：
- cannot but + 原形動詞
- cannot help but + 原形動詞
- cannot help + 動名詞

注意 此處 help 是及物動詞，作「抑制」或「忍住」解，相當於 avoid 或 prevent 之意，故用動名詞作受詞。

例 I cannot but to laugh each time I hear the joke. (✗)
→ I can't but laugh each time I hear the joke. (✓)
= I can't help but laugh each time I hear the joke.
= I can't help laughing each time I hear the joke.
每次我聽到這個笑話都忍不住笑出來。

Patty couldn't but cry upon learning that her son was killed in a car accident. (✓)
= Patty couldn't help but cry as soon as she learned that her son was killed in a car accident.
= Patty couldn't help crying the moment she learned that her son was killed in a car accident.
佩蒂一聽到她兒子在車禍中喪命時痛哭失聲。

b cannot help it / oneself 忍不住 (做那件事) 嘛

例 I know I shouldn't smoke for my health's sake, but I just can't help that. (✗)
→ I know I shouldn't smoke for my health's sake, but I just can't help it. (✓)

= I know I shouldn't smoke for my health's sake, but I just can't help myself.　我知道為了健康著想我不應抽菸,可是人家忍不住嘛。

小試身手

1. 我知道我不應該喝太多,但我就是忍不住嘛。
   I know I shouldn't have too much drink, but I just ＿＿＿＿＿ ＿＿＿＿＿＿＿＿.

2. Mindy can't help feeling nervous before she goes on stage.
   提示 用 can't but 改寫句子。
   Mindy ＿＿＿＿＿＿＿＿＿ nervous before she goes on stage.

   Ans　1. can't; help; it / myself　2. can't but feel

Unit 153　probable、likely、possible 怎麼用?

a　probable [ˈprɑbəbl̩]（很可能）、likely [ˈlaɪklɪ]（有可能）、possible [ˈpɑsəbl̩]（或許）均表「可能的」,有下列用法:

❶ probable 只用於下列這種句型:
　　It is probable that...

例　Because of the traffic jam, I am probable to be late for work this morning. (✗)

或:Because of the traffic jam, it is probable for me to be late for work this morning. (✗)

→ Because of the traffic jam, it is probable that I'll be late for work this morning. (✓)　由於交通阻塞,我今天早上上班很可能會遲到。

❷ likely 可用於下列兩種句型:
　　{ It is likely that...
　　 人 / 事物 + be likely to + 原形動詞

例　Because of the traffic jam, it is likely for us to be late for work this morning. (✗)

→ Because of the traffic jam, we are likely to be late for work this morning. (✓)

= Because of the traffic jam, it is likely / probable that we'll be late for work this morning.

由於交通阻塞，我們今天早上上班可能會遲到。

It is likely that the plan will fail. (✓)

= The plan is likely to fail.　這個計畫可能會失敗。

❸ possible 可用於下列兩種句型：

{ It is possible that...　或許……
{ It is possible for 人 to + 原形動詞　某人或許會……

例 It is possible that the general manager will resign next month. (✓)

= It is possible for the general manager to resign next month.

總經理下個月或許會辭職。

b probable, likely 及 possible 既已有「可能」的意思，不得再與表「可能」的助動詞 may 或 might 並用。

例 It may be probable that it will rain anytime. (✗)

或：It is probable that it may rain anytime. (✗)

→ It is probable that it will rain anytime. (✓)

= It is likely that it will rain anytime.

= It may rain anytime.　隨時都有可能下雨。

小試身手

選出錯誤的句子。

Ⓐ Is it probable that Jay will have a concert in Taiwan?
Ⓑ It is possible that we will move to another city next month.
Ⓒ It is likely that Jane will go camping this weekend.
Ⓓ It may be likely that we'll have a shower this afternoon.

Ans Ⓓ

Unit 154　peek、peep、peak、pique 怎麼用？

a peek [pik] *vi.* 偷窺 (= **peep** [pip])

例　I peeked / peeped through the keyhole and found nobody inside. (✓)　我從鑰匙孔偷窺，沒看到裡面有人。

A peeking Tom is a man who enjoys secretly watching women taking off their clothes. (✗)

→ A peeping Tom is a man who enjoys secretly watching women taking off their clothes. (✓)　偷窺狂是喜歡偷看女人脫衣的男子。

b peak [pik] *n.* 頂峰，巔峰

例　James is on the sunny side of 50 and is in the peak of his career. (✗)

→ James is on the sunny side of 50 and is at the peak / summit of his career. (✓)　詹姆士還不到 50 歲，正值他事業的高峰。

補充　be on the sunny side of 50　不到 50 歲
be on the dark side of 50　50 多歲，快 60 歲了

It took us 3 hours to get to the peak / summit / top of the mountain. (✓)　我們花了 3 個小時才登上山頂。

c pique [pik] *n.* 怨恨 (不可數)

例　The guest left in a fit of pique when the show host insulted him to his face. (✓)　節目主持人當著來賓的面侮辱他時，他憤然離席。

小試身手

1. Julia gave a quick (pique / peak / peep) behind the curtain and found her naughty son hiding there.
2. The team reached the (pique / peak / peep) of the mountain just before sunset.
3. The boy left in a fit of (pique / peak / peep) and never returned again.

Ans　1. peep　2. peak　3. pique

Unit 155　reply、answer、respond 怎麼用？

a　reply [rɪˋplaɪ] 是不及物動詞，表「回答」、「答覆」或「回應」，不可直接接名詞作受詞，須接介詞 to，方可接名詞作受詞。

例　Tom refused to reply my question. (✗)
→ Tom refused to reply to my question. (✓)
= Tom refused to answer my question.
湯姆拒絕回答我的問題。

b　reply 亦可作及物動詞，可用 that 子句或直接引句作受詞。

例　When I asked Amy whether we could be friends, she replied / answered, "You're not my cup of tea." (✓)
　　　　　　　直接引句
當我問艾咪我倆是否可作朋友時，她回道：「你不是我喜歡的那種人。」

= When I asked Amy whether we could be friends, she replied / answered that I was not her cup of tea.
　　　　　that 子句 / 間接引句
當我問艾咪我倆是否可作朋友時，她回說我不是她的菜。

c　respond [rɪˋspɑnd] 表「回應」，用法與 reply 完全相同，可作不及物動詞，不可直接接名詞作受詞，須接介詞 to，方可接名詞作受詞。

例　When I asked him when he would retire, the CEO didn't respond my question. (✗)
→ When I asked him when he would retire, the CEO didn't respond to / reply to my question. (✓)
我問執行長他何時退休，他沒回答我的問題。

注意　respond 或 reply 可接直接引句作受詞。而公文書信常使用 respond 取代 reply。

When I asked him when he would retired, the CEO responded / replied, "Sometime next year." (✓)
我問執行長他何時退休，他回道：「明年某個時候吧。」

Please respond to our letter by the end of this month. (✓)
請閣下月底前回覆本公司的信函。

d answer [ˈænsɚ] 可直接用名詞、that 子句（間接引句）或直接引句作受詞。

例 Why didn't you answer to my question then? (✗)
→ Why didn't you answer (或 reply to) my question then? (✓)
你當時為什麼不回答我的問題？

I asked Lindy if she needed my help with her report, and she answered / replied, "I can do it myself." (✓)
我問琳蒂是否需要我協助她寫報告，她回道：「我自己可以寫完。」

→ I asked Lindy if she needed my help with her report, and she answered / replied that she could do it herself. (✓)
我問琳蒂是否需要我協助她寫報告，她回道她自己可以寫完。

e 下列情況只可使用 answer：
{ answer the door　應門
{ answer the phone / call　接電話

例 Somebody is knocking on the door. Go answer it!
有人在敲門。快去應門！

The phone is ringing. Go answer it!
電話鈴響了。快去接電話。

小試身手

1. Please have Linda (reply / answer) to my email first thing tomorrow morning.

2. John, please ＿＿＿ the door. I think it's the delivery man.
Ⓐ reply to　Ⓑ respond to　Ⓒ answer to　Ⓓ answer

Ans 1. reply　2. Ⓓ

CH 3

常見多種易混淆用字

163

Unit 156 in a hurry、in a rush、in haste 怎麼用？

a   in a hurry、in a rush 及 in haste 可作副詞片語用，均表「匆匆地」，修飾句中動詞。

例   Upon seeing the cop, the pickpocket ran away in a hurry / a rush / haste. (✓)   扒手一見到條伯伯便匆匆逃跑了。

注意 上句的 in a hurry, in a rush 及 in haste 均修飾片語動詞 ran away。

b   in a hurry 及 in a rush 亦可置 be 動詞之後，當形容詞片語，表「匆忙的」，修飾主詞。in haste 則無此用法。

例   Tell me why you are always in such haste. (✗)
→ Tell me why you are always in such a hurry / rush. (✓)
告訴我你為何老是那麼匆忙。

小試身手

I apologize for the messy handwriting; I wrote the note in _____.（選錯的）

Ⓐ a rush   Ⓑ haste   Ⓒ a hurry   Ⓓ hasty

Ans Ⓓ

Unit 157 rubbish、garbage、trash、junk 怎麼用？

a   rubbish [ˈrʌbɪʃ]、garbage [ˈgɑrbɪdʒ] 及 trash [træʃ] 均為同義不可數名詞，均表「垃圾」或「無用的廢物」，不可說：a rubbish / a trash / a garbage (✗) 或 several / a few / many rubbishes / trashes / garbages (✗)
應說：a piece of rubbish / trash / garbage   一件垃圾
some / a lot of / lots of rubbish / trash / garbage   一些 / 許多垃圾

164

例　Hank picked up a~~ ~~garbage and threw it into the garbage can. (✗)
→ Hank picked up a piece of garbage and threw it into the garbage can. (✓)　漢克拾起一件垃圾把它扔進垃圾桶裡。
What Jack said was a~~ ~~garbage. (✗)
→ What Jack said was garbage. (✓)
傑克所說的話全是廢話。

b　junk [dʒʌŋk] 亦為不可數名詞，指「用不到的新或舊的東西」、「沒有價值或無用的東西」、「廢物」。

例　I don't use that bike any more. It has become garbage~~ ~~ to me. (✗)
→ I seldom use that bike any more. It has become junk to me. (✓)
我很少用到那輛腳踏車。對我而言，它已成了廢物。
A lot of fast food such as hamburgers and fries is considered junk food. (✓)　許多速食像是漢堡及薯條等被視為垃圾食物。

小試身手

公園地上有許多垃圾所以沒有人喜歡去那裡。
There ＿＿＿＿ ＿＿＿＿ (l)＿＿＿＿ (o)＿＿＿＿ ＿＿＿＿ on the ground in the park, so no one likes to go there.

Ans　is; a; lot; of; garbage / trash / rubbish

Unit 158　dislike、unlike、like 怎麼用？

a　dislike [dɪsˋlaɪk] 是及物動詞，表示「不喜歡」，之後用名詞、代名詞或動名詞作受詞。

例　Robert dislikes to~~ ~~be called Bobby. (✗)
→ Robert dislikes being called Bobby. (✓)
勞勃特不喜歡被喚作巴比。
I dislike Ted because he often lies. (✓)
我不喜歡泰德，因為他常撒謊。

165

I dislike heavy metal music because I think it's too noisy. (✔)
我不喜歡重金屬音樂，因為我認為它太吵了。

b hate [het] 是及物動詞，表「痛恨」、「不喜歡」，之後可接名詞、代名詞、動名詞或 to 引導的不定詞片語作受詞。

例 Peter hates speaking in public. (✔)
= Peter hates to speak in public.
= Peter dislikes speaking in public.　彼得不喜歡公開演講。

c like、love 均為及物動詞，均表「喜歡」，可用名詞、代名詞、動名詞或 to 引導的不定詞片語作受詞。

例 I like / love music. (✔)　我喜歡音樂。
I like / love to sing. (✔)
= I like / love singing.　我喜歡唱歌。
I don't like / love singing. (✔)
= I don't like / love to sing.
= I dislike singing.　我不喜歡唱歌。

d like 可作介詞，表「像」，通常放在句首，之後接名詞、代名詞或動名詞作受詞。unlike 亦通常放在句首，作介詞，表「不像」，之後接名詞、代名詞或動名詞作受詞。

例 Like George, I enjoy reading. (✔)　就像喬治一樣，我也喜歡閱讀。
Not like Peter, I never fool around. (✗，無 not like 的用法)
→ Unlike Peter, I never fool around. (✔)
不像彼得，我這個人從不會鬼混。

Unlike speaking, writing demands strict grammar. (✔)
不像口說，寫作要求文法嚴謹。

小試身手

1　Jason (doesn't like / dislikes / unlike) to eat vegetables, which makes his mom worry.

2. Unlike (running / to run / to running), swimming is a low-impact exercise.

> Ans 1. doesn't like   2. running

Unit 159 lately、recently、in the near future 怎麼用？

a lately [ˈletlɪ] 與 recently [ˈrisn̩tlɪ] 為同義副詞，均表 (過去這一段時間內的)「最近」，多與現在完成式或現在完成進行式並用。

例 I was very busy recently / lately. (✗)
→ I have been very busy recently / lately. (✓)
= I have been very busy of late.
我最近很忙。

注意 recently 可置句首、句中或句尾，lately 多只置句尾。

Recently, Kelly has been feeling listless. (✓)
= Kelly has recently been feeling listless.
= Kelly has been feeling listless recently.
凱莉最近一直感到無精打采。

Lately, Kelly has been feeling listless. (罕)
→ Kelly has been feeling listless lately / of late. (✓)

b recently 亦可表「不久前」，等於 a short while ago，與過去式並用。

例 I recently called John, but he was not at home. (✓)
= I called John a short while / a couple of days ago, but he was not at home. 我不久前 / 幾天前打電話給約翰，不過他不在家。

c in the near future 表 (未來一段時間內的)「最近」，與 will 並用。

例 I will call John again recently / lately. (✗)
→ I will call John again in the near future. (✓)
最近我會再打電話給約翰。

CH 3 常見多種易混淆用字

167

小試身手

1	Judy ＿＿ ill lately. She needs to see a doctor. Ⓐ is　Ⓑ was　Ⓒ has been　Ⓓ will be
2	John and I ＿＿ married in the near future. Ⓐ are　Ⓑ were　Ⓒ have been　Ⓓ will be

Ans 1. Ⓒ　2. Ⓓ

Unit 160　lightning、lightening、lighting 怎麼用？

a lightning [ˈlaɪtnɪŋ] n. 閃電

例　I see a bolt of lightening in the dark clouds. (✗)
→ I see a bolt / flash of lightning in the dark clouds. (✓)　我在烏雲裡看見一道閃電。

b lightening [ˈlaɪtənɪŋ] 是動詞 lighten（表「減輕」、「明亮」、「使明亮」）的現在分詞或動名詞。

例　Thanks a lot, Peter. Your timely help has lightened my workload. (✓)
多謝了，彼得。你及時的幫助減輕了我的工作負擔。

It was only 5 a.m., but the sky was lightning in the east. (✗)
→ It was only 5 a.m., but the sky was lightening in the east. (✓)
當時才凌晨五點，但東方的天空已經出現魚肚白。

c lighting [ˈlaɪtɪŋ] 是動詞 light（表照亮）的現在分詞或動名詞。

例　Thank you for lightning up my life. (✗)
→ Thank you for lighting up my life. (✓)　謝謝妳照亮了我的生命。

小試身手

1　Mary planned on (lightening / lighting / lightning) her wardrobe (衣櫥) by donating some of her old clothes to charity.

2. A bolt of (lightening / lighting / lightning) illuminated (照亮) the darkened sky; then it started to rain.

Ans 1. lightening   2. lightning

Unit 161 「修理某物」是 need to be repaired、need being repaired 還是 need repairing?

某物 + need to be + 過去分詞　某物需要被……
= 某物 + need + 動名詞

例 The car needs to repair. (✗)
→ The car needs to be repaired. (✓)
= The car needs repairing.　這輛車需要被修理了。
非：The car needs being repaired. (✗)
The table and chairs need to clean again. (✗)
→ The table and chairs need to be cleaned again. (✓)
= The table and chairs need cleaning again.
這張桌子和幾張椅子需要再擦洗一下。
非：The table and chairs need being cleaned again. (✗)

小試身手

The machine needs ＿＿＿ today, or we won't be able to work tomorrow.

Ⓐ fixing　　Ⓑ to be fixing　Ⓒ to fix　　Ⓓ being fixed

Ans Ⓐ

Unit 162 crossroad、crossroads、intersection 怎麼用？

表「十字路口」可使用 crossroads (單複數同形) 或 intersection (複數為 intersections)

例 Turn left at the first crossroad, and you'll find the library on your right-hand side. (罕)

→ Turn left at the first crossroads, and you'll find the library on your right-hand side. (✓，常用)

= Turn left at the first intersection, and you'll find the library on your right-hand side.
在第一個十字路口左轉，你就會看到圖書館在你的右手邊。

Todd's career life is at a crossroads.
陶德的職業生涯正處於關鍵時刻。

小試身手

那間舊書店就位在曼因街與艾滿街的十字路口。
The old bookstore is located at the ＿＿＿ where Main Street meets Elm Street.

Ans crossroads / intersection / crossroad

Unit 163　even though、although、though 怎麼用？

a　even though、although 及 though 均表「雖然」、「即使」，其中 even though 語氣較強，其次是 although，而 though 多用於口語。此三個連接詞均引導副詞子句，修飾主要子句。主要子句之前不可再置連接詞 but (但是)，否則造成錯誤的雙重連接。

例 Even though / Although / Though I worked hard, but I failed the test. (✗)

→ Even though / Although / Though I worked hard, I failed the test. (✓)

= I worked hard, but I failed the test.
雖然我很用功，可是我考試還是沒及格。

b even though、although 及 though 亦可置主要子句之後，此時兩個子句之前可置逗點，亦可不置逗點。

例 Peter bought his wife a gold necklace, although she told him not to. (✓)　雖然彼得的妻子叫他不要這樣做，他還是買了一條金項鍊給她。

c even 是副詞，表「甚至」，不可視作連接詞使用。

例 ~~Even~~ I worked hard, I failed the test. (✗)
→ Even though I worked hard, I failed the test. (✓)
即使我很努力了卻還是考不及格。

Donna can't even dance, so there is no chance she'll be a dancer.
　　　　　　　adv.　v.

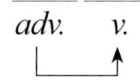

多娜連跳舞都不會，因此她不可能會成為舞者。

d though 可作副詞，表「然而」，置句尾。此時 though 之前通常置逗點。

例 → Tom is rich and nice, ~~but~~ Amy doesn't want to marry him, though. You know, he is 80 and she's just 18.
(✗，but 與 though 均表「然而」、「但是」，意思重疊。)

→ Tom is rich and nice. Amy doesn't want to marry him, though. You know, he is 80 and she's just 18. (✓)

= Tom is rich and nice, but Amy doesn't want to marry him. You know, he is 80 and she's just 18.
湯姆有錢人又好，不過艾咪卻不想嫁給他。你是知道的，他已 80 歲，而她才 18 歲。

注意 though 或 although 作連接詞也可表「然而」，所引導的副詞子句置主要子句之後。故上列 d 項的例子亦可改寫成：

Tom is rich and nice, though / although Amy doesn't want to marry him.

= Tom is rich and nice, but Amy doesn't want to marry him.

CH 3　常見多種易混淆用字

171

小試身手

1 選出錯誤的選項。

Ⓐ Although the weather is cold, Jimmy is still going swimming.

Ⓑ Tanya was tired, though she continued working on her project late into the night.

Ⓒ Abby wanted to go to the party, but she had to finish her homework first.

Ⓓ Though Andy had doubts about his abilities, but he decided to give it a try anyway.

2 即使正在下大雨，他們還是決定要去公園散步。

_____ _____ it was raining heavily, they decided to go for a walk in the park.

Ans 1. Ⓓ 2. Even; though

Unit 164 scenery、scene、view、landscape 怎麼用？

a scenery 是不可數名詞，指「風景」，不可說：a scenery, two sceneries...。

例 There are ~~many~~ beautiful scener~~ies~~ in Nantou. (✗)

→ There is a lot of beautiful scenery in Nantou. (✓) 南投有許多美麗的風景。

I'm deeply attracted by the magnificent mountain scener~~ies~~ around Puli. (✗)

→ I'm deeply attracted by the magnificent mountain scenery around Puli. (✓) 埔里周邊宏偉的山景深深吸引著我。

b scene 是可數名詞，多指犯罪、車禍、槍擊等不愉快的事故「現場」或「地點」，但也可指「景色」、「風景」，此時的 scene 與 view 同義。

例 I saw a police car rush to the scene of the traffic accident / the scene of the crime. (✔) 我看到一輛警車往車禍現場 / 犯罪現場疾駛而去。

A trip to Ethiopia enables you to see in person many beautiful rural scenes / views in the countryside. (✔)
到伊索比亞走一趟可以讓你看到鄉間許多美麗的農村景色。

The couple made a scene on the street. (✔)
這對情侶在大街上大吵大鬧，真丟人。

c landscape 是可數名詞，指陸上風景，尤指「鄉間風景」，常用單數。

例 I dream of living in a clean and beautiful landscape in Switzerland someday. (✔) 我夢想有朝一日能住在瑞士一處乾淨又美麗的風景區。

d scenic spot 表「景點」，是可數名詞。

例 There are many scenic spots around Taiwan. (✔)
臺灣周遭有許多景點。

Alishan is doubtless a beautiful scenic spot worth visiting time and again. (✔) 阿里山無疑是個值得一再遊覽的美麗景點。

小試身手

1. The crime (scenery / scene / landscape) was disturbing; just glancing at it was enough to give me nightmares.

2. The amazing _____ along Taiwan's north coast attract numerous tourists every year. (選錯的)
   Ⓐ scenic spots Ⓑ scenes
   Ⓒ landscapes   Ⓓ scenery

Ans 1. scene   2. Ⓓ

CH 3 常見多種易混淆用字

173

Unit 165 　one... the other...、one... another... the other... 怎麼用？

a "one... the other..." 表「一個……另一個……」，用於限定的兩者。換言之，"one... the other..." 要與 two 並用。

例　I have two sports cars. One is white, and another is blue. (✗)

→ I have two sports cars. One is white, and the other is blue. (✓)
我有兩輛跑車。一輛是白色的，另一輛是藍色的。

b "one... another... the other..." 用於限定的三者。換言之，"one... another... the other..." 要與 three 並用。

例　Andy has three brothers. One is a teacher, the other is a policeman, and another is a chef. (✗)

→ Andy has three brothers. One is a teacher, another is a policeman, and the other is a chef. (✓)
安迪有三個兄弟。一個當老師，一個當警察，還有一個當主廚。

小試身手

1. 湯尼有兩個兄弟姊妹。一個熱愛打籃球，另一個熱愛游泳。
Tony has two siblings. _____ loves to play basketball, while _____ _____ loves swimming.

2. 茱蒂有三件洋裝。一件是藍色的、另一件是粉紅色的，還有另一件是黑色的。
Judy has three dresses. _____ is blue, _____ is pink and _____ _____ is black.

Ans 1. One; the; other　2. One; another; the; other

174

Unit 166　one... another...、some... others...、數字... the others... 怎麼用?

a "one... another..." 表「一個……另一個……」，用於非限定的兩者。

例　Hobbies vary from person to person. One might enjoy fishing, while the other might be fond of hiking. (✗)

→ Hobbies vary from person to person. One might enjoy fishing, while another might be fond of hiking. (✓)　嗜好因人而異。
某甲也許喜歡釣魚，而某乙也許喜歡健行。

b "some... others..." 表「某些……另一些……」，用於非限定的兩群。

例　Hobbies vary with people. Some might enjoy fishing, whereas the other might be fond of hiking. (✗)

→ Hobbies vary with people. Some might enjoy fishing, while others might be fond of hiking. (✓)

c 明確數字 + 名詞... the others / the rest..."　若干……其他都……

例　The test was so difficult that only two / eight students passed it, and others all failed. (✗)　　明確數字

→ The test was so difficult that only two / eight students passed it, and the others all failed. (✓)

這次考試太難，因此只有兩位 / 八位同學考過，其他同學全都不及格。

小試身手

1. 女生的穿著依個人喜好決定。有些女生喜歡穿裙子，其他則喜歡穿褲子。
The choice of clothing for girls is determined by personal preferences. ＿＿＿＿ like to wear skirts, while ＿＿＿＿ like to wear pants.

2. Two of the team members went for a walk, while ＿＿＿＿ ＿＿＿＿ stayed inside to chat.

Ans　1. Some; others　2. the; others 或 the; rest

Unit 167　last week、this week、next week 怎麼用？

以下由 last、this、next 引導的時間副詞片語之前不得置介詞 in：

last week　上星期	this week　這個星期	next week　下星期
last month　上個月	this month　這個月	next month　下個月
last year　去年	this year　今年	next year　明年

例　I ran into Peter ~~in~~ last week. (✗)
→ I ran into Peter last week. (✓)　上星期我巧遇彼得。

I've been very busy ~~in~~ this month. (✗)
→ I've been very busy this month. (✓)　這個月我一直很忙。

What are you going to do ~~in~~ next week? (✗)
→ What are you going to do next week? (✓)　你下星期要做什麼？

I'm planning to take a trip to Europe sometime ~~in~~ next year. (✗)
→ I'm planning to take a trip to Europe sometime next year. (✓)
明年我計劃找個時間到歐洲去旅行。

We'll hold a meeting ~~on~~ this coming Friday. (✗)
→ We'll hold a meeting this coming Friday. (✓)
＝ We'll hold a meeting on Friday.　這個星期五我們會召開會議。

We'll talk about it ~~on~~ next Monday. (✗)
→ We'll talk about it next Monday. (✓)　下星期一我們會討論這件事。

小試身手

我們下週三要去游泳。
We will go swimming _____ _____.

Ans　next; Wednesday

Unit 168 on the way、in the way、by the way 怎麼用?

a on the / one's way { to + 地方名詞　往……途中
　　　　　　　　　　　　+ 地方副詞 }

例　I ran into Peter on the / my way for the post office. (✗)
→ I ran into Peter on the / my way to the post office. (✓)
我在往郵局途中碰到彼得。

I saw a terrible traffic accident on the / my way for work. (✗)
→ I saw a terrible traffic accident on the / my way to work. (✓)
我在上班途中目睹一起可怕的車禍。

Be sure to buy me a newspaper on your way to here / home. (✗)
→ Be sure to buy me a newspaper on your way here / home. (✓)
　　　　　　　　　　　　　　　　　　　　　　adv.　　adv.
你在到我這裡 / 回家途中務必買一份報紙給我。

理由　here 及 home 是副詞，不可作介詞的受詞。

b be on the way to + V-ing　即將……
　= be close to + V-ing

例　I'm well on the way to finish the report. (✗)
→ I'm well on the way to　finishing the report. (✓) 我快要完成報告了。
　　　　　　　　　　　　介詞　動名詞

c in the / one's way　擋住 (某人的) 去路

例　There's a big rock in the way, so I guess we'll have to take a detour. (✓)　有一顆巨石擋住了去路，因此我想我們得繞道了。

Don't let anything get in the way of your dreams. (✓)
別讓任何東西阻礙你的夢想。

d by the way, ...　順便一提 / 對了，……

例　We have to finish the work by 5 p.m.— by the way / incidentally, what time is it now? (✓)
我們必須在下午 5 點以前完成這工作 —— 對了，現在幾點了？

小試身手

1. 倒下的樹擋住路了，所以我們只好找另一條路繼續健行。
   The fallen tree was ____ ____ ____, so we had to find another way to continue the hike.

2. 我就快完成今年夏天最完美的度假計畫了。
   I'm ____ ____ to ____ (make) a perfect vacation plan for this summer.

3. 我今天在廣播聽到了你最喜歡的樂團，順便一提，我買了下個月演唱會的門票。
   I heard your favorite band on the radio today, and ____ ____ ____, I bought tickets to their concert next month.

Ans 1. in; the / our; way 2. on; the; way; making 3. by; the; way

Unit 169 pick、pick up、pick out、pick on 怎麼用？

a pick + 水果　摘水果

例 We had a great time picking up apples in the orchard last weekend. (✗)
→ We had a great time picking apples in the orchard last weekend. (✓)
上個週末我們在果園裡摘蘋果摘得很高興。

b pick up 物 / pick 物 up　將某物拾起

例 Pick the trash and throw it into the garbage can. (✗)
→ Pick up the trash and throw it into the garbage can. (✓)
把垃圾撿起來丟進垃圾桶內。

178

c **pick up a language** （從生活中）學習某種語言

例 I pic~~k~~ed a little Spanish while staying in Mexico. (✗)
→ I picked up a little Spanish while staying in Mexico. (✓)
我待在墨西哥期間學了一點西班牙語。

d **pick 人 up / pick up 人** 接某人

例 It's your turn to pick our children up after school. (✓)
輪到你小朋友放學後去接他們。

e **pick 人 / 物 out** 挑選出某人 / 某物

例 I felt honored when I knew I was picked out from more than one hundred candidates for the job. (✓)
獲知我是從一百多個候選名單中被挑選出來接受這個職務時，甚感榮幸。

f **pick on 人** 故意挑剔某人

例 Stop picking on me, or I'll tell the teacher. (✓)
別再找我麻煩，否則我會告訴老師。

小試身手

1. 泰迪住在日本的期間學會了日語。
Teddy _____ _____ Japanese while he lived in Japan.

2. 上週末我們去大湖採草莓。
We went to _____ some strawberries in Dahu last weekend.

3. 那個女生故意找漢克麻煩來引起他的注意。
That girl _____ _____ Hank to get his attention.

Ans 1. picked; up   2. pick   3. picked; on

Notes

Chapter 4

Unit 170 ▶▶▶ Unit 188

▶ 常見卻易用錯的單字 / 片語 / 句型

你是否曾因為用錯介詞被扣分？
你是否曾因為用錯單字 / 片語 / 句型 / 文法而被貽笑大方？

魔鬼藏在細節裡！正是這些看似微不足道的錯誤讓你的句子、談話、文章等失去說服力，甚至讓人產生負面觀感！本章收錄常見卻常用錯的單字 / 片語 / 句型 / 文法，幫助你考試、寫作、聊天不踩雷，輕鬆應對當高手。

Unit 170 record 的用法

a record [ˈrɛkəd] 作名詞，表「紀錄」，有下列重要片語：

1. set a record　　　創下紀錄
2. break the record　破紀錄
3. keep / hold the record　保持紀錄

例　The runner set a new record for the 100-meter dash. (✓)
這位賽跑選手創下了百米賽跑的新紀錄。

The swimmer had kept / held the world record for 10 years before it was broken early this year. (✓)
這位游泳選手連續保持 10 年的世界紀錄，直到今年初才被打破。

b record [ˈrɛkəd] 亦可作形容詞，之後接名詞。

例　Unemployment in that country reached a recorded high in July. (✗)
→ Unemployment in that country reached a record high in July.
(✓，此處 high 是名詞，與 level 同義)
該國的失業率於七月達到歷史新高。

A recorded number of candidates were competing for the job. (✗)
→ A record number of candidates were competing for the job. (✓)
角逐這項工作的應徵者數量空前。

c record [rɪˈkɔrd] 作動詞，表「記錄、錄音(影)」。

例　Ted recorded his voice because he needed to know how it sounded.　泰德錄下了他的聲音，因為他得知道他聲音聽起來怎麼樣。

小試身手

1. According to the news, the temperature in Taipei hit a _____ high today.
Ⓐ recording　Ⓑ recorded　Ⓒ record　Ⓓ being recorded

2	The athlete _____ a world record for the high jump. Ⓐ did　　Ⓑ took　　Ⓒ made　　Ⓓ set
3	The weather station _____ the fastest wind speed ever at 231 miles an hour. Ⓐ listened　　Ⓑ recorded　　Ⓒ blew　　Ⓓ paced

Ans　1. Ⓒ　2. Ⓓ　3. Ⓑ

Unit 171　as well 的用法

as well 視作副詞，表「也」，有下列用法：

a A and B as well + 複數動詞　A 以及 B 都……

例　~~Both~~ Jim and I as well enjoy music.（✗，Both 是贅字）
　　Jim and I as well enjoy music.（✓，口語上較少用）
　　= (Both) Jim and I enjoy music.　吉姆和我都喜歡音樂。

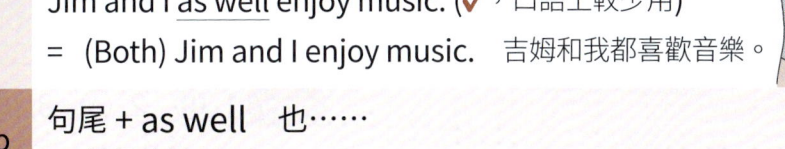

b 句尾 + as well　也……
　　= 句尾 (,) + too

例　Dana is ~~both~~ pretty and clever as well.（✗，both 是贅字）
　　→ Dana is pretty and clever as well.（✓）
　　= Dana is pretty and clever (,) too.　黛娜美麗又聰明。
　　I like painting, and I enjoy taking pictures as well.（✓）
　　= I like painting, and I enjoy taking pictures (,) too.
　　= I like painting, and I also enjoy taking pictures.
　　我喜歡畫畫，也喜歡拍照。

c as well 亦可與助動詞 may 或 might 並用，形成下列固定片語：
　　may as well + 原形動詞（語氣較強烈）　不妨 / 最好 / 不然就……
　　= might as well + 原形動詞（語氣較緩和）

例　It's getting dark, so we might as well go home now.
　　天色暗了，因此我們現在不妨就回家吧。

It's raining so hard, you may as well stay home for a while.
雨下得那麼大，你就不妨在家裡多待一下。

小試身手

1. Amber and her boyfriend as well ＿＿＿ dancing.
   Ⓐ loves　　　　　Ⓑ loving
   Ⓒ been loving　　Ⓓ love

2. In view of the heavy traffic on the highway, you might as well ＿＿＿ a train.
   Ⓐ take　　Ⓑ taking　　Ⓒ took　　Ⓓ taken

3. 選出錯誤的句子。
   Ⓐ You are energetic and creative, too.
   Ⓑ You are both energetic and creative as well.
   Ⓒ You are energetic and creative as well.
   Ⓓ You are energetic and also creative.

Ans 1. Ⓓ　2. Ⓐ　3. Ⓑ

Unit 172　rather than 的用法

rather than 表「而非……」，可作連接詞或介詞，用法如下：

a rather than 作連接詞時，可連接對等的詞類。連接主詞時，動詞按「第一個主詞」作變化。

例　Ray is <u>selfish</u> rather than <u>generous</u>. (✓)
　　　　　adj.　　　　　　　　*adj.*
雷非但不慷慨，反而很自私。

I chose <u>coffee</u> rather than <u>tea</u>. (✓)　我選擇咖啡，沒選擇茶。
　　　　　n.　　　　　　　　*n.*

<u>Ted</u> rather than I ~~am~~ wrong. (✗)

→ <u>Ted</u> rather than I is wrong. (✓)

184

= Ted, not I, is wrong.

= Ted instead of me is wrong. 錯的是泰德而非我。

＊instead of 是片語介詞，故用 me 作受詞，非 instead of I。

b **rather than 亦可作介詞，等於 instead of，之後接動名詞作受詞。**

例 Rather than driving, Andy bikes to work. (✔，少用)

= Instead of driving, Andy bikes to work.

安迪不是開車上班，而是騎自行車上班。

注意 已知 rather than 亦可作連接詞，之後接原形動詞，故上句亦可改寫成：Rather than drive, Andy bikes to work. (✔，常用)

小試身手

1. My friends rather than Amy _____ going to the KTV.
   Ⓐ is　　Ⓑ are　　Ⓒ would　　Ⓓ be

2. Rather than _____, my brother takes a bus to school.
   Ⓐ walk　　Ⓑ to walk　　Ⓒ walked　　Ⓓ be walking

3. I would like to be friends with you rather than _____.
   Ⓐ against you
   Ⓑ would like to compete against you
   Ⓒ compete against you
   Ⓓ competing against you

Ans　1. Ⓑ　2. Ⓐ　3. Ⓒ

Unit 173　would rather 的用法

would rather 表「寧願……」，有以下用法：

a **would rather + 原形動詞 + than + 原形動詞　寧願……也不願……**

例 I would rather stay home than to go out. (✗)
　→ I would rather stay home than go out. (✔)
　　　　　　　原形動詞　　　　原形動詞

我寧願待在家裡也不願外出。

I was speechless when she told me she would rather live with a pig than ~~to~~ marry me. (✗)

→ I was speechless when she told me she would rather live with a pig than marry me. (✓)
她告訴我她寧願跟一隻豬生活也不願嫁給我時，我無言以對。

b　I would rather 之後可直接接 that 引導的名詞子句作受詞，形成下列的「假設語氣」句型：

❶ 與**現在事實**相反，that 子句的動詞用過去式 (be 動詞一律用 were)。

例　I would rather (that) it ~~rains~~ now. (✗)

→ I would rather (that) it rained now. (✓)

＝ I wish (that) it rained now. (But it is not raining now.)
我真希望現在就下雨。(可是現在並未下雨。)

I would rather (that) he were here. (✓)

＝ I wish (that) he were here. (✓) (But he isn't here now)
我真希望他現在就在這裡。(可是他現在並不在這裡。)

❷ 與**過去事實**相反，that 子句的動詞用過去完成式 (had + 過去分詞)。

例　I would rather (that) you ~~told~~ me the truth yesterday. (✗)
　　　　　　　　　　　　　過去式

→ I would rather (that) you had told me the truth yesterday. (✓)
　　　　　　　　　　　　　過去完成式

＝ I wish (that) you had told me the truth yesterday.
(But you didn't tell me the truth yesterday.)
我真希望你昨天把真相告訴我就好了。(但你昨天並未把真相告訴我。)

小試身手

1　Dennis would rather watch TV at home than ＿＿＿ basketball with his friends.
　Ⓐ play　　Ⓑ plays　　Ⓒ played　　Ⓓ be playing

2　I would rather that the fairy tale ＿＿＿ true.
　Ⓐ be　　Ⓑ is　　Ⓒ was　　Ⓓ were

3 I would rather I _____ a car 3 years ago.
Ⓐ bought　　　　　　　Ⓑ have bought
Ⓒ had bought　　　　　Ⓓ would have bought

Ans 1. Ⓐ　2. Ⓓ　3. Ⓒ

Unit 174　other than 的用法

a　other than 視作介詞，表「除……之外」，與 except 或 with the exception of 同義，多用於否定句中，也可往前移到句首。

例　The man has nothing other than an old dog. (✓)
　　　　　　　否定句

=　The man doesn't have anything other than an old dog.
　　　　　　　　　　　　否定句

=　The man has nothing except (for) an old dog.

=　The man doesn't have anything with the exception of an old dog.　這個人除了一隻老狗外，其他什麼都沒有。

b　other than 亦可用於肯定句中，此時等於 besides、in addition to，表示「除了……之外，尚有……」。

例　Today, English is spoken in many countries other than the UK.

=　Today, English is spoken in many countries besides / in addition to the UK.　如今，除了英國外，有許多國家也都說英語。

c　比較用法如下：

	用法	意思等同
other than 除了……之外	用於否定句中	except 或 with the exception of
	用於肯定句中	besides 或 in addition to

187

小試身手

1. You should say nothing except the truth.
   提示 用 other than 改寫句子。
   You should say nothing _____.

2. I like to eat cauliflower. I also like to eat broccoli.
   提示 用 other than 開頭合併句子。
   _____, I also like to eat broccoli.

   Ans 1. other than the truth 2. Other than cauliflower

Unit 175　none other than 的用法

none other than 強調意料之外的發現，後只能接「人」。用法如下：
be none other than + 人　（想都沒想到）竟然是 / 正是某人

例　The new staff member was no other than my ex-girlfriend. (少見)
→ The new staff member was none other than my ex-girlfriend. (✓)　這位新來的員工竟然是我的前女友。
The man talking on the phone is none other than my dad. (✓)
正在講電話的那位男士不是別人，正是我老爸。

小試身手

The chef in this restaurant is my childhood friend.
提示 加入 none other than 改寫句子。
The chef in this restaurant _____.

Ans is none other than my childhood friend

Unit 176　do nothing but 的用法

do nothing but 表「除了……之外」，之後直接接原形動詞，不需加不定詞 to：

例　Ben did nothing but to watch TV all morning. (×)
→ Ben did nothing but watch TV all morning. (✓)
班整個早上除了看電視外啥事都不做。

You can do nothing but to apologize to her. (×)
→ You can do nothing but apologize to her. (✓)
你除了對她道歉別無他途。

注意　do nothing but 也可拆分為下列用法，之後一樣直接接原形動詞：

There is nothing we can do but to wait patiently. (×)
→ There is nothing we can do but wait patiently. (✓)
我們除了等待外別無他法。

小試身手

1. I could do nothing ＿＿＿ to my mom complain about my dad.
Ⓐ listened　Ⓑ to listen　Ⓒ but listen　Ⓓ but to listen

2. There is nothing you can do but practice again and again.
提示　用 do nothing but 改寫句子。
＿＿＿＿＿＿＿＿＿＿＿＿＿＿＿＿＿＿＿＿ again and again.

Ans　1. Ⓒ　2. You can do nothing but practice

Unit 177　do without 的用法

do without 表示「沒有某物 / 某人也行 / 也過得去」，後接人或物，用法及延伸如下：

a　此處的 do 是不及物動詞，之後不得接受詞，且本片語多與助動詞 can 或 cannot 並用。

189

先生：I can do ~~it~~ without money, but I can't do ~~it~~ without you.（✗，意思不清）
我沒錢就可以做這件事，但沒有你我就不能做這件事。

→ I can do without money, but I can't do without you.（✓）
沒錢我日子還是過得去，可是沒妳我日子就過不了了。

太太：I can do without you, but I can't do without money.（✓）
沒你我日子還是可以過得去，可是沒錢我就過不了了。

b have to do without...　沒有……也只好撐過去了

例　You've grown up, son. From now on, you'll have to do without me.（✓）
兒子，你已長大了。從今起，沒有我，你一切都得靠自己了。

c how 人 did without...　（當年）某人沒有……日子是怎麼過的

例　I don't know how my grandparents did without cellphones in those days.（✓）
我不知道當年沒有手機的時代我爺爺奶奶日子是怎麼過的。

小試身手

1. 我想知道我爸媽剛結婚沒錢時日子是怎麼過的。
I'd like to know _____ my parents _____ _____ money when they first got married.

2. 我想我沒錢會沒辦法過日子。
I don't think I can _____ _____ money.

Ans　1. how; did; without　2. do; without

Unit 178　It is time that... 的用法

a "It is time that..." 表「現在該是……的時候了」，而事實卻非如此，故 that 子句的動詞應採過去式，表示與現在事實相反的假設語氣。

190

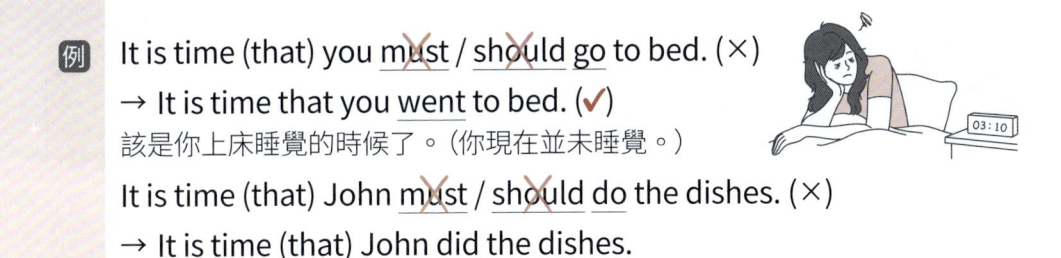

例　It is time (that) you ~~must~~ / ~~should~~ go to bed. (✗)
→ It is time that you went to bed. (✓)
該是你上床睡覺的時候了。(你現在並未睡覺。)

It is time (that) John ~~must~~ / ~~should do~~ the dishes. (✗)
→ It is time (that) John did the dishes.
該是約翰洗碗筷的時候了。(他現在並未洗碗筷。)

b　上列各句亦可改寫成：

It is high time (that) you went to bed. (✓)
= It is about time (that) you went to bed.
It is high time (that) John did / washed the washes. (✓)

c　"It is time that..." 的結構中，that 子句不論主詞為第幾人稱的 be 動詞一律為 were (非 was)。

例　It is high time he / you / they were in bed.
該是他 / 你 / 他們入睡的時候了。(他 / 你 / 他們現在並未入睡。)

d　"It is time that..." 亦可被下列句構取代：

例　It is time you went to bed. (✓)
= It is time for you to go to bed.
但英美人士不會說：It is ~~about~~ / ~~high~~ time for you to go to bed. (✗)

小試身手

1. Hank, it is time that you _____ for your own health.
   Ⓐ were exercising　Ⓑ exercises
   Ⓒ exercised　Ⓓ exercising

2. It is time for Linda to do her homework.
   提示 用 It is time that... 改寫句子。
   It is time that _____.

Ans　1. Ⓒ　2. Linda did her homework

Unit 179　can't... enough 的用法

a "can't... enough" 表「再……也不為過」，即「非常……」。

例　You were such a big help. I can't thank you so much. (✗)
你真是幫了大忙。我不能那麼地謝謝你。（語意不通）

→ You were such a big help. I can't thank you enough. (✓)
你真是幫了大忙。我再怎麼謝謝你也不夠 / 我非常謝謝你 / 我感謝極了。

The chocolate is so tasty that I can't get enough of it. (✓)
這巧克力很好吃，我非常喜歡它。

Honey, I can't get enough of your love. (✓)
親愛的，你給我的愛越多越好。

b "can't be too + 形容詞" 亦表「再……也不為過」。

例　You can't be too careful when dealing with this problem. (✓)
= You can't be careful enough when dealing with this problem.
你處理這個問題時再小心也不為過 / 要非常小心。

小試身手

1　You have seen us through so many difficulties. _____
　Ⓐ We can thank you enough.　Ⓑ We can't thank you.
　Ⓒ We can thank you.　　　　Ⓓ We can't thank you enough.

2　You can't be fast enough during a race.
　提示　用 ...too ... 改寫句子。
　_____ during a race.

Ans　1. Ⓓ　2. You can't be too fast

192

Unit 180　for the past few years 的用法

a | for / during / over / throughout | the past / last + 數字 + | days / weeks / months / years

過去若干天 / 週 / 月 / 年以來（持續做某件事）

上述時間副詞片語在句中出現時，動詞應使用現在完成式 (have / has + 過去分詞) 或現在完成進行式 (have / has been + V-ing)。

例　I had lived here for the past twenty years. (✗)
過去完成式

→ I have lived here over the past twenty years. (✓)

或：I've been living here | for / over / during / throughout | the last twenty years. (✓)
　　現在完成進行式

過去 20 年來我都住在這裡。

I have been learning French throughout the past few months. (✓)
過去這幾個月來我一直都在學法語。

b | in the past / last + 數字 + days / weeks / months / years
過去若干天 / 週 / 月 / 年以來（偶而做某件事，不常做某件事）

例　I have only seen the man once in the past three months. (✓)
過去三個月來我只見過這個男子一次。

小試身手

1. My students _____ for this dance over the past few months.
   Ⓐ practicing　　　　　Ⓑ have had been practicing
   Ⓒ are practicing　　　Ⓓ have been practicing

2. Ben _____ on stage twice in the last two weeks.
   Ⓐ is performing　　　Ⓑ has performed
   Ⓒ has had performed　Ⓓ has been performed

Ans　1. Ⓓ　2. Ⓑ

Unit 181　經常與 "on" 搭配的名詞怎麼用？

介詞 on 常與表直線性 (如從甲地到乙地；從某時到某時) 的活動並用。
be on duty　　值勤；值班 (e.g. from 9 a.m. to 5 p.m.)
be on call　　(需要隨叫隨到的) 待命
be on a trip / a journey / an excursion [ɪkˋskɝʒən] / a hike　旅行 / 遠足 / 健行 (從甲地到乙地)
be on business　　出差 (從甲地到乙地)
be on a mission　　出任務 (從甲地到乙地)
be on a diet　　節食 (從某時節食到某時)
be on fire　　著火 (從某時燒到某時)
be on the air　　在電臺 / 電視臺播放中 (從某時到某時)
be on vacation　　渡假 (美) = be on holiday　渡假 (英) (從某時渡假到某時)

例　Dad is at duty and won't be back until tomorrow morning. (✗)
→ Dad is on duty and won't be back until tomorrow morning. (✓)
老爸正在值班，要到明天早上才會回家。

There are doctors and nurses on call around the clock at the ER (emergency room). (✓)　急診室 24 小時都有醫生和護士待命。

Peter and his family are on vacation on a small island off the coast of Florida.　彼得與家人正在佛羅里達州外海的一個小島上渡假。

The program will be in the air (在天空中) at 8 p.m. (✗)
→ The program will be on the air (廣播) at 8 p.m. (✓)
本節目將於晚上 8 點播出。

小試身手

1. 房子著火了！快打 119！
The house is _____ _____ ! Call 119—hurry!

2. 下週三我就會在度假中。
I will be _____ _____ next Wednesday.

Ans 1. on; fire　2. on; vacation / holiday

Unit 182　如何連接兩個句子？

兩句之間只有逗點，無連接詞連接，是錯誤的結構，
如：Ben forgot about Elaine's birthday, this made her angry. (✕)
改正方式有以下四種：

1 將逗點刪除，改成句點，形成兩個獨立的句子，即：

例　Ben forgot about Elaine's birthday.
This / That / It made her angry. (✓)　班忘了伊蓮的生日。這讓她很生氣。

2 將逗點保留，之後 this 改成具有連接詞功能的關係代名詞 which，引導形容詞子句，修飾之前的主要子句，使兩句形成連接關係，即：

例　Ben forgot about Elaine's birthday, which made her angry.
　　　　　主要子句　　　　　　　　　　形容詞子句
班忘了伊蓮的生日。這讓她很生氣。

3 用連接詞連接兩句，即：

例　Ben forgot about Elaine's birthday, and this / that / it made her angry. (✓)

或：Ben forgot about Elaine's birthday, so this / that / it made her angry. (✓)

或：Because Ben forgot about Elaine's birthday, this / that / it made her angry. (✓)　班忘了伊蓮的生日。因此這讓她很生氣。

注意 不可同時使用兩個連接詞連接兩句，即：

Because Ben forgot about Elaine's birthday, ~~so~~ this / that / it made her angry. (×)

4 使用分號 (;) 連接兩句，即：

例 Ben forgot about Elaine's birthday; this / that / it made her angry.
班忘了伊蓮的生日。這使她很生氣。

小試身手

1. The man has long legs. This helps him run fast.
   提示 使用 which 引導的形容詞子句，使兩句形成連接關係。
   The man has ＿＿＿＿＿＿＿＿＿＿＿＿＿＿＿＿＿＿＿＿＿ run fast.

2. 提示 用 so 改寫上列句子。
   The man has ＿＿＿＿＿＿＿＿＿＿＿＿＿＿＿＿＿＿＿＿＿ run fast.

Ans 1. long legs, which helps him
2. long legs (,) so this helps him

Unit 183 如何使用現在完成式 the present perfect tense (have / has + 過去分詞)？

a 現在完成式可單獨存在，譯成「已經／曾經……」，條件是現在完成式不可與某個明確的過去時間副詞或副詞片語並用。

例 I have finished all my work this afternoon. (×)
　　　　　　　　　　　　　　過去時間副詞片語

I have met him five years ago. (×)
　　　　　　　過去時間副詞片語

Dad has called me then. (×)
　　　　　　　過去時間副詞

上列句子改正如下：

1 刪除句中的過去時間副詞或副詞片語，保留現在完成式。

例 I have finished all my work. (✓)
= I have (already) finished all my work.

= I have finished all my work (now).
我(現在)已經把所有工作做完了。
I have been there (before). (✓)　我曾過去那裡。
Dad has (already) called me. (✓)　老爸已經打了電話給我。

2 保留句中的過去時間副詞或副詞片語，將現在完成式改成過去式，即：

例　I finished all my work this afternoon. (✓)
　　　過去式　　　　　　過去時間副詞片語
今天下午我把所有的工作都做完了。

I was there | two years ago |.
　　　　　　| yesterday |
　　　　　　| in 2020 |

兩年前／昨天／2020 年我在那裡。

Dad called me this morning / at 9 a.m.
今天早上／上午 9 點老爸打電話給我。

b　現在完成式與現在式並用。過去完成式與過去式並用。

例　I had sprained my left ankle, and it still hurts. (✗)
　　　過去完成式　　　　　　　　　　　　　　現在式

→ I had sprained my ankle, and it still hurt yesterday.
　　過去完成式　　　　　　　　　　　　過去式
我的左腳踝扭傷了，昨天仍會痛。

或：I have sprained my left ankle, and it still hurts now. (✓)
　　　現在完成式　　　　　　　　　　　　　　現在式
我的左腳踝扭傷了，現在仍會痛。

或：I sprained my left ankle two months ago, and it still hurts now. (✓)
　　　過去式　　　　　　　過去時間副詞片語

兩個月前我把左腳踝扭傷了，現在仍會痛。

CH 4

常見卻易用錯的單字／片語／句型

197

小試身手

選出錯誤的句子。

Ⓐ Judy was there at the car accident scene this morning.
Ⓑ I had hurt my wrist, and I still felt the pain yesterday.
Ⓒ My friend has played the piano for five years; she still plays it now.
Ⓓ Tony had lost his toy, and he is still looking for it.

Ans Ⓓ

Unit 184 如何使用過去完成式 the past perfect tense (had + 過去分詞)？

a 過去完成式 (had + 過去分詞) 不可單獨存在。

例 The train had left. (✗)　火車已經離開了。

b 過去完成式必須與過去式並存。先發生的動作用過去完成式，後發生的動作用過去式。

例 Jimmy said that the train had left. (✓)　吉米說火車已經離開了。
　　　　過去式　　　　　過去完成式

By the time we got to / arrived at the station, the train had left. (✓)
　　　　　　　過去式　　　　　　　　　　　　　　　過去完成式

等到我們趕到 / 抵達車站時，火車已經離開了。

c 只要有明確的過去時間副詞或副詞片語出現時，句中動詞只能用過去式。

例 Jimmy said (that) the train had left　at 5 p.m. (✗)
　　　　　　　　　　過去完成式　過去時間

→ Jimmy said the train left　at 5 p.m. (✓)
　　　　　　　過去式　過去時間

或: Jimmy said the train had left. (✓)

吉米說火車於下午五點離開。

Anna told me (that) she had met Peter yesterday morning. (✗)
　　　　　　　　　　　過去完成式　　　　　　過去時間

→ Anna told me she met Peter yesterday morning. (✓)
　　　　　　　　　　過去式

或:Anna told me she had met Peter. (✓)
安娜告訴我她昨天早上見過彼得。

小試身手

Lynn ate her breakfast at seven thirty. Lynn left for school at eight.
提示 用 before 合併句子。
Lynn had _____ she _____.

> Ans eaten her breakfast before; left for school

Unit 185　如何使用比較級句構 comparative structures?

a　比較對象要一致，否則形成錯誤比較。

例　The color of this car is different from that car.
　　　顏色　　　　　　　　　　　　　　車子
(✗，比較對象不一致)

→ The color of this car is different from the color of that car.
　　　顏色　　　　　　　　　　　　　　　顏色
(劣，比較對象一致，但 color 重複，car 亦重複)

→ The color of this car is different from that of that one. (✓)
　　　單數　　　　　　　　　　　　　　　　單數
這輛車的顏色與那輛不同。

The engine of this car is more powerful than the engine of that one. (劣，engine 重複)

→ The engine of this car is more powerful than that of that one. (✓)
這輛車的引擎馬力要比那一輛 (的引擎) 大。

CH 4　常見卻易用錯的單字／片語／句型

199

Students of this school study harder than that school.
　　　　　　學生　　　　　　　　　　　　學校
(✗，比較對象不一致)

→ Students of this school study harder than students of that school.
　　　　　　學生　　　　　　　　　　　　　　　　學生
(劣，students 重複)

→ Students of this school study harder than those of that school. (✓)
　　　　　　複數　　　　　　　　　　　　　　　複數
這所學校的學生比那所學校的（學生）用功多了。

The report Ed wrote was much better than the report I wrote.
(劣，report 重複)

→ The report Ed wrote was much better than the one I wrote. (✓)
艾德寫的報告比我寫的好。

b 同範圍的比較：
比較句構中，若比較的對象屬於相同的範圍，為避免與自己比較，than 之後有以下變化：

例 David is more diligent than any student in his class. (✗)
大衛比他班上任何學生（包括他自己）都用功。（不合邏輯）

David is more diligent than all the students in his class. (✗)
大衛比他班上所有學生（包括他自己）都用功。（不合邏輯）

David is more diligent than anyone in his class. (✗)
大衛比他班上任何人（包括他自己）都用功。

以上句子應改正如下：

David is more diligent than any other student in his class. (✓)
= David is more diligent than all the other students in his class.
= David is more diligent than anyone else in his class.
大衛比他班上任何學生（不包括他自己）都用功。

c 不同範圍的比較：
在不同的範圍比較時，不會產生與自己相比較的狀態，故 than 之後接 "any + 單數名詞"、"all the + 複數名詞" 或 "anyone" 均可。

例 John and I are in the same class. He is not the best student in our class, but he is better than any other student in Mary's class.
(✗，in my class 與 in Mary's class 是兩個不同範圍)

→ John and I are in the same class He is not the best student in our class, but he is better than any student / all the students / anyone in Mary's class. (✓)

約翰與我同班。在我們班上他並不是最好的學生，但他比瑪麗班上的任何學生／全部學生／任何人都厲害。

小試身手

1. 我哥比我家所有成員都高。
   My brother is ＿＿＿＿＿＿＿ members in my family.

2. 我的房子比隔壁社區的任何房子都大。
   My house is ＿＿＿＿＿＿＿ house in the next neighborhood.

Ans 1. taller than all the other　2. bigger than any

Unit 186　如何使用最高級的句構 superlatives？

請注意以下最高級句型的句構：

例 Tokyo is the largest city in Japan, and Yokohama is the second larger. (✗)

→ Tokyo is the largest city in Japan, and Yokohama is the second largest. (✓)　東京是日本最大的城市，橫濱則是第二大。

= Yokohama is the largest city in Japan, second only to Tokyo.
橫濱是日本最大的城市，僅次於東京。

小試身手

臺北是臺灣最大的城市，臺中則是第二大。
Taipei is the (l)＿＿＿＿ city in Taiwan; Taichung is the ＿＿＿＿ ＿＿＿＿.

Ans largest; second; largest

201

Unit 187　he who、one who、those who、people who 怎麼用？

表「凡是……的人」，可使用 he who... / one who... / those who... / people who...

例　He who is optimistic is healthy in both body and mind. (✓)
　　主詞　形容詞子句　動詞　主詞補語

= One who is optimistic is healthy in both body and mind.

= Those who are optimistic are healthy in both body and mind.

= People who are optimistic are healthy in both body and mind.

凡是樂觀的人身心都很健康。

小試身手

凡是行善的人總是帶給他人喜樂。
_____ _____ practice kindness always bring joy to others.

Ans　Those / People; who

Unit 188　whoever、whomever 怎麼用？

whoever 等於 anyone who（任何……的人），who 是關係代名詞，在所引導的形容詞子句中作主詞，之後接動詞。whomever 等於 anyone whom（任何被……的人），whom 亦是關係代名詞，在所引導的形容詞子句中作受詞，換言之，whom 之後接主詞，再接及物動詞或介詞，使 whom 作其受詞。

例　Give this money to whomever need it. (✗)
　→ Give this money to anyone whom needs it.
　　　　　　　　　　　　受詞　　vt.

(✗，needs 之前應有主詞)

→ Give this money to anyone who needs it. (✔)
　　　　　　　　　　　　　主詞　　vt.

= Give this money to whoever needs it.
　　　　　　　　　　　　動詞

把這筆錢送給任何需要它的人。

The boss will hire who~~ev~~er I recommend. (✗)
　　　　　　　　　　　　　　　vt.

→ The boss will hire anyone who I recommend. (✗)
　　　　　　　　　　　　　　主詞　　vt.

→ The boss will hire anyone whom I recommend. (✔)
　　　　　　　　　　　　　　受詞　　　vt.

= The boss will hire whomever I recommend.

老闆會僱用我推薦的任何人。

小試身手

向你最信任的人尋求建議是重要的。

It is important to seek advice from _____ _____ you trust most.

Ans anyone; whom

Notes

Chapter 5

Unit 189 >>> Unit 204

> 生活用語類

與外國朋友聊天時，常因為表達不夠清楚而需要一再重述嗎？
想跟外國朋友談天說地，一句話到了嘴邊卻常卡住怕說錯嗎？
好好地跟外國朋友說話，卻老是因為講錯話被笑嗎？
如果這些症狀很常發生，小心你已經變成「詞不達意魔人」！

本章節蒐集最常見到的口語表達小謬誤，幫你揪出最容易踩雷的英文常用語，讓你講話不再卡卡，變身「英語口說達人」！

Unit 189 「幸會」是 Nice to meet you. 或 Nice meeting you.?

與人初次見面時，應說 "(It's) Nice to meet you."，相當於中文「幸會」。與初次見面的人寒暄一陣子後，要道別時，應說 "(It's) Nice meeting you."，相當於中文「這次的相見很棒」。

例 Jane: Fred, this is Mary. Mary, this is Fred.
　Fred: Nice meeting you, Mary. (✗)
Mary: Nice meeting you, too, Fred. (✗)
→ Jane: Fred, this is Mary. Mary, this is Fred.
　Fred: Nice to meet you, Mary. (✓)
Mary: Nice to meet you too, Fred. (✓)

阿　珍：佛瑞德，這位是瑪麗。瑪麗，這位是佛瑞德。
佛瑞德：幸會，瑪麗。
瑪　麗：我也很高興見到你，佛瑞德。

Peter: It's getting late. I gotta be going. Nice meeting you. Bye. (✓)
David: Nice meeting you, too. Take care. (✓)

彼得：天色晚了，我得走了。這次的相見很棒。再見。
大衛：我也一樣。保重。

小試身手

Ⓐ It's nice to meet you.　Ⓑ Nice meeting you.

　Ted: Hi, Linda. I'm Ted. ＿1＿ I've heard so much about you.
Linda: Hi, Ted. Likewise. I'd like to chat with you and get to know you more. But something came up, and I really have to go now. I'm sorry. Let's chat some other time. ＿2＿
　Ted: OK. See you later!

Ans 1. Ⓐ　2. Ⓑ

Unit 190 「當老師不容易」是 As a teacher is not easy. 或 Being a teacher is not easy.?

a
表示「當老師不容易」，不可說：As a teacher is not easy. (×)

理由 as a teacher 是介詞 as (表「當」，作為) 引導的介詞片語，不能作主詞。

應說：Being a teacher is not easy. (✓)

理由 動名詞或動名詞片語視作名詞，可當主詞，且要用單數動詞。

例 Learn English is a lot of fun. (×)

理由 learn 是動詞，不能當主詞，故應改成動名詞 learning，

即：Learning English is a lot of fun. 學英文很有趣。

b as a teacher 之前可置動詞 work，即：

例 The man works as an English teacher in that school. 那位男士在那所學校擔任英文老師。

小試身手

當職業婦女是非常具有挑戰性的。

_____ a working mom _____ very challenging.

Ans Being; is

Unit 191 「我的職業是教學」是 My job is a teacher. 或 My job is teaching.?

a
主詞是人時，be 動詞之後的名詞亦必須是人。主詞不是人時，be 動詞之後的名詞當然也不是人。
(看來我是人，不是個東西，哈！)

例 John is a soldier. (✓) 約翰是個軍人。
　　人　　　　人

The book is a good read. （✓，此處 read 是名詞，指「讀物」）
　　　物　　　　　　物

這本書是本值得看的好書。

故下列句子是錯誤的：

My job is a teacher. （✗）
　　非人　　　人

→ My job is teaching. （✓）　我的職業是教學。
　　非人　　非人

或：I'm a teacher. （✓）　我是個老師。
　　人　　　人

b　不過儘管主詞是人，有時亦可用物作主詞補語。

例　Thanks for the coffee. You are such a peach.
　　　　　　　　　　　　　人　　　　　　物

（✓，peach 是「桃子」，此處指「好人」）

= Thanks for the coffee. You are such a nice person.

謝謝你給我這杯咖啡。你人真好。

That guy is a pest. (pest 是「害蟲」，此處指「討厭的人」)
那個傢伙是個討厭鬼。

小試身手

My wife is (a salesperson / to sell clothes).
Her job is (a salesperson / selling clothes).

Ans a salesperson; selling clothes

Unit 192　job、work、career 怎麼用？

a　job 指「職場上的工作」、「職業」，是可數名詞。
　　work 則指「一般要做的工作」，為不可數名詞。

208

例 I found a work at a bank. (✗)
→ I found a job at a bank. (✓)
我在一家銀行找到了一份工作。

What's your job? (✓)
What's your occupation?
= What line of work are you in?　您是幹哪一行的 / 您的職業是什麼？

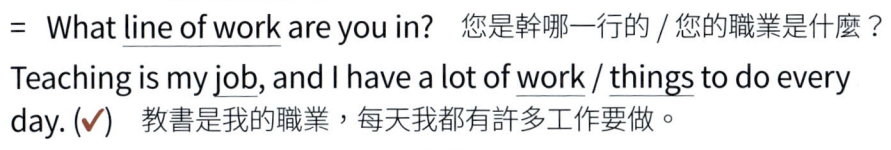

Teaching is my job, and I have a lot of work / things to do every day. (✓)　教書是我的職業，每天我都有許多工作要做。

What are you going to do after job? (✗)
→ What are you going to do after work? (✓)　下班後你要做什麼？

Peter is at job now. (✗)
→ Peter is at work now. (✓)　彼得現在正在上班。

Lucy has been out of job for half a year. (✗)
→ Lucy has been out of work / jobless for half a year. (✓)
露西失業已有半年了。

b career 指「終身的職業」。

例 Mr. Li worked as an English teacher soon after he left the military in 2001, and has remained so ever since. Teaching English is his career.
2001 年李先生自軍中退役後沒多久就當了英文老師。從此就未換過工作。教英文已成了他的終身職業。

小試身手

| 1 | Dan's (work / job / career) is cooking. He is a chef. |
| 2 | My dad has been a soldier for twenty years. It is his lifelong (work / job / career). |

Ans 1. job　2. career

Unit 193 「電話是打來找你的」是 It's your telephone. 或 It's your phone call.?

a
It's your ~~telephone~~ / ~~phone~~. Go answer it. (✗)
這是你的電話機 / 手機。去接它。
→ It's your telephone call / phone call. Go answer it. (✓)
這是你的電話。去接它。

b
Thank you for your ~~telephone~~ / ~~phone~~. (✗)
謝謝你的電話機。
→ Thank you for your phone call. (✓)
= Thank your for calling. (更佳)
謝謝你的來電。

小試身手

這通電話是找你的。你要接嗎？
The (phone / phone call) is for you. Are you going to take it?

Ans phone call

Unit 194 「手機沒電了」是 My cell phone has no electricity. 或 My cell phone ran out of battery.?

a 表「我的手機沒電了。」不可說：

例
My cell phone has ~~no~~ electricity. (✗，洋涇濱英語)
應說：My cell phone is completely discharged. (✓，正式)
或：My cell phone ran out of battery / power. (✓)
也可說：My phone is out of juice. (✓，口語)
= My phone is out of battery.

210

= My phone died.
= My phone is dead.

b 表示電池仍有電，可說：

例 That battery is still good.　那顆電池仍有電。

補充 表示電池沒電，可說 This battery is dead.　這顆電池沒電了。

小試身手

你的手機電池還有電嗎？我的沒電了。

Is your cell phone battery still ＿＿＿? Mine is ＿＿＿.

Ans good; dead

Unit 195 「你方便……嗎」是 Are you convenient to V? 或 Is it convenient for you to V?

a convenient 是形容詞，表「方便的」，指從事某事「很方便」，不可修飾人。

中文：你今天下午方便(有空)嗎？

英譯：Will you be convenient this afternoon? (✗)

→ Will you be available / free this afternoon? (✓)
　　　人

= Will you have time this afternoon?
　　　人

注意 此處 available、free 是形容詞，表「有空／方便的」，修飾人。

b convenient 多出現下列句構：

Is it convenient for 人 to V?　某人從事……方便嗎？

例 Are you convenient to give me a ride now? (✗)

→ Is it convenient for you to give me a ride now? (✓)

你現在方便可以讓我搭個便車嗎？

I'm not convenient to see you now. (✗)

→ It isn't convenient for me to see you now. (✓)　我現在不方便見你。

211

c. **convenient** 亦可修飾表事物的名詞或動名詞。

例 For most students, biking to school is far faster and more convenient than walking (to school). (✓)
對大部分學生而言，騎自行車上學要比走路上學快並方便得多。

City life is more convenient than country life.
都市生活要比鄉間生活方便。

小試身手

你今天晚上方便跟我談談嗎？（使用 convenient）
_____ talk with me tonight?

Ans Is it convenient for you to

Unit 196 「今天星期幾」是 What day is today? 或 What date is today?

a 表「今天星期幾？」，正確的英文說法如下：

例 A: What day is it　today? (✓)
　　　　　　　主詞　副詞

B: It is Friday (today).
= It's Friday (today).
= Friday.

A：今天是星期幾？
B：(今天是) 星期五。

上列問句也可改成：

A: What day is today?
　　　　　　主詞

B: (Today is) Friday.

A：今天是星期幾？
B：(今天是) 星期五。

b 表「今天是幾月幾號？」，正確的英文說法如下：

例 A: What is today's date? (✔)
= What's today's date?
= What is the date today?
= What's the date today?
B: (It's) July 18th. （今天是）7月18日。

注意 英美人士為了避免 day 與 date 造成聽覺的混淆，故不會說：
What date is it today?（聽起來太像：What day is it today?）

小試身手

A: _____
B: Thursday.
Ⓐ What day is it?　　　Ⓑ What's today's date?
Ⓒ What's today's day?　Ⓓ What date is it today?

Ans Ⓐ

Unit 197　「你是在跟我開玩笑嗎」是 Are you kidding me? 還是 Are you joking me?

kid 可作及物或不及物動詞，表（對某人）「開玩笑」；joke 可作不及物動詞，表「開玩笑」，之後不得接受詞。

例 A: I'm going out with a famous actress.
B: You must be joking me! (✗)
→ You must be kidding me! (✔)
= You must be kidding!
= You must be joking!
= You've gotta be kidding (me)!
A：我現在正跟一位知名的女演員約會。
B：你一定在開玩笑吧！

> **小試身手**
>
> A: These chicken wings taste amazing.
> B: _____ They are terrible! (選錯的)
> Ⓐ Stop kidding me!
> Ⓑ Are you joking me?
> Ⓒ You have to be kidding me!
> Ⓓ You've gotta joke!
>
> Ans Ⓑ

Unit 198 「不知道」是 have no idea 或 have no ideas?

a have no idea 等於 don't know，表「不知道」，之後直接接疑問詞 (who、whom、where、what、how...) 引導的名詞子句或名詞片語 (how to...、where to...)。

例
I have no ideas about what we should do next. (✗)
→ I have no idea what we should do next. (✓)
= I don't know what we should do next.
我不知道接下來我們要做什麼。

I have no idea what to do next. (✓)
我不知道接下來要做什麼。

Sam has no idea how to solve the problem. (✓)
山姆不知道如何解決這個問題。

b have no idea about + 名詞 / 代名詞　對……不知道

例　I have no idea about the project.　有關這項企畫我一無所知。

小試身手

1. 我不知道要怎麼把歌唱好。
   I have ＿＿＿ ＿＿＿ ＿＿＿ to sing well.

2. Judy doesn't know anything about the birthday surprise.
   提示 用 ... has no idea... 改寫句子。
   Judy ＿＿＿＿＿＿＿＿＿＿＿＿＿＿＿＿＿ the birthday surprise.

Ans　1. no; idea; how　2. has no idea about

Unit 199　"do you think" 當插入語要怎麼用？

a　do you think 與 疑問詞（who、what、when、where 等）引導的名詞子句並用時，疑問詞應置 do you think 之前。

b　凡以助動詞 do、does、did 起首的問句，其答句必以 yes / no 起首。

例　A: Do you think where he lives? (×)
B: Yes, I do. (×)
A：你認為他住在哪裡嗎？
B：是的，我認為他住在哪裡。

上列對話不合邏輯，應改成：

A: Where do you think he lives? (✓)
B: I think he lives there. / I don't know. (✓)
A：你認為他住在那裡嗎？
B：我認為他住在那裡。／ 我不知道。

Do you think who can do it? (×)
→ Who do you think can do it? (✓)　你認為誰可以做這件事？

Do you think who you are? (×)
→ Who do you think you are? (✓)　你以為你算老幾？

215

但:A: Do you know who can do it? (✓)
B: Yes, I do. / No, I don't. (✓)
A：你知道誰會做這件事？
B：是的，我知道。/ 不，我不知道。

小試身手

Where will the concert take place?
提示 加入 do you think 改寫句子。
Where _____ take place?

Ans do you think the concert will

Unit 200 「視若無睹」是 turn a blind eye to 或 turn one's blind eyes to?

在敘述對某事「視若無睹」時，應說 "turn a blind eye to + 事物"：

例 Jerry turns his blind eyes to his wife's faults. (✗)
→ Jerry turns a blind eye to his wife's faults. (✓)
= Jerry is blind to his wife's faults.
傑瑞對妻子的過錯視若無睹。

小試身手

Betty didn't do anything about her son's lies.
提示 用 turn a blind eye 改寫句子。
Betty _____ her son's lies.

Ans turned a blind eye to

Unit 201 「充耳不聞」是 turn a deaf ear to 或 turn one's deaf ears to?

在敘述對某事「充耳不聞」時，應說 "turn a deaf ear to + 事物"：

例 Paul turns his deaf ears to my advice. (✗)
→ Paul turns a deaf ear to my advice. (✓)
= Paul is deaf to my advice.　保羅對我的勸告充耳不聞。

小試身手

The father ignored the loud noises his child was making.
提示 用 turn a deaf ear 改寫句子。

The father _____ the loud noises his child was making.

Ans　turned a deaf ear to

Unit 202 "how to + V" 要怎麼用?

"how to + V" 是名詞片語，視作名詞，在句中作及物動詞的受詞，不可自成一個問句。

不可說：How to spell that word? (✗)
應　說：Could you tell me how to spell that word? (✓)
您可否告訴我那個字是怎麼拼的？
(本問句中 how to spell that world 作及物動詞 tell 的直接受詞)
或: How do you spell that word? (✓)　那個字您是怎麼拼的？
(本問句中 you 是主詞 that word 作及物動詞 spell 的受詞)

217

小試身手

I need to know: How do you pronounce the word?
提示 用 ... how to... 合併句子。
I need to know _____.

Ans how to pronounce the word

Unit 203 「一小時之後」是 in an hour 或 after an hour?

a "in + 一段時間" 指從現在算起「一段時間之後」。

例 I'll be back after an hour. (✗)
→ I'll be back in an hour. (✓)　一個小時後我就會回來。
The meeting will take place after two minutes. (✗)
→ The meeting will take place in two minutes. (✓)
會議會在兩分鐘後召開。

I'll graduate from college | in two years / two years from now |. (✓)

兩年後我就大學畢業了。

b "after + 一段時間" 指過去或未來某事發生之後「經過一段時間」。

例 Take this medicine tonight. If you still don't feel good after two days, go see a doctor immediately. (✓)
今晚就服用這個藥。兩天後你若仍感到不舒服就立刻去看醫生。

Jane and I met in 2020, and we got married in two years. (✗)
→ Jane and I met in 2020, and we got married | after two years / two years later |.
我和阿珍於 2020 年相識，兩年後我們便結婚了。

小試身手

1. Dennis _____ promoted to the manager of the company in three years.
  Ⓐ is Ⓑ was Ⓒ has been Ⓓ will be

2. Candy wanted to study all day, but she got bored _____ only two hours.
  Ⓐ at Ⓑ after Ⓒ before Ⓓ with

Ans 1. Ⓓ 2. Ⓑ

Unit 204 「身上沒帶錢」是 have no money with me 或 have no money on me?

表「某人身上沒帶錢」，

不可說：I have no money around me. (✗)
應　說：I have no money with me. (✓)
　　　= I have no money on me.
　　　= I don't have any money on me.
　　　= I don't have any money with me.
我身上沒帶錢。

小試身手

蓋瑞身上沒帶錢，所以我借他 500 元。
Gary had _____ _____ _____ him, so I lent him 500 dollars.

Ans no; money; with / on

Notes

實用文法篇

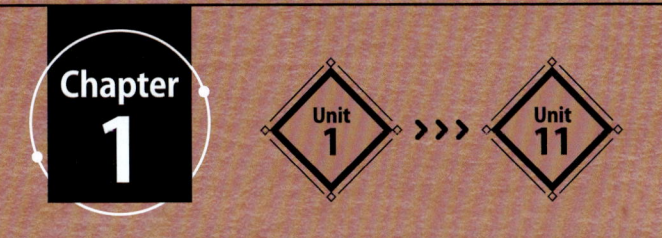

Chapter 1　Unit 1 >>> Unit 11

與時態相關的錯誤

「時態」是英文學習的基礎，但許多人會在這個簡單卻又複雜的領域迷失。其實，最大的挑戰來自於中英文思維的差異！

本章節教你如何正確使用時態，並找出那些常見的時態錯誤，提供清晰又實用的規則和範例。幫助你在時態的迷宮中找到精準的方向，能克服使用時態的障礙，讓你的英文句子更加流暢又正確！

Unit 1

大眾交通工具(如火車、高鐵、地鐵、公車、飛機等)按時刻表出發或到達時,多使用現在式

例 Our flight <u>will depart</u> at 8:30 a.m., so we must leave home at 5 a.m.
　　　　　　　未來式

(較不自然)

→ Our fight <u>departs</u> at 8:30 a.m., so we must leave home at 5 a.m. (佳)
　　　　　　現在式

我們的航班早上 8 點半出發,因此我們必須在 5 點出門。

例 The train <u>will arrive</u> at 10 p.m., so it's time for us to go to the
　　　　　　未來式

station now. (較不自然)

→ The train <u>arrives</u> at 10 p.m., so it's time for us to go to the
　　　　　　現在式

station now. (佳)

火車會在晚上 10 點到站,現在該是我們趕往車站的時候了。

當然,這些交通工具在不強調抵達或駛離的時間之下,可與任何時態並用,讀者並不需要死記。只要中文說得通,英文亦復如此。

例 Our flight <u>will take off</u> in ten minutes.
　　　　　　未來式

我們的班機將於十分鐘後起飛。

Our flight <u>has taken off</u>.　　我們的班機已起飛了。
　　　　　　現在完成式

Our flight <u>took off</u> on time.　　我們的班機(當時)準時起飛了。
　　　　　過去式

小試身手

公車下午 5 點發車,所以我們現在可以去車站了。

The bus _____ (leave) at 5 p.m., so we can go to the station now.

Ans　leaves

Unit 2　表示真理或現在仍存在的行動或狀況時，始終使用現在式

例　John studies hard.　約翰很用功。
　　　　現在式

　　In addition, he is gentle and polite.　此外，他溫文有禮。
　　　　　　　　　現在式

　　He wins my respect.　他贏得我的尊敬。
　　　現在式

小試身手

地球繞著太陽轉。

The Earth _____ (revolve) around the Sun.

Ans　revolves

Unit 3　中文有「(正)在……」時，英文就要使用進行式

句型如下：
主詞 + be 動詞 (am、are、is / was、were / will be) + 現在分詞 (V-ing)

a　現在進行式
　　句型：主詞 + am / are / is + 現在分詞 (V-ing)　現在正在……

例　I have dinner now. Call me again later. (✗)

→ I'm having dinner now. Call me again later. (✓)
　　現在進行式

我現在正在吃飯。稍後再打電話給我。

例　It rains hard at the moment. I suggest we stay here until it lets up. (✗)

→ It is raining hard at the moment. I suggest we stay here until it
　　現在進行式

lets up. (✓)　目前正在下大雨。我建議待在這裡直到雨停。

223

b 過去進行式

句型：主詞 + was / were + 現在分詞 (V-ing)　當時正在……

例 I wrote a letter when Dad entered the room. (✗)
　　過去式

老爹進入房間時，我寫信。（中文也不通順）

→ I was writing a letter when Dad entered the room. (✓)
　　過去進行式

老爹進入房間時，我正在寫信。／我正在寫信時，老爹就進入房間了。

例 John and his brother played video games when their mother
　　　　　　　　　　　　過去式

opened the door. (✗)

→ John and his brother were playing video games when their
　　　　　　　　　　　　　　過去進行式

mother opened the door. (✓)　媽媽開門時，約翰和他弟弟正在打電玩。

c 未來進行式

句型：主詞 + will be + 現在分詞 (V-ing)　將會在……

例 When you wake up tomorrow morning, honey, I will make
　　　　　　　　　　　　　　　　　　　　　　　　未來式

breakfast in the kitchen. (✗)

→ When you wake up tomorrow morning, honey,
I will be making breakfast in the kitchen. (✓)
　　未來進行式

親愛的，你明早醒來時，我將會在廚房裡弄早餐。

小試身手

1. 安妮正在看小說，這時便停電了。
Annie _____ (read) a novel when the power went out.

2. 你今晚到家時，我將會在打掃臥房。
When you arrive home tonight, I _____ (clean) the bedroom.

Ans　1. was reading　2. will be cleaning

Unit 4 條件句使用現在式，主要子句使用未來式

when（當）、if（如果）、once（一旦 = as soon as）、unless（除非）等連接詞所引導的副詞子句與主要子句並用時，這些副詞子句均只能使用現在式，主要子句則使用未來式。中文句子亦是如此。

中文：如果我將有錢，我將會買一輛跑車。(×，有兩個 will / 將，不通順)

→ 如果我有錢，就會買一輛跑車。(✓)

同理：If I will have money, I will buy a sports car. (×)
　　　　　未來式　　　　　　　未來式

→ If I have money, I will buy a sports car. (✓)
　　　現在式　　　　　　未來式

例 Unless you will tell me the truth, I will never forgive you. (×)
　　　　　未來式　　　　　　　　　　未來式

→ Unless you tell me the truth, I will never forgive you. (✓)
　　　　　現在式　　　　　　　　　未來式

除非你向我說實話，我將永遠不會原諒你。

小試身手

選出錯誤的句子。
Ⓐ If it rains tomorrow, we will cancel the picnic.
Ⓑ Unless you study hard, you will not pass the exam.
Ⓒ If Susan will call me, I will meet her at the café.
Ⓓ If they finish the project on time, they will receive a bonus.

Ans Ⓒ

Unit 5 現在完成式

句型：主詞 + have / has + 過去分詞　已經 / 曾經……

a 使用現在完成式時，助動詞 have / has 譯成「已經」，千萬不要出現表示過去的時間副詞或片語。

例　I have finished all the homework yesterday. (×)
　　　現在完成式

→ I have finished all the homework. (✓)
　　現在完成式

= I've already finished all the homework. (✓)

= I already finished my homework. (✓)
　　副詞　　過去式

我已經把所有的功課都做完了。

＊already 是副詞，表「已經」，可與現在完成式並用，也可直接與過去式動詞並用。

注意　句中只要出現表示過去的時間副詞或片語時，只能使用過去式動詞。

例　I finished all the homework yesterday.
　　過去式

我昨天把所有的功課都做完了。

例　I met Peter two days / months / years ago.
　　過去式

我兩天前／兩個月前／兩年前見到彼得。

例　David was born in 2013.　大衛出生於 2013 年。
　　　　過去式

b 現在完成式助動詞 have / has 亦可與副詞 before，形成下列結構：
主詞 + have / has + 過去分詞 + before　曾經……

例　I have read the book ever before. (×)

→ I have read the book before. In fact, I read it　 two years ago. (✓)
　　現在完成式　　　　　　　　　　　　　　過去式　表過去的時間副詞片語

我曾經看過這本書。事實上，我兩年前就拜讀過它。

c ever before 可用於現在完成式的問句或比較句中。

例　Did you read the book before? (×)

→ Have you ever read the book before? (✓)

= Have you read the book before? (✓)　你看過這本書嗎？

注意　ever 不可隨意用於現在完成式的肯定句中。

例　I have ever read the book. (✗)
　→ I have read the book before. (✓)　我曾看過這本書。
　但在比較句構中就可使用 ever 或 ever before。

例　John is the best student (that) I have ever taught.
　　　　最高級
　約翰是我教過最棒的學生。

例　John is studying much harder than ever.
　= John is studying much harder than ever before.
　約翰比以前用功多了。

CH 1 與時態相關的錯誤

小試身手

1. 重組：ever seen / Have you / before / a beautiful sunset / such
_____?

2. Eric _____ to a new house last month.
   Ⓐ moves　Ⓑ was moving　Ⓒ moved　Ⓓ has moved

3. 我們以前從未見過如此精彩的表演。
   We _____ (see) such an amazing performance before.

Ans　1. Have you ever seen such a beautiful sunset before
　　　2. Ⓒ　3. have never seen

Unit 6　過去完成式

句型：主詞 + had + 過去分詞　已經 / 曾經……

a　我們已知使用現在完成式的句子可單獨存在，但不得與表示過去的時間副詞或片語並用，即：

例　I have called Peter. (✓)
　現在完成式

　I have called Peter this morning. (✗)
　現在完成式　　過去時間副詞片語

227

只要句中出現表過去的時間副詞或片語，該句只能採過去式，即：

I called Peter this morning. 我今天早上已經打了電話給彼得。
　過去式　　　過去時間副詞片語

b 然而過去完成式不能單獨存在，一定要有過去式搭配。兩個動作都發生在過去時，先發生的動作採過去完成式，後發生的動作採過去式。

例 John had finished all the work. (✗) 約翰已經把所有工作都做完了。
　　　　過去完成式

→ John had finished all the work before he left the office. (✓)
　　　過去完成式　　　　　　　　　　　　　過去式
約翰離開公司前就已把所有的工作都做完了。
由上得知，過去完成式一定要與過去式搭配才有意義。

例 Jim says that he had been to Tokyo several times. (✗)
　　現在式　　　　過去完成式

→ Jim said that he had been to Tokyo several times. (✓)
　　過去式　　　　過去完成式
吉姆說他曾去過東京好幾次。

例 Trust me. I had called Peter first thing this morning. (✗)
　　　　　　過去完成式　　　　　　　過去時間副詞片語

→ Trust me. I called Peter first thing this morning. (✓)
　　　　　　過去式　　　　　　　過去時間副詞片語
相信我。我今天一大早就打電話給彼得了。

或:Trust me. I have called Peter. (✓)
　　　　　　　現在完成式
相信我。我已經打了電話給彼得。

注意 過去完成式亦可與介詞 by 引導的過去時間副詞片語並用。

例 By the time I got to the station, the train had left. (✓)
　　　　　　過去式　　　　　　　　過去完成式

= When I got to the station, the train had left. (✓)
　　　過去式　　　　　　　　過去完成式
等到我抵達車站時，火車已經離開了。

例 I had finished two thirds of the work by 3 p.m. yesterday.
　　　過去完成式　　　　　　　　　　　　過去時間副詞片語
到昨天下午 3 點時，這份工作我已完成了三分之二。

小試身手

1. We _____ our tickets before the movie started.
   Ⓐ had bought　　　Ⓑ have bought
   Ⓒ buy　　　　　　Ⓓ bought

2. 當我們抵達公車站時，公車已經開走了。
   By the time we arrived at the bus stop, the bus _____ (leave).

Ans　1. Ⓐ　2. had left

Unit 7　未來完成式

句型：主詞 + will have + 過去分詞　將已……
未來完成式多與表到未來某時的時間為止的副詞片語或現在式副詞子句並用。

例 By 10 a.m. tomorrow, I will have finished the report.
　　　　　　　　　　　　　　未來完成式
到了明天上午 10 點，我將已完成這份報告。

例 By the time you show up, I will have left.
　　　現在式　　　　未來完成式
= When you show up, I will have left.
　　現在式　　　　未來完成式
你出現的時候，我將已離去了。

小試身手

1. By this time tomorrow, they _____ the contract.
   Ⓐ will have signed　　Ⓑ have signed
   Ⓒ will sign　　　　　Ⓓ are signing

2. The construction of the building will be completed in June.
提示 用未來完成式改寫句子。
The construction of the building ＿＿＿＿＿＿＿＿＿＿ by next June.

Ans 1. Ⓐ 2. will have been completed

Unit 8 現在完成進行式

句型：主詞 + have / has + been + 現在分詞　一直以來都在從事……

現在完成進行式與現在完成式均可表「一直都在從事……」，但前者表示所從事的動作未來還會持續下去，後者則表示動作持續到現在為止，未來可能會持續但也可能不再持續下去。

例 I have learned English for 10 years.
　　　現在完成式
我學英文已有 10 年了。（未來可能會持續學下去，也可能會終止學習）

比較 I have been learning English for 10 years.
　　　　現在完成進行式
我學英文已有 10 年了。（未來還會持續學英文）

求職面試時，面試官可能會提出下列問題：

Could you tell me about your English learning trip?
你可否告訴我我你學習英文的歷程？

你的答句若是：

I have learned English for 10 years.　我學了十年英文。

而另一位應徵者的答句是：

I have been learning English for 10 years.　我已經學英文十年了。

面試官極有可能勾選這位應徵者，而非你。

例 I have lived in Taipei for 20 years, but I'm sick of the hustle and
　　現在完成式
bustle of city life. So, I've decided to move to the countryside early next year.
我住在臺北已有二十年，但是我很厭惡都市生活的熙攘與喧鬧。因此我已決定明年初要搬到鄉下去。

例 I have been living in Taipei for 20 years, and I enjoy the conveniences
　　　現在完成進行式
of city life. To some degree, Taipei is my hometown.
我住在臺北已有二十年，很喜歡都市生活的諸多方便。就某程度而言，臺北就是我的故鄉。

小試身手

他們從上週開始一直在進行這個專案。

They _____ (work) on this project since last week.

Ans　have been working

Unit 9　過去完成進行式

句型：主詞 + had been + 現在分詞　過去一直都在從事……

如同過去完成式一樣，過去完成進行式不能單獨存在，一定要與過去式並用。

例　Mr. Johnson had been teaching English for more than 20 years.
　　　　　　　　　過去完成進行式
(✗，句中無過去式動詞襯托)

→ Mr. Johnson told me that he had been teaching English for more
　　　　　　　 過去式　　　　　　　過去完成進行式
than 20 years. (✓，有過去式動詞 told 襯托)
強森先生告訴我他一直教英文有二十多年了。

→ Mr. Johnson had been working as an English teacher for more
　　　　　　　　過去完成進行式
than 20 years before he retired. (✓)
　　　　　　　　　　過去式
強森先生退休前一直擔任英文老師達二十多年。

小試身手

選出錯誤的句子。

Ⓐ Tina had been studying for three hours before she took a break.
Ⓑ They had been living in London for ten years when they decided to move.
Ⓒ Jimmy had been working at the company for two years.
Ⓓ By the time we arrived at the station, the train had already left.

Ans Ⓒ

Unit 10　未來完成進行式

句型：主詞 + will have been + 現在分詞　將會一直從事……
未來完成進行式表示某動作將會一直持續下去到未來某時，之後該動作還會持續下去。

例　By October 8, I will have been working for my company for 5 years.
到 10 月 8 日為止，我在公司服務將滿 5 年。

例　When I turn 30, I will have been studying Japanese for 10 years.
我滿 30 歲時，學日文將達 10 年了。

小試身手

再過兩個小時，我們將已經連續駕駛八個小時了。
Two hours from now, we ＿＿＿＿ (drive) for eight hours straight.

Ans will have been driving

Unit 11 "be 動詞 + 形容詞" 通常不可能使用進行式，即無 "be + being + 形容詞" 的用法

例　Mary is being beautiful. (✗)　瑪麗正在美麗。(✗，中文無此說法)
　　　　　　　 adj.
　→ Mary is beautiful. (✓)　瑪麗很美麗。

例　Peter is being an English teacher. (✗)
　　　　　　　　　　　　n.
彼得正在是英文老師。(✗，中文無此說法)
　→ Peter is an English teacher. (✓)　彼得是英文老師。

例　We were being young and naive 10 years ago. (✗)
十年前我們正年少又無知。(✗，中文無此說法)
　→ We were young and naive 10 years ago. (✓)
十年前我們年少又無知。

注意 有些形容詞可使用 "主詞 + am / are / is / was / were + being + 形容詞" 的結構。

例　John is usually polite, but for some reason he is being rude now.
約翰通常挺有禮貌的，但不知怎的他現在正在耍粗魯。

例　We all know Paul is a naughty boy, and he is being naughty again.
我們都知道保羅是個搗蛋鬼，他又在搗蛋了。

例　Luke has a crush on Jane. Look, he is being so gentle with her.
小魯對小珍很有好感。瞧，他正對她獻殷勤呢。

使用以上這種結構 (be + being + adj.) 的形容詞有個特性，即它們都是某人的個性 (如 foolish, generous, shy, funny, rude, gentle, naughty, selfish 等)。我們平常描述這個人時，都採 "be + adj." 的結構，如：

Paul is selfish / shy / funny…　保羅很自私 / 害羞 / 搞笑……。

但在某刻保羅流露出上述個性的「行為」時，就可說：

Paul is being selfish / shy / funny…(again).
保羅 (又) 在流露自私 / 害羞 / 搞笑……的個性了。

233

小試身手

選出正確的句子。

Ⓐ Emily is being beautiful tonight.
Ⓑ My brother was just being funny at the party.
Ⓒ Jack is being a doctor for now.
Ⓓ The weather is being nice today.

Ans Ⓑ

Chapter 2

Unit 12 >>> Unit 32

> 與否定句相關的錯誤

「否定句」聽起來簡單,但其實有不少藏在細節裡的陷阱!很多人會在這個部分踩到雷,尤其是當句子結構變得複雜時。

別擔心!本章節全面剖析與否定句相關的各種誤區,從基礎否定句到進階否定倒裝句等的實用技巧,逐步幫你拆解每個語法疑惑。你就能避免常犯的錯誤,輕鬆表達出更精準的英文!

Unit 12 初學者常犯有關否定句的錯誤

初學英文的朋友常會造下列的否定句：

例 I <u>not</u> <u>have</u> any money. (×)
　　　副詞　動詞
我沒有錢。

上列英文句中，not 是副詞，不能直接置動詞前修飾該動詞。須在 not 之前先置助動詞 do、does 或 did，形成 do not / does not / did not + 原形動詞。即：

I <u>not</u> <u>have</u> any money. (×)
　　　　現在式動詞

→ I <u>do not</u> <u>have</u> any money. (✓)　我沒有錢。
　　　　　　　原形動詞

例 John <u>not</u> <u>lives</u> here. (×)
　　　　　　　現在式動詞

→ John <u>does not</u> <u>live</u> here. (✓)　約翰不住在這裡。
　　　　　　　　　原形動詞

例 Peter <u>not</u> <u>handed in</u> his homework this morning. (×)
　　　　　　過去式片語動詞

→ Peter <u>did not</u> <u>hand in</u> his homework this morning. (✓)
　　　　　　　　　原形片語動詞

彼得今天早上沒有交作業。

小試身手

重組：to / did / the party / go / not

Maria _____.

Ans did not go to the party

Unit 13　助動詞後面加 not

句中若已有一般助動詞（如 can、could、may、might、will、would、should）或完成式助動詞（have、has、had，表「已經」）時，直接在這類助動詞之後置 not 即可。

肯定句：I can do it.　這件事我做得來。
→ I can not do it. (✗，應改成 cannot)
→ I cannot do it. (✓)
= I can't do it. (✓)　這件事我做不來。

例　You may not go out after dark. (✓，非 maynot)
　= You must not go out after dark. (✓)　你不可以天黑後外出。
　＊may 亦可以表示「可能」。

例　John may or may not attend the party.
　約翰可能會參加這個派對，但也可能不會。

例　You should not do anything against your conscience.
　= You shouldn't do anything against your conscience.
　＊conscience [ˈkɑnʃəns] n. 良心
　你不應做任何違背你良心的事。

例　I will not be at home tonight.
　= I won't be at home tonight.　我今晚不在家。
　比較 I won't be home tonight.　我今晚不會回家。

例　David is worried because his son has not returned home yet.
　= David is worried because his son hasn't returned home yet.
　大衛很擔心，因為他兒子還沒回家。

小試身手

將以下句子用否定句改寫。

1　Nancy can finish the project by Friday.

2. They should attend the meeting tomorrow.
_____

> Ans　1. Nancy cannot / can't finish the project by Friday.
> 　　　2. They should not / shouldn't attend the meeting tomorrow.

Unit 14　用 not 還是 no？

已知 not 是副詞，故不能修飾名詞，只有形容詞方可修飾名詞。故我們不可說：

例　I have not money. (✕)
　　動詞　副詞　名詞

若要改正本句，應將副詞 not 改為限定詞 no，視作形容詞，可修飾名詞，即：

I have no money. (✓)
動詞 形容詞 名詞

= I don't have any money. (✓)　我沒有錢。
　助動詞　動詞　形容詞

此時，有些讀者可能仍不懂下列句子是錯的：

I have not money. (✕)

理由是 have 之後有 not 時，have 是助動詞，have not 之後必接動詞的過去分詞形，以形成現在完成式，即：

have not + 過去分詞　尚未……

例　I have not finished my work yet. (✓)　我尚未完工。
　　　　　過去分詞

〈 小試身手 〉

Sammy has (not / no) idea about the meeting.

> Ans　no

Unit 15　not any 的用法

已知 not 是副詞，故 not 之後也可接形容詞 any，再接名詞。而 not any 就等於形容詞 no，之後接名詞。

例　There is not anyone here.
＝ There is no one here.　這裡沒有任何人。

例　I don't see any books on the desk.
＝ I see no books on the desk.　桌上我看不到任何一本書。

例　Not anyone knows the answer to the question. (✗)
→ No one knows the answer to the question. (✓)
沒有人知道這個問題的答案。

注意　not 需置於助動詞後，不可直接修飾主詞 anyone。

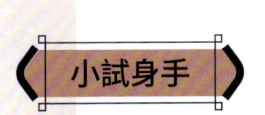

小試身手

There is not anyone in the classroom.
提示　用 No one 改寫句子。

Ans　No one is in the classroom.

Unit 16　It is no good 與 It is not good 意思不同

a　no good 等於 no use，表「沒有用」，由此得知，此處 good 是名詞，表「用途」，用於下列句構：
It is no good + V-ing　從事……是無用的
＝ It is no use + V-ing

239

例 It is no good to learn without thinking. (✗)
→ It is no good learning without thinking. (✓)
= It is no use learning without thinking. (✓)
= It is useless to learn without thinking. (✓)
= It is of no use to learn without thinking. (✓)
只顧學習卻不思考是沒用的。/ 學而不思則罔。

例 It is no use crying over spilled milk.
為濺出來的牛奶哭泣是無用的。/ 覆水難收。（諺語）

b　It is not good to V　……是不好的

例 It is not good taking advantage of someone's sympathy. (✗)
→ It is not good to take advantage of someone's sympathy. (✓)
利用某人的同情很不妥。

小試身手

抱怨天氣是沒有用的。

It is no good ＿＿＿＿ (complain) about the weather.

Ans　complaining

Unit 17　避免雙重否定

例 Paul doesn't know nothing about it. (✗，雙重否定)
→ Paul doesn't know anything about it. (✓)
= Paul knows nothing about it. (✓)　保羅對這件事一無所知。

例 I don't have no money. (✗，雙重否定)
→ I don't have any money. (✓)
= I have no money. (✓)　我沒有錢。

小試身手

選出錯誤的句子。
Ⓐ Jennie doesn't have any idea about the project.
Ⓑ There isn't any reason to worry.
Ⓒ Matt can't find no information about that topic.
Ⓓ Lisa knows nothing about cooking.

Ans Ⓒ

Unit 18　yet 與 already 做副詞的用法比較

a yet 須與 not 並用，採下列句型：
主詞 + have / has + not + 過去分詞 + yet　尚未 / 還未……
already 表「已經」，多用於肯定句中。

例　It's 1 a.m. now, and I haven't already finished my homework. (✗)
→ It's 1 a.m. now, and I haven't finished my homework yet. (✓)
現在是清晨 1 點了，而我還未做完功課。

b yet 亦可用於完成式疑問句中，表「已經」，採下列句型：
Have / Has + 主詞 + 過去分詞 + yet?

例　It's (already) 1 a.m. now. Have you finished your homework yet?
現在（已經）是清晨 1 點了。你已把功課做完了嗎？

注意　already 與 yet 均可用於完成式疑問句中，意思略有不同。

Have you finished your homework yet?
你已把功課做完了嗎？（我不知道實際的情況，故我在問你）

Have you already finished your homework?
你已把功課做完了吧？（我不知道實際的情況，但我猜想你大概已做完功課了）

c	have yet to + 原形動詞　至今尚未…… = have not + 過去分詞 + yet

例　We have yet decided how to deal with the problem. (✗)
　→ We have yet to decide how to deal with the problem. (✓)
　= We haven't decided how to deal with the problem yet. (✓)
　我們到目前為止尚未決定如何解決該問題。

d	be 動詞 + yet + to + 原形動詞　至今尚未…… = have not + 過去分詞 + yet

例　We are yet to decide how to deal with the problem.
　= We have yet to decide how to deal with the problem.
　= We haven't decided how to deal with the problem yet.
　= We haven't decided how to deal with the problem as yet.
　到目前為止我們尚未決定如何處理這個問題。

　注意 so far 與 as yet 均表「到目前為止」，惟 so far 可用於肯定或有否定意味的句子，而 as yet 則用於有否定意味的句子。

例　So far, I've visited over 30 countries. (✓，肯定句)
　到目前為止，我已走訪了三十多個國家。
　但：As yet, I've visited over 30 countries. (✗，as yet 不可用於肯定句中)

例　So far / As yet, I haven't finished my homework. (✓)
　到目前為止，我還未把功課做完。
　So far / As yet, I have only finished one third of my homework.
　(✓，only 表「僅僅」，有否定意味)
　到目前為止，我僅做完了三分之一的功課。

e	yet 亦可做對等連接詞，與 but (但是) 同義，可連接對等的兩個單字、詞組或子句。

例　Peter is rich and quite handsome, yet he is not my cup of rea. (此處 yet 是連接詞，等於 but)
　= Peter is rich and quite handsome, and yet he is not my cup of tea. (and 是連接詞，故此處 yet 是副詞)
　= Peter is rich and quite handsome, but he is not my cup of tea.

= Peter is rich and quite handsome. However, he is not my cup of tea.

= Peter is rich and quite handsome; however, he is not my cup of tea.
彼得有錢人又帥，但是 / 不過他卻不是我的菜。

= Though / Although / Even though (雖然) Peter is rich and quite handsome, he is not my cup of tea.

= Peter is rich and quite handsome; he is not my cup of tea / I don't like him, though.　雖然彼得有錢人又帥，他卻不是我的菜。

注意 此處 though 是副詞，置句尾，表「然而」，等於副詞 however。though 及 however 作副詞時，並非連接詞，故兩句要用分號（；）連接。

小試身手

1	The train hasn't arrived (yet / already). We're still waiting at the station.
2	Dora has (yet / already) completed the project ahead of the deadline.
3	選出錯誤的句子。 Ⓐ We have yet to decide how to solve the problem. Ⓑ It's 9 a.m. now, and I haven't finished my breakfast yet. Ⓒ They have not finished their assignment yet. Ⓓ I have yet understood this concept fully.

Ans　1. yet　2. already　3. Ⓓ

Unit 19　否定倒裝句

否定副詞如 never (從不)、seldom (很少)、rarely (很少)、little (一點也不) 等，及否定副詞片語如 by no means (絕不)、in no way (絕不)、under no circumstances (絕不) 等若置句首時，採問句式倒裝句構。

| a | 陳述句主詞之後有 be 動詞，如下列句構：
主詞 + be 動詞 + 否定副詞 / 片語

= 否定副詞 / 片語 + be 動詞 + 主詞 |

例 Frank is never easy to communicate with. (✓)
→ Never Frank is easy to communicate with. (✗)
→ Never is Frank easy to communicate with. (✓)
法蘭克一直以來很難溝通。

例 Andy is by no means a man (whom) you can trust. (✓)
→ By no means Andy is a man (whom) you can trust. (✗)
→ By no means is Andy a man (whom) you can trust. (✓)
安迪絕不是個你可信賴的人。

例 We will never work with such a selfish man. (✓)
Never we will work with such a selfish man. (✗)
→ Never will we work with such a selfish man. (✓)
我們絕不願跟這樣自私的人共事。

| b | 陳述句主詞之後有助動詞（如 should、can、must、will、完成式助動詞 have、has 等），如下列結構：
主詞 + 助動詞 + 否定副詞 / 片語

= 否定副詞 / 片語 + 助動詞 + 主詞 |

例 Under no circumstances you should do things like that. (✗)
→ Under no circumstances should you do things like that. (✓)
你在任何情況下都不應做像那樣的事。

例 I cannot hardly sing in tune. (✗，not 是否定副詞，hardly 等於 almost not，表「幾乎不」，亦是否定副詞，故 not 應刪除，以免形成錯誤的雙重否定結構)
→ I can hardly sing in tune. (✓)
= Hardly can I sing in tune. (✓)
我唱起歌來幾乎五音不全。

例 Never I have been to Myanmar before. (✗)
→ I have never been to Myanmar before. (✔)
= Never have I been to Myanmar before. (✔) 我從未去過緬甸。

C 陳述句主詞之後只有動詞，須使用助動詞 do、does、did，如下列結構：
主詞 + 否定副詞 / 片語 + 動詞
= 否定副詞 / 片語 + do、does 或 did + 主詞 + 原形動詞

例 Rarely Dad sings. (✗)
→ Dad rarely sings. (✔)
= Rarely does Dad sing. (✔)
= Seldom does Dad sing. (✔) 老爸很少唱歌。

例 Never John studied when he was young. (✗)
→ John never studied when he was young. (✔)
→ Never does John studied when he was young. (✗)
　　　現在式助動詞　過去式
→ Never did John study when he was young. (✔)
　　　過去式助動詞　原形動詞
約翰年輕時從不唸書。

小試身手

1. Under no circumstances (we should / should we) leave the room.

2. We will by no means allow such behavior.
提示 用倒裝句改寫句子。

Ans 1. should we　2. By no means will we allow such behavior.

Unit 20 用"否定副詞 / 片語 + 問句"的倒裝句構表「一……就……」

表「一……就……」也可使用"否定副詞 / 片語 + 問句"的倒裝句構。惟要了解這類倒裝句構之前，我們必須熟悉下列常態句構：

As soon as + 主詞 + 過去式動詞, 主詞 + 過去式動詞　一……就……
= Once + 主詞 + 過去式動詞, 主詞 + 過去式動詞

例　As soon as he saw the policeman, the thief ran away.
　　　　　　　　過去式　　　　　　　　　　　　　過去式

= Once he saw the policeman, the thief ran away.
　　　　過去式　　　　　　　　　　　　過去式

= The moment he saw the policeman,
　　　　　　　　　過去式

the thief ran away.
　　　　　　過去式

這個賊一見到警察就跑掉了。

a 上列句子亦可改以 "no sooner... than..." (「沒有比……更快……」即「一……就……」)，結構如下：

主詞 + had + no sooner + 過去分詞 + than + 主詞 + 過去式動詞
　　　└─────過去完成式─────┘

例　The thief had no sooner seen the policeman than he ran away.
　　　　　　└────過去完成式────┘　　　　　　　　　　　　　過去式

這個賊先看到警察 (用過去完成式表示過去先發生的動作)，不過這個動作沒有比 (than) 他後來跑掉快多少 (no sooner)，即：這個賊一看到警察就跑掉了。

由於 no sooner 是否定副詞片語，故置句首時，過去完成式助動詞 had 應與主詞倒裝，即成：

No sooner had the thief seen the policeman than he ran away.
這個賊一看到警察就逃跑了。

b 否定副詞 hardly 及 scarcely（幾乎不）亦可採下列句構：
主詞 + had hardly / scarcely + 過去分詞 + when + 主詞 + 過去式動詞　一……就……

例　The thief had hardly seen the policeman when he ran away.
　　　　　　過去完成式　　　　　　　　　　　　　　過去式

= The thief had scarcely seen the policeman when he ran away.
　　　　　　過去完成式　　　　　　　　　　　　　　　過去式

當這個賊逃跑時，他差一點沒看到警察。
即：這個賊一看到警察就逃跑了。

注意　由於 hardly 及 scarcely 是否定副詞（表「幾乎不」），故可置句首，過去完成式助動詞 had 應與主詞倒裝，即成：

Hardly had the thief seen the policeman when he ran away.
= Scarcely had the thief seen the policeman when he ran away.

請用英文翻譯下列中文句子：
我一到家便開始下雨了。

示範譯句

As soon as I got home, it began to rain.
= Once I got home, it began to rain.
= The moment I got home, it began to rain.
= I had no sooner gotten home than it began to rain.
= I had hardly gotten home when it began to rain.
= I had scarcely gotten home when it began to rain.
= No sooner had I gotten home than it began to rain.
= Hardly had I gotten home when it began to rain.
= Scarcely had I gotten home when it began to rain.

注意

1 表「一……就……」的英文
　　常態句多使用 as soon as、once 或 the moment，如上例。

247

2 若表示條件句時，只使用 as soon as、once 或 the moment。

例 As soon as I have enough money, I will buy a car.
　　　　現在式　　　　　　　　　未來式

= Once I have enough money, I will buy a car.

= The moment I have enough money, I will buy a car.

= Upon having enough money, I will buy a car. 我一有錢就會買車。
　　介詞

不可說

I no sooner have enough money than I will buy a car. (✗)

I hardly have enough money when I will buy a car. (✗)

I scarcely have enough money when I will buy a car. (✗)

小試身手

1	南希一聽到這個消息，就打電話給她的朋友。 Once Nancy _____ (hear) the news, she _____ (call) her friend.
2	The moment Steve opened the door, the dog ran out. 提示 用 No sooner... than... 的倒裝句型改寫句子。

Ans　1. heard; called
　　　2. No sooner had Steve opened the door than the dog ran out.

Unit 21　表「如此……以致於……」的句型

a　so + { adj. / adv.
　　　　 adj. + a / an + 單數名詞 } + that...

　　such + { a / an + 單數名詞
　　　　　複數名詞
　　　　　不可數名詞 } + that

如此地 / 如此的……以致於 / 因此……

以上句構常態用法如下：

例 John studies so hard that our teacher likes him very much.
　　　　 v.　　　 adv.

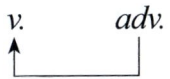

約翰如此用功，因此我們老師很喜歡他。

例 Nick is so nice to us that we all like to work with him.
　　　　　　 adj.

尼克如此善待我們，因此我們大家都喜歡與他共事。

例 It's such a cold day that I just feel like staying home.
　　　　　　　 單數名詞

天氣那麼冷，因此我只想待在家中。

例 They are such fun books that I enjoy reading them time and again.
　　　　　　　　 複數名詞

它們是那麼有趣的書，因此我很喜歡一而再、再而三地閱讀它們。

例 It is such good weather that I've decided
　　　　　　　 不可數名詞
to go hiking today.
天氣這麼好，因此我決定今天要去健行。

b　so 之後可置含形容詞的「單數」可數名詞，由於 so 是副詞表示「如此地」，故應先接形容詞，再接不定冠詞 a 或 an，再接該單數名詞。

例 Mary is a so beautiful girl that many boys have a crush on her. (✗)

→ Mary is so beautiful a girl that many boys have a crush on her. (✓)
　　　　　 adv.　　 adj.　　 單數名詞

= Mary is such a beautiful girl that many boys have a crush on her. (✓)

瑪麗是那麼美麗的女孩，因此許多男孩都在暗戀她。

c　so 是副詞，可與數量形容詞 "few / many + 複數名詞" 搭配，亦可與 "little / much + 不可數名詞" 搭配。

例 I have such little money that I can't lend you any. (✗)

→ I have so little money that I can't lend you any. (✓)

我錢太少，因此沒什麼錢可借給你。

CH 2　與否定句相關的錯誤

例	We still have <u>such</u> much time left that we might as well take in a movie. (✗)
	→ We still have <u>so</u> much time left that we might as well take in a movie. (✓)　我們所剩的時間仍很充裕，因此我們不妨看場電影吧。
例	<u>Such</u> few people showed up at Jamie's birthday party that he felt upset. (✗)
	→ <u>So</u> few people showed up at Jamie's birthday party that he felt upset. (✓)　傑米的生日宴會中現身的人這麼少，因此他心中很不是滋味。
d	由 b 項得知，在 "so... that..."（如此……以致於……）的結構中，so 是副詞，只可先置形容詞，再置不定冠詞 a 或 an，再置單數可數名詞。
例	Mr. Smith is <u>a so honest man</u> that we all respect him. (✗)
	→ Mr. Smith is <u>so honest a man</u> that we all respect him. (✓)
	= Mr. Smith is <u>such an honest man</u> that we all respect him. (✓)　史密斯先生是一個非常誠實的人，我們都很尊敬他。
e	"too... to..."（太……而不……）亦可與含有形容詞的單數可數名詞並用，形成下列結構：
	too + adj. + a / an + 單數名詞 + to + 原形動詞　太……而不……
例	David is <u>a too lazy boy</u> to do anything well. (✗)
	→ David is <u>too</u> <u>lazy</u> <u>a</u> <u>boy</u> to do anything well. (✓)　　　　　　　　　　adj.　單數可數名詞　　大衛是個太懶的孩子，因此什麼事情都做不好。
	= David is <u>too</u>　<u>lazy</u> to do anything well. (✓)　　　　　　　　adv.　adj.　　大衛太懶，因此什麼事情都做不好。
f	如同 so 一樣，too 之後亦可與 "much + 不可數名詞"、"little + 不可數名詞"、"many + 複數名詞" 並用。
例	I have <u>too much work</u> to do today.　我今天要做的工作太多了。
例	We had <u>too little time</u> to visit the museum.　我們沒什麼時間參觀博物館。
例	Peter has <u>too many things</u> to deal with almost every day.　彼得幾乎每天都有太多的事情要處理。

小試身手

1
The movie was very exciting.
I couldn't stop watching it.
提示 用 so... that... 合併句子。

2
Tim is a very smart student.
Tim always gets top marks.
提示 用 such... that... 合併句子。

Ans
1. The movie was so exciting that I couldn't stop watching it.
2. Tim is such a smart student that he always gets top marks.

Unit 22　so... that... 及 such... that... 的倒裝

"so... that..." 及 "such... that..." 的句構中，若將 so 或 such 及其之後所搭配的詞類置句首時，亦可用問句式倒裝結構：

a 主詞 + be 動詞 → be 動詞 + 主詞

例　The animal is so dangerous that you cannot be too cautious around it. (✓)

So dangerous the animal is that you cannot be too cautious around it. (✗)

→ So dangerous is the animal that you cannot be too cautious around it. (✓)　這動物非常危險，你對牠再小心也不為過。

b 主詞 + 助動詞 (如 can、will、may、should、have) → 助動詞 + 主詞

例　We've done so much that we can take a break now. (✓)

→ So much we have done that we can take a break now. (✗)

→ So much have we done that we can take a break now. (✓)
我們做了那麼多事情，因此現在可以休息一下。

例　You can sing so well that you will make a great singer someday. (✓)
　　→ So well you can sing that you will make a great singer someday. (✗)
　　→ So well can you sing that you will make a great singer someday. (✓)
你歌唱得這麼好，因此有朝一日會成為一位很棒的歌手。

| c | 主詞 + 一般動詞 → do、does、did + 主詞 + 原形動詞 |

例　John came home so late that he was told off by his father. (✓)
　　→ So late John came home that he was told off by his father. (✗)
　　→ So late did John come home that he was told off by his father. (✓)
約翰太晚回家，因此被他爸爸訓斥了一頓。

例　The widow lives such a poor life that we all sympathize with her. (✓)
　　→ Such a poor life the widow lives that we all sympathize with her. (✗)
　　→ Such a poor life does the widow live that we all sympathize with her. (✓)　這位寡婦生活得那麼貧苦，因此我們都很同情她。

注意 such 也可做代名詞，表「如此的地步」，之後不加任何名詞。

例　When I heard the good news, my excitement was such (= such excitement) that I jumped up and down.
　　→ When I heard the good news, such was my excitement that I jumped up and down.　我聽到這個好消息時，興奮得蹦蹦跳跳。

《 小試身手 》

用倒裝句改寫以下句子。

1　The food was so delicious that everyone wanted more.

2　They made such significant progress that the manager praised them highly.

Ans　1. So delicious was the food that everyone wanted more.
　　　2. Such significant progress did they make that the manager praised them highly.

252

Unit 23　little 做否定副詞時的倒裝

little 做否定副詞時可置句首，採問句式倒裝句構，形成下列固定片語：
Little did I / he / we / they know that...　我 / 他 / 我們 / 他們一點都不知道……

例　I little knew that Henry and Jane are getting married next weekend. (✗)

→ Little did I know that Henry and Jane are getting married next weekend. (✓)

= I didn't know (at all) that Henry and Jane are getting married next weekend. (✓)
我一點都不知道亨利與阿珍下週末就要結婚了。

注意　但 little 亦可與現在式助動詞 do 並用，形成下列倒裝句構：

Little do + 複數名詞 (如 people、teachers、students、parents) + know that...　一般 (人、老師、學生、父母) 都不知道……

例　Little do people know how hard it is to be a chef.
一般人都不知道當主廚是多麼困難的一件事。

Little do students know the importance of mastering English grammar.　一般學生都不知道精通英文語法的重要性。

小試身手

我完全不知道這個專案會在隔天被取消。
_____ (little) I know that the project would be canceled the next day.

Ans　Little did

Unit 24　"only + 時間副詞" 的倒裝

only + 時間副詞 (如 then、later) + 問句式倒裝句

a　主詞 + 動詞 → do / does / did + 主詞 + 原形動詞

253

例　Only then I knew that my girlfriend had been cheating on me. (✗)
→ Only then did I know that my girlfriend had been cheating on me. (✓)　只有到那時我才知道我女友一直在劈腿騙我。

b　主詞 + be 動詞 → be 動詞 + 主詞

例　Only later I was aware that my father was not my biological father, but I loved him nonetheless. (✗)
→ Only later was I aware that my father was not my biological father, but I loved him nonetheless. (✓)
直到後來我才了解老爸並非我的生父，但我仍然愛他。

c　主詞 + 助動詞 → 助動詞 + 主詞

例　I will keep earning money. Only then I can take better care of my family. (✗)
→ I will keep earning money. Only then can I take better care of my family. (✓)　我會繼續賺錢。只有這樣我才能把家人照顧得更好。

小試身手

重組：I / Only / realize / then / did

_____ my passion for my career.

Ans　Only then did I realize

Unit 25　only when、only after 的倒裝

a　"Only when" 引導的副詞子句或 "Only after" 引導的副詞子句視作 "Not until" 引導的否定副詞子句，之後的主要子句亦採問句式倒裝句構。

例　Only when John told me the truth I knew how much he had loved me all those years. (✗)
→ Only when John told me the truth did I know how much he had loved me all those years. (✓)

254

= <u>Only after John told me the truth</u> <u>did I know</u> how much he had loved me all those years. (✔)

= <u>Not until John told me the truth</u> <u>did I know</u> how much he had loved me all those years. (✔)

<u>只有當約翰對我吐真言時</u> / <u>只有在約翰對我吐真言之後</u> / <u>直到約翰對我吐真言</u>，我才知道那些年來他有多愛我。

小試身手

選出錯誤的句子。

Ⓐ Only when Debby finished her homework did she go out to play.
Ⓑ Only after the meeting started I realized I had forgotten my notes.
Ⓒ Not until the rain stopped did we go outside.
Ⓓ Only when Andy apologized did Amy forgive him.

Ans Ⓑ

Unit 26　only 之後接介詞片語的倒裝

only 之後接介詞片語（如 "only by..." 唯有，藉由、"only after..." 唯有在……之後、"only in this way" 唯以這種方式）及 not until 之後接時間名詞均視作否定副詞片語，出現在句首時，之後的主要子句一律採問句式倒裝句構。

例　<u>Only by</u> working hard <u>you can</u> fulfill your goals. (✘)
→ <u>Only by</u> working hard <u>can you</u> fulfill your goals. (✔)
你唯有藉由努力才能實踐你的目標。

例　<u>Only after</u> lunch <u>you may</u> leave. (✘)
→ <u>Only after</u> lunch <u>may you</u> leave. (✔)
唯有吃過午餐後你才能離開。

例　<u>Not until</u> 10 p.m. <u>I finished</u> all the work. (✘)
→ <u>Not until</u> 10 p.m. <u>did I finish</u> all the work. (✔)
直到晚上 10 點我才把所有工作做完。

255

> **小試身手**
>
> 重組：problem / be / the / can / solved
> Only in this way ＿＿＿＿＿＿＿＿＿＿＿＿＿＿＿＿＿＿＿＿＿.
>
> **Ans** can the problem be solved

Unit 27　比較 only if 與 if only 的不同

a only if 視作否定副詞連接詞，表「只要……就……」，置句首，之後的主要子句採問句式倒裝句構。

例　Only if you promise to be true to me I will marry you. (✗)
→ Only if you promise to be true to me will I marry you. (✓)

若上列句中的主要子句置句首時，則不採倒裝句構。

I will marry you only if you promise to be true to me. (✓)
= I will marry you as long as you promise to be true to me. (✓)
你只要保證對我忠誠，我就會嫁給你。

b if only... 表「要是……的話就好了」，自成一個完整句，用於假設語氣。

1 與過去事實相反，動詞使用過去完成式 (had + 過去分詞)。

例　If only I had taken your advice at the time. (✓)
　　　　　過去完成式

(But I didn't take your advice at the time.)
　　　　過去式
我當時若是聽了你的忠告就好了。(可是我當時並未聽從你的忠告。)

例　If only I had been there last Sunday. (✓)
　　　　　過去完成式

(But I wasn't there.)
　　　　過去式
上星期天我若是在那裡就好了。(可是我當時並不在那裡。)

2 與現在事實相反，動詞使用過去式。(若是 be 動詞，不論主詞是第幾人稱，均為 were。)

例 If only Jeff <u>knows</u> the truth. (✗)
→ If only Jeff <u>knew</u> the truth. (✓)
　　　　　　　過去式

(But he <u>doesn't know</u> the truth.)
　　　　　　現在式

要是傑夫 (現在) 知道這個真相就好了。(但是他現在並不知道真相。)

例 If only | I am | there. (✗)
         | he is |

→ If only | I were | there. (✓)
          | he were |

(But | I am | not there.)
     | he is |

要是我 / 他 (現在) 在那裡就好了。(可是我 / 他現在並不在那裡。)

注意 現在英美人士在口語中多用 was 取代 were。

故: If only | I | was there. (可)
           | John |
           | he |

但: If only | you (你 / 你們 / 妳 / 妳們) | was there. (✗)
           | they |
           | we |

→ If only | you | were there. (✓)
          | they |
          | we |

小試身手

1　Only if you study hard (you will / will you) pass the exam.

2　If only they _____ (catch) the earlier train, they would have arrived on time.

Ans　1. will you　2. had caught

257

Unit 28　用 also、too、as well 表「也」

表「也」時，可使用 also、too、as well，只用於肯定句中。also 置 be 動詞或助動詞之後，若與動詞並用，則置該動詞之前；too 及 as well 則置於句尾。

a　be 動詞

例　Megan enjoys singing, and she <u>also is</u> fond of dancing. (✗)
→ Megan enjoys singing, and she <u>is also</u> fond of dancing. (✓)
= Megan enjoys singing, and she is fond of dancing, <u>too</u>. (✓)
= Megan enjoys singing, and she is fond of dancing <u>as well</u>. (✓)
梅根喜歡唱歌，也喜歡跳舞。

b　助動詞

例　Megan can sing, and she <u>can also</u> dance.
= Megan can sing, and she can dance, <u>too</u>.
= Megan can sing, and she can dance <u>as well</u>.
梅根會唱歌，也會跳舞。

c　動詞

例　Megan sings well, and she <u>dances</u> gracefully <u>also</u>. (✗)
→ Megan sings well, and she <u>also dances</u> gracefully. (✓)
= Megan sings well, and she dances gracefully, <u>too</u>. (✓)
= Megan sings well, and she dances gracefully <u>as well</u>. (✓)
梅根歌唱得很好，舞也跳得很優雅。

注意　so 可做副詞，表「也」，也用於肯定句中，so 之後採問句式倒裝句構。

1　be 動詞

例　Peter is handsome, <u>so are you</u>. (✗，兩句無連接詞連接)
→ Peter is handsome, <u>and</u> <u>so are you</u>. (✓)
= Peter is handsome, <u>and</u> <u>you are</u>, <u>too</u>. (✓)　彼得很帥，你也一樣。

2　助動詞

例　John has left, <u>so</u> <u>have they</u>. (✗)

→ John has left, and so have they. (✓)
= John has left, and they have, too. (✓) 約翰已離開了，他們也離開了。

3 動詞

例 Paul studies hard, so do you. (✗)
→ Paul studies hard, and so do you. (✓)
= Paul studies hard, and you do, too. (✓) 保羅很用功，你也是。

小試身手

1. Jenny enjoys reading books, and she (also / too / as well) likes watching movies.

2. 選出正確的句子。
   Ⓐ David is good at cooking, and he also is good at painting.
   Ⓑ Tim plays the guitar well, and also he sings well.
   Ⓒ Ken is a great singer, so does his brother.
   Ⓓ Linda has finished her homework, and so have they.

Ans　1. also　2. Ⓓ

Unit 29　用 neither、nor、not either 表「也不」

表「也不」時，採用下列句構：
否定句, and neither + 問句式倒裝句構
= 否定句, nor + 問句式倒裝句構
= 否定句, and... not either
注意 nor 是連接詞，故之前不置 and。

a be 動詞

例 Peter isn't happy today, neither am I. (✗，兩句無連接詞連接)
→ Peter isn't happy today, and neither am I. (✓)
= Peter isn't happy today, nor am I. (✓)
彼得今天不快樂，我也不快樂。

b 助動詞

例 I have never been to Singapore, neither has my friend David. (✗，兩句無連接詞連接)

→ I have never been to Singapore, and neither has my friend David. (✓)

= I have never been to Singapore, nor has my friend David. (✓)

= I have never been to Singapore, and my friend David hasn't either. (✓)　我從沒去過新加坡，我朋友大衛也沒去過。

c 動詞

例 David doesn't like singing, and neither do I.
= David doesn't like singing, nor do I.
= David doesn't like singing, and I don't either.
大衛不喜歡唱歌，我也一樣。

▎小試身手▎

Molly doesn't have a car, and her brother doesn't either.
提示 用 neither 改寫句子。

Ans Molly doesn't have a car, and neither does her brother.

Unit 30　用 Me, too.、Me either.、Me neither. 表「我也是」

兩人對話時，肯定句可用 "Me, too."（我也是，逗點可加可不加）做為簡答。否定句則用 "Me either." 或 "Me neither." 做為簡答。

a 肯定句

例 A: Taylor enjoys hiking.　　甲：泰勒喜歡健行。
　　　　　　動詞

B: Me, too. (口語)　乙：我也是。
= So do I. (正式)
　　助動詞

260

例 A: Nicole is fond of singing.
　　　　　　be 動詞

B: Me, too. (口語)
　　So am I. (正式)
　　　　be 動詞

甲：妮可喜歡唱歌。
乙：我也是。

b 助動詞

例 A: Terry will study abroad next year.
　　　　　　助動詞

B: Me, too. (口語)
　　So will I. (正式)
　　　　助動詞

甲：泰瑞明年要出國念書。
乙：我也是。

c 否定句

例 A: Mandy hasn't finished the work.
　　　　　　　助動詞

B: Me either. (多用)
= Me neither. (少用)
= Nor have I. (正式)
　　　助動詞
= Neither have I. (正式)
　　　　助動詞

甲：曼蒂工作尚未做完。
乙：我也沒做完。

例 A: My sister is not willing to sing in public.
　　　　　　　　be 動詞

B: Me either. (口語)
= Me neither. (口語)
= Nor am I.
= Neither am I. 　我也一樣。

甲：我妹妹不願意在公眾場合唱歌。
乙：我也是。

CH 2

與否定句相關的錯誤

261

小試身手

A: I haven't been to Paris.
B: ＿＿＿＿＿

Ⓐ Me, too.　Ⓑ Me either.　Ⓒ So have I.　Ⓓ Neither I have.

Ans Ⓑ

Unit 31　not only... but (also)...
表「不僅……而且……」

a "not only... but (also)..." 表「不僅……而且……」，可連接對等的單詞、片語、副詞子句、主要子句。

1 對等的主詞（動詞按最近的主詞做變化）

例　Not only <u>you</u> but (also) <u>he</u> <u>are</u> to blame for the mistake. (✗)
　　　　　　主詞　　　　主詞

→ Not only you but (also) <u>he</u>　<u>is</u> to blame for the mistake. (✓)
　　　　　　　　　　　　最近的主詞

不僅是你而且連他都必須對該錯誤負起責任。

2 對等的形容詞

例　Sally is not only <u>beautiful</u> but (also) <u>clever</u>.　莎莉不僅漂亮又聰明。
　　　　　　　　　　adj.　　　　　　　　adj.

3 對等的副詞

例　Peggy works not only <u>diligently</u> but (also)
　　　　　　　　　　　　adv.
efficiently.　佩姬不僅工作勤奮而且又有效率。
<u>adv.</u>

4 對等的片語

例　I'm interested not only <u>in singing</u> but (also) <u>in dancing</u>.
我不僅對歌唱有興趣，也對跳舞有興趣。

5 對等的副詞子句

例　Tim succeeded not only <u>because he worked hard</u> but (also) <u>because he worked efficiently</u>.
提姆之所以成功不僅是因為他努力，而且也因為他工作有效率。

b 放句首時 "Not only... but (also)..." 不可直接連接對等的主要子句，即不可說：

例　Not only John is handsome, but (also) he is clever. (✗)

理由　第一個主要子句句首有否定副詞片語 Not only，故該主要子句應採問句式倒裝句構；第二個主要子句之前的 but also 應刪除 also，或將 also 置 be 動詞後，即：
Not only is John handsome, but he is (also) clever. (✓)
或：Not only is John handsome, but he is clever as well. (✓)
約翰不僅是個帥哥，而且也很聰明。

例　Not only David works hard, but also he treats people nicely. (✗)
→ Not only does David work hard, but he (also) treats people nicely. (✓)　大衛不僅工作勤奮，待人也很好。

小試身手

The movie was interesting.
It was also very educational.
提示　用 not only... but also... 合併句子。

Ans　The movie was not only interesting but (also) very educational.

Unit 32　感嘆詞 boy 置句首也採問句式倒裝

boy 亦可當感嘆詞，相當於「哇塞！」、「媽呀！」、「乖乖隆地咚！」置句首，之後也採問句式倒裝。

例　Boy, is she beautiful!　哇塞！她真美！
Boy, am I so tired!　媽呀！我累趴了！
不過以 boy 起首的倒裝句多出現在口語中，一般寫作不會採用。

小試身手

The weather is hot today!
提示 用 Boy 做感嘆詞開頭改寫句子。

Ans Boy, is the weather hot today!

Chapter 3

Unit 33 ▶▶▶ Unit 43

> 搞懂句子、主要子句、副詞子句、形容詞子句、名詞子句之間的區別及功能

你是否曾在閱讀或寫作時,被複雜的句子結構搞得暈頭轉向?是不是常常在面對英文句子時,覺得頭大?

本章節專注於句子結構的深入解析,清楚區分各類子句的功能和用法,讓你不再對複雜句型感到困惑。無論是閱讀理解還是寫作表達,這裡都能幫助你輕鬆駕馭句子結構,讓英文實力更上一層樓!

Unit 33 句子

句子就是起首就有名詞（如 John、Peter、Mr. Wang、money）或代名詞（it、you、he、I、they、we），之後接動詞（walk、want、run、hate）及其他詞類，形成意義完整又合乎邏輯的句意，句尾有句點、驚嘆號或問號。

一般而言，句子包括<u>陳述句</u>、<u>一般疑問句</u>、<u>特殊疑問句</u>、<u>感嘆句</u>及<u>命令句</u>。

a 陳述句
主詞 + 動詞（+ 其他使語句完整的詞類，如名詞、形容詞、副詞等）

例　<u>David</u> <u>sings</u> beautifully.　大衛歌唱得很動聽。
　　　主詞　動詞

例　<u>I</u>　<u>enjoy</u> listening to oldies.　我喜歡聽老歌。
　　主詞　動詞

例　After saying goodbye to his wife, <u>Ben</u>　<u>took</u> a bus to work.
　　　　　　　　　　　　　　　　　　　主詞　　動詞

跟愛妻道別後，班便搭公車上班去了。

b 一般疑問句（即可用 Yes / No 回答的問句，均由陳述句變化而成）

❶ 主詞 + be 動詞

→ be 動詞 + 主詞

例　<u>Danny</u> <u>is</u> a diligent student. (陳述句)
丹尼是個用功的學生。

→ Is Danny a diligent student? (一般疑問句)

(Yes, he is. / No, he isn't.)

丹尼是個用功的學生嗎？
(是的，他是。/ 不，他不是。)

例　<u>Peter and David</u> <u>are</u> willing to go hiking with us tomorrow morning. (陳述句)
明天早上彼得和大衛願意與我們去健行。

→ <u>Are Peter and David</u> willing to go hiking with us tomorrow morning? (一般疑問句)

(Yes, they are. / No, they aren't.)

明天早上彼得和大衛願意與我們去健行嗎？

(是的，他們願意。/ 不，他們不願意。)

2 主詞 + 助動詞 (如 can、will、should、shall、must、may、would、could 等) + 原形動詞

→ 助動詞 + 主詞 + 原形動詞

例 <u>You can</u> handle the problem. (陳述句)

你能處理這個問題。

→ <u>Can you</u> handle the problem? (一般疑問句)

(Yes, I can. / No, I can't.)

你能處理這個問題嗎？

(是的，我能。/ 不，我不能。)

3 主詞 + 完成式助動詞 (have、has、had) + 過去分詞

→ 完成式助動詞 + 主詞 + 過去分詞

例 <u>Paul has</u> finished his work. (陳述句)

保羅已經把他的工作做完了。

→ <u>Has Paul</u> finished his work? (一般疑問句)

(Yes, he has. / No, he hasn't.)

保羅已經把他的工作做完了嗎？

(是的，他已做完了。/ 不，他沒做完。)

4 主詞 + 動詞

→ 助動詞 (Do、Does、Did) + 主詞 + 原形動詞

例 Peter <u>bought</u> a brand-new car last week. (陳述句)
　　　　過去式動詞

彼得上星期買了一部新車。

→ <u>Did</u> Peter　　<u>bought</u> a brand-new car last week? (✗)
　過去式助動詞　過去式動詞

→ <u>Did</u> Peter <u>buy</u> a brand-new car last week? (一般疑問句)
　　　　　　原形動詞

267

(Yes, he did. / No, he didn't.)
彼得上星期買了一部新車嗎？
(是的，他買了。/ 不，他沒買。)

例 Mr. Johnson and his family live in a small fishing village. (陳述句)
　　　主詞　　　　　　　現在式動詞
強生先生與他家人住在一座小漁村裡。

→ Does Mr. Johnson and his family live in a small fishing village?
　　　　複數主詞　　　　　　原形動詞
(✗，本問句主詞為複數)

→ Do Mr. Johnson and his family live in a small fishing village? (✓)
　　　複數主詞

(Yes, they do. / No, they don't.)

或：Does Mr. Johnson live with his family in a small fishing village? (✓)
　　　　單數主詞

(Yes, he does. / No, he doesn't.)　強生先生和他家人住在一座小漁村裡嗎？

C 特殊疑問句 (此類問句起首為疑問詞，如 what、when、where、who、why、how 等，不可用 Yes / No 回答)

1 主詞 + be + 疑問詞 → 疑問詞 + be + 主詞

中文：他是誰？
英文：He is who? (✗)
→ Who is he? (✓)

中文：你今天早上在做什麼？
英文：You this morning were doing what? (✗)
→ What were you doing this morning? (✓)

2 主詞 + 一般助動詞 (can、will、shall、should、would、could 等) + 原形動詞

→ 一般助動詞 + 主詞 + 原形動詞

中文：我可以如何為您效勞嗎？(店員對顧客用語)
英文：I can how help you? (✗)
→ How can I help you? (✓)

3 主詞 + 完成式助動詞 (have、has、had) + 過去分詞

→ 完成式助動詞 + 主詞 + 過去分詞

中文：這房間好亂。你剛才做了什麼事？

英文：The room is so messy. You have just done what?（✗）

→ The room is so messy. What have you just done?（✓）

4 主詞 + 動詞

→ 助動詞 (do、does、did) + 主詞 + 原形動詞

中文：你如何拼這個字？

英文：You how spell the word?（✗，中式英文）
　　　主詞　　現在式動詞

→ How you　spell the word?（✗）
　　　主詞　　動詞

→ How do you spell the word?（✓）
　　　　　　　原形動詞

中文：約翰何時開始與妳約會的？

英文：John when started going out with you?（✗，中式英文）
　　　主詞　　　過去式動詞

→ When did John　start going out with you?（✓）
　　　　　　主詞　　原形動詞

注意 who（誰）及 what（什麼）是疑問代名詞，在特殊疑問句中可做主詞，此時中英文結構完全相同。

中文：誰偷了我的錢？
　　　主詞

英文：Who　stole my money?
　　　主詞　動詞　　受詞

中文：誰應對此事負責？
　　　主詞

英文：Who　should be held responsible for it?
　　　主詞　助動詞

269

中文：什麼事發生了？（正常說法為：發生什麼事了？）

英文：<u>What</u> <u>happened</u>?
　　　　主詞　　動詞

d 感嘆句
以 what（多麼的）或 how（多麼地）起首，結構如下：
以 what 起首的感嘆句，what 之後可接單數名詞、複數名詞或不可數名詞。

❶ What + a / an + 形容詞 + 單數名詞 + 主詞 + 動詞!

例：<u>What a beautiful car</u> <u>you</u> <u>have</u>!　你的車好美呀！
　　　　　單數名詞　　　　主詞　動詞

例：<u>What a nice man Mr. Wu</u> <u>is</u>!　吳先生是多麼好的一個人呀！
　　　　　單數名詞　　　　　主詞　動詞

❷ What + 形容詞 + 複數名詞 + 主詞 + 動詞!

例：<u>What well-bred children</u> <u>you</u> <u>have</u>!　你的孩子們多麼有教養呀！
　　　　複數名詞　　　　　主詞　動詞

❸ What + 形容詞 + 不可數名詞 + 主詞 + 動詞!

例：<u>What beautiful music</u>　<u>it</u>　<u>is</u>!　多動人的音樂啊！
　　　不可數名詞　　　　主詞　動詞

以 how 起首的感嘆句，how 之後接副詞或形容詞，不得再接名詞。

❹ How + 副詞 + 主詞 + 動詞！

例：You study how hard!（✗，中式英文）
→ <u>How hard</u> you study!（✓）　你多麼用功啊！/ 你讀書多努力啊！
　　　副詞

例：You are how polite!（✗，中式英文）
→ <u>How polite</u> you are!（✓）　你好有禮貌唷！
　　　形容詞

注意 How 之後可接非修飾主語的形容詞，而是接修飾其他單數可數名詞的形容詞；此時該名詞絕不能是複數名詞或不可數名詞。口語英文中已少用此表達方式。

How + 形容詞 + a / an + 單數名詞 + 主詞 + 動詞!
= What + a / an + 形容詞 + 單數名詞 + 主詞 + 動詞!

270

例 How nice boys they are! (✗)
→ What nice <u>boys</u> they are! (✓)　他們是多麼好的孩子啊！
　　　　　複數名詞

例 How a nice boy Jimmy is! (✗)
→ How <u>nice</u>　<u>a boy</u> Jimmy is! (✓)
　　　形容詞　單數名詞
= What a nice boy Jimmy is! (✓)　吉米真是個好孩子！

感嘆句除了以 what 或 how 起首外，一般陳述句之後加驚嘆號也可稱之為感嘆句。

例 Wow! You're such a nice man!　哇塞！你真是個大好人！

例 It's really boiling hot today!　今天真是熱斃了！

e 命令句
句子以原形動詞起首，表示「命令、懇求」之意。

例 Be quiet!　安靜！
　原形動詞

例 Let me do it.　讓我做這件事。
　原形動詞

例 Leave me alone.　讓我獨自一個人。/ 別管我。
　原形動詞

注意

❶ 否定命令句句首置 don't 或 never，再加原形動詞。

例 Don't smoke here.　別在這裡抽菸。
　　　　原形動詞

例 Don't be so lazy.　別那麼懶。
　　　　原形動詞

例 Don't never lie again.
(✗，否定助動詞 don't 不可與否定副詞並用，否則造成錯誤的雙重否定)
→ Don't ever lie again. (✓)
= Never lie again. (✓)　絕對不要再說謊了。

❷ 肯定命令句句首可置 do，表示「務必」之意，有更強調的意味。

例 Be quiet!　安靜！
→ Do be quiet!　務必要安靜！

271

例 Take an umbrella with you. It may rain anytime.
隨身帶把傘。隨時可能會下雨。

→ Do take an umbrella with you. It may rain anytime.
務必要隨身帶把傘。隨時可能會下雨。

小試身手

1. John has a beautiful house!
   提示 用 What 作感嘆句改寫句子。

2. Lisa finished her assignment yesterday.
   提示 用一般疑問句改寫句子。

3. A: _____ did you meet him?
   B: I met him yesterday.
   Ⓐ What　　Ⓑ When　　Ⓒ Who　　Ⓓ Where

Ans　1. What a beautiful house John has!
　　　2. Did Lisa finish her assignment yesterday?
　　　3. Ⓑ

Unit 34　主要子句 + 副詞子句

a　陳述句可單獨存在，成為一個句子。

例 Arthur is easy to get along with. (✔, 陳述句，同時也是個句子)
亞瑟很好相處。

I like Arthur. (✔, 陳述句，同時也是個句子)
我喜歡亞瑟。

b　兩個句子並列一定要有連接詞連接，否則屬錯誤的結構。

例 I like Arthur, he is easy to get along with. (✗, 兩句無連接詞連接)

272

→ I like Arthur <u>because</u> he is easy to get along with. (✓，句子)
　　　　　　　連接詞

我喜歡亞瑟，因為他很容易相處。

上列句中，"I like Arthur" 是主要子句，"because he is easy to get along with" 是副詞連接詞 (because) 引導的副詞子句，整個副詞子句視作副詞，修飾主要子句。

c 常用的副詞連接詞（亦稱從屬連接詞）有 when（當）、while（當）、as（因為；當）、once（一……就……）、as soon as（一……就……）、as long as（只要……）、although（雖然）、though（雖然）、even though（雖然）、if（如果）、even if（就算是）、by the time（等到……時）。以上這些連接詞置任何一個陳述句句首時，該句就是副詞子句，不能獨立存在，必須依主要子句而存在。

例 Because Arthur is easy to get along with. (✗，句意不全)
因為亞瑟很容易相處。(✗)

→ I like Arthur <u>because he is easy to get along with.</u> (✓)
　主要子句　　　　　　副詞子句

我喜歡亞瑟，因為他很容易相處。

例 By the time I got to the airport. (✗，句意不全)
等到我趕到機場時。

→ <u>By the time I got to the airport,</u> <u>the plane had taken off.</u> (✓)
　副詞子句　　　　　　　　主要子句

等到我趕到機場時，飛機已經起飛了。

例 If you promise to be true to me. (✗，句意不全)
如果你承諾對我忠誠。

→ <u>If you promise to be true to me,</u> <u>I will marry you.</u> (✓)
　副詞子句　　　　　　　　主要子句

你若承諾對我忠誠，我就會嫁給你。

注意 副詞子句可置主要子句之後，此時，副詞子句與主要子句之間不置逗點。副詞子句亦可置主要子句之前，此時，副詞子句之後要置逗點，再接主要子句。

例 Because Arthur is easy to get along with, I like him very much.
= I like Arthur very much <u>because</u> he is easy to get along with.

例 The plane had taken off by the time I got to the airport.
= By the time I got to the airport, the plane had taken off.

例 I will marry you if you promise to be true to me.
= If you promise to be true to me, I will marry you.

小試身手

Daniel didn't come to the party.
He was tired.
提示 用 ... because... 合併句子。

Ans Daniel didn't come to the party because he was tired.

Unit 35　主要子句 + 主要子句

對等連接詞 and（而且）、or（否則）、but（但是）可連接兩個對等的陳述句（即主要子句），形成一個長句。

例 Eric is rich, but he is stingy.　艾瑞克很有錢，但是他很吝嗇。
　　主要子句　　　主要子句

例 You'd better take my advice, or you'll be sorry.
　　　　主要子句　　　　　　　主要子句
你最好接受我的建議，否則你會後悔的。

例 I enjoy singing, and I'm very much into dancing, too.
　　主要子句　　　　　　主要子句
我喜歡唱歌，而且我也很喜歡跳舞。

小試身手

請填入適當的連接詞。

The movie was interesting, ＿＿＿＿ the ending was disappointing.

Ans but

274

Unit 36　命令句 + 主要子句

命令句 + or / or else（否則）+ 主要子句
命令句 + and（那麼）+ 主要子句

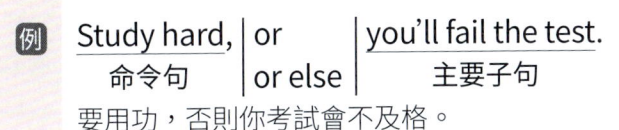

例　Study hard, | or | you'll fail the test.
　　　命令句　　| or else |　　主要子句

要用功，否則你考試會不及格。

= If you don't study hard, you'll fail the test.
　　　副詞子句　　　　　　　主要子句

你若不用功，考試就會不及格。

例　Study hard, and you'll ace the test.　要用功，那麼你就會順利通過考試。
　　　命令句　　　　　主要子句

= If you study hard, you'll ace the test.　你若用功，就會順利通過考試。
　　　副詞子句　　　　　主要子句

小試身手

請填入適當的連接詞。

Finish your homework, ＿＿＿＿ you cannot play games.

Ans　or (else)

Unit 37　形容詞子句

形容詞子句由關係代名詞（who、whom、which、that）、關係代名詞所有格（whose）、關係副詞（where、when、why）所引導，這種子句通常置名詞之後，修飾該名詞。功能如同形容詞一樣，故稱形容詞子句。

例　Gary is a kind　　man.　蓋瑞是個好人。
　　　　　形容詞　　名詞

275

例 Gary is a kind man, whom I have known for years.
　　　　　　　　名詞　　　　　形容詞子句

蓋瑞是個好人，我認識他好多年了。

例 Thank you for lending me such a fun book, which I've read at
　　　　　　　　　　　　　　　　　　　名詞　　　形容詞子句

least three times.
感謝你借給我那麼有趣的一本書，我已讀了至少三遍了。

例 This is the small town where I was born.
　　　　　　　　　　名詞　　　形容詞子句

這是我出生的小鎮。

上列各句若不使用這些關係詞所引導的形容詞子句，會造成兩個主要子句無連接的錯誤句構。

例 Gary is a kind man, I have known him for years. (✗，兩個主要子句無連接詞連接)

例 Thank you for lending me such a fun book, I have read it at least three times. (✗，兩個主要子句無連接詞連接)

例 This is the small town I was born in it. (✗，兩個主要子句無連接詞連接)

那麼，我們應如何連兩句呢？

1 使用分號 (;)

例 Gary is a kind man, I have known him for years. (✗)
→ Gary is a kind man; I have known him for years. (✓)

2 使用破折號 (—)，表示「也就是說」

例 John is an honest man—he never lies.
約翰是個老實人 —— 他從不說謊。

3 使用連接詞

例 Gary is a kind man, and I have known him for years. (✓)

例 Because Gary is a kind man, so we all respect him. (✗，Because 與 so 均為連接詞，形成錯誤的雙重連接)
→ Because Gary is a kind man, we all respect him. (✓)

= Gary is a kind man, so we all respect him. (✓)
蓋瑞是個好人,我們都很尊敬他。

4 使用關係詞(含關係代名詞、關係代名詞所有格,關係副詞引導形容詞子句,修飾之前的主要子句句尾的名詞)

例 Gary is a kind man, we all respect him. (✗,兩句無連接詞連接)

→ Gary is a kind man, him we all respect. (✗,兩句無連接詞連接)

= Gary is a kind man, whom we all respect. (✓)
　　　名詞　　關係代名詞引導的形容詞子句

例 John is an honest man, he never lies. (✗,兩句無連接詞連接)

→ John is an honest man who never lies. (✓)
　　　　　　　　　　　關係代名詞引導的形容詞子句

例 Thank you for lending me such a fun book, I've read it at least three times. (✗,兩句無連接詞連接)

→ Thank you for lending me such a fun book, it I've read at least three times. (✗,兩句無連接詞連接)

→ Thank you for lending me such a fun book, which I've read at least three times. (✓)

例 This is the small town I was born in it 20 years ago.
　　　　　主要子句　　　　　　　　主要子句
(✗,兩個主要子句無連接詞連接)

→ This is the small town in it I was born 20 years ago.
　　　　　主要子句　　　　　　　　主要子句
(✗,兩個主要子句無連接詞連接)

→ This is the small town in which I was born 20 years ago. (✓)
　　　　　　　　　　名詞

277

= <u>This is the small town</u>　<u>where I was born 20 years ago.</u> (✓)
　　主要子句　　　關係副詞引導的形容詞子句，修飾 the small town

20 年前，我出生在這個小鎮。

小試身手

1	This is the park ＿＿＿ we used to play soccer every Sunday. Ⓐ who　　Ⓑ where　　Ⓒ whom　　Ⓓ which
2	The restaurant ＿＿＿ serves the best pasta is near my house. Ⓐ who　　Ⓑ whose　　Ⓒ which　　Ⓓ where

Ans　1. Ⓑ　2. Ⓒ

Unit 38　細談關係代名詞、關係代名詞所有格、關係副詞的用法

a 使用關係代名詞 who、whom 時，之前的先行詞 (即名詞) 必須是人。who 在其所引導的形容詞子句中做主詞；whom 則在其所引導的形容詞子句中做受詞。

例　This is <u>Dora</u>,　<u>she</u> is a good friend of mine. (✗)
　　　先行詞　　主詞

→ This is <u>Dora</u>, <u>who</u> is a good friend of mine. (✓)

這位是朵拉，她是我的一位好友。

例　Doug is an honest boy, we all like <u>him</u>. (✗)

→ Doug is an honest boy, <u>him</u> we all like. (✗)

→ Doug is <u>an honest boy</u>, <u>whom</u> we all like. (✓)

道格是個老實的孩子，我們大家都喜歡他。

例　Chloe is a helpful coworker, we all enjoy working with <u>her</u>. (✗)

→ Chloe is a helpful coworker, we all enjoy working with <u>whom</u>. (✗)

→ Chloe is a helpful coworker, <u>with whom</u> we all enjoy working. (✓，可)

278

→ Chloe is a helpful coworker, whom we all enjoy working with. (✔，佳)

克洛伊是個樂於助人的同事，我們都很喜歡和她一起工作。

b 使用關係代名詞 which 時，可代替之前的整個主要子句或主要子句句尾表示靜物、動物、植物等名詞。

例 Many people say David is a liar, I don't believe it. (✘，兩句無連接詞連接)

→ Many people say David is a liar, it I don't believe. (✘)
　　　　主要子句

→ Many people say David is a liar, which I don't believe. (✔)
　　　　主要子句

許多人都說大衛是個騙子，這點我不相信。

例 Many people say David is a liar, I think it is true. (✘，兩句無連接詞連接)

→ Many people say David is a liar, I think which is true. (✘，which 應移至形容詞子句句首，盡量靠近被修飾的主要子句)

→ Many people say David is a liar, which I think is true. (✔)
　　　　主要子句

許多人都說大衛是個騙子，這點我認為是真的。

例 I bought a watch, it cost me only NT$200. (✘，兩句無連接詞連接)
　　　　　物

→ I bought a watch, which cost me only NT$200. (✔)

我買了一只錶，它才花了我新臺幣兩百元。

例 This is a watch I have never seen it before.
　　　主要子句　　　　　主要子句

(✘，兩句無連接詞連接)

→ This is a watch I have never seen which before. (✘，which 應緊接被代替的名詞之後)

→ This is a watch (which) I have never seen before. (✔)

這是一只我從來沒見過的手錶。

c 使用關係代名詞所有格 whose 時，用以代替人稱代名詞的所有格 (如 his, her 等)。

例 Here comes Cindy, her father used to be my teacher.
　　　主要子句　　　人　　　　　　主要子句
(✗，兩句無連接詞連接)

→ Here comes Cindy, whose father used to be my teacher.
　　　　主要子句　　　　　　　形容詞子句
(✓，關係代名詞所有格 whose 引導形容詞子句，修飾之前的先行詞 Cindy，並形成兩句由 whose 產生連接)
辛蒂來了，她爸爸以前是我的老師。

例 This is Darren, I have a crush on his sister. (✗，兩句無連接詞連接)
　　主要子句　　　　主要子句

→ This is Darren, I have a crush on whose sister. (✗，whose sister 應緊接在先行詞 Darren 之後)

→ This is Darren, whose sister I have a crush on. (✓)

這位是達倫，我暗戀他的妹妹。

注意 whose 的先行詞也可指東西或動物。

例 I once saw a cat its tail was exceptionally long.
　　　主要子句　　　　　　主要子句
(✗，兩句無連接詞連接)

→ I once saw a cat whose tail was exceptionally long. (✓)
　　　　　　　先行詞

我有一次曾見到一隻尾巴特別長的貓。

d 關係副詞有 when、where、why 三種，均由 "介詞 + which" 轉變而成。

❶ where 的先行詞是表示地方的名詞

例 I live in Taipei, there are many tall buildings in it. (✗，兩句無連接詞連接)

→ I live in Taipei, there are many tall buildings in which. (✗，in which 應緊接先行詞 Taipei 之後)

→ I live in Taipei, in which there
　　　　　　　　地方名詞
are many tall buildings. (✔)

= I live in Taipei, where there are many tall buildings. (✔，佳)
我住在臺北，那裡有許多高樓。

例 The place which I live is a small fishing village. (✘，live 表「居住」是不及物動詞，which 無法做 live 的受詞，我們不能說：" I live a small fishing village." 而要說 "I live in a small fishing village.")

→ The place in which I live is a small fishing village. (✔)

= The place where I live is a small fishing village. (✔，佳)
我住的地方是個小漁村。

例 Look at the mountaintop, there is a white house on it. (✘，兩句無連接詞連接)

→ Look at the mountaintop, there is a white house on which. (✘，on which 應緊鄰接在地方名詞之後)

→ Look at the mountaintop, on which there is a white house. (✔)

= Look at the mountaintop, where there is a white house. (✔，佳)
看那山頂，上面有一棟白色的屋子。

例 The old man was sitting on the chair, under it there was an old dog. (✘，兩句無連接詞連接)

→ The old man was sitting on the chair, under which there was an old dog. (✔，具體指出位置，可不用 where 代換)
老先生正坐在椅子上，椅子下有一條老狗。

2 when 的先行詞是表示時間的名詞

例 Mr. Wang was born in 1945, in that year the Second World War ended. (✘，兩句無連接詞連接)

→ Mr. Wang was born in 1945, in which the Second World War ended. (✔，可)

→ Mr. Wang was born in 1945, when the Second World War ended. (✔，佳)　王先生於 1945 年出生，那一年第二次世界大戰結束了。

281

3 why 的先行詞是 the reason

例 Harry is too selfish. That is the reason which he has few friends.
(✗，which 無法在所引導的形容詞子句中做主詞，因為已有主詞 he；which 也無法做受詞，因為及物動詞 has 之後已有受詞 few friends，故 which 之前應置介詞 for，形成 for which（因為這個理由）)

→ Harry is too selfish. That is the reason for which he has few friends. (✓，可)

→ Harry is too selfish. That is the reason why he has few friends. (✓，佳)　哈利太過自私。那就是他朋友很少的原因。

注意

a the reason 可省略，保留 why；也可省略 why，保留 the reason，即：

例 Harry is too selfish. That is the reason he has few friends.
= Harry is too selfish. That is why he has few friends.

b the reason why 也可改用 the reason that 取代，後者多用於口語中。

例 I know the reason why Dana quit her job.
= I know the reason that Dana quit her job.　我知道黛娜辭職的原因。

小試身手

1	漢克終於找到他考試不及格的原因。 Hank finally found the reason ＿＿＿ he failed the exam.
2	我長大的那個村莊這些年已有很大的變化。 The village ＿＿＿ I grew up has changed a lot over the years.

Ans　1. why　2. where

Unit 39　形容詞子句限定修飾與非限定修飾的區別

a　關係代名詞、關係代名詞所有格或關係副詞之前的先行詞若是專有名詞（如 Peter、Taipei、New York）、書報雜誌名稱（如 *USA Today*、*Newsweek*、*Time*、*The Washington Post*）、國名（如 Japan、Vietnam）、機構名稱（如 the United Nations）等，這些專有名詞已具有其特殊性，之後的關係詞所引導的形容詞子句可有可無，不須再強調該專有名詞的特殊性，因此關係詞之前一定要加逗號，翻譯成中文時依序翻譯。此稱<u>非限定</u>的形容詞子句。

英文：I live in <u>Taipei</u>, <u>which</u> is a big city.
　　　　　　　　專有名詞

中文：我住在臺北，這是個大都市。

英文：I subscribed online to <u>*Time*</u> magazine, <u>which</u> I like to read
　　　　　　　　　　　　　專有名詞
　　　because it keeps me informed of what's going on in the world.

中文：我在線上訂閱了《時代》雜誌，我很喜歡看，因為它讓我了解世界大事。

英文：Standing by the window is <u>Peter</u>,
　　　　　　　　　　　　　　　專有名詞
　　　<u>whose</u> sister is my wife.

中文：站在窗邊的是彼得，他姐姐是我老婆。

英文：My English teacher is <u>Mr. Li</u>, <u>who</u> is patient with us students.
　　　　　　　　　　　　　專有名詞

中文：我的英文老師是李老師，他對我們學生很有耐心。

英文：I went to college in <u>2008</u>, <u>when</u> I met my wife-to-be.
　　　　　　　　　　　　專有名詞

中文：我於 2008 年唸大學，就在那年我認識了我後來的妻子。

b 若先行詞是普通名詞，本身不具特殊性時，該先行詞之後不置逗號，使其後關係詞所引導的形容詞子句發揮限定修飾先行詞的功能，翻譯成中文時，先將形容詞子句翻譯成「……的」，再翻譯先行詞。

英文：Ian is a boy , who never lies. (×)
　　　　普通名詞　　形容詞子句

中文：伊恩是個男孩，他從不說謊。
　　　（不具特殊性）

→ 英文：Ian is a boy who never lies. (✓)

中文：伊恩是個從不說謊的男孩。

英文：This is a book, which I enjoy reading. (×，a book 不具特殊性，不加逗號)

中文：這是書，我喜歡看這本書。

→ 英文：This book is a must-read, which I never get tired of reading. (✓)
　　　　　　　　　　　（有特殊性）

中文：這是一本必讀的書，我讀它從不感到厭煩。

c 有些名詞雖是普通名詞，卻有其獨一性時，之後的形容詞子句採非限定修飾，即關係詞之前需置逗號。常用的這類獨一性名詞有 my mother（媽媽只有一個）、my father（爸爸只有一個）、my grandmother（奶奶／外婆只有一個）、my grandfather（爺爺／外公只有一個）、president（國家元首只有一個）、boss（公司頂頭上司只有一個）等。

英文：Here comes my mother who is an English teacher. (×)
中文：我那位當英文老師的媽媽來了。(×，暗示我還有一位當校長、女工或計程車司機等的媽媽)

英文：Here comes my mother , who is an English teacher. (✓)
中文：我媽媽來了，她是個英文老師。(✓)

英文：Mr. Smith is our president who is nice to his people but strict with his officials. (✗)

中文：史密斯先生是善待百姓但嚴格對待官員的我們的總統。(中文不通順，且暗示另外還有一位總統)

英文：Mr. Smith is our president , who is nice to his people but strict with his officials. (✓)

中文：史密斯先生是我們的總統，他善待百姓，且嚴格對待官員。(中文順暢)

小試身手

1. Taiwan is an island (which / , which) is famous for its food.
2. I have a friend (who / , who) lives in New York.

Ans 1. , which　2. who

Unit 40　that 取代關係代名詞 who、whom、which

that 可取代 who、whom、which 當做關係代名詞用，但有三個條件：

a that 之前不可有逗號。

例 I respect Bill, that never lies. (✗)
→ I respect Bill, who never lies. (✓)　我尊敬比爾，他從不說謊。

例 Gone with the Wind is one of the few novels which / that I enjoyed reading. (✓)《亂世佳人》是少數幾部我很喜歡看的小說。

Gone with the Wind is a well-written novel, that I enjoyed reading. (✗)
→ Gone with the Wind is a well-written novel, which I enjoyed reading. (✓)《亂世佳人》是本寫得很好的小說，我很喜歡看。

b that 之前不得有介詞。

例 Tom is my colleague, with that I enjoy working. (✗)
　　　　　　　　　　　　介詞

→ Tom is my colleague, with whom I enjoy working. (✓)
　　　　　　　　　　　　　　介詞

= Tom is my colleague, whom I enjoy working with. (✓)
湯姆是我的同事，我喜歡與他共事。

但：Tom is one of the few colleagues, that I enjoy working with. (✗)

→ Tom is one of the few colleagues whom I enjoy working with. (✓)

= Tom is one of the few colleagues that I enjoy working with. (✓)

= Tom is one of the few colleagues with whom I enjoy working. (✓)
湯姆是少數幾個我喜歡與他們共事的同事之一。

C 有最高級形容詞修飾的名詞，之後的關係代名詞只可用 that 取代 who、whom、which。

例　Jane is the best student whom I've ever taught. (✗)
　　　　　最高級形容詞

→ Jane is the best student that I've ever taught. (✓)
珍是我教過最棒的學生。

例　What is the most difficult job which you have ever done? (✗)
　　　　　最高級形容詞

→ What is the most difficult job that you have ever done? (✓)
你以前曾做過最難的工作是什麼？

【小試身手】

選出錯誤的句子。

Ⓐ The car that I bought last year is still in great condition.
Ⓑ The teacher, whom I admire, has published several books.
Ⓒ This is the most beautiful place that I have ever visited.
Ⓓ The movie, with that I went to see last weekend, was very exciting.

Ans Ⓓ

Unit 41　who 做形容詞子句受詞時的注意事項

在現代口語中，英文為母語人士者常用 who 當形容詞子句中的主詞，也當形容詞子句的受詞，取代 whom。但 whom 之前有介詞時，仍使用 whom，不使用 who。

例　Here comes Michael, whom I just ran into
　　　　　　　　　　　　　受詞
　　this morning. (✓，正式)

→ Here comes Michael, who I just ran into
　　　　　　　　　　　　受詞
　　this morning. (✓，口語)

麥可來了，今天早上我還跟他巧遇。

例　The colleague, to who I sent the email, replied quickly. (✗)
　　　　　　　　　介詞

→ The colleague, to whom I sent the email, replied quickly. (✓)
　　　　　　　　　介詞　受詞

我寄電子郵件的同事很快就回覆了。

小試身手

The classmate, with (who / whom) I studied yesterday, passed the exam.

Ans　whom

Unit 42　關係代名詞 whom、which 做受詞的省略用法

關係代名詞 whom 或 which 在限定修飾的形容詞子句中做受詞時，可予省略。

例　The man whom you saw this morning is my father.
　　　　　　受詞　　及物動詞

287

= The man you saw this morning is my father.
你今天早上見到的那位男士是我父親。

例 The book which Bob is reading is a French novel.
　　　　　受詞　　進行式及物動詞

= The book Bob is reading is a French novel.
鮑伯正在看的那本書是法文小說。

小試身手

The movie which we watched last night was very interesting.
提示 請以省略關係代名詞改寫句子。

Ans The movie we watched last night was very interesting.

Unit 43 關係代名詞 who、whom 接插入語用法

關係代名詞 who 及 whom 之後接插入語，如 I think（我認為）、I feel（我覺得）、in my view（以我之見）時，這些插入語不會改變 who 或 whom 應該使用的格（主格或受格）。

例 Chris is the man I think　　who　　can handle the problem.
　　　　　　　　　　　主詞（故用主格）　動詞

(✗，who 應置插入語之前)

→ Chris is the man whom I think can handle the problem.
　　　　　　　　　　主詞　　　　動詞

(✗，whom 應改成主格 who，以做形容詞子句的主詞)

→ Chris is the man who I think can handle the problem. (✓)
　　　　　　　　　主詞　　　　動詞

克理斯是我認為能解決這個問題的人。

例 Carrie is a competent co-worker, in my view, we should all support her. (✗，兩句無連接詞連接)
及物動詞

→ Carrie is a competent co-worker, in my view, we should all support whom. (✗，做動詞 support 的受詞，關係代名詞 whom 應緊接先行詞 co-worker 之後)

→ Carrie is a competent co-worker whom, in my view, we should all support. (✓) 凱莉是個很稱職的同事，以我之見，我們都應該支持她。

小試身手

Betty is the artist (who / whom), in my view, creates the most creative works of art.

Ans who

289

Notes

Chapter 4

Unit 44 >>> Unit 49

名詞子句

「名詞子句」是英文句子中超級重要的無名英雄，它能擔任主詞、受詞、補語，甚至是介詞的受詞，讓句子變得更生動有趣！

本章節帶你輕鬆搞懂名詞子句的構造與功能，並解析其在不同情境中的應用，無論是日常會話或寫作中都能正確使用名詞子句，提升你的英文水準，做個英文達人不是夢！

Unit 44 何謂名詞子句？如何形成名詞子句？名詞子句有什麼功能？

中文的句子(陳述句)可直接當主詞，之後加動詞及其他詞類，形成一個更長的句子。英文句子則無此錯誤結構。

a 陳述句做主詞 + 動詞及其他詞類

中文：安迪整天鬼混令他父母擔心極了。(✓)
　　　陳述句做主詞　　　動詞

英文：Andy fools around all day worries his parents sick. (✗)
　　　陳述句做主詞　　　動詞

在英文的概念中，直述句自成一個獨立句子，即：
Andy fools around all day.

此時應將直述句改成名詞子句(即句子變成的名詞，如同一般名詞，可做主詞)。

只要在陳述句之前加一個連接詞 that 即成名詞子句，如下：
that Andy fools around all day

b 由於名詞子句視同一個名詞，故句首的 that 首字母 t 小寫，子句句尾無句點，就如名詞一樣，名詞子句只是句中的一個部分。由於名詞可做主詞、受詞或 be 動詞之後的補語，故名詞子句亦可當主詞、受詞或 be 動詞的補語。

例 Andy fools around all day. (✓，句意完整)　安迪整天鬼混。
　 主詞　動詞

→ That Andy fools around all day
　 主詞(視作單數主詞)
worries his parents sick. (✓)
動詞
安迪整天鬼混令他父母擔心極了。

c that 子句作及物動詞的受詞時，that 可省略。

例 I just can't believe (that) Ashley is so musically talented.
　　　　　及物動詞　　　　　　名詞子句
我真不敢相信艾希莉有如此的音樂天分。

例　My understanding is _____ (that) Becky sings well.
　　　　　　　　　不完全及物動詞　　名詞子句做主詞補語
　　就我所知，貝琪歌唱得很好。

小試身手

莉娜在繪畫上很有天賦讓她的朋友們感到驚訝。
_____ Lena is very talented at drawing amazes her friends.

Ans　That

Unit 45　特殊疑問句改成名詞子句

a 中文的特殊疑問句可以當主詞，之後加動詞或其他詞類，形成一個更長的句子。

中文：傑克在什麼地方仍是個謎。(✓)

英文：Where is Jack still remains a mystery. (✗)
　　　問句結構 (不可做主詞)

應改成兩個句子，即：

Where is Jack? It still remains a mystery. (✓，問句與陳述句各自獨立)
　問句　　　　　陳述句

b 但我們亦可將疑問詞起首的特殊疑問句改成名詞子句，步驟如下：

1 有 be 動詞的特殊疑問句

問　　句：Where are we going?

名詞子句：where we are going　我們要去哪兒

問　　句：Who is he?

名詞子句：who he is　他是誰

293

2 有一般助動詞 (如 can、will、should...) 及完成式助動詞 (如 have / has / had + 過去分詞) 的特殊疑問句

問　　句：When will David come back?

名詞子句：when David will come back
　　　　　大衛將何時回來

問　　句：What have you done?

名詞子句：what you have done
　　　　　你做了什麼事

3 有助動詞 do / does / did 的特殊疑問句

問　　句：Why did the boy leave home?

名詞子句：why the boy did left home　這男孩子為什麼離家出走

問　　句：Where does John live?

名詞子句：where John does lives　約翰住在哪裡

以上這些由特殊疑問句變化而成的名詞子句與 that 引導的名詞子句一樣，在句中可當主詞、及物動詞的受詞或 be 動詞之後的補語。

例　Why did the boy leave home is beyond me. (✗)
　　　　　　問句

→ Why the boy left home is beyond me. (✓)
　　　名詞子句做主詞

這男孩子為何離家出走非我所了解。

例　I don't know where does Peter live? (✗)
　　　　　　　　　　問句

→ I don't know where Peter lives. (✓)　我不知道彼得住在哪裡。
　　　vt.　名詞子句做受詞

例　I have no idea (about)　　why did the boy leave home? (✗)
　　　　介詞，此介詞實際上並不使用　　　　問句

→ I have no idea why the boy left home. (✓)
　　　　　名詞子句作省略的介詞 about 的受詞

我不知道為什麼這男孩離家出走。

294

例　Tell me how should I do it? (✗)

→ Tell me how I should do it. (✓)　告訴我這件事我該怎麼做。
　　名詞子句做 Tell 的直接受詞

小試身手

請將問句改寫成名詞子句，並填入句子中。

1. What time does the train leave?
I need to know _____.

2. Why did Carey cancel the meeting?
We are trying to understand _____.

> Ans　1. what time the train leaves
> 　　　2. why Carey canceled the meeting

Unit 46　一般疑問句改名詞子句

a　一般疑問句（即句首無疑問詞的問句，可用 Yes / No 回答）亦可藉由疑問詞 whether（是否）改成名詞子句。

1 be 動詞 + 主詞 → 主詞 + be 動詞

問　　句：Is Chris going to come?
　　　　　(Yes, he is. / No, he isn't.)

名詞子句：whether Chris is going to come　克里斯是否會來

2 一般助動詞 / 完成式助動詞 + 主詞
→ 主詞 + 一般助動詞 / 完成式助動詞

問　　句：Can you do it?
　　　　　(Yes, I can. / No, I can't.)

名詞子句：whether you can do it　你是否能做這件事

問　　句：Has Bella finished her homework?

名詞子句：whether Bella has finished her homework
　　　　　貝拉是否已做完功課

3 以助動詞 do / does / did 起首的問句變成名詞子句時，採下列步驟：

　　a 在問句前先置 whether

　　b 刪除 do / does / did

　　c whether 之後接問句的主詞

　　d 再將問句的原形動詞恢復應有的時態動詞

問　　句：<u>Does</u>　Charlie <u>know</u> the truth?
　　　　　現在式助動詞　　　原形動詞

名詞子句：<u>whether</u> Charlie <u>knows</u> the truth　查理是否知道真相
　　　　　　　　　　第三人稱單數現在式動詞

問　　句：<u>Did</u>　　Elaine <u>tell</u> you the truth?
　　　　　過去式助動詞

名詞子句：<u>whether</u> Elaine <u>told</u> you the truth　伊蓮是否有告訴你真相
　　　　　　　　　　　　過去式動詞

問　　句：<u>Do</u>　　they <u>like</u> it?
　　　　　現在式助動詞　原形動詞

名詞子句：<u>whether</u> they <u>like</u> it　他們是否喜歡它
　　　　　　　　　　　現在式動詞

b 如同 that 子句與 what、when、why、where、how 疑問詞引導的名詞子句一樣，whether 引導的名詞子句亦視同名詞，在句中可做主詞、受詞、be 動詞之後的主詞補語。

1 主詞

例　<u>Whether will Elva come</u> depends on the weather. (✗)

　→ <u>Whether Elva will come</u> depends on the weather. (✓)
艾娃是否會來要依天氣而定。

例　<u>Whether can John do it</u> remains to be seen. (✗)

　→ <u>Whether John can do it</u> remains to be seen. (✓)
約翰是否能做這件事有待觀察。

例 Whether is Mary willing to marry me is not known yet. (✗)

→ Whether Mary is willing to marry me is not known yet. (✓)

瑪麗是否願意嫁給我尚不得而知。

2 受詞

例 I am curious (about) whether David has already left.
　　　　　　　介詞，可省略

我很好奇大衛是否已經離開了。

例 I don't know whether this fruit can be eaten.
　　　　　vt.

我不知道這個水果可不可以吃。

3 be 動詞之後的主詞補語

例 We are all set. The only problem is whether can we get the funds we need. (✗)

→ We are all set. The only problem is whether we can get the funds we need. (✓)

我們都準備就緒了。唯一的問題是我們是否能拿到我們所需的那筆資金。

注意

1 whether 引導的名詞子句做及物動詞的受詞或 be 動詞之後的補語時，whether 可被 if 取代。

例 I don't know whether Jason can do it.
　　　　　vt.

= I don't know if Jason can do it.　我不知道傑森是否能做到。

例 The only problem is whether we can get the funds.

= The only problem is if we can get the funds.

唯一的問題是我們是否能取得資金。

2 whether 引導的名詞做主詞時，whether 不可被 if 取代。

例 Whether Peter will come remains to be seen. (✓)

彼得是否會來還說不準。

但: If Peter will come remains to be seen. (✗)

3 whether 亦可與 not 並用。

例 I don't know whether Jason can do it or not. (✓)

= I don't know whether or not Jason can do it. (✓)

297

= I don't know if Jason can do it or not. (✓)
我不知道約翰是否能做這件事。

但：I don't know if or not Jason can do it. (✗)

❹ whether 子句當主詞時，whether 就不能被 if 取代。

例 Whether Jason will do it or not doesn't concern me. (✓)

= Whether or not Jason will do it doesn't concern me. (✓)
傑森是否要做這件事不關我的事。

但：If Jason will do it or not doesn't concern me. (✗)

If or not Jason will do it doesn't concern me. (✗)

❺ whether 亦可當副詞連接詞，表「不論是否」，引導副詞子句，修飾主要子句。

例 Whether it rains or not, we will go camping as scheduled. (✓)

= No matter whether it rains or not, we will go camping as scheduled. (✓)

= We will go camping as scheduled whether or not it rains / whether it rains or not. (✓)　不論下不下雨，我們都會按計劃去露營。

但：If it rains or not, we will go camping as scheduled. (✗)

If or not it rains, we will go camping as scheduled. (✗)

❻ 至此，我們已經了解名詞子句有三種：

① that 子句

例 I know that it pays to learn English.　我知道學英文是值得的。

② whether 子句

例 Nobody cares about whether you will join us (or not).
你是否要加入我們，沒人在乎。

③ 疑問詞子句

例 Tell me what you'll do this afternoon, please.
請告訴我你今天下午要做什麼。

我們可用女生的名字「戴慧怡」永遠記住這三種名詞子句：

戴：that 子句

慧：whether 子句

怡：疑問詞子句

即：that (戴)、whe (慧)、疑 (怡)

298

小試身手

選出錯誤的句子。

Ⓐ Whether John will pass the exam remains uncertain.
Ⓑ I don't know if or not Mike can come.
Ⓒ The main question is whether or not we can solve this issue.
Ⓓ Whether or not it rains, we will go for a picnic.

Ans Ⓑ

Unit 47 「戴慧怡」名詞子句

a 「戴慧怡」名詞子句出現在下列結構時，由於修飾形容詞，立刻成為副詞子句。

例 I am worried that something is wrong with Adam. He looks a bit
　　　 adj.　　　　　　副詞子句

upset today.　我擔心亞當不太對勁。他今天看起來有點不快樂的樣子。

例 I am curious whether Annie can do it.
　　　adj.　　　　副詞子句

我很好奇安妮是否能做這件事。

例 I am not quite sure where David lives.
　　　　　　　adj.　　副詞子句

我不太確定大衛住在哪兒。

b 「慧怡」名詞子句可做介詞的受詞，「戴」名詞子句則不可。

例 I'm worried about that something is wrong with Adam. (✗)
　　　　　　 介　　　　　名詞子句

→ I'm worried that something is wrong with Adam. (✓)
　　　　adj.　　　　　　副詞子句

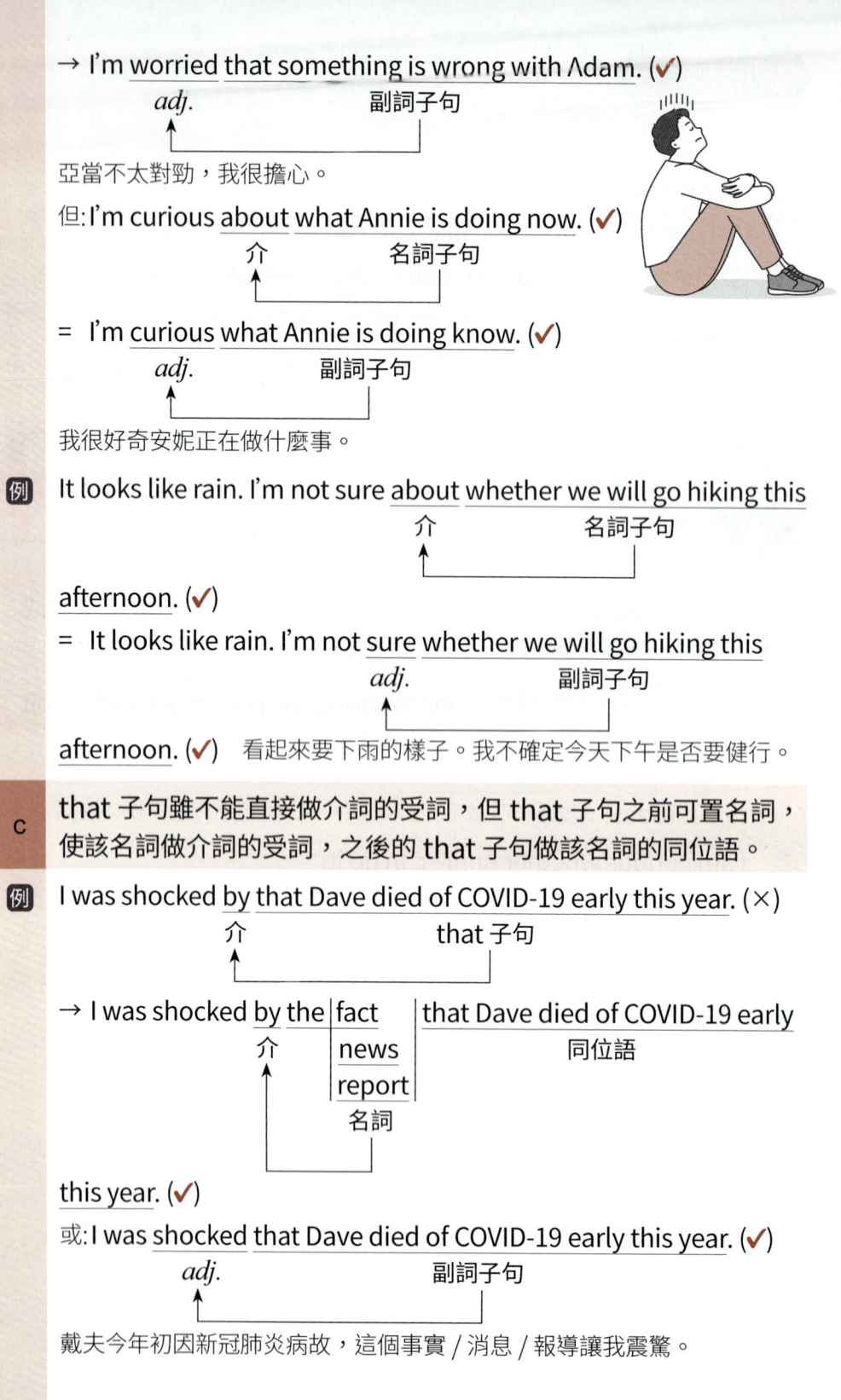

亞當不太對勁，我很擔心。

但：I'm curious about what Annie is doing now. (✓)
　　　　　　介　　　　　　名詞子句

= I'm curious what Annie is doing know. (✓)
　　　adj.　　　　　　副詞子句

我很好奇安妮正在做什麼事。

例 It looks like rain. I'm not sure about whether we will go hiking this
　　　　　　　　　　　　　　　　介　　　　　　名詞子句

afternoon. (✓)

= It looks like rain. I'm not sure whether we will go hiking this
　　　　　　　　　　　　　　　adj.　　　　　　副詞子句

afternoon. (✓)　看起來要下雨的樣子。我不確定今天下午是否要健行。

C　that 子句雖不能直接做介詞的受詞，但 that 子句之前可置名詞，使該名詞做介詞的受詞，之後的 that 子句做該名詞的同位語。

例 I was shocked by that Dave died of COVID-19 early this year. (✗)
　　　　　　　　介　　　　　　that 子句

→ I was shocked by the | fact | that Dave died of COVID-19 early
　　　　　　　　　介　　| news |　　　　　同位語
　　　　　　　　　　　 | report|
　　　　　　　　　　　　　名詞

this year. (✓)

或：I was shocked that Dave died of COVID-19 early this year. (✓)
　　　　　　　adj.　　　　　　副詞子句

戴夫今年初因新冠肺炎病故，這個事實 / 消息 / 報導讓我震驚。

d 不過 that 子句可置介詞 in 或 except 之後，此時 in that（因為）或 except that（只不過）視作副詞連接詞，引導副詞子句，修飾之前的主要子句。

例 John is nice in that he often helps the poor.
　　　主要子句　　　　　　副詞子句

　　= John is nice because he often helps the poor.
　　約翰人真好，因為他常幫助貧困的人。

例 The apartment is pretty good except that the rent is a bit high.
　　這間公寓挺不錯的，只不過租金有點貴。

小試身手

選出正確的句子。
Ⓐ I am interested about that Tom won the award.
Ⓑ We are curious that how the movie ends.
Ⓒ John is very kind in that he always donates to charities.
Ⓓ Ida is worried about that her project will fail.

Ans Ⓒ

Unit 48　引導 that 子句相關的片語

a now (that)...
now (that) 亦視作副詞連接詞，等於「如今既然」，受到 now 的影響，所引導的副詞子句動詞應使用現在式或現在完成式。

例 Now that we were alone, you could tell me the truth.（✗）
　　　　　　　過去式　　　　　　過去式

→ Now (that) we are alone, you can tell me the truth.（✓）

= Since / Because we are alone, you can tell me the truth.（✓）
既然我們獨處了，你可以把真相告訴我了。

301

b given that...

that 之前亦可置 given，此處 given 是介詞，表「考慮到」或「有鑑於」，之後可接 that 子句或名詞做受詞。

例 | Given | his age, the old man did a great job.
   | Considering |
   | In view of |

考慮到這位老先生的年紀，他的表現算是很不錯了。

例 | Given that | Jimmy has been learning English for
   | Considering that |
   | Given the fact that |
   | In view of the fact that |

only three years, he did quite well in the English speech contest.
有鑑於吉米學英文才三年，他在英文演講比賽中的表現算是相當棒了。

c provided / providing that...

provided that = providing that，均視作副詞連接詞，與 if (如果) 同義，引導副詞子句，修飾主要子句。

例 I'll buy you a fancy mountain bike | provided that | you pass
                                      | providing that |
                                      | on condition that|

the exam.
= I'll buy you a fancy mountain bike if you pass the exam.
你若通過這場考試，我就會買一臺很炫的登山車給你。

d seeing that...

seeing that... = because... = considering that... 由於 / 因為……

例 Seeing that you've graduated from college, you'll have to find a job soon. 由於你已大學畢業，你得盡快找到工作。

> 小試身手

1. 有鑑於他有限的資源，馬克還是成功取得了好成績。
   _____ his limited resources, Mark managed to achieve great results.

2. 如果你保證會小心駕駛，我就讓你借我的車。
I'll let you borrow my car _____ you promise to drive carefully.

Ans 1. Given / Considering / In view of
     2. provided (that) / providing (that)

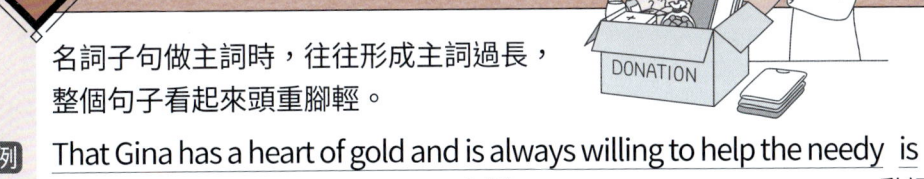

Unit 49　以 it 代替名詞子句

名詞子句做主詞時，往往形成主詞過長，整個句子看起來頭重腳輕。

例 That Gina has a heart of gold and is always willing to help the needy is
    　　　　　　　　　　主詞　　　　　　　　　　　　　　　　　　　　動詞
known to all of us. (✓，但主詞過長)
吉娜有一顆善良的心，總是願意幫助貧困的人，這點我們都知道。

例 Whether everyone should attend the meeting (which is) scheduled for 10 a.m. tomorrow hasn't been decided yet. (✓，但主詞過長)
我們是否要參加預定在明天早上 10 點召開的會議，這點尚未決定。

此時，我們可用代名詞 it 代替過長的名詞子句，而將該名詞子句移至句尾，形成下列結構：
It + 動詞… + 過長的名詞子句
故上列兩句可改寫為：

例 It is known to all of us that Gina has a heart of gold and is always willing to help the needy. (✓，佳)

例 It hasn't been decided yet whether everyone should attend the meeting (which is) scheduled for 10 a.m. tomorrow. (✓，佳)

小試身手

Whether the students will complete their project on time remains uncertain.

提示 用 "It + 動詞 + 名詞子句" 的結構改寫句子。

Ans It remains uncertain whether the students will complete their project on time.

Notes

Chapter 5

Unit 50 >>> Unit 67

> 動狀詞

「動狀詞」是連結動作與語法結構的重要橋樑，幫助我們豐富語句結構，創造出更多元、更靈活的表達方式！無論是表達目的、原因，還是描述動作的狀態，動狀詞都能在句子中發揮關鍵作用。

本章節將深入探討動狀詞的各種形式，包括不定詞、分詞及動名詞，並介紹它們在不同語境中的應用與區別。無論是在簡化句子結構還是提升語句精確度，動狀詞能幫助你讓語言表達更精確、更有趣！

Unit 50 動狀詞的種類

動狀詞包括不定詞、分詞及動名詞，茲分述如下：

a 不定詞

❶ 原形不定詞：sing

❷ to + 原形動詞：to sing

例　I can <u>sing</u>.　我會唱歌。
　　　　　原形不定詞

例　I want him <u>to sing</u>.　我想要他唱歌。

b 分詞

❶ 現在分詞：如 washing、singing、repairing

❷ 過去分詞：如 washed、sung、repaired

例　Mom is <u>singing</u>.　老媽正在唱歌。
　　　　　　現在分詞

例　The song is so popular that it has been <u>sung</u> by many people.
　　　　　　　　　　　　　　　　　　　　過去分詞

這首歌太流行，許多人都唱過。

c 動名詞

如 singing、dancing、writing

例　I <u>enjoy</u> <u>singing</u>.　我喜歡唱歌。
　　 vt.　動名詞 (做 enjoy 的受詞)

例　<u>Singing</u> is my hobby.　唱歌是我的嗜好。
　　動名詞 (做本句的主詞)

小試身手

My boyfriend wants me ____ with him.

Ⓐ come　　Ⓑ to come　　Ⓒ comes　　Ⓓ coming

Ans Ⓑ

Unit 51　原形動詞 / 原形不定詞

原形動詞也稱作原形不定詞，可置於以下位置或與特殊動詞並用：

a 置助動詞 will、would、shall、should、can、could 之後。

例　I will call you back first thing tomorrow morning.
　　我明天早上第一件事就是回電給你。

例　You should finish all the work before leaving.
　　你應該在離開前完成所有工作。

b 與使役動詞 make、let、have 並用。

例　Dad made me to wash his car this afternoon. (✗)
　　→ Dad made me wash his car this afternoon. (✓)
　　老爸叫我今天下午洗他的車子。

例　I'll have Stan to take care of the matter. (✗)
　　→ I'll have Stan take care of the matter. (✓)
　　我要叫史坦處理這件事。

例　Tom won't let me to touch his brand-new car. (✗)
　　→ Tom won't let me touch his brand-new car. (✓)
　　湯姆不讓我碰他的新車。

注意　get 亦可做使役動詞，採下列句型：

get + sb + to + 原形動詞　叫某人從事……

例　I'll get Stan take care of the matter. (✗)
　　→ I'll get Stan to take care of the matter. (✓)
　　= I'll | have | Stan take care of the matter. (✓)
　　　　　| make |
　　我會叫史坦處理這件事。

注意　以上使役動詞只有 make 可採被動語態，即：

例　Dad made me wash his car. (✓)
　　→ I was made to wash Dad's car. (✓)　我被要求洗老爸的車。
　　Dad let me wash his car. (✓)
　　→ I was let to wash Dad's car. (✗)

Dad got me to wash his car. (✓)
→ Dad was gotten to wash his car. (✗)

> 小試身手

The teacher made the students (to complete / complete) their assignments.

Ans complete

Unit 52　不定詞片語：to + 原形動詞

"to + 原形動詞"則為我們常說的不定詞片語，有三種功能：

a 不定詞片語當名詞用，表示尚未實現且不一定會實現的計畫、夢想等。

中文：娶阿珍是我的夢想。(✓，中文的動詞可直接當主詞)

英文：Marry Jane is my dream. (✗，英文的動詞不可直接當主詞)

從句尾的 dream (夢想) 得知，「娶阿珍」只是個夢想，這個動作未來不一定會實現，故應採 to 引導的不定詞片語當主詞，即：

例　To marry Jane is my dream. (✓)

中文：環遊世界是我明年的計畫。

英文：Travel around the world is my plan for next year.

(✗，此處 Travel 是動詞，不可當主詞)

→ To travel around the world is my plan for next year. (✓)

1 由上得知，名詞不定詞片語做主詞時，be 動詞之後的名詞一定為表示意願、目標、計畫等名詞，常用的此類名詞如下：
aim (目的)、attempt (企圖)、decision (決定)、goal (目標)、plan (計畫)、desire (渴望)

2 名詞不定詞片語如同「戴慧怡」名詞子句一樣，可用 it 代替，即：

例 To marry Jane is my dream.
= It is my dream to marry Jane. 娶阿珍是我的夢想。

例 To get admitted to a top-notch university is my plan for next year.
= It is my plan for next year to get admitted to a top-notch university.
考上一流大學是我明年的計畫。

* top-notch [tɑpˋnɑtʃ] a. 一流的，頂尖的

b 名詞不定詞片語當及物動詞的受詞，此時這些及物動詞通常表示意願、企圖、期待、希望、決定要……等，常用的動詞如下：wish (希望)、hope (希望)、decide (決定要)、intend (企圖)、attempt (企圖)、want (想要)、expect (期待)、strive (努力要)、desire (渴望)、yearn (渴望)、long (渴望)。

例 I hope visiting my grandparents sometime next year. (✗)
→ I hope to visit my grandparents sometime next year. (✓)
我希望明年找個時間去探視我爺爺奶奶。

例 What I want saying is that David is a man we can trust. (✗)
→ What I want to say is that David is a man we can trust. (✓)
我想要說的是大衛是我們可以信賴的人。

例 I | desire | being with you forever and a day. (✗)
　　| yearn |
　　| long　 |
→ I | desire | to be with you forever and a day. (✓)
　　| yearn |
　　| long　 |
我渴望能跟你廝守在一起直到海枯石爛。(直到永遠再加一天)

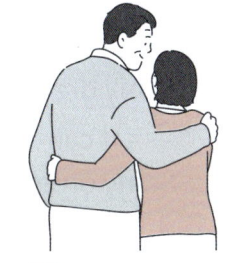

c to 引導的不定詞片語亦可置名詞之後做形容詞，修飾該名詞，但該名詞必須做不定詞片語中及物動詞的受詞，否則就要做介詞的受詞。

例 Don't you think this is a good place to live?
　　　　　　　　　　　　　　　　 名詞　　不及物動詞

(✗，不能說：I live a good place. 應說：I live in a good place.)
故上列問句應改為：

例 Don't you think this is a good place　　　to live in? (✓)
　　　　　　　　　　　　　　　　　　形容詞片語，修飾 a good place
你不覺得這是個好住處嗎？(a good place 做 to live in 的受詞)

例 Paul is a nice co-worker　to work. (✗)
　　　　　　　名詞　　　不及物動詞
不可說：I work a nice co-worker.
　　　　　　　　　vi.
應　說：I work with a nice co-worker.
故上列句子應改成：

例 Paul is a nice co-worker to work with.
保羅是個可以共事的好同事。(a nice co-worker 做 to work with 的受詞；且不定詞片語 to work with 視作形容詞，修飾 a nice co-worker)

例 I have something to　do now. (✓，something 做及物動詞 do 的受詞)
　　　　　　　　　　及物動詞
我現在有事要做。(to do 是不定詞片語，視作形容詞，修飾代名詞 something)

d　to 引導的不定詞片語亦可做副詞用，可置句首或句尾，修飾句中動詞或整個主要子句。

例 I came all the way here to see my dream girl, Mary.
= I came all the way here in order to see my dream girl, Mary.
= I came all the way here so as to see my dream girl, Mary.
我一路來這裡為了要見見我的夢中情人瑪麗。

但: with a view to、with an eye to、for the purpose of 亦表「為了要」、「目的是要」，這三個片語的 to、of 是介詞，故之後應接動名詞做受詞。

例 I came all the way here with a view to see my dream girl, Mary. (✗)
→ I came all the way here with a view to seeing my dream girl, Mary. (✓)
= I came all the way here with an eye to seeing my dream girl, Mary. (✓)
= I came all the way here for the purpose of seeing my dream girl, Mary. (✓)

注意 to 引導的不定詞片語與 in order to 引導的不定詞片語可置句首或句尾；so as to 引導的不定詞片語只能置句尾。

例　To get admitted to a top-notch university, you'll have to study hard. (✓)

= In order to get admitted to a top-notch university, you'll have to study hard. (✓)

= You'll have to study hard to get admitted to a top-notch university. (✓)

= You'll have to study hard in order to get admitted to a top-notch university. (✓)

= You'll have to study hard so as to get admitted to a top-notch university. (✓)

想要考上一流的大學，你就非努力不可。/ 你必須努力以便考上一流的大學。

但: So as to get admitted to a top-notch university, you'll have to study hard. (✗)

小試身手

選出錯誤的句子。

Ⓐ Finish the project is our main goal this month.
Ⓑ Linda plans to join the gym next week.
Ⓒ Tom expects to finish his work by tomorrow.
Ⓓ This is the best book to read during the holidays.

Ans Ⓐ

Unit 53　so as to 與 so that

"so as to + 原形動詞"（以便，為了要）源自 so that 引導的副詞子句。so that 等於 in order that，是副詞連接詞，所引導的副詞子句表示某目的。句型如下：

主要子句 + | so that　　　 | + 主詞 + 助動詞 (can, may, will 等)
　　　　　| in order that |
+ 原形動詞

311

例　You'll have to study hard so that you can get admitted to a top-notch university.

= You'll have to study hard in order that you can get admitted to a top-notch university.

= You'll have to study hard so as to get admitted to a top-notch university.

= You'll have to study hard in order to get admitted to a top-notch university.
你必須用功讀書以便考上一流的大學。

小試身手

Kelly practices piano every day so as to become a professional pianist.
提示　用 "so that" 句型改寫句子。

Ans　Kelly practices piano every day so that she can become a professional pianist.

Unit 54　與原形不定詞並用的特殊句構

a　do nothing but + 原形不定詞　除了……以外，什麼都沒 / 不做

例　Victor does nothing but to idle around all day. (✗)
Victor does nothing but idled around all day. (✗)
→ Victor does nothing but idle around all day. (✓)
維克多什麼也不做只是每天鬼混。

例　This weekend, I'll do nothing but to take a good rest. (✗)
→ This weekend, I'll do nothing but take a good rest. (✓)
這個週末我什麼都不做只是好好休息。

312

例　When I was in college, I did nothing but to study every day. (✗)
　→ When I was in college, I did nothing but studied every day. (✗)
　→ When I was in college, I did nothing but study every day. (✓)
唸大學時，我幾乎每天什麼都不做就只是讀書。
但: be doing nothing but V-ing

例　Ted is doing nothing but watch TV now. (✗)
　→ Ted is doing nothing but watching TV now. (✓)

泰德現在什麼都不做就只是在看電視。

b | choose / expect / want / desire | nothing but to + 原形動詞　什麼都不要，只要……

上列「選擇」、「期望」等動詞原本就可接 to 引導的不定詞片語做受詞，如 "choose to V"、"expect to V"、"want to V"、"desire to V"，故上述片語在 nothing but 之後亦加 "to + 原形動詞"。

例　I wanted nothing but slept. (✗)
　→ I wanted nothing but to sleep. (✓)　我什麼都不想，只想睡覺。

例　I desire nothing but have a house of my own. (✗)
　→ I desire nothing but to have a house of my own. (✓)
或: I desire　nothing　　　but　　　a house of my own. (✓)
　　　vt.　　　n.　　　(= except)　　　n.
　　　　└──── 共做 desire 的受詞 ────┘

我什麼都不想要，只想要一棟屬於自己的房子。

c be interested in nothing but (interested in) + 動名詞 / 名詞
除了……之外，其他都不感興趣

例　Paul is interested in nothing but to sing. (✗)
　→ Paul is interested in nothing but singing / music. (✓)
　　　　　　　　　　　　　介　　　　動　　名

保羅除了唱歌 / 音樂外，其他都不感興趣。

313

| d | cannot but + 原形不定詞　忍不住……
= cannot help + 動名詞
= cannot help but + 原形不定詞
此處的 help 等於 stop 或 resist，表「抗拒」。 |

例　Upon hearing the sad news, the woman <u>couldn't but to cry</u>. (✗)

→ Upon hearing the sad news, the woman <u>couldn't but cry</u>.
(✓，但少用)

= Upon hearing the sad news, the woman <u>couldn't help crying</u>. (✓，常用)

= Upon hearing the sad news, the woman <u>couldn't help but cry</u>.
(✓，常用)　這名婦人一聽到這悲傷的消息就忍不住哭了。

| e | have no | choice
option
alternative | but to + 原形動詞 |

除了……之外別無選擇

例　Because of the heavy rain, we <u>have no choice but cancel</u> the camping trip. (✗)

→ Because of the heavy rain, we <u>have no choice but to cancel</u> the camping trip. (✓)

由於下大雨的關係，我們除了取消這趟露營之行外，別無選擇。

小試身手

| 1 | 南茜只想在漫長的一天結束後放鬆一下。
Nancy wanted nothing but ＿＿＿＿ (relax) after a long day. |
| 2 | 湯姆忍不住為這次旅行感到興奮。
Tom cannot help ＿＿＿＿ (feel) excited about the trip. |

Ans　1. to relax　2. feeling

Unit 55 分詞的種類

a 現在分詞：（原形動詞 + ing）

原形動詞	→	現在分詞
keep（保持）	→	keep<u>ing</u>
sing（唱歌）	→	sing<u>ing</u>

b 過去分詞：（原形動詞 + ed）

原形動詞	→	過去分詞
want（要）	→	want<u>ed</u>
ask（問；要求）	→	ask<u>ed</u>

c 不規則變化

英文的動詞變化成現在分詞或過去分詞並非上述幾個例字那麼單純，請看下例：

原形動詞	→	現在分詞
write（寫）	→	wri<u>ting</u>（非 writeing）
die（死亡）	→	d<u>ying</u>（非 dieing）
cut（切，割）	→	cut<u>ting</u>（非 cuting）

原形動詞	→	過去分詞
write（寫）	→	writ<u>ten</u>（非 writed）
read [rid]（閱讀）	→	read [rɛd]（非 readed）

因此，要想掌握這些動詞變化唯有藉由閱讀英文文章勤查字典，一點一滴地累積知識，並養成寫英文日記的習慣。無需死記硬背，不出三年就會完全通曉。

小試身手

請填入正確的現在分詞與過去分詞。

原形動詞	→	現在分詞	→	過去分詞
write	→	_____	→	_____
ask	→	_____	→	_____

Ans writing; written; asking; asked

Unit 56 分詞與時態及主被動語態的關係

a 現在分詞可形成下列各類進行式：

1 現在進行式：主詞 + am / are / is + 現在分詞

例 I am having / eating breakfast.
我正在吃早餐。

例 The sun is rising.
太陽正在升起。

2 過去進行式：主詞 + was / were + 現在分詞

例 Minnie was writing a letter then.
蜜妮當時正在寫信。

3 未來進行式：主詞 + will be + 現在分詞

例 Vic will be working this time tomorrow.
明天此時維克會在上班。

4 現在完成進行式：主詞 + have / has been + 現在分詞

例 Sean has been learning English for six years.
尚恩六年來一直都在學英文。

5 過去完成進行式（與過去式搭配）：主詞 + had been + 現在分詞

例 I had been working for four hours when / by the time Terry arrived.
　　　　　　　　　　　　　　　　　　　　　　　　　　　　　　過去式

泰瑞到的時候，我一直都在工作已達 4 小時之久。

6 未來完成進行式（與現在式搭配）：主詞 + will have been + 現在分詞

例 By the time our boss will arrive at the office, the meeting will have been going on for at least an hour. (✗)

→ By the time / When our boss arrives at the office, the meeting
　　　　　　　　　　　　　　　　　現在式
will have been going on for at least an hour. (✓)
等到我們老闆抵達辦公室時，會議將已開了至少一個小時。

316

b 過去分詞可形成被動語態，且只有及物動詞才可形成被動語態。

1 如何判斷動詞為及物動詞或不及物動詞？

先造兩個下列有空格的中文句子：

我 ＿＿＿＿ 他。

他被我 ＿＿＿＿ 。

2 在上列兩個空格中隨意放置相同的英文動詞並譯成中文，如果兩句中文都很通順，這個英文動詞就是及物動詞；若有任何一句中文不通順就是不及物動詞。

茲以 punish（處罰）為例：

我 __punish__ 他。

他被我 __punish__ 。

中文：我 __處罰__ 他。（通順）

他被我 __處罰__ 。（通順）

由上得知，punish 是及物動詞 (*vt.*)，在主動語態（主詞 + 及物動詞 + 受詞）中，punish 之後一定要有受詞，否則就須採被動語態（主詞 + be + 過去分詞）。

例　I punished Sam. 我處罰了山姆。（主動語態）
　　主詞　及物動詞　受詞

　　Sam was punished by me. 山姆被我處罰了。（被動語態）
　　　　　　過去分詞

再以英文動詞 happen（發生）為例：

我 __happen__ 車禍。

車禍被我 __happen__ 。

中文：我發生車禍。（尚通順）

中文：車禍被我發生。（不通順）

由中譯立即得知 happen 是不及物動詞 (*vi.*)，因此之後不能直接置受詞，故無下列被動語態的英文句子：

例　A car accident was happened this morning (×)
今天早上一起車禍被發生了。（不通順）

CH 5 動狀詞

317

換言之，不及物動詞又能用於主動語態。

A car accident | happened | this morning. (✓)
　　　　　　　| took place |
　　　　　　　| occurred |

今天早上發生了一起車禍。（通順）

c 及物動詞在句中出現的句型：

1 主動語態

a 主詞 + 及物動詞 + 受詞

例　Molly finished the work early this morning.
　　主詞　　vt.　　受詞
　　今天一早茉莉就把工作做完了。

b 主詞 + be + 及物動詞變成的現在分詞 + 受詞

例　I am doing nothing now.　我現在沒在做什麼事。
　　主詞　vt.　　受詞

例　Steve has been learning English for 5 years.
　　主詞　　　vt.　　　受詞
　　史提夫持續學英文達五年之久。

c 主詞 + 助動詞 + 原形及物動詞 / 過去分詞 + 受詞

例　Believe it or not, I can play the piano.　信不信由你，我會彈鋼琴。
　　　　　　　　　　　　　vt.　受詞

例　I have finished all the work.
　　　　過去分詞　　受詞
　　我把所有的工作都做完了。

2 被動語態

例　I did it.

　　It was done by me.　這件事被我處理完了。
　　　被動語態

例　The portrait was painted in the 17th century.
　　　主詞　　被動語態
　　這幅畫是十七世紀(被)畫的。

例　All the work has been finished.　所有的工作都(被)做完了。
　　　　　　　　被動語態

d 不及物動詞在句中出現的句型：
不及物動詞之後無受詞，故不可出現在被動語態中。換言之，不及物動詞只能採 "主詞 + 不及物動詞" 的主動語態。

例 Mr. Li was fainted in the middle of his speech. (×)
→ Mr. Li fainted in the middle of his speech. (✓)
　　　　vi.
李先生在他演講進行到一半時昏倒了。

例 A car accident was happened early this morning. (×)
→ A car accident happened early this morning. (✓)
今天一大早就發生了一場車禍。

注意 be 動詞之後若接不及物動詞時，這些動詞均應改為現在分詞，形成進行式。

例 A beautiful girl was danced with Peter. (×)
　　　　　　　　　vi.
→ A beautiful girl was dancing with Peter. (✓)
　　　　　　　　　過去進行式
一位美女在和彼得跳舞。

例 I've been waited for you for over an hour. (×)
　　　　　vi.
→ I've been waiting for you for over an hour. (✓)
　　　現在完成進行式
我一直等你等了一個多小時了。

小試身手

1. A beautiful song ____ by the choir last night.
   Ⓐ sing　　Ⓑ was sung　　Ⓒ sang　　Ⓓ is singing

2. By next month, I ____ Spanish for a year.
   Ⓐ will have been learning　　Ⓑ will be learning
   Ⓒ have been learning　　Ⓓ have been learned

Ans 1. Ⓑ 2. Ⓐ

Unit 57 分詞片語的應用與連接詞的使用

a 句中若有兩個動詞,其所代表的動作有先後次序時,第二助動詞應有連接詞 and 連接。

例 Aaron locked the door rushed to the bus stop. (✗,動詞 locked 與 rushed 無連接詞連接)

→ Aaron locked the door and rushed to the bus stop. (✓)
亞倫把門鎖好便匆匆趕往公車站了。

b 兩個動詞所代表的動作同時發生時,無須置連接詞,第二動詞變成現在分詞。

例 Dad sat in the armchair read a newspaper. (✗)

→ Dad sat in the armchair reading a newspaper. (✓)　老爸坐在扶手椅 (同時在) 看報。

例 Bob stood up smoking a cigarette. (✗)
鮑伯 (邊) 站起來 (邊在) 抽菸。(不合邏輯,兩個動作不可能同時發生,故第二動詞 smoked 之前應有連接詞 and 連接,即先站起來,再抽菸)

→ Bob stood up and smoked a cigarette. (✓)
鮑伯 (先) 站起來 (再) 抽菸。(合乎邏輯)

注意 句中兩個動詞,有逗點相隔,不論這兩個動詞所代表的動作是否同時發生,第二個動詞一定變成現在分詞。若是 be 動詞 (is, was, are, were) 一律變成現在分詞 being,再予省略。

例 Cathy lay back on the couch, looked as if she was tired. (✗)

→ Cathy lay back on the couch, looking as if she was tired. (✓)
　　(lie 的過去式)
凱西躺在長沙發上,看起來好累的樣子。

例 Gary came back from work, was tired and listless. (✗)

→ Gary came back from work, was tired and listless.
　　　　　　　　　　　　　　　(being)

即:Gary came back from work, tired and listless. (✓)
蓋瑞下班回家,既疲累又無精打采。

＊listless [ˈlɪstləs] *a.* 無精打采的

例 I left home was young and came back was old. (✗，left 與 was、came 與 was 均無連接詞連接)

→ I left home ~~was~~ young   and   came back ~~was~~ old.
　　　　　　　(being)　(連接 left 及 came)　　　　　(being)

即：I left home │ young 　　　　│ and came back │ old.　　　　│ (✓)
　　　　　　　 │ a young man │ 　　　　　　　 │ an old man. │

少小離家老大回。

比較下列兩句：

例 The little boy walked all the way back to cry. (✗，不合邏輯)
小男孩一路走回來目的是要哭。

→ The little boy walked all the way back crying. (✓，合乎邏輯)
小男孩一路哭著走回來／邊走邊哭。

注意 否定句的分詞變化：

例 The little boy stood there, (he) did not know what to do. (✗，did 之前無連接詞 and 連接)

→ The little boy stood there, and (he) did not know what to do.
(✓，兩句有 and 連接)

→ The little boy stood there, did not knowing what to do. (✗，did 之前無連接詞 and 連接，故應刪除 did，動詞 know 變成現在分詞)

即：The little boy stood there, not knowing what to do. (✓)
小男孩站在那裡，不知道該做什麼。

C 兩句在一起應有連接詞 and (同時) 或 so (因此) 連接。

例 Henry hadn't finished his work, and / so he started to worry.
(✓，兩個主要子句有 and 或 so 連接)
亨利工作沒做完，同時／因此他開始擔心。

1 兩個主要子句若無連接詞 and 或 so 連接時，此時第一個主要子句的動詞或完成式助動詞 have、has、had 要變成現在分詞，且相同的主詞應省略。

例 Henry having not finished his work, he started to worry. (✗，not 要置 having 之前)

→ Not having finished his work, Henry started to worry. (✓)
亨利工作沒做完，他開始擔心。

例 ~~Henry was~~ not finished with his work, ~~he~~ started to worry. (✗)
　　　　being

→ Being not finished with his work, Henry started to worry. (✗)

→ Not being finished with his work, Henry started to worry. (✓)

= Not finished with his work, Henry started to worry. (✓)

亨利工作沒做完，開始擔心了。

例 Paul was tired and sleepy, he went to bed immediately. (✗，兩句無連接詞 and 或 so 連接)

→ ~~Paul was~~ tired and sleepy, ~~he~~ went to bed immediately.
　　　being

→ Being tired and sleepy, Paul went to bed immediately. (✓)

= Tired and sleepy, Paul went to bed immediately. (✓)

保羅又累又睏，立刻就上床睡覺了。

2 由上得知：

兩句無連接詞連接時，往往第一個主要子句要變成分詞片語，也就是分詞構句。

第一步：刪除相同的主詞。

第二步：之後的動詞要變成現在分詞，若是 is, was, are, were 等 be 動詞時，一律變成 being。

第三步：being 可省略。

例 ~~Tim was~~ not interested in studying, ~~he~~ found a job right after he
　　　being

graduated from high school. (✗)

→ Being not interested in studying, Tim found a job right after he graduated from high school. (✗)

→ Not (being) interested in studying, Tim found a job right after he graduated from high school. (✓)

= Not interested in studying, Tim found a job right after he graduated from high school. (✓)

提姆對讀書不感興趣，高中畢業後立刻找了一份工作。

> **小試身手**
>
> Tom had finished his homework, and he went out to play.
> 提示 請用分詞片語結構（分詞構句）改寫句子。
>
> > Ans Having finished his homework, Tom went out to play.

Unit 58 獨立分詞片語

a 兩個句子在一起，無連接詞連接，且主詞不同時：
第一步：保留不同的主詞。
第二步：之後的動詞變成現在分詞，be 動詞一律變成 being，完成式助動詞（have、has、had）則變成 having。

例 The sun had set, the cowboys rode their horses back to the ranch. (✗)
　　　主詞不同

→ The sun having set, the cowboys rode their horses back to the ranch. (✓)
太陽已西下，牛仔們騎著馬回到牧場。

注意 不同主詞所形成的分詞片語。由於獨立修飾不同的主詞，此類分詞片語稱作獨立分詞片語，而這樣的結構就稱為獨立分詞構句。

例 All things were considered, we decided to cancel the plan.
　　　　　　　主詞不同
（✗，兩句無連接詞連接）

→ All things were considered, we decided to cancel the plan. (✓)
　　　　　being

= All things considered, we decided to cancel the plan. (✓)
全盤考慮後，我們決定放棄該計畫。

323

b 若第一個主要子句的主詞是主角，第二個主要子句的主詞是配角，此時可保留第一個主要子句，第二個子句則形成分詞片語。

例 Ryan was watching TV, his wife was knitting beside him.
　　　第一個主要子句　　　　第二個主要子句
（✗，兩句無連接詞連接）

→ Ryan was watching TV, his wife ~~was~~ knitting beside him.
　　　　　　　　　　　　　　　　　(being)
　　　　　主詞不同

即：Ryan was watching TV, his wife knitting beside him. (✓)
　　　　　　　　　　　　　獨立分詞片語，修飾 his wife

萊恩在看電視，他的老婆在他旁邊編織。

例 If the weather permits, we will go hiking tomorrow. (✓)
　　連接詞

天氣許可的話，我們明天將會去健行。

Weather permits, we'll go hiking

　　　　主詞不同

tomorrow.（✗，兩個主要子句無連接詞連接）

→ Weather ~~permits~~, we'll go hiking tomorrow.
　　　　　permitting

即：Weather permitting, we'll go hiking tomorrow. (✓)
　　　獨立分詞，修飾 weather

= We'll go hiking tomorrow, weather permitting. (✓)

小試身手

請用獨立分詞片語修正句子。

1. The guests had left, the hosts began cleaning up.

2. The sun was shining, the children played in the park.

Ans 1. The guests having left, the hosts began cleaning up.
　　　 2. The sun shining, the children played in the park.

Unit 59 限定修飾的形容詞子句簡化成分詞片語

限定修飾的形容詞子句（即關係代名詞之前無逗點）中，若關係代名詞作主詞時，該形容詞子句可化簡成分詞片語。
第一步：刪除作主詞的關係代名詞 who 或 which。
第二步：將 who 或 which 之後的動詞變成現在分詞，若動詞是 be 動詞（如 is、was、are、were），一律變成 being，再予省略。

例 The girl who is talking to her classmate is my daughter. (✓)
　　　　　主詞

→ The girl ~~who is~~ talking to her classmate is my daughter.
　　　　　　(being)

即：The girl talking to her classmate is my daughter.
正在跟同學說話的女孩是我女兒。

例 A book which is worth reading is worth reading time and again. (✓)
　　　　　主詞

→ A book ~~which is~~ worth reading is worth reading time and again.
　　　　　(being)

即：A book worth reading is worth reading time and again. (✓)
值得看的書值得一看再看。

小試身手

The man who is waiting at the bus stop is my uncle.
提示 用分詞片語結構簡化句子。

Ans The man waiting at the bus stop is my uncle.

Unit 60 非限定形容詞子句不可簡化成分詞片語

非限定的形容詞子句 (即關係代名詞前有逗點)，通常不可簡化為分詞片語。

例 I respect Tom, who never fails to help the poor. (✓)
我尊敬湯姆，他總是幫助窮困的人。

但: I respect Tom, ~~who~~ never ~~fails~~ to help the poor.
　　　　　　　　　　　　　failing

→ I respect Tom, never failing to help the poor. (✗)

我尊敬湯姆，我總是幫助窮困的人。(語意不通)

注意 非限定修飾的形容詞子句句構若為 "關係代名詞 + be + 名詞" (也就是主詞的地位) 時，則仍可化簡，形成同位語。

例 I'm going to call on Peter, who is a good friend of mine. (✓)
→ I'm going to call on Peter, ~~who is~~ a good friend of mine.
　　　　　　　　　　　　　　　(being)
即: I'm going to call on Peter, a good friend of mine. (✓)
　　　　　　　　　　　　　　　　　同位語

我將拜訪彼得，我的一位好友。

例 Joe, who is my co-worker, is to be promoted to sales manager next month. (✓)
→ Joe, ~~who is~~ my co-worker, is to be
　　　　(being)
promoted to sales manager next month.
即: Joe, my co-worker, is to be promoted to sales manager next
　　主詞　同位語
month. (✓)

我的同事喬下個月就要升遷為業務經理了。

例 David is a man of his word, which is a fact that is known to all of us. (✓)

→ David is a man of his word, ~~which is~~ a fact ~~that is~~ known to all of us.
　　　　　　　　　　　　　　　　　(being)　　　(being)

即: David is a man of his word, a fact known to all of us. (✓)
大衛是個言而有信的人，這是我們大家都知道的事實。

小試身手

The Eiffel Tower, which is a famous landmark in Paris, attracts millions of tourists each year.
提示 將非限定形容詞子句改寫為同位語。

Ans The Eiffel Tower, a famous landmark in Paris, attracts millions of tourists each year.

Unit 61　簡化副詞子句為分詞構句

once、unless、though、when、if、while 等六個連接詞所引導的副詞子句，其主詞若與主要子句的主詞相同時，亦可化簡為分詞構句，步驟如下：

1 刪除主詞。
2 之後的動詞變成現在分詞。
3 動詞若為 be 動詞 (is, was, are, were)，一律變成現在分詞 being 之後，再予省略。

例 Once I'm available, I'll give you a call. (✓)

→ Once ~~I am~~ available, I'll give you a call.
　　　　　(being)

即: Once available, I'll give you a call. (✓)
一旦有空，我會打電話給你。

例 Though I have little money, I lead a happy life. (✓)

→ Though ~~I have~~ little money, I lead a happy life.
　　　　　having

327

即：Though having little money, I lead a happy life. (✓)
雖然我錢不多，日子卻過得很快樂。

例 When I am tired, I don't feel like doing anything. (✓)
→ When ~~I am~~ tired, I don't feel like doing anything.
　　　　(being)
即：When tired, I don't feel like doing anything. (✓)
當我累的時候，我什麼事都不想做。

例 Unless you are told otherwise, do as I say. (✓)
→ Unless ~~you are~~ told otherwise, do as I say.
　　　　　(being)
即：Unless told otherwise, do as I say. (✓)
除非另外有人告訴你怎麼做，否則就照我的話去做。

注意

1 once 引導的副詞子句簡化為分詞構句時，多為 "once + (being) + 形容詞"，實際使用時 being 一律省略。

例 Once I am rich, I'll definitely buy a house. (✓)
→ Once ~~I am~~ rich, I'll definitely buy a house.
　　　　(being)
即：Once rich, I'll definitely buy a house. (✓)
我一旦有錢，肯定會買一棟房子。

例 Once I have money, I'll definitely buy a house. (✓)
→ Once having money, I'll definitely buy a house. (罕)

2 If 引導的副詞子句，即使其主詞與主要子句的主詞相同，也鮮少簡化為分詞構句。

例 If I have money, I'll definitely buy a house. (✓)
→ If having money, I'll definitely buy a house. (罕)

但：If necessary = if it is necessary　如有必要
If possible = if it is possible　如有可能

例 If I'm necessary, I can come to your assistance anytime. (✗)
→ If it is necessary, I can come to your assistance anytime. (✓)
= If necessary, I can come to your assistance anytime. (✓)
= If needed, I can come to your assistance anytime. (✓)

= If need be, I can come to your assistance anytime. (✓)
如有必要，我隨時可前來幫助你。

例　Give me a call if you are possible. (✗)
　→ Give me a call if it is possible. (✓)
　= Give me a call if possible. (✓)　如有可能，打一通電話給我。

小試身手

Once Tina is finished, she will join us for dinner.
提示 用分詞片語結構簡化句子。

Ans Once finished, Tina will join us for dinner.

Unit 62　形容詞＋身體部位名詞變成的過去分詞：描述身體部位

表示身體部位的名詞可變成過去分詞當形容詞用，置被修飾的名詞前。

例　Who is that girl with the big eyes? (✓)
　→ Who is that big-eye girl? (✗)
　→ Who is that big-eyed girl? (✓)　那位大眼女孩是誰？

例　The red-hair girl is my girlfriend. (✗)
　→ The red-haired girl is my girlfriend. (✓)　那位紅髮女孩是我女友。

例　The one-leg soldier was highly praised as a hero. (✗)
　→ The one-legged [ˈlɛɡɪd] soldier was highly praised as a hero. (✓)
那位獨腳的戰士被視作英雄大受讚揚。

例　The bare-foot farmer is my father. (✗)
　→ The bare-footed farmer is my father. (✓)
這位打赤腳的農夫是我父親。

> **小試身手**
>
> The (broken-arm / broken-armed) player still managed to finish the game.
>
> **Ans** broken-armed

Unit 63 分詞作形容詞用

a 有些分詞可做形容詞用，可置名詞前修飾該名詞；亦可置 be 動詞之後，做主詞補語。

例 The teacher raised a confused question. (×)
　　　　　　　　　感到困惑的
→ The teacher raised a confusing question. (✓)
　　　　　　　　　令人困惑的
老師提出一個令人困惑的問題。

b 現在分詞有「主動」的概念；過去分詞則有「被動」的概念。使用現在分詞做形容詞時，表示「令人……的」；使用過去分詞做形容詞時，表示「感到……的」或「受到……的」。

例 The question was so confused that all the students were confusing. (×)　這個問題那麼感到困惑，以致所有學生都令人困惑了。
→ The question was so confusing that all the students were confused. (✓)　這個問題那麼令人困惑，因此所有學生都感到困惑了。

例 The injuring soldiers were rushed to the hospital. (×)
這些令人受傷的戰士被火速送往醫院。
→ The injured soldiers were rushed to the hospital. (✓)
這些受傷的戰士被火速送往醫院。

例 The news was excited, and those who heard it were exciting. (×)
這個消息感到興奮，凡是獲悉的人都令人興奮。
→ The news was exciting, and those who heard it were excited. (✓)
這個消息令人興奮，凡是獲悉的人都感到興奮。

例　None of the audience were interesting in the speech because it was not interested at all. (✗)
聽眾對這演講全都不令人興趣，因為它一點都不感到興趣。

→ None of the audience were interested in the speech because it was not interesting at all. (✓)
聽眾對這演講全都不感興趣，因為它一點都不令人產生興趣。

例　Who's that charmed lady in the corner? (✗)
　　　　　感到著迷的

→ Who's that charming lady in the corner? (✓)
　　　　　令人著迷的
角落裡那位魅力四射的小姐是誰呀？

C　此外現在分詞含有「進行」的概念；過去分詞則有「完成」的概念。即：現在分詞可表「正在……的」或「即將……的」；過去分詞則表「已經……的」。

例　The retiring teacher made a farewell speech.
這位即將退休的老師發表了一篇告別演講。

例　I ran into the retired teacher in Japan three years later.
三年後我與這位已退休的老師在日本偶遇。

例　I'm thirsty. Get me some boiling water to drink. (✗)
我好渴。拿一些正在沸騰的水給我喝。（✗，正在沸騰的水喝不得，會把食道燙熟的）

→ I'm thirsty. Get me some boiled water to drink. (✓)
我好渴。拿一些已煮沸過的水給我喝。

例　Don't stand in the fallen rain, or you'll get soaking wet. (✗)
不要站在已降落到地面上的雨中，否則你全身都會溼透的。（✗，不合邏輯）

→ Don't stand in the falling rain, or you'll get soaking wet. (✓)
不要站在正在下的雨中，否則你會全身溼透的。

> **小試身手**

1. The movie was so (boring / bored) that I almost fell asleep.
2. Everyone was (exciting / excited) about the upcoming event.

Ans 1. boring　2. excited

Unit 64　主詞補語的誤用：副詞與形容詞的分辨技巧

避免錯用副詞取代形容詞作主詞補語。

例 Everyone is born freely. (✗)　每個人都是自由地被生下來。
　　　　　　　↑adv.

理由 freely 修飾動詞片語 is born (出生)，「自由地出生」表「按自己的意願隨時隨地出生」，不合邏輯。

→ Everyone is born free. (✓)　人人生而自由。/ 每個人出生時是自由的。
　　　　　　　↑adj.

本句原為：Everyone is born and is free. (✓)

將 and 刪除，則成

Everyone is born is free. (✗，兩個 is 動詞無連接詞連接)

此時應將第二個動詞變成現在分詞 being，再將 being 省略，即成下列正確的句子：

Everyone is born (being) free.
即：Everyone is born free. (✓)

同理

Everyone is born equally. (✗)　人人皆是平等地生下來。(不知所云)
　　　　　　　↑adv.

→ Everyone is born equal. (✓)
　　　　　　　↑adj.

人人生而平等。(形容詞 equal 是主詞 Everyone 的補語)

例　Bob was born deafly. (✗)　鮑伯是以耳聾的方式生下來。(不知所云)
　　　　　　　　adv.

→ Bob was born deaf. (形容詞 deaf 是主詞 Bob 的補語)
　　　　　　　　adj.

鮑伯生下來就是聾的 / 就聽不見聲音。

小試身手

這水果嚐起來很甜。
This fruit tastes _____.

Ans sweet

Unit 65　with 引導的情狀片語

a　情狀介詞片語是一種表示情況或狀態的片語，由介詞 with 引導，之後先加受詞，再加動詞變成的現在分詞或過去分詞。如果是及物動詞，可變成"現在分詞 + 受詞"，如果是不及物動詞，一律變成現在分詞，結構如下：

with + 受詞 + 及物動詞變成的現在分詞 (+ 受詞)
with + 受詞 + 及物動詞變成的過去分詞
with + 受詞 + 不及物動詞變成的現在分詞

b　情狀介詞片語附屬於句子中，可置句首，多半都置句尾。

例　With you sit beside me, I can hardly concentrate on my work. (✗)
　　　　　　vi.

→ With you sitting beside me, I can hardly
　　　　　　　現在分詞
concentrate on my work. (✓)
有你坐在我身旁，我幾乎無法專心工作。

333

例 It's so cold today that the old man is sitting on the bench with his hands and legs shiver. (✗)
　　　　　　　　　　　　　　　　　　　　　　　　　　　　　vi.

→ It's so cold today that the old man is sitting on the bench with his hands and legs shivering. (✓)
　　　　　　　　　　　　　　　　　　　　　　　　現在分詞

今天好冷，老先生坐在長椅上手腳發抖。

例 Danny lay on the ground with his eyes close. (✗)
　　　　　　　　　　　　　　　　　　　　　vt.

→ Danny lay on the ground with his eyes closed. (✓)
　　　　　　　　　　　　　　　　　　　　過去分詞

丹尼閉著雙眼躺在地上。

例 The bad guy approached the girl with his right hand hold a knife. (✗)
　　　　　　　　　　　　　　　　　　　　　　　　　　　　vt.　受詞

→ The bad guy approached the girl with his right hand holding a knife. (✓)
　　　　　　　　　　　　　　　　　　　　　　　　　　　　現在分詞

= The bad guy approached the girl with a knife (held) in his right hand. (✓)
　　　　　　　　　　　　　　　　　　　　　　　　　過去分詞

壞蛋右手握著一把刀朝著女孩走去。

小試身手

選出錯誤的句子。

Ⓐ The man stood by the door with his arms cross.
Ⓑ The teacher looked at the students with his arms folded.
Ⓒ The cat lay on the sofa with its tail wagging.
Ⓓ Dennis entered the room with his shoes covered in mud.

Ans Ⓐ

334

Unit 66 常用的獨立分詞片語

下列為常用的獨立分詞片語，置句首，不修飾句中的主詞，而是作副詞片語用，修飾整個句子。值得注意的是，這些獨立分詞片語均含現在分詞，而非過去分詞。

例 Generally spoken, men are physically stronger than women. (✗)
→ Generally speaking, men are physically stronger than women. (✓)
= In general / On average / By and large, men are physically stronger than women. (✓)
一般而言，男人體格要比女人強壯。

例 Strictly spoken, Paul is not cut out for the job. (✗)
→ Strictly speaking, Paul is not cut out for the job. (✓)
嚴格地說，保羅並不適合這個工作。

小試身手

嚴格來說，運動對身心健康都很重要。
_____, exercise is important for both physical and mental health.

Ans Strictly speaking

Unit 67 動名詞

動名詞與現在分詞外形一模一樣，均是"動詞 + ing"。但動名詞是動詞變成的名詞，因此如同名詞一樣，在句中可作主詞、及物動詞的受詞、介系詞之後的受詞、補語或同位語。

a 動名詞做主詞

例 Write is my hobby. (✗)
　　動詞

335

→ <u>Writing</u> is my hobby. (✓) 寫作是我的嗜好。
　　動名詞

例 <u>Learn</u> English is a time-consuming process;
　　動詞
it can't be done overnight. (✗)

→ <u>Learning</u> English is a time-consuming process; it can't be done
　　動名詞
overnight. (✓) 學習英文是個費時的過程，無法在一夕之間就可完成。

例 <u>Marry</u> Jenna was a nightmare for me. (✗)
　　動詞

→ <u>Marrying</u> Jenna was a nightmare for me. (✓)
　　動名詞
娶珍娜對我來說是場惡夢。(✓，已經娶)

注意 <u>To marry</u> Sandy is Peter's dream. (✓，尚未娶)
　　　不定詞片語
娶珊蒂是彼得的夢想。

b 動名詞做及物動詞的受詞

例 Evan <u>denied</u> <u>to steal</u> my money. (✗)
　　　　 vt.　　不定詞片語

→ Evan <u>denied</u> | stealing | my money. (✓) 伊凡否認偷了我的錢。
　　　　　　　　 | having stolen |

常用的此類動詞如下：

acknowledge	承認	miss	想念
admit	承認	permit	允許
advise	建議	postpone	延遲
allow	允許	practice	練習
anticipate	期待	prevent	阻止
delay	延誤，延遲	suggest	建議
detest	討厭	recommend	建議
enjoy	喜歡	advise	建議
fancy	想要	propose	建議
finish	做完	resist	抗拒

keep (continue)	繼續	resent	痛恨
mention	提及	risk	冒險
mind	在乎		

例 I have finished writing the report. 我寫完報告了。

注意 過去分詞 finished 亦可做形容詞，表「做完的」，通常採 "be finished with + 名詞" 的結構。故上句亦可改寫如下：

I'm finished with the report.

= I'm done with the report. 我寫完報告了。

例 The young couple decided to delay having children until they got better jobs. 這對年輕夫婦決定延後生育直到有更好的工作為止。

例 I suggest to cancel the camping trip because of the heavy rain. (✗)

→ I | suggest / recommend / propose | canceling the camping trip because of the heavy rain. (✓) 由於大雨的關係，我建議取消露營之行。

例 I miss to go camping with you while we were in college. (✗)

→ I miss going camping with you while we were in college. (✓)

= I miss the days (when) I went camping with you while we were in college. (✓)
我懷念大學時跟你露營的那段日子。

例 Don't risk to swim in the pond alone. (✗)

→ Don't risk swimming in the pond alone. (✓)
別冒險一個人獨自在池塘游泳。

例 We don't allow to smoke here. (✗)

→ We don't | allow / permit | smoking here. (✓)

= We don't | allow / permit | anyone to smoke here. (✓)
人

= We forbid anyone | to smoke / from smoking | here. (✓)

我們不允許 / 禁止任何人在此處吸菸。

CH 5

動狀詞

337

例　I dislike to smoke. (✗)
　→ I dislike / resent smoking. (✓)　我不喜歡 / 痛恨吸菸。

c　有些及物動詞可接 to 引導的不定詞片語或動名詞 (片語)，意思不變。常用的此類及物動詞如下：

start	開始	like	喜歡
begin	開始	hate	痛恨
love	喜歡		

例　I started to learn / learning English when I was 18.　我 18 歲就開始學英文。

例　When did you begin to write / writing the report?　這份報告你什麼時候開始寫的？

例　I love / like to sing / singing whenever I have free time.
　只要有空，我就會唱歌。

例　I hate to tell / telling lies.　我討厭說謊。

d　有些及物動詞之後可加動名詞或不及物動詞加受詞，但意思有別。常用的這些及物動詞如下：

❶ mean to…　有意要……
　mean + V-ing　意即 / 意思就是……

例　I meant / intended to help James, but he refused to be helped.
　我有意要 / 打算要幫助詹姆士，他卻拒絕接受幫助。

例　Moving to a new school means making new friends.
　轉到新學校意即能交到新朋友。

❷ try to V　設法要……
　try + V-ing　試試……

例　I know the job is tough, but I'll try to do the best I can (do) to finish it.
　我知道這工作很艱難，但我會設法盡全力完成它。

例　I tried calling Bobby several times, but no one answered the phone.
　我試著打了數通電話給巴比，但電話都沒人接。

338

例 If this way doesn't work, try meeting him in person.
如果這個方法行不通，試試看與他親自見面。

3 stop to V　停下來改做某事
　　stop + V-ing　停止做某事

例 Emily stopped to take a photo of the beautiful sunset.
艾蜜莉停下來拍了一張美麗的夕陽照。

例 Kent stopped writing to say hello when he saw me.
肯特看到我時，便停筆跟我打招呼。

4 quit to V　辭職以便從事
　　quit + V-ing　辭職；停止從事

例 Justin quit (his job) to work for a bigger company.
賈斯汀辭職改為一家更大的公司效命。

例 Luke quit playing video games to please his girlfriend.
路克不打電動以取悅他的女友。

5 remember to V（未來）　記得要去做……
　　remember + V-ing（過去）　記得曾經做……

例 Remember to call me no later than 9 a.m. tomorrow morning.
記得要在明天早上 9 點以前打電話給我。

例 Years have passed by, but I still remember biking around Taiwan with you in our early twenties.
多年過去，但我仍記得我們二十出頭歲時曾一起騎車環臺。

6 forget to V　忘了要……
　　forget + V-ing　忘了曾……

例 Don't forget to bring me back the book next week.
別忘了下星期要把書還給我。

例 I'll never forget seeing the Eiffel Tower in Paris.
我永遠不會忘了曾看到巴黎的艾菲爾鐵塔。

小試身手

| 1 | They postponed (to travel / traveling) until next year. |
| 2 | Jennifer loves (to cook / cook) for her family on weekends. |

Ans　1. traveling　2. to cook

Notes

Chapter 6

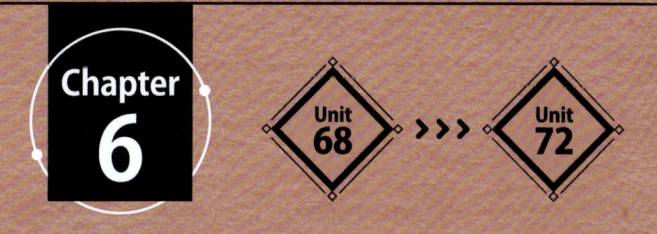

Unit 68 ▶▶▶ Unit 72

▶ 假設語氣

「假設語氣」就像是一種穿越時間的語言魔法，讓你能談論不真實的情況、假設的事件，甚至是心中的想望！無論是想表達「如果我中了大獎」的美好幻想，還是回顧「如果當時我做了不同選擇」的遺憾，假設語氣都是一項重要的語法工具。

本章節將拆解假設語氣的各種樣貌，告訴你如何在日常生活中輕鬆運用這些結構，讓你言之有物！

Unit 68 純條件的假設語氣

a 使用純條件的假設語氣時，if 子句的動詞使用現在式，表示一個條件，主要子句則使用未來式助動詞，如：will、shall、must、ought to、should、can 等。

例 If you are here, I would tell you the truth. (✗)
　　　現在式動詞　過去未來式助動詞

→ If you are here, I will tell you the truth. (✓)
　　　現在式動詞　未來式助動詞
你現在若在這裡，我就會把真相告訴你。

b 連接詞如 once（一旦）、when（當）、as long as（只要）、as soon as（一旦）、before（在……之前）、unless（除非）、if（如果），均可用現在式表示純條件的副詞子句。只有主要子句會出現助動詞 will 表「將」，條件句（即副詞子句）採現在式，不得再使用 will。

例 Once | I will have money, I will buy a car. (✗)
　 If 　|　未來式助動詞　　未來式助動詞
　 我 | 一旦 | 將會有錢，我將會買車。
　 　 | 若　 |

→ Once | I have money, I will buy a car. (✓)
　 If 　|　現在式動詞　未來式助動詞
　 我 | 一旦 | 有錢，就會買車。
　 　 | 若　 |

例 I will not do anything before he will arrive. (✗)
　　未來式助動詞　　　　　　　未來式助動詞
在他將抵達之前，我將什麼都不做。

→ I will not do anything before he arrives. (✓)
　　未來式助動詞　　　　　　　現在式動詞
在他抵達之前，我不會做任何事。

例 If you want to pass the test, you must study hard. (✓)
　　　現在式動詞　　　　　　未來式助動詞
你若想考試過關，就須努力讀書。

> 小試身手

1. 如果艾妮塔早到，我會到車站見她。
   If Anita _____ (come) early, I _____ (meet) her at the station.

2. 布蘭登一到家，就會打電話給朋友。
   As soon as Brandon _____ (get) home, he _____ (call) his friend.

Ans 1. comes; will meet   2. gets; will call

Unit 69 與現在事實相反的假設語氣

a 現在事實使用現在式表示。

例 I'm not rich now. 我現在沒錢。
   現在式動詞

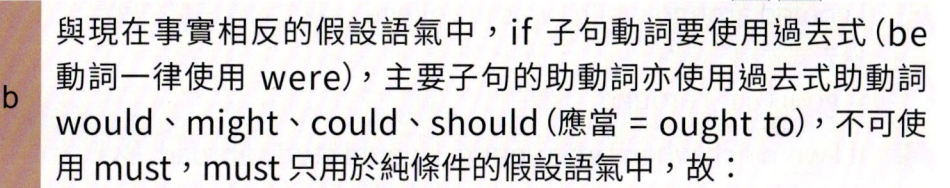

b 與現在事實相反的假設語氣中，if 子句動詞要使用過去式（be 動詞一律使用 were），主要子句的助動詞亦使用過去式助動詞 would、might、could、should（應當 = ought to），不可使用 must，must 只用於純條件的假設語氣中，故：

例 If I'm rich, I would buy a car. (×)
   現在式動詞　過去式助動詞

→ If I were rich, I would buy a car. (✓)
   過去式動詞　過去式助動詞

我若是現在有錢，就會買車。（事實是，我現在沒錢。）

例 If I have more free time, I would travel the world. (×)
   現在式動詞　　　　　　　過去式助動詞

→ If I had more free time, I would travel the world. (✓)
   過去式動詞　　　　　　　過去式助動詞

如果我有更多空閒時間，我就會環遊世界。（事實是，我現在沒空。）

CH 6　假設語氣

343

小試身手

如果他們有時間，就會來和我們一起吃晚餐。
If they _____ (have) time, they _____ (join) us for dinner.

Ans had; would join

Unit 70　與過去事實相反的假設語氣

過去事實要用過去式動詞表示。假設語氣的 if 子句應使用過去完成式 (had + 過去分詞)，主要子句則採 "would / could / should / might ｜ have + 過去分詞" 的句構。

例　I was poor when I was young.　我年輕時很窮。
　　　過去式動詞

例　I goofed around while I was in college.　我念大學時都在鬼混。
　　過去式動詞
　　＊ goof [guf] around　瞎混

例　If I were rich when I was young, I would study abroad. (✗)
　　　　過去式動詞　　　　　　　　　　　　過去式動詞

　→ If I had been rich when I was young, I would have studied
　　　　過去完成式

　　abroad. (✓)　我年輕時若富有的話，就會出國深造了。

例　I could do it if you had helped me. (✗)
　　過去式助動詞

　→ I could have done it if you had helped me. (✓)
　　　過去完成式

如果你當時幫我，我就能完成這件事了。

> **小試身手**
>
> 如果他們當時聽從你的建議，他們可能已經成功了。
> If they _____ (listen) to your advice, they _____ (succeed).
>
> **Ans** had listened; might have succeeded

Unit 71　與未來狀況相反的假設語氣

if 子句中的主詞之後要置助動詞 should（表「萬一」），若假設的可能性低，主要子句要使用過去式助動詞（和與現在事實相反的假設語氣相同）。但若假設的可能性高時，主要子句要使用現在式助動詞（與純條件假設語氣相同）。

a 低可能性：

If + 主詞 + should + 原形動詞, 主詞 + | would / could / might / should / ought to | + 原形動詞

例　It's sunny today. But if it should rain, we would cancel the activity.
今天陽光普照。不過萬一下雨，我們就會取消活動。

b 高可能性：

If + 主詞 + should + 原形動詞, 主詞 + | will / can / may / should / ought to | + 原形動詞

例　It's a cloudy day. If it should rain, we will cancel the activity.
今天是陰天。萬一下雨，我們就會取消活動。

小試身手

這裡通常不會有很大的風。但萬一明天起風，我們可能會延後戶外音樂會。

It's usually not very windy here. But if it should be windy tomorrow, we _____ (postpone) the outdoor concert.

Ans　might postpone

Unit 72　使用假設語氣應注意事項

a　省略 if 讓「何秀華」搬家：
if 子句有過去完成式助動詞（had + 過去分詞）、助動詞 should（萬一）或 be 動詞 were 時，可將 if 省略，並將 had（何）、should（秀）、were（華）移置句首。

例　If I had met Ken, I certainly would have told him the truth.
　　= Had I met Ken, I certainly would have told him the truth.
　　我若當時遇到肯，肯定會告訴他真相。

例　If you should make the same mistake again, I might punish you.
　　= Should you make the same mistake again, I might punish you.
　　萬一你再犯同樣的錯，我也許就會處罰你了。

例　If you were late for work again, you would surely be fired.
　　→ Were you late for work again, you would surely be fired.
　　你上班若再遲到的話，肯定會遭開除。

b　It is | time / about time / high time | + that 引導的過去式子句
該是……的時候了（實際卻非如此）

例　Stop playing video games, son. It is time that you should go to bed. (✗)

→ Stop playing video games, son. It is time that you went to bed.
(✓) 兒子，別再打電動了。該是你睡覺的時候了。

例 It is about time that we must leave. (✗)

→ It is | about | time that we left. (✓)　該是我們離開的時候了。
　　　　| high |

c

but for + 名詞　（現在）若非 / 要不是……
= If it were not for + 名詞
= Were it not for + 名詞

but for + 名詞　（當時）若非 / 要不是……
= If it had not been for + 名詞
= Had it not been for + 名詞

例 But for your advice, I wouldn't be helping him.
= If it were not for your advice, I wouldn't be helping him.
= Were it not for your advice, I wouldn't be helping him.
(現在) 要不是你的建議，我才不會幫他呢。

例 But for your help ten years ago, I might have ended up in jail.
= If it had not been for your help ten years ago, I might have ended up in jail.
= Had it not been for your help ten years ago, I might have ended up in jail.　十年前要不是有你的幫助，我可能早就鋃鐺入獄了。

d 對過去事物的猜測有下列三種句型：

❶ must have + 過去分詞　一定曾經……

例 The road is wet. It must rain last night. (✗)
→ The road is wet. It must have rained last night. (✓)
馬路是溼的。昨晚一定下過雨。

❷ may have + 過去分詞　很可能曾經……

例 Dan looked tired. He may stay up late last night. (✗)
→ Dan looked tired. He may have stayed up late last night. (✓)
丹看起來很疲累。昨晚他很可能熬夜太晚了。

347

3 cannot have + 過去分詞　不可能曾經⋯

例　Jerry is honest. He <u>may not have lied</u> to you yesterday afternoon. (✕)

→ Jerry is honest. He <u>cannot have lied</u> to you yesterday afternoon. (✓)　傑瑞很老實。昨天下午他不可能向你撒謊的。

注意　若表猜測的句構為疑問句時，不可使用 "May...have + 過去分詞?" 而要使用 "Can...have + 過去分詞?"。

例　The road is wet. <u>May it have rained</u> last night? (✕)

→ The road is wet. <u>Can it have rained</u> last night? (✓)
馬路是溼的。昨晚可能下過雨了嗎？

◀ 小試身手 ▶

1	It is high time that we (must leave / left) for the airport.
2	If you should need assistance, please call me. 提示　將 if 省略改寫句子。

Ans　1. left
　　　2. Should you need assistance, please call me.

Chapter 7

Unit 73 >>> Unit 90

▸ 其他常見的混淆用法

英文學習中,是不是常會遇到一些讓人頭痛的混淆用法?有些語句聽起來差不多,但意思和用法卻天差地遠!有些語法問題,看似差異不大,卻讓你摸不著頭腦,甚至讓人抓狂!

在本章節中,我們將針對一些常見的混淆用法進行詳細解析,透過深入探討這些常見錯誤,讓你「一眼看穿」它們,便能輕鬆駕馭英文,擺脫那些常見的語法陷阱,轉而成為你的英語優勢!

Unit 73　every 連接二個主詞時應用單數還是複數動詞？

every + 單數主詞 + and + 單數主詞 + 第三人稱單數動詞

例　Every student and teacher know that exams are unfair to some. (✗)
→ Every student and teacher knows that exams are unfair to some. (✓)
每個師生都知道對某些人而言考試並不公平。

小試身手

Every boy and girl in the class (has / have) a new notebook.

Ans　has

Unit 74　everyone 與 every one 的不同

a　everyone 指「每個人」，尤指天下所有人，之後不可加介詞 of。every one 則指同類東西的「每一個」或指某人類團體的「每一個人」，之後要加介詞 of。

例　Every one should fight for freedom. (✗)
→ Everyone of us should fight for freedom. (✗)
→ Everyone should fight for freedom. (✓)
= Everybody should fight for freedom. (✓)
= Every one of us should fight for freedom. (✓)
= We all should fight for freedom. (✓)
= All of us should fight for freedom. (✓)
每個人 / 所有人 / 我們大家都應為爭取自由而奮鬥。

例　I have five apples, and I guarantee that everyone of them is sweet. (✗)
理由 everyone 指「每個人」，此處應改為 every one，指「五顆蘋果中的每一顆」。

→ I have five apples, and I guarantee that every one of them is sweet. (✓)
我有五顆蘋果，而且我保證它們每一顆都很甜。

b　each 亦可直接做代名詞，every 則不行。

例　Paul and I are good friends. Each one of us has a bike. (✓)
　=　Paul and I are good friends. Each of us has a bike. (✓)
但：Paul and I are good friends. Every of us has a bike. (✗)
→ Paul and I are good friends. Every one of us has a bike.
(✗，保羅與我是兩個人，故不可使用 Every one)
我和保羅是好友。我們每個人都有一輛自行車。

小試身手

1. (Everyone / Every one) in the group was excited about the new project.
2. The teacher asked (everyone / every one) of us to present our ideas.

Ans　1. Everyone　2. every one

Unit 75　「敲門」是 knock the door 或 knock on the door？

a　knock 表「敲」門 / 窗戶時，視為不及物動詞，必須接 on 或 at 方可接 door 或 window 做受詞。

例　Somebody is knocking the door. Go answer it. (✗)
→ Somebody is knocking on / at the door. Go answer it. (✓)
有人在敲門。快去應門。

例　I knocked the window, but I saw no one inside the room. (✗)
→ I knocked on / at the window, but I saw no one inside the room. (✓)　我敲了窗戶，但房間裡我看不到一個人。

b knock 若表「擊倒」或「擊昏」某人，則為及物動詞，有下列用法：
knock sb down　將某人擊倒
knock sb out　將某人擊昏

例　The boxer knocked his opponent down in the first round.
= The boxer knocked down his opponent in the first round.
拳擊手在第一回合就把對手擊倒了。

例　The policeman knocked the bandit out as he tried to run away.
= The policeman knocked out the bandit as he tried to run away.
匪徒企圖逃逸時，警察就把他擊昏了。
* bandit [ˋbændɪt] n. 土匪

注意 上列各例的受詞若改為代名詞時，該代名詞要置 knocked 之後。

例　The boxer knocked down him in the first round. (✗)
→ The boxer knocked him down in the first round. (✓)

例　The policeman knocked out him as he tried to run away. (✗)
→ The policeman knocked him out as he tried to run away. (✓)

小試身手

Please (knock / knock on) the door before entering the room.

Ans　knock on

Unit 76　「在郊區」是 in a suburb 或 in the suburbs？

in a suburb 指「在某個郊區」，in the suburbs 泛指「在郊區」。

例　Taipei City is getting increasingly crowded, so more and more people are choosing to live in a suburb. (✗)
→ Taipei City is getting increasingly crowded, so more and more people are choosing to live in the suburbs. (✓)
臺北市日益擁擠，因此選擇住在郊區的人也就愈來愈多了。

例 George was born in the suburbs of Taichung. (✗)
→ George was born in a suburb of Taichung. (✓)
喬治出生於臺中某市郊。

例 You'll find many beautiful villas in the suburbs of Kaohsiung.
= You'll find many beautiful villas on the outskirts of Kaohsiung.
在高雄市郊你會發現許多美麗的別墅。
* outskirts [ˈaʊtˌskɝts] n. 市郊 (恆用複數)

小試身手

Debbie prefers living _____ because it's quieter.
Ⓐ in suburbs Ⓑ in a suburb Ⓒ in the suburb Ⓓ in the suburbs

Ans Ⓓ

Unit 77 「在城裡」是 in town 或 in the town？

a in town 泛指「在城裡」，表示未離開這個城鎮。out of town 則表示「不在城裡」，town 之前均不可置定冠詞 the。

例 I live in Taipei. I'm in the town most of the year, but I'll be out of the town for two weeks, starting next Monday. (✗)
→ I live in Taipei. I'm in town most of the year, but I'll be out of town for two weeks, starting next Monday. (✓)
我住臺北。一年大部分時間我都在城裡，不過下星期一開始我會出門在外兩個星期。

b in the town 則指「在某個特定的小城鎮裡」。

例 There is nothing to see in the (small) town, but in the countryside, the scenery is beautiful beyond description.
這個 (小) 城鎮沒啥看頭，但在鄉間，景色就美不勝收了。

小試身手

Anna will be in (town / the town) next week, so we are going to meet for coffee.

Ans town

Unit 78 「天黑」是 after darkness 或 after dark？

a dark 可做名詞，指「天黑」，表「天黑之後」，應說 after dark，而非 after darkness。表「天黑之前」，應說 before dark，而非 before darkness。

例 You should avoid going out alone after darkness. (✕)
→ You should avoid going out alone after dark. (✓)
= You should avoid going out alone after nightfall. (✓)
天黑之後，你應避免獨自外出。

例 Be sure to come back before darkness. (✕)
→ Be sure to come back before dark. (✓)
務必在天黑之前回來。

b darkness 亦為名詞，指「黑暗」或「暗處」。有下列重要用法：

例 I watched the train leave until it disappeared into the dark. (不自然)
→ I watched the train leave until it disappeared into the darkness. (✓)
我看著火車離去直到消失在黑暗中。

c dark 做名詞時，亦形成下列重要片語：
keep sb in the dark about sth　將某事把某人蒙在鼓裡

例 Kevin kept his mother in the darkness about the news of his father's sudden death. (✕)
→ Kevin kept his mother in the dark about the news of his father's sudden death. (✓)
凱文把他母親蒙在鼓裡，不讓她知道父親突然過世的消息。

d dark 亦可做形容詞，表「黑暗的」。

例 It's getting dark. Let's go find a youth hostel for the night.
天色漸漸暗了。咱們去找間青年旅館過夜吧。

例 Don't always look on the dark side of life. Look on the bright side instead. 別老是看著人生的黑暗面。相反地，要看 (人生的) 光明面。

小試身手

Gina promised to return before (dark / darkness).

Ans dark

Unit 79 「甚至」是 even 或 even though 或 even if？

a even 是副詞，表「甚至」，不可當連接詞使用。換言之，even 不可用以連接兩句。

例 The question is quite easy, even a five-year-old child could answer it. (✗，兩句無連接詞連接)

→ The question is quite easy. Even a five-year-old child could answer it. (✓，Even 是副詞，表「甚至」或「連」)
這個問題很簡單。甚至 / 連五歲的孩子都可回答得出來。

b even 與 though 並用，形成連接詞 even though，表「雖然」、「縱然」，引導副詞子句，與主要子句形成連接。

例 Even though he is rich, Mr. Li is not arrogant.
= Although / Though he is rich, Mr. Li is not arrogant.
李先生雖然富有，卻不驕傲。

c even if 亦是連接詞，表「就算」，用於假設語氣，所引導的副詞子句也許是事實，也許非事實。

例 Even if you give me all you have, I won't marry you.
就算你把你的一切都給了我，我也不會嫁給你。

355

小試身手

1. 雖然安琪拉很用功讀書，她還是考試不及格。
   _____ Angela studied hard, she still failed the test.

2. 就算丹尼斯道歉，我也不會原諒他。
   _____ Dennis apologizes, I won't forgive him.

> Ans 1. Even; though   2. Even; if

Unit 80 「像家一樣舒適」是 homey 或 homely？

a 在美式英語中，homey [ˈhomɪ] 是形容詞，表「像家一樣舒適的」；homely [ˈhomlɪ]，表「相貌平庸的」，是 ugly「醜的」委婉語，鮮少人會使用這個字。

例 I often visit that restaurant because of its homely atmosphere. (✗)
→ I often visit that restaurant because of its homey atmosphere. (✓)
我常光顧那家餐廳，因為它有賓至如歸的氛圍。

例 A: Who's that homely girl sitting by the window? (千萬不要使用本字)
B: Don't be so rude!
甲：坐在窗邊那個內在美的女孩是誰呀？
乙：不要這麼沒禮貌！

記住 世上所有女孩都是美麗的，只不過是有些女孩更美而已！

b 在英式英語中，homely 與 homey 同義，均表「如在家一般舒適的」。

小試身手

我喜歡到奶奶的家走走，因為那裡有一種像家一樣舒適的氛圍。
I love visiting my grandmother's house because of its _____ atmosphere.

> Ans homey

Unit 81　provide「提供」與 provided that「如果」的用法

a　provide [prəˋvaɪd] 是及物動詞，表「提供」，用於下列結構：
provide sb <u>with</u> sth　提供某人某物
= provide sth <u>for</u> sb

例　Don't worry. I'll <u>provide</u> you <u>the</u> right tools. (✗)
→ Don't worry. I'll <u>provide</u> you <u>with</u> the right tools. (✓)
= Don't worry. I'll <u>provide</u> the right tools <u>for</u> you. (✓)
別擔心，我會提供你合適的工具。

b　provided that 視作連接詞，表「只要」或「如果」，與 if 或 as long as 同義。均引導副詞子句，修飾主要子句。

例　Provided that we have enough money, we can complete the project right on time.
= | Providing that | we have enough money, we can complete the
　 As long as
　 If
project right on time.
如果我們錢夠的話，就可準時完成該企劃案。

小試身手

The manager will provide us _____ a list of tasks for the meeting.
Ⓐ for　　Ⓑ with　　Ⓒ of　　Ⓓ in

Ans　Ⓑ

Unit 82 「拿給我」是 Give me it. 或 Give it to me.?

give (給予)、bring (帶來)、show (展現)、teach (教導)、write (寫)、buy (買)、sell (賣)、read (讀)、tell (告訴)、lend (借給) 等動詞可做授與動詞，採下列句型：

授與動詞 + 物 + 介詞 to / for + 人
= 授與動詞 + 人 + 物 (更常用)

例 Please give a call to me this afternoon. (較不自然)
= Please give me a call this afternoon. (更常用)
請在今天下午打電話給我。

例 Bella wrote a letter to Ian last Sunday. (✓)
= Bella wrote Ian a letter last Sunday. (✓，更常用)
上禮拜天貝拉寫了一封信給伊恩。

例 Dan sold his bike to Lisa yesterday. (佳)
= Dan sold Lisa his bike yesterday. (可)
丹昨天把他的腳踏車賣給莉莎了。

例 Mrs. Smith teaches English to me. (✓)
= Mrs. Smith teaches me English. (✓，更常用)
史密斯老師教我英文。

例 Go buy a newspaper for me, son. (✓)
= Go buy me a newspaper, son. (✓，更常用)　兒子，去幫我買份報紙。

注意 上列授與動詞之後的物是代名詞 (it 或 them) 時，不宜省略介詞。

例 Give me the book. (✓，更常用)
= Give the book to me. (✓)　給我那本書。
但：Give me it. (劣)
→ Give it to me. (✓)

例 Tell me the story. (✓，更常用)
= Tell the story to me. (✓)　告訴我那個故事。
但：Tell me it. (劣)
→ Tell it to me. (✓)

358

例 Show me the money. (✓，更常用)
= Show the money to me. (✓)　亮出你的錢來。
但:Show me it. (劣)
→ Show it to me. (✓)

例 Bring me the books. (✓，更常用)
= Bring the books to me. (✓)　把那些書帶給我。
但:Bring me them. (劣)
→ Bring them to me. (✓)

小試身手

told / the good news / me / Iris / to

Ans　Iris told the good news to me.

Unit 83　「比較少」要用 less 還是 fewer？

less 與 fewer 均可做形容詞，表「較少的」，惟前者修飾不可數名詞（如 money、water、air、information 等）；後者修飾可數名詞且一定是複數（如 families、girls、boys、trees、people 等）。less 是 little（沒多少）的比較級，fewer 是 few（沒幾個）的比較級。

例 Matt has few money. (✗，money 是不可數名詞，不可說 a money，two moneys，five moneys。)
→ Matt has little money. (✓)　麥特沒多少錢。

例 Matt has little money, but I have fewer money than him. (✗)
→ Matt has little money, but I have less money than him. (✓)
麥特沒多少錢，不過我的錢比他更少。

例 Owen has little friends, but I have even less friends than him.
(✗，friend 是可數名詞，如 a friend、two friends、six friends、many friends。)
→ Owen has few friends, but I have even fewer friends than him.
(✓)　歐文沒幾個朋友，而我的朋友比他的更少。

例 As the temperature is dropping drastically, <u>less and less people</u> are going out for exercise. (✗，老美常犯這個錯誤。)

→ As the temperature is dropping drastically, <u>fewer and fewer people</u> are going out for exercise. (✓)
由於氣溫驟降，出門運動的人愈來愈少。

例 It seems that Mr. Zelenskyy is getting <u>fewer and fewer support</u> from the US. (✗，support 是抽象名詞，不可數)

→ It seems that Mr. Zelenskyy is getting <u>less and less support</u> from the US. (✓)
看來澤倫斯基先生正逐漸失去美國的支持。

小試身手

The company has (few / less) information about the new product than expected.

Ans less

Unit 84　「一分耕耘，一分收穫。」英文怎麼說？

音譯：Even game win, even so whole. (✗)
中譯：甚至遊戲贏，甚至如此全部。(✗，瘋子才會講這樣的話。)
正確的英文：No pain, no gain. (✓，諺語)
　　　　　　沒有辛苦，就沒有收穫。
即：一分耕耘，一分收穫。

另一個類似的諺語如下：
　　As you sow, so shall you reap. (✓，諺語)
= You reap what you sow. (✓)
實際正確翻譯為：種什麼因，得什麼果。
即：善有善報，惡有惡報。

360

> 小試身手

一分耕耘，一分收穫。
No _____, no _____.

Ans pain; gain

Unit 85 「不入虎穴，焉得虎子？」英文怎麼說？

音譯：Blue who say, and whose. (✗)
中譯：藍色誰說，以及誰的。(✗，瘋子才會講這樣的話)
正確的英文：Nothing ventured, nothing gained. (✓，諺語)
即：If you venture nothing, you will gain nothing. (✓)
　　如果你什麼事情都不敢冒險嘗試，就不會有所得。
即：不入虎穴，焉得虎子？

> 小試身手

不入虎穴，焉得虎子？
Nothing _____, nothing _____.

Ans ventured; gained

Unit 86 「喝湯」是 drink soup 或 eat soup？

西式餐飲中，「湯」多為濃湯，有菜有肉，視作一道菜，故表「喝」湯要用 eat 而非 drink。

例　Don't drink the soup until it cools down. (✗)
　→ Don't eat the soup until it cools down. (✓)
　湯涼了再喝。

例　Some people drink soup to lose weight. (✗)
　→ Some people eat soup to lose weight. (✓)　有些人靠喝湯瘦身。

CH 7
其他常見的混淆用法

361

> **小試身手**
>
> 請不要太快喝湯；它還很燙。
> Please don't _____ the soup too quickly; it's still too hot.
>
> Ans　eat

Unit 87　「如何稱呼……」是 How do you call...? 或 What do you call...?

例　How do you call a baby cow in English? (✗)
你如何／以什麼方式用英文稱呼小牛呀？(✗，用嘴還是手？本問句不合邏輯)

→ What do you call a baby cow in English? (✓)
你用英文稱呼小牛為什麼呀？
即：在英文中小牛叫做什麼呀？(合乎邏輯)
答句：We call a baby cow a calf. (✓)

也許受了中文影響，我們見到老外，就直接把「我怎麼稱呼您呀？」直譯成：
How do I call you? (✗)

理由　由於 How 是副詞，修飾動詞 call，因此在老外聽來，本句的意思是「我該用什麼方式打電話給你？」因而無以言對。

應說：What should I call you? (✓，但有點不禮貌)　我該稱呼您為什麼？
更好的說法為：
What should I call you, please? (✓)
或：What's your name, please? (✓)
= May I have your name, please? (✓，更好)　請問您貴姓？

How do you call a man without a body and a nose? (✗)
→ What do you call a man without a body and a nose? (✓)
我們已知，表「你將某人稱做什麼？」，英文應說：
What do you call a man...? (✓)　你把某人稱呼為什麼？
而非：How do you call a man...? (✗)
你如何／以什麼方式將某人稱呼……？

故：How do you call a man without a body and a nose? (✗)

→ What do you call a man without a body and a nose? (✓)
你會把一個沒有身體和鼻子的人稱做什麼？

答案：Nobody nose. (Nobody knows. 的諧音)

小試身手

你怎麼用英文稱呼這種樹？
_____ do you call this type of tree in English?

Ans　What

Unit 88　「聖誕節當天」是 on Christmas 或 at Christmas？

a 表「聖誕節」當天，應說 on Christmas Day，on Christmas 則為較口語的說法。

例　I'll be on duty on Christmas. (較口語)

→ I'll be on duty on Christmas Day (December 25th). (✓)
聖誕節（十二月二十五日）當天我要值班。

b 表「聖誕節前後放假這幾天」（約 12 天）應說：at Christmas。

例　I'll be going hiking with my friends at Christmas.
聖誕節前後這幾天我會和我朋友去健行。

c on Christmas Eve　平安夜

例　We'll have a big party at Christmas Eve. (✗)

→ We'll have a big party on Christmas Eve. (✓)
平安夜當晚我們會舉行一場大型派對。

d Easter 一字亦有相同的用法：

例 What are you planning to do on Easter Day?
復活節當天你有什麼打算？

例 I'll be flying to Tokyo on vacation at Easter.
復活節這幾天我會搭機到東京度假。

> 小試身手

We'll decorate the Christmas tree (on / at) Christmas Eve.

Ans on

Unit 89 「回家」是 go to home 或 go home？

a home 可做副詞，修飾動詞（如 come、go、leave、arrive、get 等）。

例 I leave from home at 7:30 a.m. and come back to home at 5 p.m. every day. (✗)
→ I leave home at 7:30 a.m. and come (back) home at 5 p.m. every day. (✓)
我每天早上七點半出門，下午五點回家。

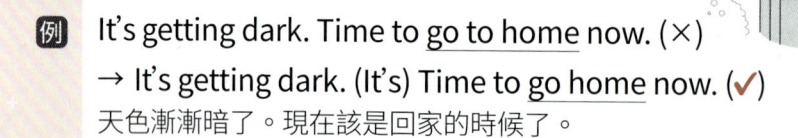

例 It's getting dark. Time to go to home now. (✗)
→ It's getting dark. (It's) Time to go home now. (✓)
天色漸漸暗了。現在該是回家的時候了。

例 By the time I arrived at home, it was almost 2 in the morning. (✗)
→ By the time I arrived home, it was almost 2 in the morning. (✓)
等到我抵達家門時，已經是清晨兩點了。

b home 亦可做名詞，與介詞 at 形成固定搭配。

例 What do you often do at the home? (✗)
→ What do you often do at home? (✓) 你在家時通常做什麼事？

364

比較

例 I'm home now.
　　　　 副詞

= I've | got
　　　 | arrived | home now.   我到家了。
　　　 | come (back)| 副詞

例 I'm at home now.　我現在待在家中 (沒外出)。
　　　 home 是名詞

c 下列問句多使用 home 取代 at home。

例 Anybody home?　有人在家嗎？(敲門時用語)
(由 Is there anybody at home? 化簡而成。)

◆ 小試身手 ◆

Bill arrived (home / at home) early this morning.

Ans　home

Unit 90　意志動詞

a 意志動詞有「建議」、「要求」、「命令」、「規定」等四大類，之後接 that 子句作受詞時，that 子句恆使用助動詞 should，而 should 往往予以省略，保留之後的原形動詞。

1 建議：advise、move (提議)、propose、recommend、suggest、urge (呼籲)
2 要求：ask、demand、desire、insist (堅持要求)、request、require
3 命令：order、command
4 規定：rule、regulate

例 Because of the heavy rain, many parents suggested that the hiking tour must be canceled. (×)

365

→ Because of the heavy rain, many parents suggested that the hiking tour should be canceled. (✓)

= Because of the heavy rain, many parents suggested that the hiking tour be canceled. (✓)
由於下大雨的關係，許多家長建議取消這趟徒步旅行。

例 The boss demanded that we had to finish the project by 5 p.m. (✗)

→ The boss demanded that we should finish the project by 5 p.m. (✓)

= The boss demanded that we finish the project by 5 p.m. (✓)
老闆要求我們下午 5 點以前完成該企畫。

例 I insist that you must not work with that selfish guy. (✗)

→ I insist that you should not work with that selfish guy. (✓)

= I insist that you not work with that selfish guy. (✓)
我堅持要求你不得與那個自私的傢伙共事。

注意 insist 亦可表「堅信」，suggest 亦可表「暗示」，此時若接 that 子句作受詞時，that 子句採一般時態。

例 Steve's words | suggest | that he is jealous of you.
　　　　　　　 | imply　|
史提夫的話語暗示他很忌妒你。

例 I | insist　　　　| that Paul lied to me.　我堅信保羅沒對我說實話。
　 | am sure　　　|
　 | am convinced |

b　that 子句若置意志動詞變成的名詞之後，而與該名詞形成同位語時，that 子句也要使用助動詞 should，而 should 往往予以省略，保留之後的原形動詞。

例 It is my | suggestion | that you'd better study abroad upon graduation from high school. (✗)
　　　　　| proposal　 |

→ It is my | suggestion | that you should study abroad upon graduation from high school. (✓)
　　　　　| proposal　|

= It is my | suggestion | that you study abroad upon graduation from high school. (✓)
　　　　　| proposal　|
我建議你高中畢業後馬上出國留學。

例 My advice is that Nelly <u>must</u> learn Japanese if she wants to work in Tokyo. (×)

→ My advice is that Nelly <u>should</u> learn Japanese if she wants to work in Tokyo. (✓)

= My advice is that Nelly <u>learn</u> Japanese if she wants to work in Tokyo. (✓)　我的建議是娜莉若想在東京工作就應學日文。

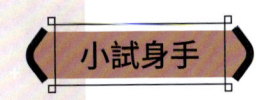

小試身手

The teacher suggested that the students (must submit / submit) their homework tomorrow.

Ans submit

國家圖書館出版品預行編目(CIP)資料

英語地雷大冒險：解鎖你不知道的錯誤用法 /
賴世雄作. -- 初版. -- 臺北市：常春藤數位出版股
份有限公司, 2025.01
  面；　公分. --（常春藤生活必讀系列；BA24）
  ISBN 978-626-7225-78-3（平裝）

1. CST：英語　2. CST：讀本

805.18　　　　　　　　　　　　　　113020356

常春藤生活必讀系列【BA24】
英語地雷大冒險：解鎖你不知道的錯誤用法

作　　者	賴世雄
編輯小組	許嘉華・畢安安・Nick Roden
設計組長	王玥琦
封面設計	王穎緁
排版設計	王穎緁・林桂旭
法律顧問	北辰著作權事務所蕭雄淋律師
出 版 者	常春藤數位出版股份有限公司
地　　址	臺北市忠孝西路一段 33 號 5 樓
電　　話	(02) 2331-7600
傳　　真	(02) 2381-0918
網　　址	www.ivy.com.tw
電子信箱	service@ivy.com.tw
郵政劃撥	50463568
戶　　名	常春藤數位出版股份有限公司
定　　價	399 元

ⓒ常春藤數位出版股份有限公司 (2025) All rights reserved.　　Y000011-3562

本書之封面、內文、編排等之著作財產權歸常春藤數位出版股份有限公司所有。未經本公司書面同意，
請勿翻印、轉載或為一切著作權法上利用行為，否則依法追究。

如有缺頁、裝訂錯誤或破損，請寄回本公司更換。　　　　【版權所有　翻印必究】